Twenty Tiny Tales

(and a few tails!)

*Elaine J. Bradley's
Book of Short Stories*

Copyright © 2019 Elaine J. Bradley

The moral right of the author has been asserted.

Apart from any fair dealing for the purposes of research or private study, or criticism or review, as permitted under the Copyright, Designs and Patents Act 1988, this publication may only be reproduced, stored or transmitted, in any form or by any means, with the prior permission in writing of the publishers, or in the case of reprographic reproduction in accordance with the terms of licences issued by the Copyright Licensing Agency. Enquiries concerning reproduction outside those terms should be sent to the publishers.

These stories and their characters are purely fictitious, although some of the tales were inspired by small, actual and sometimes personal incidents.
Enjoy!

Matador
9 Priory Business Park,
Wistow Road, Kibworth Beauchamp,
Leicestershire. LE8 0RX
Tel: 0116 279 2299
Email: books@troubador.co.uk
Web: www.troubador.co.uk/matador
Twitter: @matadorbooks

ISBN 978 1838590 345

British Library Cataloguing in Publication Data.
A catalogue record for this book is available from the British Library.

Printed and bound in Great Britain by 4edge Limited
Typeset in 11pt Adobe Caslon Pro by Troubador Publishing Ltd, Leicester, UK

Matador is an imprint of Troubador Publishing Ltd

Twenty Tiny Tales

To my husband Ian for his support and encouragement to have these stories published.

To Bill and Jenny Frost. Bill discovered Matador for me: a brilliant find, and Jenny has proof read all of my stories several times.

To Joan and David Russell, my other proof readers, and to Karyl Quigley, my artist friend, who designed my book cover.

Thank you all so much.

Contents

The Museum of Childhood	1
Flower Power	15
Second Chance	23
Port Logie Story	27
A Friend in Need	32
A Debt Repaid	39
One Guid Turn Deserves Another	55
Dicing with Death	63
All in a Day's Walk	72
One Step Too Far	77
They Shoot Rabbits Don't They?	89
A Watertight Alibi	121
Amber Alert	140
Epiphany and Atonement	163
One Week Left	187
The Luck of the Devil	195
That's What Friends Are For	205
The Revenge of Benj	231
The Power of Pain	257
Charity Begins At Home	266
Scoop The Pool	295
A Real Murder Mystery	304

The Museum
of Childhood

The Museum of Childhood was an old four-storey building set in the middle of the main street. It was well hidden among a mixture of pubs, eating places, and tourist shops, the latter of which contained a variety of tartan gifts, Loch Ness Monsters in various guises, flags of Scotland, shortbread and tablet. There was no "shop front" to the museum, just a narrow entrance opening inside to a small foyer and ticket counter. On the Royal Mile, even on cold, wet evenings there was always an abundance of passers-by. However, most people, unless they were tourists specifically looking for the museum, would pass it by without a glance. Even so it was open seven days a week for the tourist season, which was March to October, and only closed for two days midweek during the winter months.

Sadie, a twenty-two-year-old graduate, had secured a temporary post there, commencing at the beginning of October when the museum was less busy, the high season over and the children back to school. Her contract was to produce a new catalogue/brochure for the museum, which would include floor plans and showcase plans identifying specific exhibits of particular interest. There was no charge for entry to the museum and its viability relied upon grants and donations, so Sadie was also looking at ways to increase the popularity and profitability ensuring the future of the museum. She had spent her first week studying the existing material, walking the building floor after floor, measuring dimensions and poring over layouts and she currently had the basic floor plans, to scale, on her laptop.

She had enjoyed the last few weeks. Working largely alone, with occasional consultation meetings with key museum personnel, had been both interesting and challenging. She'd listened in to the guided tours given to school parties, and noted down the items that most interested the modern-day children. She had also documented the questions they had asked. As a result, Sadie had put forward suggestions for some new interactive activities using replicas of toys and classroom equipment from previous decades and generations. Her list so far included skipping ropes, tops and whips, yo-yos and a variety of dressing-up props with attire from bygone days. She was currently working on a 1940's school environment, where visiting groups would be able to access a classroom and sit at the old student desks, use pens with nibs and loose ink, practise writing, use reading schemes of the day and learn songs: both those taught in music lessons and those sung in the schoolyard.

The next key stage of Sadie's project was a cataloguing of each exhibit, precisely, with its position in the relevant display case, and a brief history and explanation of individual pieces. It was now late October and she had chosen to work on the two days when the museum was closed, to maximise her undisturbed time and enable her to sit in each room in turn with her laptop set up.

The quiet of the museum was strange after the frantic preceding days of half term, with visitors, old and young, milling about and a museum staff presence on every floor. It was tranquil now though and easier to set up her portable workstation exactly where she wanted it without being in anyone's way, or impeding the progress of visitors to the museum.

The first day had been very productive and by 5pm Sadie was ready to call it a day. It was dark outside, as the clocks had changed to GMT the previous weekend, and once Sadie had switched the last light off, the interior of the museum was illuminated only by the dim security lights, which cast an eerie glow on the glass cases on the lower floor. Quickly Sadie stepped outside, laptop under her arm, locked the door and the outer shutter and hurried off towards the bright lights of the local eateries.

The following day, Sadie worked to a similar pattern, stopping only for a twenty-minute lunch break, and anxious to get back to her cataloguing. She had completed the plan and descriptions of items on the ground floor, which were baby and infant toys, teethers, prams, cradles, baths and clothing on one side of the room, and various mechanical toys of yester-year on the other. There were ancient machines, which required a coin (originally old currency, of course) to be inserted to display a scene, or play a tune. A Punch and Judy Tent showed lurid, caricatured puppets, which Sadie couldn't help thinking would have terrified rather than amused its contemporary children. Grotesque!

When Sadie finally wound up for the day, it was 6.15 and she was absolutely starving. "Pizza Hut tonight," she decided. She made a quick check of the whole floor. Once again the rest of the skeleton team had already left and for the first time that day Sadie was very much aware of the stillness of the building. As she flicked the main light switch, and was left standing alone in the semi-darkness, she glanced around at the strange shadows and reflections thrown by the dim lighting and the glass cases. She caught sight of a distorted face and jumped – stupid! It was only Mr Punch – reflected by the light, strangely warped as it shone on the showcase on the opposite wall. Still, Sadie shivered, it wasn't a very pleasant sight. If she was a child, she really wouldn't like Mr Punch. His face would give her nightmares, she was sure of it.

Sadie quickly stepped outside, locked the door and shutter, and made her way towards the streetlights and people! Strange that she should feel safer on the dark, and today damp, Royal Mile than in the warm comfort of the museum.

As she devoured her pizza and salad, Sadie thought about her tasks for the next day. The museum would be open to visitors again and she was sure that there was at least one school party booked in, so perhaps it would be better to work on the top floor where she would be less intrusive. The fourth floor was a long gallery with various tableaux along one side, so that visitors ascended the stair to it at one end, walked along the viewing corridor and down the steps at the other end. The gallery was dimly lit to create atmosphere, while the individual rooms were lit in a style appropriate to the era with Victorian and Edwardian types of lighting. Compared to the other floors, Sadie found it gloomy and just a bit oppressive.

Still, it had to be done!

The next day saw Sadie with a collapsible table and her laptop set up at one end of the fourth-floor gallery, where there were two 1940's style classrooms. A grim-faced schoolteacher complete with mortar board and gown dominated the scene, standing beside his high desk which had a step up to it and was designed to command a view of every pupil in the classroom.

Upon his desk were a large bottle of red ink, an inkwell, quills, three leather-bound books, a small globe and the school bell. On a hook at the side of the desk was hung the dreaded leather strap.

A chart picturing the leaves and fruits of various trees was mounted on one wall and a blackboard showing a lesson in cursive handwriting was attached to another wall, adjacent to a map of the world. The classroom clock hung behind the teacher's desk.

Several rows of old, dark wood pupils' desks faced that of the teacher. They were worn, and written and carved upon (a strapping offence for sure!) and were spread with open books, wooden rulers and pencils. The pupils' seats were joined together: an uncomfortable-looking form of wood with iron legs. A geography lesson was in progress and an aged atlas was open on one desk. A couple of pupils were bent over the desk, quietly studying one of the books, and looking very demure and formal in shirts, ties and blazers.

Further along the gallery was a typical living room depicting the scene of a child's birthday party. The tableau contained a number of life-sized children, formally dressed and intent on playing party games. "Hunt the Thimble" was in progress, and the table was set with jellies and fairy cakes. A miniature chair held a small child clutching a monkey. Sadie smiled at the thought of modern-day children being confronted with this to celebrate their birthdays. More likely they would want to play with her laptop after a feast of burgers and chips!

Next was the sweetie shop full of jars of humbugs, soor plums, dolly mixtures, cough-candy and black bullets. Children in winter outdoor attire, complete with hats and hand-muffs gazed into the shop window. Sadie contemplated this for a while, and made a note on her computer in the form of a suggestion that the shop could be opened to the public and that visiting children could actually buy "quarters" of traditional sweets to contribute to making some income for the museum.

She was just beginning work on the final tableau: a nursery, with a magnificent old fireplace, a wonderful Victorian rocking horse and a variety of dolls, building bricks and die-cast cars strewn around the clippie rugs, when suddenly from behind her arose a plaintive chanting noise. Sadie jumped a mile! She had completely forgotten about the recording of children playing schoolyard games, which was triggered by a motion sensor as visitors entered the fourth-floor gallery. Sure enough two people had entered the far end of the passageway. They looked shocked but Sadie wasn't sure whether, like her the haunting, echoing chants had startled them or if the sight of Sadie herself, sitting hunched over her laptop in the subdued light, had alarmed them.

The schoolyard singing continued as the couple wandered along the narrow gallery: "When Mary was a teacher…" An outburst of distant, youthful laughter followed, which echoed all around and then faded as the hall was filled with "The Big Ship sails through the Alley-Alley-O…" As they approached Sadie, both smiled, and the lady remarked, "That was a bit scary. It really took us both by surprise."

Sadie nodded in agreement. "I've heard it several times, but it can still give me a bit of a shock when it suddenly starts up. I've been in here for an hour alone, in deathly silence, so it really got me this time." They all had a chuckle, then the couple moved further along, and after a few minutes Sadie heard them descending the stairs at the other end.

She carried on through the afternoon, making a note to herself that she would find out all the words to the various schoolyard songs and copy them for use in the activities she'd designed for the young visitors. It would be quite good fun to learn the accompanying actions too.

Sadie decided that after her previous late night, she would treat herself to an early finish at the museum. She could eat early then catch up on some correspondence back at the flat. She departed at 4.45 leaving two of the museum staff in attendance and with the locking up responsibilities when the museum closed at 5.30.

Sadie had fancied a change of scene, so had been working on the third floor all morning. It was the Floor of the Dolls: full of enormous display cabinets, each holding rows and rows of dolls from every generation and covering more than two hundred years. She had been given the keys to each of the glass cases, so that she could check each doll's information against its overall position in the display and whether it was chronologically so placed. She had walked round and round the room marvelling at the collection. Although she'd been in the room several times and had viewed them before, she couldn't help but see exhibits that she hadn't previously noticed.

There were very old rag dolls, hand sewn and unique, china and porcelain dolls: some in amazingly detailed, and also hand sewn, costumes. In their velvet, satin and brocade they were fashion statements covering the Victorian, Edwardian and Georgian periods. There were black dolls, including golliwogs (obviously allowable as a piece of history), oriental dolls, small figures in a variety of national costumes, and talking dolls: from those that cried "Mama" when tipped, to those with a pull cord which triggered a series of plaintive requests and statements. Some of the exhibits, whilst aged, were in pristine condition: obviously regarded as show pieces rather than toys. Others were much used and obviously loved. Some had luridly painted faces and some had real hair. There were dolls dressed in bridal and christening robes.

More modern dolls were made from rigid plastic with jointed arms and legs, then came the more pliable rubber dolls, babies with soft, moulded features, plastic kiss-curls and eyes that opened and closed. Sadie recognised quite a few of the later models: her mother still had her Tiny Tears doll from the late sixties. Sadie had been allowed to play with it when she was a child but once she had outgrown it, her mother reclaimed it and still to this day had it in her wardrobe. There were also Sindy, Paul and Patch dolls, Tressy, Barbie and Ken, Action Man and Tommy Gunn, all of which sported various accessories, from clothes to cars and weapons. Sindy had a more varied wardrobe than Sadie herself!

One of the things that struck Sadie was that nearly all of the dolls had blonde hair, blue eyes, rosy cheeks and rosebud mouths: every little girl's dream! She remembered as a child, wistfully wishing that she had been born blonde and blue-eyed.

There was one display cabinet completely devoted to Teddy Bears through the ages, the information boards telling the history of the toy, from the Teddy Roosevelt All American Bear to present-day icons such as Steiff and Charley Bears. This exhibition was obviously a favourite with the school children and all afternoon Sadie had heard exclamations of recognition and delight from the visiting primary school children.

"Oh look Paddington Bear! My mum has one, she made him some marmalade sandwiches out of foam and he has them in his hat. They've been there since before I was born."

"Look at that huge grizzly bear – he wouldn't even fit in my bedroom."

"That one's Winnie the Pooh."

One little girl looked up and pointed. "There's Super Ted: flying above everyone else."

"How many bears can you name?" asked the attending teacher.

"Rupert! Rupert the Bear! Checked trousers!"
"Pudsey! Children in Need!"
"The Three Bears!"

"This is the Teddy Bears' Picnic, isn't it?" asked one boy pointing to a tartan rug on the floor set with tiny china teacups and saucers, a plate of jam tarts, and a gathering of all shapes and sizes of bear sitting around the edge.

"Yes," agreed the teacher. "Now remember the song we have been practising ready for today? Let's give it a go... one... two... three!"

The whole group sang "The Teddy Bears' Picnic" right through and Sadie sat enthralled. When they had finished she applauded and they beamed at her. What an enjoyable afternoon, and she had to admit that she found the display of teddy bears warming and comforting compared to some of the other exhibits. The school party departed and Sadie worked on for another hour on the third floor, inspired by the children's enthusiasm. Perhaps a teddy bear quiz sheet would go down well as a future activity.

Having concluded her work on the third floor by 4.15, Sadie decided that she should go back to the fourth floor and try to finish what she started yesterday. When she arrived at the top of the stairs the schoolyard singers automatically began their chanting followed by shrill laughter, and Sadie, her heart having jumped, muttered to herself in annoyance. She couldn't help but find the voices haunting and just a bit spooky, even though she told herself she was being silly. In any case it was unlikely that anyone would come up to the fourth floor at this time to disturb her, or to set off the audio tape. She knew that the last school party had already departed, so she determinedly settled down to work.

At 5.25 Sadie's mobile phone pinged with a text. In the silence it made her jump, but she pulled it out of her bag and checked it. It was Sarah from the reception area informing her that she was leaving for the day and that it would be Sadie's responsibility to lock up later as she was the only one remaining in the building.

Sadie okayed this, reminding Sarah to lock the door behind her and that Sadie had her own key with which to unlock and re-lock the door when she wished to leave.

Sadie was close to completing her cataloguing of the gallery items and determined to finish before she left so she worked on oblivious to the time. Eventually satisfied with her final product, she turned off her laptop and made to gather her belongings up. She glanced at her watch to find that it was 6.40: the time had flown. Making a note of the time on her worksheet, she picked up her bag and computer and headed for the stairs, switching off the main lights as she passed them. As she crossed from the fourth-floor area to the staircase area she triggered the schoolyard tape again and in the darkness jumped a mile, the hairs on her neck beginning to rise. She gave a shiver and ran down the flight of stairs.

As Sadie rounded the newel post at the bottom of the staircase to the open-plan third floor she started in fright as she was confronted by a dark, human shape with a pale face and gaping expression. She let out an involuntary cry. Her nerve endings were still on edge and tingling as she realised with a gasp of relief that it was the huge, full length mirror and the reflection staring back at her was her own. But then she did a double take! A dimly lit form appeared over her left shoulder, and reflected in the glass, she knew that he, she or it, was looking straight at her. She spun around quickly to face the wan figure, peering nervously into the shadows but seeing nothing but rows of dolls' faces fixed with rosy cheeks, artificial smiles and staring blue eyes. Dolls from the last two centuries: made from china, porcelain, cloth or plastic, dolls with painted, unnatural expressions! The sea of faces was unnerving.

In the subdued light Sadie gazed around the room in trepidation, her breathing shallow and her limbs frozen as she tried to locate the source of her fear. Her heart was still pounding and she could feel the blood pumping furiously inside her head. More faces met hers as her eyes darted about uneasily, looking for what could have possibly caused the weird reflection. She was aware of nothing that could have reproduced a life-sized figure in the looking glass, so with apprehension she slowly turned back to the mirror itself, hardly daring to raise her eyes for fear of what she might see.

With tentative eyes she studied herself and the room behind her, endeavouring to identify which dolls were reflected over her left shoulder, and simultaneously trying to calm herself. She saw nothing very clearly, only the glass cases with tiered rows of dolls' faces she had seen so many times before during her cataloguing. Granted there were some she did not like… she really wasn't keen on those Victorian china dolls with their very white faces… she didn't like some of the marionettes or the clowns with their grotesque, exaggerated features. Sadie found herself shivering again…

She turned again and her eyes fell upon Puss in Boots. He really had to be the scariest of the lot: a human shaped form, dressed in a gentleman's coat and breeches, with a feathered hat and high boots. His head was feline. It was a real cat's head: a taxidermy job, Sadie thought: pale cream fur with an open, hostile mouth displaying a full set of pointed teeth, which Sadie was sure were real. He was definitely the most sinister character there, bordering on a bit sick. Would anyone in their right mind give a child this as a gift? No way would Sadie use him as a prop when reading the Puss in Boots story to children. They'd have nightmares for the rest of their lives.

All this happened so quickly and before Sadie could recover herself, the schoolyard chanting began on the floor above. "When Mary was a teacher..." Shrill voices and laughter followed, echoing eerily around the vast empty space.

But there was no one on the floor above! Or there shouldn't be... Sadie was in the museum alone as she had been on most evenings recently. What was going on? The recording was on a motion sensor... what could have set it off? The song changed to "The Big Ship sails through the Alley-Alley O..." She wondered momentarily whether one of the museum staff was having a joke at her expense, so she shouted: "Okay, you win, you've given me a real fright...stop it!"

The chanting continued...

Sadie could feel the hairs on her neck rising again and goose bumps manifesting themselves all over her taut body. She was paralysed with fear, unable to move her legs, though her brain was telling her to run. Panic completely consumed her power of reasoning. She couldn't think straight: her only thoughts were to get out fast! But how? Her legs wouldn't work...

For several moments she was rooted to the spot. Petrified! She heard screaming: piercing screeching was echoing all around her, whilst the disturbing childlike chanting and laughter went on and on... in the background...

With a jolt, suddenly Sadie realised it was she who was screaming. With a tremor throughout her body, she forced herself to close her mouth and her eyes. She covered her ears with her hands and tried to control her breathing. The singing stopped abruptly. Slowly Sadie opened her eyes, which immediately darted from side to side. She dared not look back to the mirror for fear of what she might see, but then facing out towards the room, she was confronted with the rows of lifeless, staring eyes, her own eyes immediately falling on the bared teeth of Puss in Boots.

Suddenly she became aware that everything had happened so quickly, that she was still standing in only the subdued, ghostly light of the cabinets. Stupid! "Turn the main light on," she told herself. Her hand and legs somehow obeyed her brain and she reached the main switch for the third floor. The instant brightness dazzled her momentarily and she stood transfixed, eyes roving wildly around the room. Then she bolted to the other end of the room, to the staircase leading down to the second floor, which she could see was in darkness. No way was she turning the third-floor light off! It could stay on all night for all she cared!

Once Sadie had descended the dark stairway, she groped about feverishly for the main light switch for the second floor but was unable to locate it. Panicking again she peered into the dimness, nerves completely on edge, and scalp prickling as if something was crawling on her. There were two rooms off to the side of the corridor and a faint light shone from each. It was insufficient, however, to illuminate the gloomy passageway, and although Sadie wanted to run the length of it to the next staircase she dare not for fear of the unknown ahead. The far end of the second floor was in complete darkness and she knew that there were three steps down towards the end. Uncertainly she felt her way, hands in front of her and sliding her feet across the carpet. Tears were streaming down her face although she made no sound.

The chanting started again and Sadie screamed, as shrill laughter pealed through the staircase entrance behind her. It was all the more ghostly for being two floors above and the echoes seemed to travel round and round the gallery... "The Big Ship sails through the Alley-Alley-O..." continued the high-pitched, childish voices cutting the previous silence like a knife. She ran forward, blindly now, crying hysterically and simultaneously choking and gasping for breath... she missed the first downward step and stumbled, falling down the remaining two, landing with one leg bent beneath her. Struggling with difficulty to her feet she hobbled painfully towards the entrance to the ground floor hall. She would be out of this awful, terrifying place very soon and there was no way she was coming back! She would hand her notice in tomorrow.

Suddenly the lights from the ancient machines started to flash, as if a coin had been inserted. The tableaux lit up as one, and fairground style music began to play noisily and brashly. Mr Punch's raucous voice shouted: "That's the way to do it… that's the way to do it." Sadie screamed and screamed…

―⁓―

The next morning was bright but cold. Sarah stood outside the museum pondering at the open shutters. It was not often any of the staff were in as early as she. Strange the door was locked! Usually the first to arrive would open both shutters and door. Never mind, she had her key and let herself in leaving the door unlocked as usual. Sarah sauntered through the first hall towards the staff cloakroom, then stopped aghast. A body, not immediately recognisable, lay on the floor near the Punch and Judy tent.

Sarah stared in horror… Sadie's inert body lay lifeless and rigid. Her face was contorted and frozen mid-scream, her eyes wide and terrified, and her hair, once long and dark, now completely white.

Flower Power

Clara had been a child of the Sixties. Well, to be precise, a teenager of the Sixties. How she had loved that era, totally immersing herself in its culture. In her opinion no decade since could hold a candle to it for mood, atmosphere and music. A time of pacifism, love and euphoria! Yes, the music was fantastic: vibrant but moving and spiritual. She'd embraced the whole way of life with an enthusiasm and passion that she'd never equalled since. Sure she was still living the "aging hippy" (the locals called her that!), but there were fewer of her kind and mind-set left. The world had moved on without her so to speak. Today's world was full of trouble, violence and wars, capitalism and greed, economic crisis! The newspapers were full of it. Not that Clara ever read them. She preferred her own world: time locked perhaps, but it worked for her.

Her quaint little flower shop, "Flower Power", was tucked away in a quiet side street in a bustling market town. It was her own re-creation of a gentler, more peaceful, idyllic time. The window was painted with "peace", "love" and brightly coloured flowers, and the shop sign above emblazoned with "Flower Power" joined up in a garland of ivy with scarlet poppies at either end.

As well as her shop Clara had acquired an E registration 1967 VW camper van at an exorbitant price for use as her delivery van, and had painted it herself with the Flower Power logo and a myriad of psychedelic flora. She'd taken some stick for that! Some thought it sacrilegious for a start. Clara admitted that it was a bit "in your face" and looked as if it had been painted with a spade, but it sure as hell got her noticed.

She also dressed for work in appropriate style for the Sixties image with flared trousers and Jesus sandals, psychedelic coloured, loose-fitting blouses or smocks, some tie-dyed herself, beads and her long, once dark hair, now tinged with silvery threads and hanging loose about her shoulders.

In Clara's shop Sixties music played constantly and the customers loved it. There were always individuals who would pop in for a bunch or bouquet of flowers and end up staying for an hour: listening, singing along, dancing or simply chilling out and reminiscing. Sometimes people would enter the shop, initially attracted by the music and ended up buying some flowers simply because they felt they should, having stood in the shop for the duration of eight favourite tracks. Sixties music was certainly timeless! There were also regulars who came in with personal requests: "I'm not leaving until you've put San Francisco on," was the most popular one. Always ready to oblige Clara would "fast forward" to the chosen song whilst she hand-tied and wrapped their flowers. "A Whiter Shade of Pale", "Nights in White Satin" and "Itchycoo Park" were practically daily features of her working day, interspersed with Scott McKenzie's dulcet tones about every two hours. She knew how to get people coming back!

Clara's own personal favourite was "Flowers in the Rain", and she'd turned the back wall of the shop into an amazing mural: a positive explosion of vivid colour, depicting brilliantly coloured, exotic-looking flora, with gentle raindrops falling, some about to drip from the flower petals, while an ethereal fairy with diaphanous wings sat atop a toadstool "watching flowers in the rain" – a great talking point!

It was the "Spirit of Fatima" that had initially been the inspiration for the shop though – a little out of time, but when Clara had first heard Don McLean play and sing it at a live concert in 1972, she had been moved to tears. Afterwards it had haunted her until she was determined to emulate the "Spirit of Fatima": the concept of providing far more than a floral offering to troubled minds and bodies.

After her glorious fling with the Sixties, when she had dropped out of university to travel across America to San Francisco, Clara's parents had eventually persuaded her to return and finish her degree in medicine, which she reluctantly did. She'd been a sensible, hard-working GP for nearly twenty-five years when she'd come to a major life decision – and just like that – she'd jacked it all in! She had always wanted to help people: to improve their health and their lives. In particular she was interested in mental health problems, but had long ago stopped believing that a prescription for anti-depressants was the answer. Half the population were on medication for either depression or stress-related illnesses and the NHS at the mercy of the massive pharmaceutical companies. GPs were not afforded the time they needed to use counselling skills or alternative therapies, but Clara believed that her empathy and talents lay in this direction, and that encouraging people to embrace a different lifestyle was the key to resolving many mental health issues.

So she'd set up as a florist!

Her flower arranging and choice of blooms was self-taught, as was her artwork. Clara found both activities relaxing and satisfying. Her life was now unhurried, a very real step back into the Sixties, in which she made plenty of time to talk to her customers. She probably worked even longer hours now than as a doctor for a fraction of the salary but she found her work both satisfying and enjoyable. The colourful and relaxed Sixties environment she had created was an initial topic of wonder and an instigator of conversation, and people would agree that it reminded them of better, happier and more laid-back times. On the wall adjacent to her "Flowers in the Rain" mural, Clara has scripted some of the words from the "Spirit of Fatima":

> "Where all things are known, but few are revealed,
> Where sins are forgotten and sickness is healed…"

Over the years Clara had developed an understanding of and empathy with the needs of her regular customers. Often when individuals came to the shop it was not just for flowers – they required something more: a listener, a comforter, sometimes a counsellor, and sometimes even a healer. Clara was there! She was adept at reading facial expressions and body language as they stumbled over their words, and somehow she always divined what they needed, and she responded positively and sympathetically. Ever mindful still of her Hippocratic Oath to "do no harm", she traded accordingly, and if her flowers were a little on the expensive side, the purchaser knew that over all they were good value for money and the price included that extra special something that was needed to lift a mood, brighten a day, or simply make it through the night.

Clara's stock of flowers was nothing short of amazing, and she took the greatest of pleasure in searching out new and unusual species. Of course she always kept a supply of the best sellers and most commonly known flowers: roses, carnations, chrysanthemums, lilies – she had to cater for traditional tastes to earn her bread and butter, but she delighted in having a wide range of snappy colours and different species to amaze and excite her Sixties-loving customers. She enjoyed creating sprays which not only looked stunning and unusual, but had a delightful perfume too. She believed that a bouquet should be an uplifting experience, appealing to all of the senses. The addition of some aromatic night-scented stocks, or a couple of richly perfumed tea-roses, or even the cloying but compulsive scent of oriental lilies to a mixed bouquet made such an olfactory difference. Sometimes Clara would add a couple of sprigs of lavender or even catmint to enhance the general aroma, and in the summer, even though they didn't last long, she would include some long stemmed sweetpeas from her own garden: the scent delectable!

If flowers were being purchased as a gift, Clara would take great pains to identify with both the customer and the preferences of the intended recipient: favourite flowers, favourite colour, age and personality. Her "Eighteen Yellow Roses" arrangement was a real favourite: made different by the subtle inclusion of a few sprigs of lavender, or in the spring, pussy willow. Very popular!

She would ask questions about the occasion for the tribute, and make composition suggestions based upon what she had learned about the recipient of the flowers, pointing out suitable blooms for inclusion. Nothing was ever too much trouble – she loved her work. Once Clara had completed an arrangement that particularly pleased her she would catalogue its contents and give it a name.

"Carnaby Street", for example, was a wild splash of vibrant, sharply contrasting colours: the bouquet consisting of scarlet gladioli, canary yellow lilies, brightly speckled alstromeria, and red, orange and pink giant gerbera. Purple statice sprigs were also dotted about, and in the summer Clara would add huge prize-winning dahlias in purple or red. The result was positively explosive.

"Sunshine Superman", whilst still a vivid and uplifting experience, was slightly more harmonious with its sunny colour scheme: yellow roses, lilies, carnations and gerbera, with just a touch of pale lilac in whatever flowers she had at the time (irises her preferred choice), and a trio of magnificent sunflowers, hand tied, and adorned with a contrasting ribbon, with a "smiling sunshine" just visible in the centre of the arrangement.

Popular choices included:

"All you need is Love" – predominantly full red roses, highly perfumed and intoxicating, with a hint of pale blue and a posy of lily of the valley at the front. Sometimes, if the occasion required it, she might add some Bleeding Heart with its small, fragile heart shaped blooms.

"Hi-Ho Silver Lining" – yellow and white composition with some of the blooms edged in silver glitter, wrapped in a silver cloud of tissue and cellophane and sprinkled with silver stars.

"Autumn Almanac" was a burst of bronzes, golds, oranges, yellows and crimsons. Clara also included twigs of beech, silver birch and mountain ash from her garden, which she had previously stood in a glycerine and water mix to turn them into varying autumnal shades, whilst maintaining their moisture and pliability: a bouquet made to last several weeks!

Other themed arrangements included: Purple Haze, Good Vibrations, Summer in the City and, of course, Mellow Yellow. The latter was a very special offering of a more muted, tranquil colour scheme – delicate, pale yellows, pastel peaches and rich creams. It did not have universal appeal, but Clara had designed it for a "special" brand of customer, to bring peace, harmony and balance to troubled minds. Combined with a bit of informal counselling, she was confident that at £40 it would "go" and be considered good value for money.

Her "special" clients would come into the shop looking tired and wan, or distraught and stressed like a coiled spring, and would simply say, "Clara, I really need a Mellow Yellow!" and she would sit them down at the back of the shop while she put the flower arrangement together, asking questions, listening attentively to all the problems and talking gently back. When she finally sent the client on his or her way she was confident that she had helped and knew that they were very satisfied individuals.

Whilst catering for traditional weddings and funerals, Clara also offered Sixties Specials for each occasion. She created bouquets and posies, garlands to be worn around the neck, coronets and headbands for both male and female members of a wedding party, and she even decorated hats to order in true Sixties style and colours. With every wedding she catered for she included a complimentary assortment of flowers on clips and braids to be handed out liberally to all wedding guests so that everyone could "wear some flowers in their hair".

It was Wednesday and Clara was busy with a large funeral order: the funeral of one of her regular customers who had become a personal friend. It was to be a fitting send-off for Davy, a well-known and much-loved local "hippy", only a little older than Clara herself. He'd been a gentle man, a naturalist who had lived his life quietly: walking, sketching and studying wildlife. His wishes were for an internment in a wicker casket and no funereal clothes. Orders for flowers had come flooding in.

She had already prepared the "LOVE" and "PEACE" tributes: the letters formed by using inconspicuous plastic moulds, and filled with every conceivable colour of flower. A psychedelic explosion! She had also created his name "DAVY" in garlands of green and sunshine yellow blooms atop, his favourite colours.

Now Clara was working her way through the many orders which were predominantly for Sunshine Superman and Mellow Yellow sprays, though she would try to make each one slightly different. She had set aside one hundred assorted blooms, each simply but individually wrapped so that anyone who wished to could drop their own flower and message into the grave. Her personal tribute was a flat, circular arrangement of all yellow and gold roses, with yellow lupins radiating from the central cushion so that the whole thing looked like a giant sun.

The shop was going to be closed for the afternoon while Clara attended the occasion, and her change of clothes was hanging in the back room: a long, loose cotton dress in shades of blue and green, three strings of beads and her best sandals. She had even brought her cowbell, bought in 1967, worn for years and in recent times hanging in the hall at home.

Clara had promised Davy's family, such as it was, that she would bring her Sixties music both for the service itself and afterwards. She knew Davy's favourites and had selected for the service, Donovan's "First There Is A Mountain", "Blowing In The Wind", "Where Have All The Flowers Gone?" and of course "San Francisco" which everyone would be invited to join in.

Clara was just putting the finishing touches to the ensemble of tributes, when a police car drew up to the kerb outside the shop. She glanced up and went back to her work. Two officers entered the shop, warrant cards in their hands. One spoke: "Clara Faith Hope, I am arresting you on suspicion of possession of, and with intent to supply, a controlled drug. You don't have to say anything, however, it may harm your defence if you do not mention when questioned anything you later rely on in court. Anything you say may be given in evidence. Do you understand this caution?"

Clara looked from one to the other then slowly nodded.

"It's in the flower food packages, isn't it?" asked the second officer… 'Mellow Yellow' – I believe."

She went quietly.

"Write on…"

Second Chance

Bill and Margaret befriended me when I had no one and they are still the kindest loveliest people I know. I met them at the local parade of shops and something happened between us. I was just mooching about, wondering where my next meal was coming from, when Margaret looked across and caught my eye. It was as if she knew how desperate I was and had some understanding of what it's like when you've fallen on hard times.

For me that was a magical moment, or if you believe in Him, something of a Godsend. I must have looked a real mess: I certainly felt it, and I was absolutely starving – I couldn't think of a time when I'd felt more hungry! I knew that I'd lost quite a bit of weight, and the first thing that Margaret did was offer me a sausage roll, straight from the baker's bag she was carrying. It was still warm, flaky and so tasty. To me it was ambrosia. I took it really carefully so that I didn't touch any of the other sausage rolls in the bag but then I expect that I ate it far too fast for what might be termed well mannered. Bill just smiled indulgently at how much I was enjoying it. After I'd finished and there had been a few exchanges of words, Bill said out of the blue, "Right you are coming home with us. You look as if you need a good feed. Just wait until you sample one of Margaret's proper dinners."

He wasn't kidding! They took me home with them that very afternoon, chatting both to me and to each other all the way. "Home" was a neat, unassuming little house with a garden. I love gardens! Always have! When Joni was alive we had a fantastic garden. She was positively fanatical about it, working in it every hour God sent (which as it turns out wasn't enough). Every season brought its own jobs and she would be out in all weathers. I like to think that I did my bit: I didn't know the names of all the flowers and plants and what have you, but at least I could dig. Boy could I dig! I dug for England in that garden!

I wandered around Bill and Margaret's garden, which was small but delightful, and it brought back a load of memories – Joni and I pottering around our garden in the middle of summer; she picking flowers for the house and me walking beside her carrying the basket while she put the most delicate, sweet smelling flowers in. We would sit together on the rustic seat in the rose garden, watching the sun go down. I remembered that day when she was really cross with me; I'd watered a new shrub she'd just put in and it scorched all the leaves – oops! Generally though we rubbed along just fine and I thought the world of her.

That first day with Bill and Margaret was so special: a turning point in my life. I couldn't believe that they had welcomed me into their lovely home: me, a total stranger! I mean, let's be honest, they didn't know whether they could trust me, or know that I'd once been respectable. I felt humbled by their faith in me.

Margaret put a chicken in to roast and then, once we'd got to know each other a bit better, Margaret asked me if I'd like her to cut my hair. I was a bit apprehensive at first but she certainly knew what she was doing. She even tidied my beard up, which was great because it was really starting to irritate me. Afterwards I felt better than I'd done in a good while.

Margaret's chicken was fantastic too. What a meal! I was going to leave after dinner, but Bill wouldn't let me. He insisted on a bed for the night and "see what tomorrow brings, Danny". They cobbled together a "makeshift bed" as they called it. To me it was heaven, and when they left me to my own devices, I snuggled down into the warmth of the old blankets, the sort that always have that funny but not unpleasant smell about them. I could tell that Bill and Margaret weren't well off but their house was cosy, warm and so friendly. You could tell that there was a lot of love in it and I really appreciated their kindness after what I'd been through.

I'd been going to leave the next morning but Bill insisted I stay on. They actually went out and bought me a proper bed and when they brought it in, Margaret said, "You're staying with us now, Danny. We have no family and this can be your home." At that Bill offered up his hand for a "high five" and I met it with delight.

So, I just seemed to stay. If ever anyone fell on his feet it was me. Bill and Margaret have helped me so much. They used to say that they couldn't imagine life without me now and that they would miss me so much if I ever decided to go. I can hardly believe it but I've been here for fourteen years now and feel very much part of the family. I still miss my Joni and I'll never, ever stop loving her, or forget her lovely face and the brilliant times we had together. She shouldn't have had to die. But I love Bill and Margaret and I know that I'll be all right with them because they love and trust me. They trusted me that first day we met, even though they didn't know anything about me, and that makes them very special people.

I am well fed, and I've also put on a bit of weight. My hair is always clean and tidy now: Margaret keeps me right! I've tried over the years to give as much back as I can, and despite my age I can still fetch and carry, and of course dig! I'm sixty-three now and I'm still very active and if I say so myself, don't look half bad. I know that I'll be the first to turn my toes up, and for that I'm glad. I don't want to lose another loved one ever in my whole life. Bill and Margaret look as young as ever they did when I first met them and they are the most wonderful people I've ever met. It's not everyone who would give a down and out a second chance at life.

And what a life,
Danny (Bearded Collie)
They read my name on my collar!

NOT The End

Port Logie Story

They were on their way to Port Logie along a little-used track across the spartan peninsula. The woman had binoculars and a camera around her neck, while the man carried a small back pack containing a flask of coffee, a couple of buttered scones and a small plastic bag containing their few valuables. Just enough for a day's walking and a brief stop at their destination: a small village, which had neither pub, tearoom nor shop of any kind.

They'd been once before in the late autumn of the previous year: a short, dark day with high winds, choppy seas and not another soul in sight. The place had seemed desolate, bordering on the edge of sinister. The single row of cottages was a full storey below the level of the road and one and all looked unoccupied. On their walk the previous year, the couple had visited the Fishponds, marked on their OS map, some three quarters of a mile beyond the end of the village.

The building housing the fishponds was a quaint, circular, multi-level affair, with the lowest level opening directly into the sea to allow fish to swim back and forth. The level for viewing was a circular structure hewn in the rock, with a narrow path around the edge of high rocky walls and a deep central pool.

A low cave ran off to one side and housed a series of micro-environments for various little-seen species.

Above at ground level was a reception area with a gift shop, under the jurisdiction of Rachael: a garrulous, wild-looking woman, who told visitors that she was *not* a witch despite what the locals said about her. "The village women were strange!" she'd proffered. They were a tightly knit community in what Rachael described as a "window licking" community; watching everything that went on in the village from behind their curtained windows. They believed that she cast spells upon their husbands…

On their route across the slender peninsula, the couple conversed about their previous experience of the place. They debated in fact whether the woman from the fishponds was slightly mad, or if it was the village itself that was sinister and spooky. They had not actually met any of the regular villagers on their last visit, and wondered whether in fact this in itself was proof of Rachael's sanity, and if there had been unseen faces behind the windows watching their every move. They'd speculated on whether the cottages were mainly holiday homes and therefore not always occupied. It seemed that a lack of amenities in the village might have driven people into the town, especially as inhabitants grew older. Was it simply "natural wastage" in a dying village, in which case was it The Fishpond Woman who was crazy?

As they neared the village the man exclaimed to his wife, "Look an airship over the sea! How extraordinary in a place like this. Who would have thought it!"

The hedgerows were high and the woman could not yet see the sea, or the airship.

"It's not so unusual," she remarked. "They're often used in advertising."

"Oh this is totally different. Much bigger – Zeppelin-like. Just wait until you see it."

As they rounded the last bend and the track curved down to the village and the beach, the sun shone onto a turquoise sea dotted with brightly coloured boats. The cottage roofs came into view.

"Where is it then?"

"I don't know – It's gone!" said the man full of incredulity.

"Sure you didn't imagine it?" she laughed.

They walked down to the solitary picnic table and unpacked their sack, pouring two coffees and arranging the scones on pieces of kitchen roll. As they sat enjoying the tranquillity and the warmth of the sun on their shoulders, the woman unveiled her camera and began to peer about for bird life.

"I can't think where that airship can have disappeared to so quickly," said her husband.

"Are you sure it was there in the first place?" she murmured absent-mindedly.

"Of course it was there. It was huge."

The woman focused her camera on the horizon and scanned back and forth. No sign of anything out of the ordinary. She turned her attention to a pair of common sandpipers on the beach.

"It was over there," pointing to his right and out over the bay. "Can't think where it can have gone!"

"Perhaps the breeze carried it around the headland," she offered half-heartedly, her mind on the sea edge where a variety of birds were foraging as the tide retreated.

"It's a real mystery," he persisted.

"Well it doesn't really matter, does it? It's not a life or death threat, is it?"

"It's just strange that's all. I just wish that you'd seen it. I should have taken the camera and photographed it while we were still on the track."

The woman looked at him in exasperation, then returned to her bird watching.

"All you think about are your bloody birds," he countered.

"It seems to me that you're pretty obsessed with your space ship!"

"I never said it was a spaceship!" he retorted. "I said an airship – like a zeppelin-shaped hot air balloon, and it *is* curious that it has just vanished so quickly, isn't it?"

"No! It isn't! There's a breeze: it's just been carried further along the coast! OK? Now I'm going to photograph the house martins, are you coming?" She indicated two empty-looking cottages behind them, where the deft fly-catchers flitted like lightning back and forth to their nests in the eaves.

"No, I'm going to take a walk around the headland and see what I can see."

"Fine, let's meet back at the picnic table at…" she looked at her watch, "about 1.30?" He nodded assent and they strode off in different directions.

At 1.25 she was sitting back at the rustic table and bench seat. Her camera was now trained back on the waders on the shoreline. She glanced at her watch: 1.45. She wasn't concerned, he was never on time – he'd probably underestimated the distance to the headland. It was way beyond the fishponds. She mused about his apparent obsession with the airship. It was a bit strange. In fact it wasn't really like him at all: usually he was quite happy to sit in the sun and enjoy the scenery while she chased around collecting her pictures. Oh well, he'd probably return with a bad back, the terrain out to the headland was pretty rough going. She returned pragmatically to her photography. He'd turn up soon and meanwhile she was quite content where she was.

At 2.30 she set out to look for her husband.

At 3.15 she rounded the headland herself. Nothing! No husband, no airship! Just miles of empty sea and a coastline of lethal-looking rocks, with birds dotted about on both. The woman returned to their rendezvous and sat on the bench, waiting, camera still in its case, and her mind definitely not on the birds.

At 5.30 she telephoned the emergency services.

In the ensuing days the village women who had been interviewed maintained that none of them had seen anything except a woman on her own photographing the birds, and had not at any time seen a man. All identified the woman positively from a photograph shown to them by the police but failed to identify the man. They collectively suggested that the police interview the Keeper of the Fishponds.

Local fishermen and farmers alike swear that no airship, spaceship or any unfamiliar craft has been sighted up or down the coast, or they would know about it.

That was three weeks ago. No body has yet fetched up.

A Friend in Need

Tears welled up in Laura's eyes as she looked, panic-stricken up and down the long, unfamiliar road. Lost! From Auntie Christine's to the hospital should have been easy! Uncle Jack had said it was only two miles, and that didn't seem such a long way.

She stood, undecided which way to go. In either direction the road seemed endless. Of course, she could just retrace her steps, only she felt as if she'd already walked forever and she needed to see her mum. Everyone had told her that Mum would only be in hospital for two or three days, but that was nearly two weeks ago. Auntie Christine and Uncle Jack had been very kind to her, but she just wanted to see her mum. They'd told her that apparently children were not allowed to visit – but surely she could just see her mum for a few minutes. After all it was she who had rung for the ambulance and got her into hospital.

Ten-year-old Laura was an intelligent, sensible child, mature beyond her years, but right now the almost adult common sense had deserted her and the ten-year-old child was frightened, panicky and tearful. She wanted her mum.

Laura looked at her wristwatch. It was seven o'clock: she'd been walking for an hour; having set off straight after tea when she would be least missed. She knew that visiting was until eight, and surely she must be somewhere near the hospital now. Which way? She looked left and right, trying to decide. "Left," she guessed.

She wiped her eyes and set off again, walking briskly. She must get to the hospital during visiting hours. It started to rain and she wished she'd brought a coat. The sky was grey, and the light was beginning to fade. There were few people about. Laura looked warily behind her – no one! A young couple hurried along, a good way ahead of her, an umbrella pulled down over their heads. Laura tried to keep them in sight. An occasional car passed her, splashing through the gutter water and spraying the footpath too. Soaked and cold, she walked on.

Suddenly she heard the noise of an engine, and a car pulled alongside her. A man leaned over and opened the passenger door. "Want a lift?" he asked, "Where are you going? You're soaked."

"No thank you," said Laura, hurrying past. She knew she must not accept lifts from strangers.

The car moved slowly along beside her. The man was peering out at her. He looked kind and ordinary – but… Laura began to panic again. "Go away," she shouted at the man. She looked wildly around, continuing to walk as fast as she could. The young couple were now out of sight and there was no one else about.

A slight figure loomed out of the shadows making Laura jump. A small, rough-coated dog stood there, watching her and wagging its tail slightly. Laura looked down at the creature; it was grey, with a splash of white on its chest. Its coat was wispy and bedraggled. Laura continued to walk away from the car, and the dog fell into step beside her. "It's pretending that it's my dog," she thought. "Good dog!" she said loudly.

The man in the car kept pace with her. "Sure you don't want a lift? Your dog can come too." He smiled – really a very nice smile. Laura could feel the warmth of the car heater through the open door. It was tempting… Suddenly the little dog began to bark furiously, and with a shrug the man called, "I guess that's a 'No' then!" He closed the car door and drove away.

Laura looked down at the dog. It wagged its tail more vigorously now, turning large brown, sorrowful eyes upon her. "Thank you," she whispered. The dog stayed with her pattering along in the wet beside her, its tail waving gently. At the next fork in the road Laura halted, contemplating which road she should take. The dog, however, did not hesitate and gave a small "woof" as it headed to the left. It stopped after a few metres, looking back at Laura.

"I believe you are taking me to the hospital," she said to the little creature, following it trustingly. She strode out more confidently now, matching her pace with that of her new friend. "You really are a clever dog. You scared that man away and you know where the hospital is, don't you? I'm glad you are my friend." The dog responded with a wag and an eager surge forward.

After some minutes a large building came into view. The dog gave a few staccato yaps and Laura sighed with relief. The hospital! Her companion accompanied her to the hospital doors, where it stood, mouth open and tongue lolling out the side as if it was laughing. Through the glass, Laura saw the brightly lit reception area and Uncle Jack standing at the reception desk. As he turned and saw Laura, he smiled with relief, and beckoned her inside. As she stepped through the automatic doors she turned to thank her new friend – but the dog had already vanished!

Ted Grainger had had enough of life. He was fifty-one years old and he'd been unemployed for eight months. He'd applied for 46 jobs so far and had been unsuccessful every time. "We regret to inform you…" and "Thank you for your interest but…" were everyday reading! He'd never get another job at his age. His redundancy money, which had been a bare minimum, was already dwindling.

Ted had worked since he was sixteen, and had never been out of work before. He'd never had State handouts and he wasn't about to start now. He'd rather kill himself! The final straw though had been when Sharon had left him six weeks ago. He didn't blame her: at forty-eight she looked ten years younger. She was blonde, slim attractive, while he was miserable, depressed and skint. What use had she for him? Come to think of it, he'd be worth more to her dead than alive.

It was a mild evening and Ted had walked and walked, turning his problems over in his head: his thoughts and worries racing round in circles. He hadn't been able to sleep for weeks now, and was physically and mentally exhausted. His mood tonight was at an all time low as he flung himself down on a wooden bench on the riverside. He put his aching head in his hands and closed his eyes. The swifts swooped about him catching hovering insects, but Ted was unaware of their presence. At the end of his tether, he couldn't go on like this – something had to give! Ted put his hand in his pocket and felt the bottle of tablets. He'd been carrying them around for three days now, hoping at some point that he would literally "have the bottle".

Ted sat for a long time, hardly aware of dusk turning into darkness. He jumped as he caught in his peripheral vision a small, shadowy shape sitting unobtrusively some ten feet away to his left. He peered through the gloom and identified the shape as a diminutive, rough-coated dog. It was greyish, he thought, but unrecognisable as any particular breed. Its eyes were large and dark: liquid, like two deep pools. The creature sat motionless, watching Ted intently. Its tail flicked slightly when it realised that it had attracted his attention.

"What do you want?" asked Ted. The dog continued to stare. "Go away! You're spooking me!"

The dog sidled a little closer, the very tip of its tail wagging tentatively. Before long and without him realising how it happened, Ted's hand was resting on the dog's head. For its part the creature seemed very content with the arrangement, its gaze fixed with expectation on the man's face.

"Mates now, are we?" said Ted.

Suddenly further along the riverbank, Ted heard raised voices, swearing and then the sound of a brawl breaking out. The dog stood, ears pricked and turned to the direction of the noise, listening, then moved a few paces forward. It stopped and looked over its shoulder at Ted expectantly. There was a cry! "Help, help, I'm being robbed!"

"Okay dog, it's your call," said Ted rising.

With a brief wave of the tail, the little creature set off at a run, Ted charging along behind the diminutive silhouette. As they arrived at the scene, there was one body on the ground, another two towering above, aiming kicks at head and gut. The attackers were two hefty youths of perhaps nineteen or twenty. As to the victim, it was impossible to say: it was male, his arms were covering his head, trying to protect himself from the rain of blows… blood pooled on the ground beneath him.

Ted sized up the situation and waded in. A strong bloke, fit for his age, he had no trouble dragging off one youth and despatching him to the ground with a well-aimed punch. The other turned from his "victim" to Ted, but hadn't bargained for being up against a far more experienced fighter in the older man. Ted forced the lad to his knees, one arm twisted up his back. The little dog stood guard: tail stiff and lips curled, daring the prostrate youth to move. Teamwork! Ted felt better than he had for weeks. Others had now arrived at the scene and assisted the victim to his feet, praising Ted's courage. Someone had rung the police. Amidst the clamour Ted glanced around for the dog: it had vanished…

Only a few days later Ted received a letter of thanks from the robbery victim and a glowing write-up in the local press, which resulted in an offer of employment from a local fitness centre. Sadly he never saw the little dog again.

Amy sat in her favourite armchair, her head drooping forward on her chest. These days she spent a lot of time in shallow slumber, neither awake nor quite sleeping: as if light sedation was holding her just below consciousness. She had lived a long time; more than her four score years! She couldn't remember if she was eighty five or six…

Her body gave an involuntary jerk. Amy raised her head and slowly opened her eyes. Her vision was blurred. Had she been dreaming about Trixie again? She looked around the room, gradually bringing the familiar furniture into focus. Her eyes fell upon a small, dark shape on the hearthrug. Amy stared at it, waiting for the image to become clear. At last she convinced herself that there was a miniature, rough-coated, grey dog watching her.

"Now how did you get in?" Amy smiled and stretched out a frail, bony hand towards the creature. The dog, regarding her with large, brown eyes, took a step towards her, its tail quivering with friendliness. "You look very like a young version of my little Trixie. A more faithful dog never lived and how I loved her!" murmured Amy. The dog moved closer, tail waving gently and eyes fixed intently upon Amy's face. "Have you come to keep me company?" continued Amy. "Well you're welcome. There's no denying I've been a lonely old woman since Trixie passed on. There's been many a day I've wished I could join her."

As Amy leaned forward to reach down to the dog, a sharp pain seared through her chest, causing her to clutch at herself with both hands. She leaned back feeling light-headed, and closed her eyes again. These "attacks" were not unusual. She recognised the signs – but where were her tablets? They were usually on the table next to her… Oh no!… left on the bedside cabinet. If she could just manage to get one and put it under her tongue… She leaned forward again in an attempt to get to her feet, but recoiled with the severity of the pain. She couldn't catch her breath. Perspiration broke out on the woman's forehead and her hair stuck to it damply and limply. Amy endeavoured once more to struggle to her feet, her face contorted with pain. Eventually she sank back exhausted whilst the dog looked on with anxious eyes. "I think this is the end. Did Trixie send you so that I was not alone? Faithful friend!"

The dog waited quietly, until the woman's hand fell from her chest and hung limply over the side of the chair. Then it stepped forward so that its head was touching the lifeless fingers of its mistress, and together Amy and Trixie left the room for the last time…

A Debt Repaid

It was a small, compact room: a single bed, en-suite toilet facilities and a very basic desk and chair. The décor was minimalist to say the least: plain walls all the same neutral colour and the only addition a couple of pictures, one above the head of the bed and one above the desk, facing him as he sat. There was a calendar on the desk with each date meticulously crossed off as it passed.

He'd learned that material possessions counted for very little in life and he had proven that he could get by without most things. He had few clothes now, but was clean, and showered every day. He also exercised every day, mainly walking, weather permitting. He spoke little, but thought and wrote, a great deal. His life was in that room. He slept, ate, wrote and read. There were few people in his life. His mother was now in a residential care home and had long since forgotten who he was. True Mark came to see him twice a month, but the visits were brief and a bit stilted.

They had nothing in common now, the only thing that had bound them together was gone and they had little to talk about beyond formal pleasantries, which gave way to awkward silences, when Mark would make a hasty departure: his parting words always the same, "Keep the faith!"

That was a joke!

He was twenty-seven now and had been writing prolifically in the last two years. There was so much he wanted to say: so much he needed to say. Whether lying on his bed or walking his daily circuit, his mind was continuously on the boil, and he would suddenly, urgently, have to get to his desk. Technology had passed him by, and so he scribbled feverishly: crossing out, rewriting, asterixing and inserting, drawing arrows up and down pages then finally rewriting the revised page neatly, and adding it to his manuscript.

He never talked about his work to Mark, afraid of his only friend's reaction. The book was an autobiography and obviously Mark featured in a significant number of chapters. Inevitably it contained classified information: secrets from their teenage years, their pranks, misdemeanours and loves. He had been candid about their youthful exploits and the blood brothers relationship they had vowed years before.

It was the day of Mark's fortnightly visit and neither party was particularly looking forward to it. Mark was seated in his usual place sporting a sharp suit, silk tie and highly polished black shoes, when his friend walked in, wearing his usual casual attire. They greeted each other in a half-hearted fashion.

"So what's new, Boy?" asked Mark.

"Not much around here," said *Boy*.

"You look as though you've lost even more weight since I was last here."

"Under 140 now."

"Good God, you used to be 210, back in the day. It's time you got some flesh back on those bones…" he paused, "and got some weight training done again. You look like a wraith."

"No motivation any more, and other priorities now," responded the tired voice.

"What other priorities can you possibly have?" snorted Mark derisively.

"Do me a favour!"

"I thought I'd already done you a favour! I saved your miserable goddamn life – remember? You still owe me one. If it hadn't been for me you would have drowned in that canal fifteen years ago – and I still come and see you every fortnight. You never return the compliment do you?"

"Let it go, Mark. I've paid you back tenfold. If I could turn back the clock, I'd just as soon you'd let me die back then."

"Come on mate – we're still blood brothers, aren't we? Watching each other's backs all the way, like we promised." They talked perfunctorily for a while about the weather and Mark's latest promotion at work, then: "Anyway gotta go, Boy. Got a red hot date tonight: you know how it is!"

He was back at his desk, rereading the third chapter of his manuscript: the story of two twelve-year-old boys larking about near the canal, the dark, still waters below them; a sheer edge from the path to the water. Two boys: pushing and shoving, laughing and daring: then suddenly, himself, falling, hitting the silent water below with a mighty splash. Screaming in fright and going down and down, mouth open, involuntary gulping in the evil-tasting water, then everything going into slow motion around him, unable to see, and his ears hearing only distant, muffled sounds as if from another world. He seemed not to be struggling any more, but moving in harmony with the water, as if in a somnambulistic state.

He was only vaguely aware of someone grasping him and dragging or towing him along with them. It was a not unpleasant sensation – rather as if he was floating through the air without any effort.

There was a gap in his memory from this point, and he next remembered lying on his side on the tow path, a man kneeling beside him, rubbing his back and urging him to cough up water. His unfocused eyes fell upon two other figures a short distance off: a boy and a woman. The boy, he was sure, was Mark and he appeared to be wearing the lady's coat around his shoulders. Water was streaming down his legs.

Only later did he hear the full story: that he had fallen into the canal, cried out, and Mark, who knew that he couldn't swim, had jumped in and rescued him. A couple out walking further along the path had heard the splash, seen a commotion and hurried along. The man had dragged him out in a semi-conscious state, and then helped Mark, his rescuer, out. The woman had wrapped her coat around the shivering Mark, commending his prompt action in saving his friend's life.

So it was in the next day's newspaper, and a few weeks later Mark received a special award for bravery from the Mayor, something he has never let his friend forget.

From that time on he was forever repaying Mark for his life: buying him pints when his friend had spent all of his money, lending him money, which was rarely repaid, backing off when they both had eyes for the same girl… That was the worst!

As soon as he'd clapped eyes on Katie, he just knew she was the one. She was petite with dark, shoulder length hair, an elfin face and a quiet voice: a gentle, unassuming lass: shy, and almost always dressed down in T-shirt and jeans. When he'd asked her out for a drink she had blushed and falteringly declined, telling him that she didn't drink alcohol and didn't really like to go to pubs. He changed the offer to a coffee, with the added invitation that she could choose a venue where she would feel comfortable. She had accepted!

Katie had chosen a small, quaint coffee shop called Campbell's: off the beaten track and patronised apparently by groups of mature ladies out shopping. There was waitress service and the tables had immaculate white cloths, silverware and small posy vases on them. He'd felt a bit like a fish out of water, but Katie seemed quite at home and well known there. Once they had got talking, he relaxed a bit, and the genteel hum of the place assured him that no one was taking much notice of the quiet couple in the corner. They'd got on really well and Katie wasn't so shy when she was talking about college and her career expectations. She was in her final year, with exams just around the corner, and she explained to him that it didn't leave much time for socialising though it did her good to break off for a coffee or a walk sometimes. He had understood: he'd been through various training courses at work for the furtherance of his career, which required considerable time and commitment. If you wanted to get on in life you had to have focus!

There had been plenty more cups of coffee, and walks. He looked back now at these idyllic days. The girl who changed his life! It was all there in chapter five…

Back to the reality of the present!

He had days of dark thoughts, who doesn't? He experienced loneliness, even though he was surrounded by people. The worst sort of loneliness! He didn't fit in here and knew that he shouldn't be here. However, he couldn't do anything about that now: he had to stay focused on his writing because that is what helped him to get through every day.

Sometimes he would turn back to a previously written chapter and reread it. Reliving the memory as if it was yesterday: the milestones and landmarks of his life. Whatever else, he never suffered from writer's block. He had so much to say, even if he told the tale clumsily. He wrote page after page feverishly, the words tumbling out like a waterfall. There were few significant characters: himself, Mark... Katie, who in a sense was only a fleeting, transient character, but such a turning point, and so much influence upon his life: then and now! She was the reason he needed to write... and was able to transform his thoughts into the written word.

He'd reached the penultimate chapter – at least he thought he had. He wasn't sure that he would know when to stop writing. Maybe he would just keep on scribbling for the rest of his life or perhaps he would suddenly have "written himself out". A bit like Forrest Gump with his running!

When Mark had visited yesterday they'd gone through the usual meaningless ritual. Mark was full of himself. Another new girlfriend: stunning, sexy, good job! Nothing new there, then! All Mark's women were of the same ilk and he was temporarily besotted, but once he'd shagged them a couple of times that was it. They had nothing else to offer him and he certainly didn't have anything to offer them. He simply ditched them and moved on.

It had been like that with Katie. Once Mark had met her, he wanted her. It was as simple as that! He'd used every trick in the book to get her as well, but Katie would have none of it. That was when Mark started putting the pressure on him. He'd tried it all: he had fallen for her "big time": give him a break because he was certain she was "the one". Then he told him that Katie had been two-timing him and that he should give her the push. He'd seen her with Jim S... so he should blow her out. Needless to say none of those ploys had worked.

Then came: "You know you owe me. I saved your bloody life! At least give me a chance. Katie can decide which of us she wants, but she ain't going to do that if she hasn't seen what she could have instead of what she's got."

"No!"

"Are you going to blow all our years of friendship for someone you've only known for a few months? What happened to the 'blood brothers' pact? What happened to 'thanks for saving my life, pal'? You really can be a piece of shite."

He remembered replying, "What do you want me to do? Finish with her? How do you know that she'll go out with you even if I do? I love her Mark and I'm not letting her go."

He and Katie had a gentle relationship, something that Mark had never understood. It had taken time for Katie to trust and to blossom. He hadn't rushed their relationship, but let things take their course at a pace that Katie was comfortable with. When they had finally made love, it was at Katie's instigation. It was her first time and she was nervous, but he had done everything to ensure that it had been slow and gentle and fulfilling for her.

His thoughts jumped now to the last time he had seen Katie. They had a "night in" at his place: he'd cooked a pasta meal, they'd shared a bottle of wine and watched a DVD, and then had an early night. He'd had to leave early the next morning for a meeting in Manchester so they'd cuddled and made love before falling asleep in each others' arms. He had reluctantly, but carefully extricated himself from the warm bed at 5am, leaving Katie asleep. As he was leaving the house at 5.50 he looked in at her and she had momentarily opened her eyes and smiled. "Go back to sleep," he'd said softly, "I'll call you later today." – and that is how he would always remember her: how he wanted to remember her.

He could not possibly have foreseen what would happen in the next 24 hours.

The meeting in Manchester had been productive and worthwhile, and just maybe would lead to a promotion for him. He gathered his belongings together as the train approached his station, making sure that his car keys were to hand. It had been a relaxing journey, much better than having to drive through Manchester during the rush hour. A good decision! He had tried to ring Katie from the train, but had been unable to obtain a signal. Instead he'd sent her a text, hoping that at some point she would receive it.

He'd alighted from the train and headed for the station car park, a fine drizzle against the receding light causing him to squint as he hurriedly found his car and got inside. Funny how he remembered these trivial details: the coldness of the car as he headed home, the short journey not enough for the heat to come through, parking the car on the road outside the house, and hurrying to the front door, key in hand. The house in darkness now!

He had faithfully recorded every detail.

He had entered the silent house, dropping his bag in the hall and taking off his coat as he walked into the kitchen. He filled the kettle and as it boiled, checked his phone. Nothing from Katie. That was strange! He'd phone her as soon as he'd made himself a cuppa. As he carried his cup and phone into the living room, he noticed Katie's handbag – exactly where he remembered seeing it last night. She must have forgotten it. Then he stopped in his tracks! How could she have forgotten it: it was where she kept the keys, for both his house and her flat, her purse and her phone. Was she still here? Was she ill? He called her name – nothing! He tried her mobile again and as he heard the ringing sound through his own phone, seconds later he jumped as he heard Katie's phone burst into life from the depths of her handbag with Mozart's "Eine Kleine Nachtmusik". Hastily he opened her bag and rummaged for the phone, so focused that he never even thought about the privacy of a girl's handbag and the fact that he would never have dreamed of doing such a thing normally. The phone showed the missed calls from him and texts received but still unread: nothing else.

He remembered standing: stunned and confused for a moment, then his brain working furiously. Where was Katie? She had to be here still! Upstairs? Asleep? Unconscious? He ran into the hall and bounded up the stairs two at a time. The bedroom door stood wide open and as he rounded the doorframe there Katie was, sprawled on her front on the bed. Her hands were tethered to the headboard and blood pooled beneath her hips. One of his own ties was tightly around her neck and it had clearly been used to choke the life out of her. He stopped aghast, unable to comprehend the scene, and then screamed and screamed! He flung himself on the bed crying hysterically, touching Katie's inert body and loosening the tie from her blue, bruised neck. Suddenly he stopped in panic; he shouldn't have touched her. He had to phone the police! They had to get whoever had done this. He ran downstairs to the phone...

Well that was the story so far! The following hours, even days, seemed like a dream: a nightmare in fact, and even now he was unable to document the various scenes in detail. Perhaps he would be able to return to this part of the narrative at some point in the future…

―⁂―

Since then he'd recorded in note form the events as he remembered them: sketchy, with gaps, and filled intermittently with his feelings for Katie, his shock, his horror and ultimately, his despair.

He'd called the police, and in what seemed like minutes, they'd arrived in force. Soon his house was full of people in white suits and boots and after a few questions in the kitchen, he was removed from the scene to the back of a police car. At the time he had thought that it was to spare him the trauma of what they needed to do to his home, and even worse, to Katie. He knew from watching crime series on the television what was likely to happen.

Two officers had interviewed him at the station and he had recounted the events of the previous evening, that morning, and his day in Manchester. Luckily, with travelling by train, he had exact times, a car park ticket still in his car, a taxi receipt from Manchester in his wallet, and the attempted calls made to Katie's mobile phone. All proclaiming his whereabouts! He had kept breaking down during the questioning but the detectives had been kind and patient. Eventually he had signed his statement, given his fingerprints for purposes of elimination, and now he had the facts all there in his manuscript.

He read on through his notes…

As he couldn't return home, he'd spent the night at Mark's flat, and his friend had provided a shoulder to cry on. He had given the police the details of his whereabouts, and the next morning two Serious Crime Officers had arrived, requiring more details of his relationship with Katie, and his movements during the previous day. Had he locked the door when he left yesterday morning? Of course he had! They had seemed particularly interested in his time of departure from the house that morning and the evidence of his journey to Manchester, and they finally revealed that Katie's death had been determined as between 05.00 and 08.00 hours. It only occurred to him then that the crime must have taken place soon after his own departure. Was someone watching the house? He wracked his brains, wondering if he had subconsciously noticed anyone in the street, or a car maybe? Finally the leading police officer had questioned him about his entry to the house on his homecoming, and having replied that he used his front door key, it suddenly struck him that there was no sign of any forced entry. Could Katie have let the person in?

The post-mortem was to be carried out that afternoon, after which he was asked to attend the police station to give a voluntary DNA sample.

He had ended up staying with Mark for two more days, as his home remained a crime scene, but he had spent much of that time back at the police station, each of the interrogations becoming more harrowing and aggressive. Then came the arrest!

"Peter James Gardner, I am arresting you on suspicion of the rape and murder of Catherine Adams. You do not have to say anything, but anything you do say may be used in evidence at your trial."

The court case, even now, was hazy in his mind. It seemed to go on for days, and much of it was too technical for him to comprehend in his dazed and bereft state. It appeared that the only DNA present at the scene was his own. His fingerprints were, of course, all over the house. Well they would be wouldn't they – it was his house for God's sake! Katie's prints were in most rooms too, and so were Mark's and a couple of his other mates. It proved nothing.

The estimated time of death had been confirmed at the post mortem and therefore stood at between 5 and 8am. The Crown Prosecution had built up a convincing case against him in terms of means and opportunity, with regard to the time, and this was strengthened by the forensic evidence presented in the form of his semen being the only DNA found in Katie's body.

On the stand, of course, he had admitted to having sexual intercourse with Katie the previous evening, maintaining truthfully that it had been consensual. The jury had, however, already heard that the trauma inflicted upon Katie's body confirmed otherwise. The girl had been raped, before being murdered by strangulation! His own statement given initially to the police contained his belief that Katie had in fact been sexually assaulted in some way. With these seemingly conflicting facts, the CP had tied him in knots until he couldn't think straight or speak coherently.

Even Mark, who had appeared as a character witness for him, had buckled under cross-examination and had "admitted" that his friend had a "bit of a temper" and also that he had told Pete that Katie was two-timing him. Now a motive as well!

It had taken the jury less than two hours to return a verdict of "Guilty". If Pete thought that his world had fallen apart with Katie's death, it had now been smashed into tiny pieces that could never be reassembled.

Was this the final chapter? He wasn't sure.

He'd been inside for three long years now and his Appeal had come and gone with no change to his circumstances. He simply could not believe what had happened to him. In the early days he'd looked forward to the visits from his solicitor and Mark, relieved to see a familiar face from the outside world, optimistic about his appeal and sure that new evidence which would exonerate him would have come to light. He had also wanted to talk to Mark about Katie, but found his friend increasingly reluctant and evasive. It seemed that Mark had completely forgotten that he had once been attracted to Katie too. When Pete tried to remind Mark of how he'd pleaded with Pete to give him a chance with her, his friend had become incensed: "That was a joke!" he'd hissed through clenched teeth. "I just wanted to get her away from you. She was bad for you, and what happened proved it."

As Pete tried to protest, Mark continued: "That girl was bad news! She was ruining our friendship. Coming between us and stirring up trouble! We go back as far as our early school days and don't you forget it."

After Mark's visit on that occasion, Pete had pondered long and hard over his friend's attitude. He had written down their conversation so that he would remember it as precisely as possible. Unsure of its significance, he had felt, nevertheless, that it was important. Did Mark know something about Katie? He could not believe that it could be anything bad…

And that was the start of his writing… he recorded everything that he and Mark discussed…

With endless time on his hands, over a period of months he began to build his autobiography. Actually that sounded a bit too grand, he was no author! He analysed his friendship with Mark, covering the milestones of their lives, and realised how it had altered over the years: long before Katie had come on the scene. Maybe back to the two twelve-year-olds, who had sworn to be Blood Brothers by each cutting one of their palms with Mark's penknife, and dramatically joining palms allowing their blood to mingle as it dripped to the ground. That was only months before the canal incident! In his long hours of musing, Pete came to the conclusion that it was after the rescue from the water when the change had occurred. Mark had become something of a local hero, whilst Pete had felt like an idiot. Mark suddenly had lots of other friends. Pete was constantly the butt of their jokes. Yet Mark would not relinquish Pete's friendship, and Pete could not, for fear of seeming ungrateful. Mark became more dominant and arrogant, Pete quieter and more resigned, and yet something endured between them.

Then came the contention over Katie. It was the first time that Pete had stood up to Mark, and he firmly held his ground. If he had to, he would sacrifice his friendship with Mark, but it would be of his friend's doing. All the facts and his own thoughts now down on paper!

In a previous chapter he had written of his meeting with Katie, the early days and their growing relationship. He had been candid about his love for her, described her own quiet intelligence and gentle, shy personality, how he had planned to marry her, although he hadn't made this particular dream known to her, and now, he never would.

Though Pete continued to receive visits from Mark, they became more and more strained. Neither of them was comfortable in the other's company, yet they were drawn together, despite having so little to talk about. In the early days of Pete's incarceration they had reminisced about their shared childhood days and the main incidents that marked them: the Blood Brothers pact, the canal incident, of course, and eventually as they travelled mentally through the years: Katie and what had followed.

"Do you believe that I could ever do something like that?" he'd asked of Mark during one visit.

"Of course not! Do you believe that I could?" Pete stared at his friend for a long moment before he replied, "No…er…no…" Their eyes met and suddenly Pete knew.

Mark gave a dismissive laugh and turned away. "Well, I'd better be off, so see ya…" As he reached the door, he turned and added, "Don't forget, you still owe me, so… Keep the faith!" and he was gone.

Back at his desk, Pete stared long and hard at the picture before him; Mark and himself at sixteen, arms around each others' shoulders, dressed in open-necked shirts of a particularly loud design, with big cheesy grins for the camera. He turned and looked at Katie smiling shyly from the wall beside his bed. He picked up his pen and began to write… The prominent aspects of the case came thick and fast.

Significance of time of death? Opportunist, who saw me leave the house? Or someone else who already knew my plans for that day?

No DNA from the rape! He came prepared and was very careful. Premeditated.

Used my tie to strangle Katie. No mess or disruption in bedroom, so someone who knew where to go? In a premeditated murder wouldn't the killer have come prepared?

No "stranger" fingerprints in house. None found on front door, doorbell or knocker.

No sign of forced entry either, so had Katie let someone in? Someone she knew?

Or did they already have a key to his house?

Mark had a key: had always held an "emergency" key since Pete had bought the house. *Mark's* prints were all over the house: had stayed over on many occasions and therefore it hadn't aroused any suspicion. *Mark* had fancied Katie, but he also resented her, for, as he saw it, coming between them. *Mark* was jealous and also thought that Pete should always let him have what he wanted. After all, HE OWED HIM!

It took days to analyse his scribblings and to carefully think each facet through. He didn't want to leave his room, ate little, carried his notepad and pen everywhere with him, and finally sat reading through a re-draft of the draft of original bullet points.

This really was the final chapter!

He'd already arranged a meeting with his solicitor, and requested that he also bring Ray Blackett with him. Friday couldn't come quick enough. Two photocopies of the whole manuscript were formally handed over; one to Peacock and Daly Solicitors and one to Ray, an author and journalist, who also had shares in a small publishing company. Pete had done his homework and with the help of Owen Daly, singled out Ray as the right man for the job.

It was several months later when Pete's work came to fruition. Thanks to Ray, one of the Nationals had run an article on the release of the book, complete with an extract from it and an overview of the original murder case, citing a request for the case to be reopened. Copies of the book went on sale the next day and Owen Daly sent Mark a personal copy in that day's post, the inscription inside read "A debt repaid"…

One Guid Turn Deserves Another

There was old Seth again, out on the rocks, picking shellfish after the retreating tide. Helen had got used to seeing him now in his old-fashioned oilskins and boots, sou'wester pulled right down, covering most of his face and neck, and carrying an old plastic bucket that looked as if it had seen better days. He was out every day, and in all weathers: the only variable factor being the tide times.

She'd watched him often in biting wind and driving rain, his head and body bent against the raging elements, stoically lumbering from rock to rock, peering into crevices or pools and then crouching down and using some kind of metal tool to prise some small, unfortunate sea critter from its home or resting place.

Helen had often wondered what manner of shellfish he collected, and whether he lived off the fruits of his activities or whether perhaps he sold them at a local market. She'd clambered over the slippery rock shelves herself, finding them equally treacherous in Wellington boots and training shoes, and had never discovered anything that she would be prepared to eat, unless marooned on a desert island.

She'd never spoken to Seth in the two months she had been in residence at Barnacle Cottage. Even if she'd been on the seashore at the same time as the old fellow, he was always too far away to speak or even to hail. She'd waved to him a few times in the early days of her convalescence but he'd never acknowledged her. He always seemed completely focused on the job in hand, and apparently never noticed her. Helen speculated on whether this was a deliberate act as she was an outsider in the small and tightly knit community.

As Helen had become fitter, she had taken to walking further afield, sometimes taking routes inland for a change of scene and slightly more strenuous geography. She strayed into the heather-clad foothills of the hilly backbone of the peninsula. Usually now she saw Seth on those wilder, inclement days when she hadn't ventured out at all. She would sit at the front window of the cottage and watch his slow, determined progress like a daily ritual for both of them.

Onwards he battled against gale force winds and battering rain and waves, always on the same stretch of coastline, presumably, she mused, his favourite and most fruitful patch. She'd often speculated on how old Seth must be: glimpses of his face, mainly covered by his headwear gave no clue. She'd caught snatches of flesh colouring but was never able to make out facial features. In truth she could not have guessed how old he was. His gait over the rough yet slippery rock surfaces gave no clue. A young person would have had as much difficulty keeping their feet as on octogenarian. The stoop, the hunched back, could have as easily been indicators of the difficulty of the terrain itself, but for some reason Helen had decided that Old Seth (as he was always referred to by the locals) must be in his seventies. Indeed, she thought, his very name suggested as much.

In the weeks Helen had lived in Barnacle Cottage, she had met a few of the inhabitants of the tiny hamlet Pelgowan, all that remained of a once thriving fishing port. Most were elderly and native to the village and a couple of the cottages had been bought as holiday homes, which mostly stood empty. When she had first arrived, her landlady Mrs MacKinnon had met her at the cottage and walked her through the primitive facilities concerning heating, lighting and plumbing, including instructions on the use of the back up generator housed in the outhouse. She had warned Helen that power cuts were a frequent feature of the peninsula.

The nearest town was thirteen miles away, and a bus ran into town and back once a day, but the hamlet was further provided for in the form of a weekly visit from a travelling shop, a van, which stocked dry and tinned goods, bread and fresh vegetables. A butcher's van came separately every Thursday.

"If you want fresh fish," Mrs MacKinnon had told her, "just see Big Angus in that blue cottage along there. He goes out regularly and he'll see you all right." She had pointed along the narrow coast road to the left.

The cottage, as Helen soon found out was The Anchorage and Big Angus had proved a valuable contact. He was a rough looking, weather-beaten, cheery bloke who could have been in his twenties or thirties, Helen decided. He was indeed "Big" at six foot three with huge muscled arms and shoulders. He now called twice a week and dropped off freshly caught fish. He sold what he caught locally and often presented Helen with fish she had never seen before, much less eaten.

When she questioned Angus about some new catch, he'd tell her a name. "Them's rock salmon or pollocks, etc. Just a bit o' butter an' pepper on and inter the oven in foil. Don't be overcooking him now or yer'll spoil 'im. Twenty minutes is all he needs!" Helen had taken the horrors at first until she'd got Angus into the habit of beheading and gutting everything for her. She coped with her new menus reasonably well now but she wished he'd stop calling them by a gender. She still didn't dare tell him that when he'd brought her a live crab, she had discreetly taken it down to the sea and let it go.

Angus never stopped for more than a few minutes to discuss the weather or the fish and would never step into the house "on account of 'is boots". Helen had asked him a couple of times about the "lone winkle picker" as she called him in her head. All she got in return was, "Ah that'll be Auld Seth. You've seen 'im 'ave you? Aye well I'm not surprised. 'E's out there in all weathers." Then a hurried, "Right I'll be off. I'll be out in boat again on Thursday, God willing, so I'll mebbes see yer then."

On another occasion Helen had asked about Seth's age. Angus mused for a few seconds. "I guess 'e'd be about 92 now. Never looks any different," was the reply. "Anyhow I'll be off, but you get them mussels real soon now – boiling water, five minutes, no more."

Angus took his leave and Helen watched him striding across to his cottage, peering out to sea as he did so. As she cooked her mussels a little later, she marvelled at Seth's resilience to the elements at such a grand old age.

As Helen settled into her new way of life, she watched the summer gradually fade into autumnal colours. The bracken on the low hillside behind the cottage yellowed, then browned, and the brambles grew laden with fruit. She spent an afternoon picking blackberries and made three pies with the fruits of her labours. When Angus called with a codling and some queen scallops, she gave him a pie.

"Why thank ye Miss Helen," he said, waving away the money she offered him for the fish. "I'll not be takin' yer money today. One guid turn deserves another! Thank ye kindly."

Helen had hoped also to take a pie to Auld Seth, but although she looked out to catch him, he was always some distance away, and she never ever saw him on the village street. She considered taking the pie out to him on the rocks, but rejected the idea as impractical when he was so busy with his shellfish and carrying his bucket. Eventually she put the spare pie in her freezer.

Autumn turned to winter, and the trees grew bare, accentuating their wind-distorted skeletons. The wind was biting and the sea rougher: dark waves rolling in and cresting at ten and twelve feet before thundering onto the rocks mottled black and green. And still Seth was out scavenging every day. As Helen became more housebound by the weather, she took to watching him at each low tide, while drinking her coffee. As low tide became later each day until it occurred through the night, she noticed that the old man would turn out just after high tide, slithering his way through the waves as they receded across the rocky shelves, and scrambling for what she guessed were mussels, cockles and winkles. Maybe the odd crab too, she supposed, before they were washed back into the murky depths of a winter sea.

Helen sat in her cottage, cosy with her coffee one particularly stormy afternoon, watching Seth performing his usual routine. Suddenly she saw the old man stumble and disappear from sight. Helen stood up, craning her neck to see him. He was gone! In panic she ran to the back door, grabbing her waterproof from the hook there, and thrusting her feet into her Wellingtons as she zipped up. She ran clumsily across the empty road and onto the rocky shelf. Her feet slid from side to side as she skittered over the wet, uneven surface, unable to see where she was stepping as the rain beat against her face. Still she could not see Seth.

She stumbled on blindly until at last she saw a bundle of dark oilskin some thirty yards away. Gasping with relief she started to run towards it, slipping on the seaweed covered rocks, all the more slimy from the relentless waves crashing against them, as the rain continued to pelt down. Throwing out her hands sideways she tried to correct her balance, but her body momentum was too great and she felt herself falling with a surreal slowness, until with a dull thud she was flat on her back, one leg trapped beneath her, in a crevice between two slabs of rock, and the elements completely overwhelming her. Groaning with pain Helen tried to sit up, but her leg twisted excruciatingly against the rocks. Crashing water seemed to hammer inside her head, while the stormy sea sounded distant to her ears.

Where was Seth? She tried to focus her eyes, peering through the driving rain and the rearing, pounding waves. Disorientated by her blurred vision and ringing ears, Helen called out the old man's name, and thought she heard his faint reply on the wind. Spurred on, she managed to extract her foot painfully from the trapped Wellington boot and began to crawl towards the sound. Further out to sea the waves rolled in higher and more terrifyingly: walls of water crashing violently against rock and spreading across the kelp and bladder wrack weed, making the dark fronds writhe and clutch at the prostrate woman.

Still she crawled on, dragging her injured bare foot, yelping as it twisted, and shuddering as she felt the sodden weed between her bloodied fingers and toes. An assortment of creatures and debris milled around her body in the raging water and surf.

At last she reached the dark mound, only to realise that it was not the old man at all, but a section of tarpaulin cast up by the sea. She looked wildly about her, sure that this was where she had seen Seth fall. Nothing! Bordering on hysteria by then, Helen shouted over and over, her voice weakening as the last of her energy was spent, the waves mounting in the storm and the rain pounding relentlessly around her. No reply came from anywhere among the rocks. Mentally and physically exhausted now, and frozen to the marrow, she turned her back on the sea, and weeping, began to drag herself inland on raw hands and knees. She had failed! What had happened to the poor old man?

Just as she knew that she could drag herself no further, that she was completely spent, Helen felt strong hands reach down to her waist and support her weight as she crawled a few more yards. The salt water continued to swirl around her, then she could feel it no more, and as she realised she was clear of the reaches of the ocean, she collapsed face down in the spongy bladder wrack.

Helen didn't know how long she had been there, when she became aware of two giant feet beside her, and then strong, muscular arms gently turning her over and supporting her head. She gave a gasp of relief and lapsed back into unconsciousness.

Unable to feel any sensation in her limbs, but sure that she was not dead, Helen opened her eyes again and found that she was now in her own bed in the cottage, warm under a heavy duvet. Mrs Ross from the next cottage was in attendance. Helen tried to speak, but Mrs Ross interjected, "Lass yer've caused some worry hereabouts! Big Angus found ye and carried ye back home. Laid in all the seaweed and in a terrible state were ye."

"What about Seth? Is he all right?" asked Helen anxiously.

"We'll talk about Seth later, lass. What possessed ye tae be gannin' ower there on sich a day? Ye could hae killed yersel'."

"I was at my front window and I saw Seth fall. He didn't get back up, so I ran out to help him, but I couldn't find him. Has someone found him? Is he all right?" Helen was becoming agitated. Then she frowned in thought: "I vaguely recollect Angus picking me up and carrying me off the shore but he was there before that. I couldn't have got off the rocks by myself, Mrs Ross. Angus saved my life."

"Nay lass, Angus said yer'd crawled over the rocks before he saw ye. Ye must have done that yersel'. Look at them bloodied hands of yours! Angus said he found ye lyin' ower the road on tide mark in all that stinkin' weed."

"Well, someone helped me get off the rocks, Mrs Ross, I remember it distinctly. I might have died if they hadn't. I couldn't drag myself any further. But did Angus find Seth?" Helen spoke the last words sharply, in exasperation.

"Lassie, Seth has been lost down there these long years. He went down on those very rocks opposite here fifteen years ago and his body were never recovered yet!"

"What!" exclaimed Helen. "Seth's dead! But I saw him. I've watched him day after day collecting shellfish in his bucket."

"There's a few seen him oft times, nearly allus in the mucky weather, which it were when he went over."

"You mean the villagers all know about… this? Everyone talks as if he is still here!"

"Because he is, Lass, and I doubt he'll still be here when we're all long gone. Seth loved this place – he winna' leave it. Looks after us, he does…" The woman's voice trailed off as she nodded pensively.

"But I asked about Seth many times and no one told me anything. I saw him often out there." She pointed to the place where only yesterday she had seen the old man fall.

"Mebbes folks didn't want to scare ye when ye said that ye'd seen him. There's many would hae packed their bags and left, Lass. Anyhow it seems like Seth's been a guid friend tae ye, which ye would've been tae him. Ye were prepared tae gan out and help him. Round here we believes as one guid turn deserves another."

Suddenly a thought came to her, "Where did Seth live, Mrs Ross?"

"Here, Lass. This were his cottage. Agnes MacKinnon is his daughter, she moved into town when the sea took him.

Dicing with Death

Jon Leder had had a love affair of over forty years with motorcycles, which had started more or less as soon as his age had reached double figures, and which was unrelenting over the subsequent decades. He had tried and test ridden just about everything he could lay hands on, as well as owning a considerable number of bikes himself. He'd cut his teeth on an ancient Bantam D3, a 125cc in olive green: an ex-post office bike, which he'd bought (without his parents' knowledge), for the grand sum of £4. It had no brakes when he acquired it, and he generally stopped it by dragging his feet, clad in his father's NCB Wellingtons, along the dirt track where he practised. This led to his first accident when boy and bike collided with a stone pillar. Luckily Jon walked away virtually unscathed but the life of the illustrious Bantam came to a sudden end. An AJS of similar vintage came next in those early years, followed by a Panther and a BSA C15. A whole range of Hondas, Suzukis and Yamahas spanning a couple of decades followed, then a Triumph Thunderbird Sport and a 250cc Aprilia. He reckoned that the total would probably work out at one for every year of his life.

As a youngster Jon had led a bit of a charmed life: his bikes leading him into one scrape after another, sometimes quite literally. He was certainly no stranger to the odd broken bone and plaster cast. Upon reaching adulthood, to the surprise of his father, his passion lessened none and he was never without at least one machine.

Over the years he'd had girlfriends who loved the bikes, and more who detested them. Plenty of women had endeavoured to persuade him to relinquish the motorbikes – but those women were long gone and the bikes remained.

In his mid-forties Jon had had one very close brush with death. His favoured machine at the time was an imported Honda Fireblade with a colour scheme of white and Cadbury's Chocolate wrapper blue… tested it… loved it… bought it! He'd had it nearly a year, and was still well impressed with its performance. He'd had a personal best of 154 mph out of her on the open road, and he knew that he'd reached his own limitations before he'd been anywhere near those of the bike. *Ah well – room for improvement when there was less traffic about.*

A Saturday afternoon in September – weather good, and he was on a road that was made for the Blade: a narrow country road that he knew like the back of his hand, with a series of excellent switchbacks and hairpin bends. Going some! Closing the gap between himself and the Ford Puma in front… a familiar right-hand bend coming up… going to have to take the Puma on the bend…

No going back now but knew he could do it! Even with a car travelling towards him, there was sufficient room to gun it through. He was almost on the bend and riding close to the centre line, but with still plenty on the right. Suddenly the Puma was braking like crazy and veering to the left…

A combine harvester was way out into the road, taking up half of the opposite lane to clear the bend, blind to his left because of the hedgerow. Saw the Puma but not the bike, that is until it was airborne minus the rider. He brought the cumbersome machine to a slow halt and realised that the rider was beneath the combine, trapped by one leg.

Jon was dazed! Confused! Two women fussing around him… one of them the driver of car maybe? Get this skid lid off… Someone saying, "Don't take his crash helmet off." Ambulance arriving. Police. A man standing just within his peripheral vision: elderly, not doing anything in particular… looked a bit like his dad. Was he hallucinating?

Although he had no recollection of his journey in the ambulance, Jon remembered arriving at the hospital and being in the X-ray Department in particular, where it was discovered that several bones in his ankle and foot were fractured. His shoulder was dislocated and he was diagnosed as having moderate concussion. His lid and leathers had saved him from much worse and he was duly patched up and some hours later despatched home.

Two weeks later Jon's mother was still trying to persuade him to give the motorcycling up – the Blade was a write-off anyway… "No chance!" Jon had exclaimed. "Far better to burn out than fade away! When I go it'll be over the handlebars: only way to go!" He went out and bought a second-hand 600cc Suzuki Bandit to tide him over until he could afford something more exciting to ride.

Three years and several motorcycles later Jon managed to fall twenty-five feet from a ladder while erecting a shop sign for a customer. He recalled thinking incredulously as he was falling, "Is this how it ends?" Not even on a bike – the irony of it!

Lying on the busy High Street road below, concussed, and with a new set of broken bones, but still conscious, Jon felt a step removed from all the commotion around him. Afterwards, in hospital, he remembered seeing amidst the people milling everywhere shouting urgently, a half-familiar figure – an elderly man, just standing gazing at him from across the street. It looked like his dad but this bloke seemed older. He remembered the bystander at his bike crash. Bit of a coincidence there! Was it his mind playing tricks on him? Had he imagined the old geezer? Or in times of trauma did he subconsciously think of his father? Maybe it was just a symptom of his concussion. He couldn't stop thinking about it though: he was sure it was the same figure.

When his business partner came in to visit him he asked him about the old bloke, but Graeme couldn't recall seeing anyone who matched the description. "I wouldn't have noticed, mate: I was too busy trying to get an ambulance and stop you being run over. You should have seen the chaos you caused! One old dear was going to drive straight over the top of you, and when I shouted at her and stopped her she said, 'I thought he was drunk!' Of course that makes it OK to mow somebody down!"

Long after visiting hours Jon was still pondering on the aged spectator at both accident scenes. The more he tried to visualise the person, the more he became convinced that the man was too old to be his dad. He wondered about his grandfather and concentrated hard on bringing his features to mind. Family members used to say that Alf was like his father, but Bill had been gone for years now and Jon couldn't picture him well enough to make a judgement. "I think you're losing your marbles!" he told himself sternly.

Weeks later, out of hospital but still in plaster, and with his ankle held together with a variety of metal accessories, Jon still couldn't quite shake off the strange experience he'd had at the scene of both of his accidents. He replayed both incidents over and over, and was quite convinced that it had been the same figure he'd seen both times and he even wondered briefly if he'd seen a ghost, then berated himself for such nonsense. A guardian angel sounded even more ridiculous!

One afternoon during Jon's convalescence, when his father had come to visit him, the two of them sat over their mugs of tea discussing the accident. Jon, though he felt foolish, mentioned the old man at the scene.

"He looked a bit like you Dad, but older, very old in fact! I wondered at the time if I was hallucinating. I even wondered if it could be Granddad. Did you and he look alike, I can't remember?"

"A bit," admitted his father, "but I doubt Bill 'ud come back to haunt you." He chuckled.

"I know it sounds mad, but it's happened at least twice and I've kept thinking about it and trying to make some sense of it. Of course, maybe I'm just mad."

"I've always thought you were! Fey, I'd call it rather than mad. In truth I always thought you were in for a short one. Never thought you'd make it past thirty the way you went on! Fighting! That car crash! And remember when you got shot in the arm? That mate o' yours Nick! Messing on with those bloody air rifles."

"Better to have something to remember though!" grinned Jon. "At least I haven't had a boring life have I?"

"Too bloody right you haven't. If you were out gallivanting somewhere, we used to sit on tenterhooks, dreading a knock on the door, because it was usually the police or Mrs Armstrong next door seeing as she was the only one with a phone in them days!"

"Didn't think my nemesis would be an old codger though. I've never been scared of anybody but I must admit he's got under my skin. I think he's a bad luck omen: a Jonah!"

"Well maybe it is your Granddad after all and he's just trying to look after you."

As the senior man took his leave, he remarked, "We've brought back a few memories this afternoon, haven't we?"

"Talked a load of shite too," added Jon. "See you next week, Dad."

Alf came jauntily up the drive bearing a bulky carrier bag: "Photos!" he announced. He carefully lifted out an aged family album. "Here, have a look through that while I make us a brew."

When he entered the living room bearing a steaming mug in each hand and two wrapped chocolate biscuits clenched between his teeth, Jon was immersed in family history. He looked up at his father. "Who is this Dad?" he indicated a faded black and white photograph in the album.

"That's your granddad: my dad. Not as you would remember him though. He'd be about in his early twenties there, I think. There's another one of him holding me as a baby. Reckon they'd be taken about the same time. Take away the hairstyle and he looks more like you at that age." Alf mused, "Yes you definitely looked more like my dad than me. Well they do say it skips a generation."

Tea forgotten, Jon flicked through the album until he came to a photograph of his grandfather as an elderly man. He studied it long and hard. "I'm beginning to think that this old bloke following me around is Granddad, you know. It seems ridiculous to believe in ghosts but I can't come up with any other explanation, other than hallucination, resulting from concussion or stress."

He took a gulp of cold tea and then made up his mind to tell his father something that had been bothering him. "You know,

Dad, when I was a kid I used to see this old man and it terrified the life out of me at the time. I've never spoken to anyone about it: not you or Mam or any of my friends. I thought everyone would just ridicule me, and you know me – I had to be the Hard Man."

"Where did you see him?" asked Alf curiously.

"Once out in the street when we used to live by the church. He was just staring at our house, and I walked right past him, down the street and back. When I came back up he was gone and I thought nothing of it. Just wondered why he was looking at *our* house.

"The second time was in my bedroom and I was sure it was the same man. He put the fear of God into me. He was just standing there! Since this latest accident I've been trying to recall more about these other incidents. I've fixed on it being Granddad because of how traumatised I was as a kid when he and Grandma moved away. The only thing is, I saw the old fellah when Granddad was still alive. Weird or what?"

"I think you're going soft in the head myself," said his father. "All these accidents! I think the surgeon must have put your brain in your right ankle by mistake."

Jon was sat in his usual comfy armchair in his small cosy living room with his afternoon pot of tea. He'd glanced through the newspaper that morning without much interest, and for the last hour had just been sitting, thinking of the past. There was a lot of it! More than he'd expected he would have. As his father had expressed years ago, he thought he "was in for a short one".

However, he'd cheated death like a cat. He must have used up eight lives now over the past seven decades. Jon pondered to himself on the irony of life. He'd lived life to the full and on the edge: exciting! Exhilarating! He'd never wanted to grow old. He'd worked at great heights and fallen, ridden the fastest bikes he could find, and written three of them off with his dare-devil stunts. He'd been in a serious car crash in his youth (though he wasn't driving the car), and had to have major surgery to his arm. As a teenager he'd been accidentally shot with an airgun, the result of a bit of horseplay between him and his best mate. Hospital again! And he'd been in more fights than he cared to remember: a regular visitor to the local A&E! They'd joked about getting a chair with his name on it.

Quality over quantity had always been his motto, and yet here he was at 82. He should never have got to be an old man. He hadn't wanted to, and he was out of his depth in this world now. Out in a blaze of glory: that's how he'd imagined it. One last bike, one last ride! And now he was beyond it.

Since Eileen had become ill and he'd spent all his time taking care of her, he'd missed his last opportunity to choose when he could go. She'd been gone for nearly eight years now and it didn't seem right. Even Sammy his faithful old dog had passed away last year, and now he didn't have anything to get up for in the morning. It didn't seem fair that he'd lasted so long.

On both occasions, the passing of his wife and his dog, he'd encountered his "old bloke" again. He'd kind of got used to him, though he was no nearer to solving the mystery of who or why. He'd fairly convinced himself that it was his grandfather, who visited him in times of misfortune, conjured out of his own stressed mind – but even so it still sounded pretty daft. He felt himself nodding into slumber…

Jon awoke from an unsolicited nap with a jump. "What the hell are you doing here?" The old man stood silently before him as if deep in thought – or far away. "You've been following me around for years and I want some answers. Why? And who are you?" then puzzled, "How old are you? You've been old since I was a kid!"

The old man smiled but remained silent. Jon studied the figure with his tired watery eyes, then observed, "You haven't changed over the years. Why? You look about the same age as me."

The figure beckoned and Jon struggled to his feet. He followed his visitor to the large mirror in the hall and stood side by side with him. He stared at only one reflection: his own. He turned sideways and looked again at his companion, who somehow didn't look so old to Jon now. It was as if he was still looking in the mirror, and suddenly he understood.

"I'm more than ready," he admitted, and as one they drifted off leaving the discarded shell on the hall floor.

All in a Day's Walk

From where I was walking I could see three cows all peering intently into the river. The bank was steep just there on both sides and I wondered what they could have seen to hold their attention so. It certainly wasn't a place where they would attempt to drink. I meandered over casually so that I didn't scare them and looked down into the water. A young calf, only a day or two old – I'd actually seen some of them being born, just that week – was stranded on a small clump of reeds in the river on the side furthest from me. It had obviously fallen over the edge and was too small to climb back out. The three adult cows were very agitated and were calling out frantically to it.

I started to panic. We'd had a fair amount of rain in the last few days and the river was quite high. If the calf moved, it would plunge into much deeper water. The situation was urgent. I looked about, there was no one in sight on either side of the river. No farm hands! No other dog walkers! What could I do?

Nothing else for it – I'd have to go in. I was a bit worried that one of the dogs might try to follow me so I put them in a "down stay" and entrusted Hatti to guard my keys, watch, mobile phone and jacket. I looked down into the water and decided that I needed to keep my shoes on – I didn't know what

I was going to encounter on the bottom! These decisions were all made in a flash and in matter of seconds I was slithering down the steep, muddy bank and into dark, turbulent water. I had a slight misgiving, too late, that I didn't have any idea how deep the water was going to be. When my feet finally touched the bottom, I was standing with my shoulders just out of the water. It was freezing and a bit scary!

I waded across towards the calf, weeds entangling my legs as I went, my feet squelching on I didn't know what. I'm not afraid of water and I consider myself to be a good swimmer but I was more than a bit anxious when I couldn't see through the murk. In retrospect, my fear for the calf must have out weighed any fear I felt on my own account, because looking back on the whole incident, I must have been mad to attempt what I did.

I reached the poor little creature and it shied away from me in terror. However, it had nowhere to go, so I was able to grasp it quite firmly around its chest. Meanwhile, all three cows were still creating a fearsome racket and stamping their hooves somewhere above my head. Suddenly one of them, presumably Mum, launched herself into the water beside me. She landed practically on top of me causing something that felt like a tidal wave and she wasn't best pleased that I'd "attacked" her baby!

I decided that discretion was the better part of valour and retreated to my own side of the river. I was concerned that the cow would persuade the calf to move away from me and put it in more danger. She wasn't happy with me still being in the river and was thrashing about causing waves and trampling down the reeds around where the calf was marooned, making its island even smaller. I was forced to get out of the river to pacify both mother and calf. This brought its own problems. Where I'd slid down, I'd made the slope smooth and muddy, so scrambling back up proved to be quite a feat. When I eventually heaved myself up onto the grass, I was covered in mud and other assorted debris, and of course, soaked to the skin.

Once I was out of the river, the cow calmed down again and also clambered out of the river. She was calling urgently to the calf to follow her, but it had neither the size nor experience to cope with the steep, slippery riverbank. It cried pitifully after its mum. There was still no one around and I could feel panic setting in again. I looked at my mobile phone lying on the grass next to Hatti. Who could I ring to help me? I didn't know the number of the farm. I racked my brains to try and think of someone who lived close by, and who would be able to turn out immediately. I tried the number of one friend but there was no reply. Okay, I was on my own: I had to do something NOW!

I got back into the water gingerly, and carefully traversed the river again. The calf watched me with frightened eyes. I was only going to get one shot at this. I had to grasp the calf and use all my strength to hoist her as high as I could in the hope that she could help herself the rest of the way and clamber to safety. I didn't want to think about what would happen if the cow jumped into the water again. I had to act quickly before that could happen.

I reached the pathetic little creature, put both arms around it and tried to lift. I hadn't bargained for what it weighed. I had foolishly imagined that because it was in water it would be lighter. Possibly it was, but there was no way I was going to be able to raise that animal two inches, let alone over two feet. Three irate faces stared down into mine. Now what?

All I could think of was to keep the calf as still as possible and stop her going underwater. The cows didn't seem to mind my presence so much, as long as I wasn't trying to wrestle with their progeny. I contented myself with gently supporting her and hoping no one objected too much. Surely someone would pass along the river path before too long and be able to either help or get help. I seemed to be there for ages getting colder and more worried by the minute: the centre of attention from both sides of the river. The dogs were beginning to wonder what I was doing, so I had three bovine faces on the one hand and four canine ones on the other, all regarding me in various stages of curiosity, anxiety and anger.

As time went on and not a soul had appeared, I became more and more despairing and frightened. I was near to tears, when suddenly all four dogs started a volley of barking. I looked up hopefully and saw a man, a stranger to me. He looked over the edge of the bank and took in the scene in seconds. "Don't Move!" he commanded. I saw him throw something on the ground and then in an instant he was in the river wading purposefully towards me. The water seemed to part easily as he forged powerfully through it. When he reached me, I realised that this was one big bloke. He must have been around six feet and sixteen stone of pure muscle. His soaked black vest showed the definition of his pectorals and deltoids. His arms were huge and bronzed. Exactly my idea of a hero!

"Stand back in case you get hurt," he warned, his arms encircling the calf easily. He took a deep breath and then, miraculously lifted the beast clear of the water, pushing it upwards, towards the bank. The cows surged forward, but were arrested for a few seconds by his shout. That was all the time he needed: a final thrust and the calf stood on dry land, reunited with her family.

I heaved a sigh of relief. "Thank you," I said, tears streaming down my face now. "I couldn't have lasted much longer."

"No problem," my wonder man replied. "You did well! It's not every day I get the opportunity to save a damsel in distress!"

I'm not sure whether he was talking about the calf or me, but in another second he had picked me out of the water, slung me over his shoulder, and wading back across the river, deposited me on the bank side. He vaulted out of the river and pulled me to my feet. "I suggest you go and get out of those clothes, and get warm," were his parting words, and then he picked up his black leather jacket from the grass, checking that his wallet was there and was gone through the trees in a flash.

I was left dazed and speechless, staring after him. I bent down to retrieve my personal belongings and noticed that in his haste to be gone he had dropped something, presumably from his wallet. I picked it up. It was a small white card, a business card, I thought. Curious, I turned it over. The front simply held the symbol of a chess piece: the black knight!

One Step Too Far

"Six years tomorrow!" thought Lynn as she turned off her computer in the Sports and Recreation Office of the Wellsfield District Council. If only she'd known six years ago how it was all going to turn out. "If only one could turn the clock back." She stood lost in her own thoughts for a moment or two and then quite abruptly, she switched off the lights and headed for the staff car park, calling goodnight to the security officer as the door swung behind her.

This was the start of her fortnight's holiday. Tomorrow was her wedding anniversary and then on Sunday they were driving up the west coast of Scotland to a holiday cottage in the highlands. She drove home, her hands and feet synchronising mechanically, whilst her brain was otherwise engaged: would she be home before Tim? She hoped so! As she rounded the last bend and the drive came into view, she could see that it was empty. She heaved a sigh of relief. Good! Only then did she start to look forward to being home. She parked her car on the left-hand side of the drive and carefully ensured that it left the right amount of space for Tim's car on the right – she didn't want trouble to start as soon as he walked in the door, not at the very beginning of the holidays.

She let herself in the front door. As she was turning her key in the lock she could hear the thundering noise on the stairs and smiled. In the next moment she was almost knocked off her feet, and she sagged beneath the weight of two heavy paws on her shoulders. Thor, the owner of these paws, was a German Shepherd Dog: large even by German Shepherd standards, he stood nearly 29 inches at the shoulder, and on his hind legs was taller than Lynn herself. He backed off and stood grinning at her; his mouth wide open and his tongue lolling out of one side. His tail thumped the hall radiator causing a dull clanging to reverberate around the silent house.

"Hello my lad! Your Mummy's home. Do you want to go for a walk?" Lynn talked to the dog as he followed her upstairs. She reflected: there was nothing better than the welcome Thor gave her every time she came in. It didn't matter whether she'd been out for five minutes or five hours, his greeting was always the same. She hurried to change into her jeans and a sweatshirt, hoping that she would get out for her walk before Tim came home. If only she could…

"Come on Thor," she called with a sense of urgency, as she ran lightly down the stairs. The dog padded behind her, his tail still wagging in anticipation. She grabbed his lead from the hall table and in another minute, the two of them were heading out of the back door and through the garden. Lynn unbolted the gate and soon they were out in the fields beyond. Once she was out of sight of the house Lynn relaxed and slowed her pace a little. She took a few deep breaths, enjoying the early evening sun, and watching Thor as he gambolled about like a giant, overgrown puppy. He was five years old. They'd bought him just a year after they were married. Both of them had wanted a dog, and Tim had been insistent on *his* dog being a German Shepherd. He was derisive of what he called "small yappers" and was always telling people that dogs were like their owners.

Perhaps this was superficially so: Thor, like Tim was certainly a handsome specimen. Yet ironically it was to the petite and gentle Lynn that the dog really attached himself. Tim was tall and broad shouldered, with dark brown hair, deep blue eyes and a very bronzed skin, summer and winter alike. At 34 years, he was a handsome man: intelligent and articulate. He ran his own business, marketing and installing computer software. Lynn, small, slim, and fair, rather than blonde, had been swept of her feet at 23 years old when he'd first singled her out from all the other girls in the office for his attentions. Whilst the rest of the office had drooled over him, Lynn had been wined and dined in style, and basked in a certain amount of glory and satisfaction, as she was cajoled into recounting the tales of where she had been taken the previous night or weekend.

Within three months of their first date Tim had asked her to marry him, and in another three months they were duly wed. Lynn had suggested waiting until the next year but Tim had scorned this idea. "Why wait?" he'd asked. "Most people are forced into a long engagement to be able to afford to get married and buy a house. We don't need to do that. I can buy a house any time I like. You can pay whatever you like for your wedding dress, I can afford it, and I want to be absolutely stunned when you come down the aisle."

They'd started looking at houses as soon as they were engaged and had finally settled (at least Tim had finally settled!) on a new four-bedroomed detached on the edge of a village development. To Lynn it was like a palace. She had begun by looking at two- and three-bedroomed semis in the local property guide, but again Tim had said, "We don't want to be moving in just a couple of years. Let's buy what we want now and enjoy it. I can afford it!" …and so they'd come to Westmoor Park!

Although it hadn't taken Lynn long to become disillusioned with married life, and to realise that she was "owned" by a dictator, it was when Thor had come into their lives the following year that the real trouble began. Tim had taken charge of the dog's early training, but in just a few weeks Thor had become so afraid of his loud voice and all too ready hand of chastisement that he would run to Lynn for protection, tail between his legs. This did not please Tim at all and he would drag the dog back to him, scolding him all the while. "A firm hand – that's what he needs."

Lynn had tried to intervene on a number of occasions when she had thought Tim was being too hard on the puppy, and this had led to violent arguments between them. Eventually Tim had cast him aside as a "stupid, soft but bloody minded animal" and eventually took little notice of him at all except to complain about the dog hair on his clothes. Lynn took over Thor's training from then on, coaxing him gently until she had his confidence, and as she also fed, groomed and walked him there soon developed a bond of trust and loyalty between them.

Meanwhile married life for Lynn was becoming more unbearable by the day. Tim was a man who liked his own way and was accustomed to getting it. Thor was just one bone of contention between them. What Lynn had admired as strength and confidence in Tim in their early days of courtship, began to manifest itself in stubborn arrogance. He had a domineering manner and frequently embarrassed her in public by being overbearing, belittling her, and generally being discourteous to shopkeepers, neighbours and her own friends and colleagues alike. She knew that the envy that the girls in her office had once had, had now turned to sympathy for what Lynn had to endure. Not that she had ever spoken a word against him to any of them, she didn't need to – but it didn't go unnoticed that when he rang the office he was abusive and abrasive with people, and he would shout down the phone at Lynn so loudly that the rest of the office could not help but be aware. At the few office social "with partner" evenings he had been to with

Lynn he had drunk far too much and began to cause trouble or embarrassment of one sort or another. He constantly boasted about his job, his wealth, his car... He made his opinions known loudly and whatever the topic of conversation was, he always managed to turn it to his favourite subject: Tim Urwin. Those "without partners" evenings the Council held, Tim quite simply forbade her to attend. Lynn felt nothing short of a prisoner.

Tim was also extremely vain and image conscious and drove a top of the range red sports car. He'd originally wanted Lynn to have a smaller version of the same – after all, what his wife drove was in effect an extension of his own image! However, she'd resisted on the grounds of practicality – there was Thor to consider, and such a large dog could not be comfortable in the rear of a sports car. Although Lynn always tried to avoid conflict with Tim as far as possible, she had stuck out on this occasion and eventually persuaded him to buy her a 1.3L Peugeot estate car. It was not often that Lynn got her own way but having done so on this occasion, she was quietly delighted with the result and very proud of her "ordinary" car. Tim had, of course, been scathing about her choice of car and had conceded only on condition that he didn't have to ever travel in it. Following the purchase, Lynn was quite prepared for Tim to be derisive and insulting about her car, and he was! But there was nothing she couldn't endure for the sake of Thor.

Over the months and then years of their life together, Lynn had become so used to submitting to Tim's will and his whims, almost automatically, she gradually became more and more introverted, withdrawing into a private world of her own where she felt reasonably safe that Tim could not reach her. Thor became her best friend and constant companion and their greatest joy was to be out walking and playing together, enjoying the sights and scents of the fields and the wooded walk behind their house. Their biggest disappointments were when

Tim decided to join them on their walks. It was an intrusion into their private world and their special relationship. Tim always seemed to have to do everything at breakneck pace and was continually urging Lynn to "step it out and get the blessed walk over with" so that they could get back home. Thor was constantly being grumbled at and bellowed at for loitering and sniffing, and Tim would fly into a rage when the dog took no notice of his irate shouts. A call from Lynn would bring the dog bounding to them, which would only enrage Tim even more and he often would swear and aim kicks at him.

Although Lynn suffered a great deal of abuse from Tim in silence, and, it had to be admitted, was rather afraid of him, she would not allow a hand to be raised against her dog, and their arguments about Thor were frequent and stormy. Tim's resentment of the dog grew worse and worse and he had threatened on several occasions to "take him to the Vet" or worse "to drop him off on a distant country road". Tim had used physical violence more than once on Lynn, usually following one of his heavy drinking sessions and a subsequent argument about Thor. The first time he struck her, Thor was in the room, restless and agitated because of the angry, raised voices. Tim's fist had barely made contact with Lynn's face, when Thor leapt at him, snarling and knocking him to the ground. Tim was badly shaken and absolutely furious. Afraid for the dog's safety, Lynn had shakily called Thor to her and he had obeyed, standing beside her, hackles still up and baring his teeth at Tim. From that time onwards it had become a most unhappy situation: Lynn feared for the dog's life and tried more than ever to avoid any confrontation with Tim, whilst Thor had made it crystal clear to both of them that he would defend his mistress with his last breath.

Over the last eighteen months Lynn had considered leaving Tim on many occasions, but so far had not summoned the courage to do so. Six years of feeling that she was a prisoner had taken its toll and she despaired of ever being able to break free. She was firmly convinced that Tim would never let her go without a great deal of resistance. He would find her wherever she went and harm either her or Thor, or alternatively would endeavour to make her life sheer hell. She knew that she had to be able to be self-sufficient to make the break. She would have to start to buy and furnish a house from scratch, and to do that she needed her job. But as long as she was tied to the Wellsfield District Council, it would be an easy matter for Tim to find her. It would take a great deal of planning to enable her to disappear from Tim altogether and she spent considerable time each day exploring every possibility she could think of. It was constantly in her mind that she and Thor would have to run away somehow…

But here she was, still married to Tim, on the eve of their sixth wedding anniversary and about to go on holiday. She desperately wished that she could look forward to the next two weeks away from work, but the prospect of the three of them being together all day in a confined space, only filled her with trepidation. They had already had arguments over the travelling arrangements. The obvious answer was to use Lynn's car, which would take all three of them and luggage. However, Tim had decided that he would drive up separately in his own car. He was not travelling in the Peugeot and that was that, he had informed her the night before last.

It was the fourth day of their holiday and the strain was showing. They'd set out that morning in a tense silence. Tim had reluctantly agreed that they would use only Lynn's car for the expedition, but with very bad grace and he was smouldering in the passenger seat ready to pounce and criticise her driving at the least excuse. For Lynn's part she was on edge but relieved to be driving herself, for Tim had been given to the most dreadful road rages since they'd left home: racing other drivers, never accepting anyone overtaking him, and driving so close to vehicles in front: people whom he said were "Sunday afternoon drivers" or "over cautious" or those "dawdling along admiring the scenery". He had terrified the life out of many other drivers, (and Lynn herself) over the years, and this week was proving no exception. In the past they had had so many rows over his reckless driving and each one just made him take even more risks and frighten her even more, as if it gave him a cruel sense of satisfaction seeing her sitting next to him so tense, her knuckles white from clutching the sides of her seat. Over all she found it better to brace herself mentally for the ordeal and to appear physically as relaxed as possible. At least that way she didn't give him the satisfaction of knowing that he had terrified her.

How many couples, Lynn wondered as she drove, would come on holiday, nearly three hundred miles each way, in two separate cars and then go out almost every day in separate cars meeting up at their destination?

The journey today was tense; the atmosphere electric. True, Lynn felt in control to a certain extent, since she was at the wheel. She carefully negotiated the narrow road with its sharp bends and cliffs to one side, with a sheer drop on the other. She was a skilful and competent driver, but that didn't stop her feeling nervous when Tim was in the car with her. Nor did it prevent Tim from continually cursing other road users and on one occasion leaning right over her and blasting on the horn at an oncoming vehicle which (in his opinion) was taking up too much road. He also had a habit of tapping on the gear lever if he thought that Lynn was in too high or too low a gear. However, as far as Lynn was concerned, putting up with this was infinitely better than using Tim's car, with him at the wheel, and going through severe mental torture for the whole journey.

She pulled into the tiny rural car park, which save for them was empty, and they got out. Lynn went straight to the back of the car and let Thor out. She watched with pleasure as he capered about, taking in as many new scents as he could. Tim, meanwhile had gone to the back of the parking area and was studying the steep, narrow pathway which led into the pass where the Macdonald cave was situated. The legend behind it was that Bonnie Prince Charlie had used this cave as a hideout on his escape to Skye. Not that Tim was much interested in that, but it did afford him some pleasure in being able to say "Been there" or "Done that". He'd done several of the Munroes himself and liked to tick them off on a map on his office wall. He usually felt that walks such as they'd planned today were well beneath his capabilities, but on this "family holiday" he grudgingly did walks every other day that suited Lynn and Thor also.

He walked back to the car and took out the rucksack they used for day excursions, threw it onto his back and demanded, "Well, are we ready to set off then? And can you get that stupid dog under control?" Lynn had told Thor to "down", receiving that instant obedience which so infuriated Tim, and put on her walking boots (she never drove in them), nodded assent and locked the car, zipping the keys carefully into the pocket of her fleece jacket.

With Tim it was never a leisurely amble along, taking time to take in and appreciate the scenery. He set off, head down, at a brisk pace and within a few hundred metres was well ahead of his wife and dog. Every so often he would stop and look behind with impatience, making it obvious that he'd waited for her to catch up, and then as soon as Lynn was within a few metres of him, he'd growl, "Right then?" and set off again. As many times before, Lynn sighed, it was never a ramble always a route march!

The path was narrow, and rocky in places, and Lynn had to use her hands to help her clamber over large boulders. It ascended quite steeply and soon they were well away from even the nearest farmhouse. Before long even the few free-ranging sheep had been left far behind, and only heather and an odd patch of gorse could be seen. The path was overgrown with heather in places, indicating that it was not a popular route with walkers, especially at this time of the year.

They'd walked for about an hour and a half, having stopped once briefly for a cup of coffee from the thermos flask, and now the terrain, although still desolate, was levelling out. The path ahead was still visible where it started to ascend again beyond the plateau they'd reached. Lynn paused for breath and to admire the view, looking down on the route they had just climbed, but Tim forged on ahead regardless, still well ahead of the other two.

Since they had set off from the car Thor had capered about making a number of detours from the path and bounding through the heather after some interesting and unfamiliar scent. Earlier he'd startled a sheep or two (he knew better than to chase them!), and put up a few grouse. Now that they'd reached a relatively flat spot, he took the opportunity to chase about again, and in doing so left the path, leaping across great mounds of heather. Before he realised it, he'd run into a peat bog and immediately began to sink. He struggled to free himself, but he was a heavy dog and was helpless against the force sucking him down.

Lynn screamed in panic. She was frozen to the spot in terror. Her scream had brought Tim running back down the path towards her. He took in the scene very quickly and began searching about for something to use to reach the dog. Before their very eyes Thor was sinking further and further into the bog and the more he struggled to free himself the faster he seemed to go further down. His eyes were wide with fear as the peat enveloped the tops of his legs.

Tim's hurried search did not yield anything he could usefully employ to reach the dog and in desperation he waded in towards the terrified animal. Once in the bog Tim had to move slowly, testing his way gingerly with each step. By the time he reached Thor, the peat was around his knees, and the dog's body was now almost submerged. Tim managed to grasp Thor firmly around his chest and took hold of his collar with his other hand. It took him several attempts to free the dog and all his strength to lift him clear of the swamp. He knew that he would be unable to carry him back to safety: he was thigh deep himself already. Using every bit of force he could muster he threw Thor as far as he could towards the path. He didn't quite make the distance but now Lynn had her wits gathered and she grabbed him and pulled with all her might before he started to sink again.

She clung to the slime covered dog, weeping with relief now that he was safe. She quickly clipped on his lead to prevent any more blunders. Then suddenly conscious of Tim's shouting, she turned to where he was attempting to drag himself through the peat, sinking lower with each step. Like the dog, every move seemed to pull him further into the seething black mass. He was still some three to four metres from solid ground, when he was a little over waist deep.

Lynn stood stupefied, her mind racing as to what to do. She looked all around. There wasn't a soul about! She knew that they hadn't passed anyone on the path all the time they had been walking. Ahead stretched only the single-track footpath with heather and bog on either side. They were still a good half hour away from the cave. All in all, she thought, it was quite a trek just to see a cave with a bit of a legend attached to it. There was probably no one else for miles around! She turned back to see the bog, slowly but very surely, engulfing her husband – the peat was now well up his chest and his eyes had in them that same look that the dog's had also had. His careful, controlled movements now abandoned Tim was now flailing his arms about in panic, desperately struggling for the edge like a man who can't swim. He began to scream…

Still Lynn watched from the path, holding tightly on to Thor's lead.

One arm became caught in the thick squelching mud and Tim was unable to free it. In vain he tried with his other arm until that too became entrapped in the heaviness of the peat. His shoulders succumbed now to the power of the bog, and his terrified eyes met Lynn's calm ones. The last thing he saw was the slow smile, which gradually appeared on her face once she was sure that the bog was deep enough to take his full height.

In another minute the peat bog looked exactly as it had before. Its surface gave no indication of the frenzied activity of the last fifteen minutes. Lynn bent and patted the dog. "Come on Thor, we'd better get home. You really need a bath. What a good job we came in my car!"

They Shoot Rabbits Don't They?

Over the summer they'd got to know each other quite well. Valerie, or Val as she preferred, had taken the seasonal cleaning job at the Sleepy Bay Caravan Site. From June until the first week of September she had arrived at 9.45 each morning except Sunday ready to put the "closed" notices on each of the toilet and shower blocks in turn while she performed her "sometimes unsavoury" tasks. Clad in overalls and rubber gloves, the size of which made her look quite diminutive, and armed with a host of chemical cleaning products, she worked her way systematically though the ladies block followed by the gents, then the disabled and parent and toddler special facilities, sanitising each from ceiling to floor. She finished her daily shift at 12.30.

Val worked discreetly and anonymously so that most holiday makers were hardly aware of her presence, staying away from the shower blocks when they had "closed" signs up. A few briefly passed the time of day as they filled their water containers or emptied their waste receptacles. Some would simply call out a "Good Morning" as they passed by, but to most she was just "the cleaner", part of the invisible smooth running of the site.

Iain and Joyce were different. They treated Val as an equal and talked to her about more than just the weather, though inevitably that played its part when holidaying in Scotland. If they were putting the kettle on, one or the other would take a cup of tea over to her as she worked.

They'd first met in early July, when they were at Sleepy Bay for a fortnight, and they continued their chats during their subsequent two weeks in August. They'd told Val of their recent retirement and how they loved this particular caravan site with its plethora of flora and fauna. Five miles away from even the nearest village it was a haven for wildlife, and they loved to stroll around the seventeen-acre site watching the scores of rabbits feeding unconcerned, and looking out for stoats and the occasional deer. They were avid bird watchers and the site boasted swallows, house martins, linnets and yellow hammers as well as many more common species.

The couple discovered that Val was 61 years old and lived in a local village: Stonybank, with her husband Robert, who was 66 years old. They had been married for 26 years, following unsuccessful prior marriages for both of them. Val had two children from her first marriage and they both lived in New Zealand. The reason Val had taken the Sleepy Bay cleaning job was to raise some extra funds to go to New Zealand.

Val, Iain and Joyce were in the same age band, Iain being 62 years old and Joyce having just had her 60th birthday earlier that year. They too were into a second marriage for both of them, having tied the knot only a year ago. It seemed that right from the start something jelled with the three of them and each morning their few minutes passed together were a sharing of life experiences. It became clear that Val was more than "just the cleaner". She was intelligent, sharp as a razor, and had a sense of humour, which appealed to Iain immediately. She brought them sample menus from the hotel where she and Robert regularly had their Sunday lunches, but while sounding delicious these proved a bit beyond the pocket of Joyce and Iain, who observed to his wife, "They must have a bob or two. You don't go there on cleaner's wages!"

When the local agricultural show was on in August, Val told them that she was exhibiting in various home baking classes, and was confident that her cheese scones and fruit loaf would be strong contenders. She confided that Robert was also competing for the first time and had made lemon curd, plum jam and some very tangy marmalade.

After the weekend of the show, Val brought Joyce and Iain half a fruit loaf and a jar of lemon curd, both of which were first prize winners. They were delicious. Robert had also taken second prize for his tangy marmalade, so all in all they had a very successful weekend, and Val was delighted.

Iain and Joyce returned home during the third week of August, for family commitments, one being the 93rd birthday of Iain's father. When they returned again to Sleepy Bay on 2nd September Val was delighted to see them and told them how much she had missed their daily conversations. The site was much quieter now, with both English and Scottish children having returned to school. Val was working her last week.

"I hope you don't think this sounds stupid," she said, "but I have missed you both so much. I was wondering if maybe the three of us could have a little outing somewhere for lunch, maybe one day next week when I have no work? Nothing fancy!" she quickly interjected. "Maybe a run down to the lighthouse: a walk then a sandwich and a cuppa?"

"That sounds like a fine idea," said Joyce.

"I could pick you up here in my car and it would save you moving your motorhome," suggested Val.

"In that case, if you drive I'll buy the lunch. It will be a nice change for me not to do the driving, especially on those narrow roads to the lighthouse," said Iain gratefully.

"Why don't you come a have a cuppa with us when you've finished your shift on your last day and we can have a proper talk about it and decide on a day?" invited Joyce.

Joyce had baked a quiche and some fruit scones for Friday, Val's last day, and they had more time to chat and get to know each other that afternoon. They discovered that they all had a love of life in the country. They all disliked having to go into town, and in particular hated shopping. They agreed unanimously that they were happiest in old comfortable clothes and they were all avid readers, although Iain and Joyce mainly read thrillers, murders and ghost stories, while Val preferred romances and chick-lit.

Iain was interested to hear about Val and Robert's plans for moving to New Zealand. He'd assumed they were just having a holiday with their family, but discovered that they were hoping to emigrate. The paperwork was all well underway and they had moved into the rented cottage they currently occupied in order to facilitate an easy departure when all the legalities were completed.

In turn Joyce and Iain recounted how they had returned home from Sleepy Bay to a burglary earlier in the year. A friend who looked after the house in their absence had arrived one morning to find the windows at the rear of the house open, having been jemmied, and the contents of drawers and cupboards in various rooms spilled out. She had no idea of what might have been taken but had phoned the police immediately.

Iain described the anguish of facing a five-hour drive home, while speculating upon what sort of mess and loss awaited them. "We were thinking the very, very worst," he admitted, "so even though it was bad enough, I think we'd imagined a great deal worse."

"So what did they take?" asked Val curiously.

Joyce pulled a face. "Jewellery, perfume, various toiletries, training shoes – new ones still in their boxes, two Marks and Spencer ladies suits, some cash that I'd carelessly left at home. No large items or electrical items were taken: TV and computers still there. No real damage apart from the windows where they got in. I've got to say – it could have been worse!"

"It's not the point though, is it? It's the fact that someone has violated your home," said Val sympathetically.

Iain described the paranoia they'd both felt about leaving their home unattended, or planning any other holidays. "We were so pleased with the new motorhome and looking forward to spending more time away in our retirement, and then this! We felt like selling the van. We didn't want to leave the house. We even felt like putting the house on the market. But you can't let the bastards grind you down. They can't rule the rest of your life!"

He paused. "It's taken us a good while to calm down and feel like we're getting back to normal and we've done as much as we can afford to make the house as secure as possible."

"It's like Fort Knox now," added Joyce. "New monitored alarm system, top-notch locking systems on the windows and doors, new kitchen windows and back door for that matter."

"The police Victim Support Officer was very helpful," chipped in Iain. "He gave us a number of anti-theft devices for around the house, including extra gadgets for windows and doors and some smart water. Plus I've put extra external lights up. It's like Blackpool illuminations now!"

"It is," agreed Joyce, "and I've smart watered and photographed just about everything in the house. You live and learn!"

"What's smart water then?" asked Val.

Joyce explained the process of marking valuables with individualised smart water so that in the event of theft, items so marked would be traceable by their unique batch of smart water. "I've marked everything I could think of: jewellery, cameras, TVs, computer equipment, expensive ornaments, leather goods – you name it and I've smart watered it, and I've got everything photographed on one SD card."

Val was incredulous. "That is really useful to know. You say the police can supply it? I think I'll have to look into that. Both Robert and I have quite expensive guns and I have some antique jewellery. Do you know if smart water will work on china?"

"Yes it would," replied Joyce. "You only put a tiny dab on, and you would put it on the underside, or in a crevice rather than painting a flat area at the front of say an ornament."

"Well would having items marked with smart water reduce their value? And what about if you wanted to sell an item you'd previously marked?"

"I honestly don't know," admitted Joyce, "I have some info at home, but to be honest you'd be better off asking the police when you obtain it. I'm sure they'll have already had questions like that."

"You know," Joyce continued, addressing Iain, "I haven't marked my new jewellery."

She turned back to Val. "I only got the replacements a couple of days before we came away, and in all the holiday preparation, I've forgotten to smart water it. I'll have to do it as soon as we get home.

"It's OK though," she said to her husband, "I've got it with me – the jewellery that is, not the smart water."

"You'd better not let it out of your sight then," he commented. "There's three grand's worth in here. Mind you don't get much for your money these days: a ring, a watch, a bangle, and a bracelet and necklace set."

"This is the watch," said Joyce displaying a gold Rotary on her wrist.

Val looked at it admiringly. "That is a lovely piece and very modern. I like it."

"Replacing my eternity ring took quite a chunk out of the settlement. I'll hardly dare wear it, but I'll have to – I can't leave it lying at home in a box."

Joyce got up and went to one of the bedroom overhead cabinets, from which she withdrew an old, battered makeup bag. "Good disguise, eh?"

She pulled out a handbag-sized pack of tissues and a couple of lipsticks, followed by a small cardboard box bearing the "Simple" name and logo. She lifted the moisturiser tub from the box, opened it and inside revealed, instead of moisturising cream another single tissue, which she withdrew to reveal a five diamond half-eternity ring. She slipped it on and showed Val her hand.

"That is beautiful," breathed the other woman.

"It wants to be for what it cost!" exclaimed Iain. "Twelve jewellery items were taken, but the insurance settlement only paid for five at today's prices. Still at least she's got what she wants, and she can wear them all at the same time!"

Joyce returned the ring to its hiding place, and by the time she sat down again Iain was asking Val about the guns she'd mentioned. "I do a bit of target shooting," he explained. "Webley Air rifle!"

Val explained that both Robert and she held firearms certificates, and that they would be coming onto the caravan site after it had closed for the winter, to "cull" the rabbits.

"Oh no!" exclaimed Joyce in horror. "We love the rabbits and other wildlife. It's why we come here."

"But there are too many of them now and we need to reduce the numbers fairly drastically. We won't touch the other species, apart from if we see any vermin while we are down here: rats, foxes, badgers, etc."

Iain and Joyce exchanged surreptitious looks of alarm and disapproval. This changed everything! Meanwhile Val prattled on, oblivious to the subtle changes in mood and body language. Iain knew that Joyce would simply shut down and contribute little to the conversation now. She despised shooters! He tried to keep the conversation going out of politeness. He also wanted to know more!

Using his own knowledge of weaponry, Iain drew Val out on the subject of their guns, wondering how much she knew. He discovered that Robert had a Berretta and "another gun" and that Val herself had a Browning. She was, however, unable to supply model numbers, although she did volunteer the information that Robert went deer stalking and would get rid of unwanted foxes and badgers for the local farmers, while she wouldn't tackle anything that big and just "despatched" rabbits, rats and squirrels.

Meanwhile Joyce had become completely silent as she pondered how easily and casually words such as "cull" and "despatch" were thrown out: words invented to justify killing small animals for what was no more than sport. It was hard to imagine this short, tubby woman, who read love stories and entered baking competitions being a shooter, or snapping the neck of a rabbit or squirrel. Joyce shuddered at the thought.

Through her musings she heard a mention of three gun safes in Val's house and wondered whether each gun had to have its own safe or whether there was an arsenal locked up in each, with a choice of weapons for all occasions. "How easily one could change one's mind about someone," she thought never dreaming that this afternoon would have ended so. How on earth could they get out of spending a day next week with this cold-hearted woman?

Gradually Iain managed to steer the conversation down other avenues, and polite conversation resumed, but the atmosphere never totally recovered. A couple of times he shot Joyce a look, imploring her to help out by joining in a little, and gradually she did. A few non-contentious stories were told, jokes were laughed at, and the afternoon wore on. Thankfully the subject of firearms was not resurrected and Val seemed in no particular hurry to take her leave.

Suddenly a large face appeared at the glass in the door of the van and Joyce jumped in fright.

"Oh it's Robert!" exclaimed Val peering out of the window beside her.

Taken aback Joyce opened the door and invited him inside.

He kicked off his muddy boots and climbed aboard. Robert was a huge man, who might have passed for either an old farmer or a retired rugby player. It occurred to Joyce that Val liked her men big, and that's why she seemed attracted to Iain. How had that thought suddenly popped into her head, she wondered? Probably because every morning Val had greeted him with: "Good Morning You Big Gorgeous Man!" Well, obviously something had registered. She looked over at the two of them. They certainly seemed to be getting on famously now.

Robert was quiet and polite, gratefully accepting a cup of tea, settling himself back comfortably on one of the sofas, and looking around at the layout of the van. "Very nice!" He nodded to Joyce, then smiled indulgently as Val continued to chatter on about her family in New Zealand. When so required, he answered her in monosyllables accompanied by a grin, which creased his friendly brown face.

Joyce took her time to study him, while the conversation went on all around her, without her being required to join in. He was a bear of a man. He looked to be a gentle giant, his brown eyes twinkling as he smiled benevolently about him, his massive, muscular frame in open and relaxed posture. Well giant he might be but he could not be gentle if he killed animals in their own environment for no good reason other than they were in the way of man.

On finishing his tea Robert took his leave telling them that he had to get back to work and make the most of the daylight hours. Val departed shortly after having arranged to collect Iain and Joyce at 11am the following Wednesday.

Neither of them made any objection to the arrangement made much earlier in the afternoon.

The day dawned dry and bright with a slight breeze, and at the appointed time Val arrived in her Nissan Micra. They set off up the narrow winding road to the lighthouse on the extreme of the peninsula. The road climbed and narrowed proportionately until the last three quarters of a mile was barely wide enough for one vehicle, and had passing places every two hundred yards. The land fell away from them on both sides, changing from closely cropped pasture with free-ranging sheep to cliff edges with sudden drops to the sea as they neared their destination. The impact of the breathtaking scenery was somewhat belittled by Val's incessant chatter as she swung the car around acute bends, rather too fast, and sometimes while looking over her shoulder to speak to Joyce who was huddled in the tiny back seat.

They arrived nevertheless at the small car park without misadventure and both Iain and Joyce were relieved to tumble out into the wind. There were another five cars already parked up but no person in sight. They all donned waterproof jackets and Val put on a wide-brimmed Aussie-style hat, then grasped Joyce's arm, tucking her own arm into it, and stepping out purposefully in a "girls together" fashion.

The walk was wild and windy, the scenery dramatic. A narrow winding path cut through bouncing heather, some in full purple flower, while other more exposed clumps had already died back to a rusty hue: just as attractive while in the throes of death. One hundred and fifty feet below the waves crashed upon evil-looking black rocks, creating a constant thunder. Gulls and cormorants flew out across the turbulent sea and a lone gannet dived and rose spectacularly and repeatedly, floating for a few moments while it scoffed its catch before rising again to take its next dive.

The peninsula boasted a number of viewpoints, many with cautionary signs concerning the danger of the cliff edges. The three visitors stood together at each point, exclaiming in admiration, and scanning the horizon for a glimpse of Ireland or the Isle of Man. Joyce began to feel uncomfortable with the powerful grasp Val had on her arm, while she was craning further and further out over the cliff edge to better view the rocks below. Suddenly Val gave an extra hard tug, yelling as she did so, then as Joyce let out a shriek of horror, Val fell about laughing. "Thought I was going to pull you over, didn't you?" she gasped through her giggles.

Every nerve ending was tingling as Joyce jerked her arm away from Val, and took a few steps inland away from the sheer drop.

"Sorry," said Val sheepishly.

"It's OK," Joyce replied, tight-lipped, and taking a firm grip of Iain's arm.

On the way back to the lighthouse tearoom the conversation was stilted, with Iain trying to cover the awkwardness by telling a few jokes. "Let's just get today over with as best we can and then we don't ever have to see the woman again," he whispered.

Once inside the tearoom, they scrutinised menus and chose their lunch options: cheese and bacon toasties for Iain and Joyce, and a bowl of homemade broccoli and stilton soup with a crusty bun for Val. A pot of tea for two was ordered and a cappuccino for Joyce. Over the delicious food the atmosphere relaxed and the three of them were soon conversing in a friendly manner. Lunch dawdled on well into the afternoon until they were the only customers left, Val telling the others about Robert's casual work at a local farm, where he was building new dry stone walls, again a way of raising extra money for New Zealand.

"There's nothing we won't turn our hands to," she said. "Robert was actually going to come with us today, but he decided that he'd better work."

As they finally left the café Val asked whether Joyce and Iain minded a detour past where Robert was working, then as they were standing outside of the car, Val realised that her car key was broken. Pulling her hand from her pocket, she displayed with a dismayed expression, the plastic casing in two pieces, and demonstrated that the remote control would not work. She tried several times to operate the gadget to no avail, so Iain took the key from her, and piecing it together held the pieces firmly in place and succeeded in unlocking the car doors.

Val gratefully took the key from him and tried the ignition. The car would not start.

"Sorry about this. I'll have to ring Robert and ask him to come and get us. We may be here a while yet! We might as well go and have another cuppa."

Val didn't seem too perturbed, much to Joyce's surprise. Time wasn't much of a problem to them, being on holiday, but she knew that Val had an elderly Jack Russell Terrier at home alone, who might well need to be out by now.

Iain meanwhile had been fiddling with the key and fob, and suddenly the car engine sprang to life. Val had just reached Robert on the mobile, and looked startled at the sound. "We're mobile," he announced, and by way of explanation, "the key is coded, and the microchip is in the fob. I've just held the plastic casing around the key and hey presto!"

Val spoke into her phone, "Iain's got the car started so we'll be with you in about, say fifteen minutes. Fifteen minutes!" she emphasised.

Joyce looked towards her husband and raised her eyebrows. In return he shrugged.

Once in the Micra Val spent a few minutes adjusting her seat, the rear-view mirror and finally her hair, before their journey got underway. Once they had retraced their route along the single-track road, Val turned left, instead of right towards the caravan site. It too was no more than a track, veering more inland and climbing steadily up the higher ground, which formed the backbone of the peninsula. They travelled the winding road, fields of gold on either side where crops had already been harvested. The hedgerows were full of small birds, with the occasional pheasant breaking cover and running across their path with startled calls. Val was forced to drive more slowly, for which Joyce was thankful, as she watched birds and rabbits scuttling off the road at the approach of the car. At last they turned right between two imposing stone pillars, which heralded the name "Windrush Farm".

"This is all Robert's work," announced Val gesticulating to both sides of the road. The stone walls were obviously very new with no signs yet of weathering, and formed a corridor all the way up to the farm buildings. They were indeed a work of art, not to mention a labour of love. Iain and Joyce were greatly impressed. The line of each was dead straight and the tops almost impossibly flat. As they drove along Val pointed out narrow access gaps to the fields on either side, and a couple of integral stiles, all cleverly designed and neatly executed. The effect was amazing, and it was fantastic that this dying art was still alive and well in this picturesque little backwater.

Robert was hard at work as Val eased the car up beside him. Chunks of stone in varying shapes and sizes lay haphazardly around him, and two parallel lines of string acted as guides to mark the section of wall Robert was currently building. Val greeted him cheerily and Robert straightened up and stepped towards the car. Iain and Joyce complimented him on the quality of his work and the big man smiled. "Ay there's a bit o' graft gone inter that."

"How long has it taken you to do all this?" asked Iain.

"Three months give or take! Couple more weeks in it yet," he replied indicating with his head towards another set of pillars, which were the wall's ultimate destination. "Val will be helping me Sunday no doubt!"

Joyce nodded to Val. "What – you do this as well? It must be pretty heavy work."

"Oh I enjoy it, and I'm very good at filling in the small gaps, aren't I Rob? I've an eye for seeing the right shaped piece of stone for the job."

Robert grinned. "She's no' a bad labourer, and I get more tea breaks when she's on t' job."

"Rob always does the top on his own," volunteered Val. "Every craftsman has his own style or mark and Rob's walls are distinctive by being flat on top: no one else does that."

Having taken a few minutes out Robert declared that he should be getting back to work, and Val and the others headed off to Sleepy Bay. Back at the site Val accepted Iain's offer of a cup of tea and the three of them climbed aboard the motorhome. Val seemed to have completely shaken off any worries she might have had about the broken key and settled back into the cushions as she chattered away.

Joyce and Iain were returning home in another three days, but revisiting Sleepy Bay in mid-October. As Val at last took her leave, with Iain's assistance with the car keys once again, she invited them to get in touch when they were back on site, and to have dinner with Robert and herself at their home.

"I can pick you up again so that you don't have to move the motorhome, and that way you can both have a drink."

"But what about you?" asked Joyce, "It means you won't be able to drink."

"Not bothered!" Val replied. "It won't hurt me for once."

"OK we'll be in touch, and thanks for today," Iain and Joyce each gave Val a parting hug and she drove away, waving from her window.

At 5.15 on Sunday afternoon Iain and Joyce arrived home and began systematically unpacking the motorhome, always their first job. Having carried everything they needed into the house, and set the first lot of washing away in the machine, they flopped down with cups of coffee, before embarking on the task of putting clean clothes, books, DVDs, and valuables in their proper places.

They'd spent their last few days going over the two meetings with Val, and more briefly Robert, and the subject was raised once again by Joyce. "I really don't want to go to their house," she said. "I find it hard to believe we can have both been so wrong about the sort of person she is, and I can't condone or ignore what she does."

"I agree," replied her husband. "The subject never once cropped up in all those weeks we talked to her over the summer. She saw you taking photographs of the birds and the rabbits and must have known what animal lovers we are."

"So how can we get out of this dinner date? Shall we just not let her know when we are back at Sleepy Bay? She might just arrive at the site unannounced, which would be pretty awkward."

"I've given it quite a bit of thought over the last few days and I think we should go. No, hear me out," he said as Joyce started to object, her expression disapproving. "This will be our last time this year at Sleepy Bay, and by next season Val and Robert will have gone to New Zealand, probably for good. We can get through one more meeting and then that will be it and we won't have had to fall out. We'll never see them again."

"I just don't know if I can keep up the pretence that everything is hunky dory between us. What if they start talking about shooting during dinner?"

"I won't let it happen, we'll have plenty of other topics, won't we? New Zealand. Robert's work. Don't worry I'll keep the conversation going and avoid anything taboo. I promise."

"All right I'll certainly try," agreed Joyce, "I just hope my feelings don't show."

"That would be a first!" teased her husband.

Coffee finished, they went about their tasks, carrying bags and boxes to appropriate rooms to empty. Joyce picked up her cameras, handbag and the old battered shoulder bag in which she kept the cosmetics bag containing her new jewellery, taking them into their bedroom. She withdrew the make-up bag and was about to place it in her bedside drawer, when she decided to have another look at her latest acquisitions. She unzipped the bag and delved inside: tissues, lipsticks, the small box – which actually felt very light! Joyce quickly opened the Simple container: the plastic tub containing her eternity ring was gone! She stared in disbelief, then rummaged through the rest of the bag's contents. The bangle, necklace and bracelet were also missing. She ran downstairs shouting for Iain.

He emerged from the garage, with a worried look. "What's wrong? You look as if you've seen a ghost!"

"My jewellery! It's gone!" she gasped. She held out the empty bag to show him.

"Calm down. It can't have gone – you've put it somewhere else, so just keep calm and think about the last time you wore it."

"But I haven't worn it since I showed it to Val. We were in the van, and after that day at the lighthouse we stayed on site for the rest of the holiday, so I haven't worn it." She paled as these thoughts sank in. "It's been stolen, hasn't it?"

"It can't have been stolen, because there's no evidence of the motorhome being broken into. The door hasn't been forced, there are no windows tampered with, and we never leave the van unlocked even if we are only across at the showers," he reasoned.

"What about here on the drive?" she questioned. "Has the van been unlocked whilst we were having coffee? Could it just have happened now?"

"No, definitely not! The van was locked whilst we were in the house, and while we were emptying it we were in and out all of the time. No one would have had time to search the van for valuables. What are the chances of someone hitting on that very locker straight away?

He continued, "Let's just go into the van now and search for where you might have put the stuff."

Every nook and cranny was searched! Every pocket was turned out. Joyce took everything out of her handbag, her old dilapidated bag, which had housed the make-up bag, her camera case and her toiletries bag. Iain looked among the food they had brought from van to house and went through the gifts they had brought home for friends, shaking wrappings out. Between them they covered every possibility they could think of to no avail.

"It has been stolen, hasn't it?" wept Joyce. "We've had another burglary."

"I must admit, it's beginning to seem like it, I just can't see how. Are you absolutely sure that the last time you saw your jewellery was the day that you showed it to Val?"

"I am! I am absolutely positive!"

"Well, I'm going to have to inform the police, though what they will be able to do I really don't know."

Over a week had passed and the police had been and gone. The motorhome had been examined and tested for forensic evidence. The results would take time DS Bennett had informed them, when he issued them with a crime number.

The same Burglary Support Officer who had seen them in the spring, came to visit them, and Joyce ashamedly confessed that the items had not been smart watered, although she told him rather tearfully that everything else in the house had been done following the earlier burglary.

When questioned about the alarm on the motorhome, Iain explained that when on a caravan site he did not set the alarm, because the second key, held by Joyce, was a basic key and she could not disarm the alarm with it. This made it impractical if they were in separate places and Joyce returned to the van first. In addition the alarm had not been set when they were having their coffee on their return home. The van was on the drive in full view of their house and those of neighbours.

"Normally when we are at home, or parked in any public place the alarm is on," he finished. "I know how this looks but we really are very vigilant, especially since the house was turned over."

Iain and Joyce were sat with their empty coffee cups and once again the theft of the jewellery was the topic of discussion. They had been round in circles, looking at every possible scenario, and were both agreed that the van could not have been broken into on their drive. They had been in the house for a bare fifteen minutes and the van had been locked.

They'd concluded that the burglary had taken place on the caravan site, but how – they could not fathom.

"Someone must have had a key!" declared Joyce. "But they must have also known about the location of the jewellery, don't you think?"

"I just can't see it. For a start the keys are never out of our possession. We both use our keys regularly throughout the day and they have not been misplaced at any time. Another thing, a few people on site know about our burglary but even if you've mentioned the replacement jewellery, they're not going to know where it was kept, or that you weren't wearing it that day. The whole thing is far too risky."

"I don't think the insurance company have been very good this time, do you? Last time I thought they were very sympathetic."

Iain smiled wryly. "Have you considered that they might think we are pulling a stroke?"

"What! You mean they think we've engineered our own burglary? That's mad."

"Well it is in a way, because if we'd wanted people to think we'd been robbed, we'd have made sure the door was jemmied, or something. However, I suppose the police and the insurance companies have to consider the possibility and, of course, there are some pretty thick people out there. I'm sure criminals are making mistakes all the time."

"You don't seriously think that the police suspect us as well do you?" Joyce said indignantly.

"I would think that they'll have to keep us on the suspect list. In fact we might be the *only* suspects."

Joyce sat for a moment then, hesitantly started: "I'm going to have to say this because I've been turning it over in my mind for days now. The person at the top of my suspect list is Val, or should I say Val and Robert."

Iain positively gaped at her. "Don't say anything yet," she continued, "wait until you've heard my reasons."

She took a deep breath, "Val was the last person to see the jewellery. And because she was in the van when I showed it to her, she knew exactly where it was kept. No one else apart from us knew that particular information. An opportunist thief would have had to rifle through all the cupboards, etc."

"Also," she continued hastily, "when could a break in have taken place? Not at a time when we are on site – too much risk of us returning to the van at any moment. If we go out for the day, we go in the motorhome, so we have everything with us. In any case the only day we *were* out was the day with Val at the lighthouse. Best opportunity of all!"

"Hang on, Val was with us all of the time," interjected Iain.

"Ah but Robert wasn't. He was working locally and he had his pick-up truck with him."

"Is this going somewhere?" asked her husband, "because I still fail to see means and motive. I know you've got it in for Val because of her being a shooter, and I don't like that either, but the girl sat in our van, had lunch with us, introduced us to her husband – invited us to dinner. Need I go on?"

"No, you need to listen to all my reasoning before you make a judgement one way or the other." She took a deep breath: "Val and Robert are saving to go to New Zealand. Reading between the lines, they will be *gone* to New Zealand soon taking as much money as they can with them. Val invites us to go out for a few hours in her car, which puts her in control of the time factor.

"Meanwhile Robert does the van over, knowing exactly what he is looking for and precisely where it is. Don't forget that both Val and Robert are familiar faces on site and probably wouldn't attract undue attention."

"OK!" said Iain. "Do you want to put some more meat on these bones?"

"Val was very interested in the burglary, wasn't she? She asked lots of questions. She wanted to know about smart water, and as a result of that she found out that the new jewellery hadn't been done. Perfect opportunity from her point of view! If we'd gone home and come back there's a good chance that it would have been smart watered while we were home.

"She arranges for us to go out in her car, leaving our motorhome unattended for several hours. Obviously as I said, she is in control of the time. We were ages in the lighthouse café.

"Then she breaks her key! Was that a coincidence, or was it planned? It gives her an excuse to phone Robert. Can you remember how she emphasised that we would be over to where he was working in fifteen minutes? And I've just had another idea," Joyce exclaimed. "It gives Robert an alibi of sorts, doesn't it? That's why she wanted us to see his work – to prove he was there."

Iain sat for several minutes analysing the scenario. Eventually he spoke. "I can see your thought process, but you haven't taken account of how Robert would get into the van. The lock wasn't smashed and the door was still locked when we got back to the site. Also we don't know for certain that the jewellery was nicked that day. It could have been any time between the Friday that Val was in our van and the Sunday we came home."

"But the fact remains that we *were* burgled and whoever it was accessed the motorhome without any evidence of forcing locks on either the door or a window. If you are saying that someone must have had a key then it could as easily be Robert as anyone, so he's still my main suspect, given that he'd probably been told exactly where my bag was."

"You do realise all of this is supposition, don't you. Circumstantial evidence if you like," said her husband. "I'm not rubbishing what you've said, but there is absolutely nothing that we could go to the police with."

"And…" he said after a pause, "they might interpret it that we are pulling a scam and trying to throw the blame onto someone else."

Joyce looked uncertain. "So what are we going to do?"

"We are going to accept their invitation to dinner when we get back to Sleepy Bay, and we are going to see if we can find out more for ourselves." Iain asserted.

It was 15th October and Joyce and Iain had been back at Sleepy Bay for four days. They were waiting for Val to arrive to take them to her home. Although they had her email address, they still did not know where they were headed, apart from "A little rented cottage on the edge of Stonybank". The village was seven miles away and comprised of three streets of terraced houses, a few stray cottages and a dark stone pub, which had been closed for over a year.

The couple were dressed casually as requested, and they each carried a fleece jacket as the evenings were turning chilly. It was dark by the time Val arrived at the picnic area outside the caravan site, where she had pre-arranged to pick them up, and blacker still when she pulled up in front of a small bungalow standing on its own two hundred metres beyond the last of the village houses. There were no streetlights this far out, but the lights from the bungalow windows illuminated the path to the door. As the three of them walked together from the car, the sound of the sea carried up to them from way below. The tide was in, the waves making a thunderous rumble against the cliffs.

Inside, Robert met them and relieved them of their garments, hanging them on a stand in the hall. He guided them into a cosy lounge with a dining table set for four at one end. Val headed straight for the kitchen.

Drinks were poured while an appetising aroma drifted in from the kitchen. Val, having donned an apron bearing those famous words "Keep Calm and Carry On" entered the room to advise that dinner would be served in thirty to forty minutes. "I'll be back in a few minutes," she called over her shoulder as she disappeared again.

Initial pleasantries exchanged, Iain began to ask Robert about his guns, telling him that he belonged to a target-shooting club at home.

"Val said that you had a Berretta and a Browning between you, but she couldn't remember any details about them or about your other guns."

Before long the two were in deep discussion about the merits of various pieces, while Joyce looked on with distaste. Robert's favoured shotgun was a 12 bore semi-automatic Berretta, which he used, he said, for taking out nuisance foxes and badgers for local farmers.

"Seven shots!" said Iain.

"Right!" confirmed Robert.

"And what do you use? Number five cartridges, I would guess."

"And you'd guess right," grinned Robert.

"So what's your second rifle?" queried Iain.

"Marlin 223 rifle, side by side."

"Very nice! Sound moderator?"

"Aye, not such a long range, of course, but a handy little weapon."

"So Val said she had a Browning?"

"So she has, but she mainly uses her air rifle. She only shoots rabbits and rats: short range stuff. The odd crow and pigeon."

Iain didn't react.

"So she won't need a licence for 12 foot pounds. What has she got then?" he asked nonchalantly.

"A Daystate Huntsman Regal: pre-charged, sound moderated and a telescopic sight. Ideal for her and best for the job!"

"Quite a collection, I'd be interested to see them some time."

"I'll give you a look after dinner mebbes. I'll just go and see if Boss needs a hand in kitchen yet."

Once Robert was out of the room Iain whispered to Joyce, "I know, I know: just stick to the plan. I have to find out what we're up against."

She nodded with a resigned expression, and Robert returned and ushered them to the table.

Dinner was served: roast sirloin of beef, Yorkshire puddings, roast and mashed potatoes and two huge tureens bearing a variety of vegetables.

"A big meal for two big men," announced Val as she brought the gravy boat through.

Robert poured four glasses of merlot and held his own up in a toast. "Health and happiness, or if ye prefer it, 'slainte and lang may yer lum reek!'"

The four touched glasses. "To your new life in New Zealand!" said Iain raising his glass again. The others followed suit.

"You must be pretty close to going now that you have your visas," said Joyce.

"We are. We're selling things at a rate of knots. Some of the rooms are practically empty," confirmed Val. "Soon there won't be a trace that we've been here at all." She looked at Robert and he smiled.

Iain and Joyce exchanged a significant look.

After a dessert of homemade raspberry pavlova, followed by an extensive cheeseboard with oatcakes, the men fell to discussing guns again. Rising from the table Robert invited Iain to take a look at his "gun room", while Joyce volunteered to help Val clear up and wash up.

~~~

In the kitchen, now scantily equipped, Joyce began to tell Val of their second burglary, hitherto not mentioned. She watched Val's reaction closely as she recounted the details.

"So what was taken?" she'd asked, a look of sheer incredulity on her face.

"Only my new jewellery," responded Joyce, "there wasn't much else of value in the motorhome. We travel light and have our cash and cards with us at all times." She paused. "We think that the thief knew exactly what he or she was after.

"We've also concluded by a process of elimination that the burglary occurred on the day that we were at the lighthouse with you, because we were on site all the rest of the holiday." She watched Val's face throughout her tale, but saw only a picture of innocence.

The other exclaimed, "Oh that's terrible! None of your new jewellery was done with that smart water you were telling me about, was it?"

"Unfortunately not," replied Joyce carefully, "but because it was replaced by the insurance company's own jeweller, and we have photographs and certificates for it, it will be difficult for burglars to sell it on. It is traceable: the police and the insurers have both confirmed that."

Joyce was sure she saw a startled look momentarily pass over Val's face before she made her reply. "Oh well, I suppose that's something."

Joyce turned to face the other woman squarely and began, "Val, no one but you knew where my jewellery was kept, or the fact that I had not marked it with smart water." She paused. "I mean *no one!*" It seems very coincidental that it was taken on the very day that you took us down to the lighthouse."

Val's face turned bright scarlet. "Are you accusing me?" she exclaimed angrily. "I was with you *all* the time."

"But Robert wasn't," said Joyce quietly. "He was working locally. He was a regular visitor to Sleepy Bay and his presence on site wouldn't attract much attention. Also you spoke to him on the phone when we were ready to set off back from the lighthouse. Were you making sure it was safe to do so? Did you think that our visit to see where he working gave him some kind of alibi? Come to think of it, was all that delay with the broken key *deliberate?*"

Val's countenance had reddened, then paled, her mouth open in shock and outrage in turn. "Do you know that is defamation of character, woman!" She shouted.

"It would be if it was untrue," agreed Joyce, "but I happen to think that it is the truth, and I believe I can prove it. Just hear me out.

"Firstly let me just say that I thought we had become friends – of a sort anyway. I realise that we don't know each other well: we haven't known each other long, but I believed you were a decent person."

"I am a decent person!" retorted Val. "It is you who is not. How can you stand in my house, after I've fed you and your husband, and make such accusations?"

"Because I'm giving you a chance, Val, to put things right. I know you have been desperate to raise money for New Zealand. I know you want to see your family and make your life there with them. Perhaps you thought another couple of thousand of easy money would help. Have you already sold your jewellery and just wanted mine? Or have you sold mine as well?

"Do you know that if Iain and I take this further it could stop you going to New Zealand at all? I believe that we have sufficient grounds to name you and Robert to the police, and then there are forensic results to come back. They might just help if the police have a couple of names to work with. That would rather scupper your plans for New Zealand, don't you think? The alternative is for you to give me back my jewellery tonight, and go to New Zealand."

Val had recovered some of her composure by now and said derisively, "You are talking absolute rubbish. I am going to tell Rob about this right now." She flounced out of the room, calling to her husband. Joyce followed.

Robert and Iain weren't in the gun room. One of the safes was open and empty, and the women heard their mens' voices outside. They followed the sound and found them in the dark at the back of the house, which faced out to sea. Iain was examining the Marlin under a security light, whilst Robert was loading an American made Benjamin airgun. They looked up as Val, her voice full of indignation, started to recount the tale.

As his wife ran out of steam, Robert cocked the rifle and held it steadily in two hands. He turned to Joyce, his expression stern. "Got any proof of all this?"

Iain cut in, "We have enough circumstantial evidence to go to the police with names and have them start an investigation. We're currently awaiting forensic results: there were fingerprints at the crime scene, so all the police need is someone to provide a match."

"I don't think so," said Robert menacingly, raising the Benjamin and taking a stance to show he meant business.

"Don't be so bloody stupid, you'd never get away with it for a start. What are you going to do – shoot both of us? First degree murder is a long, long way beyond domestic burglary. By the way, your reaction actually proves your guilt!" retorted Iain, brazening it out, and at the same time gradually manoeuvring the Marlin until he was holding it by the barrel, ready to use it as a club.

"You're out of your league there, boy," said Robert nastily. "My gun's loaded – yours isn't!"

"Your actions are just proving your guilt," Iain tried again. "Are you seriously considering upping your game to murder for a handful of jewellery? Come on man!"

Just at that moment there was a series of small flashes and clicking, which startled three of the group. Joyce, never without her small camera in her handbag, had snapped several times in rapid succession, capturing Robert holding the gun on Iain.

"Another piece of evidence," she smiled grimly.

Robert turned his head slightly towards Val, keeping the rifle trained on Iain. "Get that gun from him. Don't worry it definitely isn't loaded."

As Val approached cautiously and hesitantly, Robert commanded Iain to lower the Marlin and hand it to Val. He did so very slowly, still holding the rifle by the barrel, but watching Robert with a steady gaze. Only he saw Joyce move slowly and inconspicuously into the shadow a few yards behind Robert. Suddenly she sprang from the darkness right behind Robert and crashed a piece of rock into the back of his head. He reeled, and in that second, Iain grabbed at the air rifle, catching it by the barrel and forcing it downwards.

Robert recovered himself almost as quickly and pulled the trigger in a reflex action. Then screamed! Iain grabbed the gun and threw it a short distance. Blood trickled down Robert's neck and back as he collapsed in a groaning heap. His right foot was shattered where the 357 pellet had embedded itself.

Joyce looked in horror at the damage she had caused, while a hysterical Val fell upon her husband, tears streaming down her face. She cradled and berated him simultaneously.

"Oh Rob, what have we got into? Are you all right? Dear God – I must take you to hospital. How has it come to this? You said everything would be okay."

Iain, the calmest of all of them, took control of the situation, ignoring Robert's groans of pain and expletives. "Right, you'd better listen and start seeing some sense here! First of all Val, do you admit that between you and Robert you burgled our motorhome?"

"No, she doesn't!" said Robert through gritted teeth. "Your wife attempted to murder me."

"If that's how you want it, Robert, that's fine. All four of us here know that you are guilty, so in the absence of confessions, here's what is going to happen." Iain pulled a wad of tissues from his pocket and retrieved the Benjamin. He carefully cleaned the barrel, the only part he had held, making sure he didn't erase Robert's own prints.

"This…" he indicated the rifle, "is going over the cliff, right there," he pointed, "and so are you, along with that chunk of rock. And here's what happened. You were careless when you were tinkering with the gun, injured yourself, lost your balance, went over the edge and hit your head on a rock at the bottom. Fatally, I'm afraid. In fact, given the choice you've just made, you could say you've shot yourself in the foot." He paused.

"Actually it's probably better if I smack you in the head again first. I'm a bit stronger than Joyce."

"No, nooooo." Val started screaming, and hurled herself at Iain, who caught her wrists and restrained her.

"Then tell me the truth if you want to save your husband."

Val's face crumpled. "I'm sorry! So, so sorry! We needed some extra money, and it was my idea to begin with. When I found out that the jewellery wasn't smart watered I thought it would be easy. I shouldn't have done it – you'd both been kind to me."

"We thought you were our friend, Val," said Joyce. "We thought that you were like us at first, but you shoot little creatures and you steal from your friends. You're not like us at all. You're ruthless!"

"I'll go and get your jewellery. It's still in one of the gun safes," wept Val, "just help Rob please."

"All right, here's the deal," said Iain. "Either Rob goes over the cliff; lock stock and barrel, and of course, rock! Sad but fatal accident!" he looked over the cliff edge to the rocks below. "They look lethal!" he declared.

"You my dear, go off to New Zealand post haste to join your family, never to set foot in this hemisphere again, and count your blessings. Sound okay?"

Robert looked pleadingly at Val.

"Alternative ending then," continued Iain. "You both admit to theft. Joyce's camera on movie mode can record your confessions, just as a bit of extra insurance for us, not to be used unless we have to. Let me just assure you that if we have to, then we most certainly will.

"You return to us Joyce's jewellery, now, with some suitable recompense for all this inconvenience, and you *both* go to New Zealand, never to return. Now that seems like a pretty good offer to me, but it's only on the table for five minutes, and no, we're not leaving you alone to discuss it."

Val and Robert looked hard at each other and then Robert said, "Okay, we take the deal, but how do we know that **we** can trust *you*?"

"That's rich!" chuckled Iain. "Answer, you don't! Take it or leave it."

Joyce cut in, "We won't renege. We want you to go to New Zealand. We want our rabbits to be safe."

"By the way," added Iain, "I think 'suitable recompense' would be your guns. That'll keep everyone safe won't it? Val can prepare a Bill of Sale for me: job lot £50. You can't take them with you anyway Robbie Boy, whichever option you go for."

―――

As Joyce escorted Val back to the gun room, she asked, "There's only one aspect that has puzzled me in all of this: how did Robert get into the motorhome without forcing the locks or breaking any windows? I'm assuming he already has 'form'? A professional if you like!" She paused. "And if that is the case, how come you've been accepted for New Zealand?"

Suddenly Val recovered her composure and grinned. "It was easy, I used your set of keys."

"How?" exclaimed Joyce; incredulous. "They haven't been out of my sight – I carry them everywhere."

"Exactly!" explained Val triumphantly. "Always in the front pocket of your little walking bag, aren't they? You even take it to the showers with you, and how many times when you've been talking to me, have I seen you take it out, ready to open the van door?"

"But I would know if you'd taken it at any of those times. I use my key several times a day."

"I took it that day at the lighthouse," smirked Val. "It was easy peasy! While you were at the counter ordering lunch, you left your bag on the chair beside me. I knew exactly where the key would be. Then, when we were waiting for the food to arrive, I went to the loo and phoned Robert. I nipped outside and left the key in a pre-arranged place in the dry stone wall (which he built, by the way). I'd already told you that he had thought about joining us – just in case you spotted him. He dropped the key into the driver's door compartment of the Micra when we visited him, just as he leaned in to kiss me. Clever don't you think?"

"But what if I'd discovered the key missing when we returned to the van?"

"But you didn't did you? Because I made sure that I kept you talking and that it was Iain who opened the door. Child's play after that: as soon as you were making a cuppa and Ian was at the loo, I slipped the key back in your bag. Magician, aren't I? And you're not as clever as you thought you were!"

"Well you sound very cocky now Val but you've still been caught."

Joyce took the small padded envelope from Val and checked that the four pieces of jewellery were there, just as Iain half dragged a now dazed Robert into the room.

"Leave those safes open," he commanded. He sat the bleeding Robert in to a chair and began removing all the firearms from safe to table.

"Find some writing paper and get the details of these guns down on a Bill of Sale," he directed Val, "and then we'll go our separate ways. – And think yourselves very lucky!"

⁓

As they left Sleepy Bay a week later, Joyce looked about her with satisfaction at the scores of rabbits nibbling peacefully at the grass. "I love this place," she said. Apart from the wardens she and Iain were the last to leave the site.

"At least the rabbits are safe for another year," she added.

"And we'll be back in the spring to watch over them," Iain agreed. "But what the *hell* are we going to tell the insurance company?"

A Watertight Alibi

Wednesday Morning

Christine emerged from the steaming cubicle, stepping carefully onto the terry towelling bath mat, her blonde hair darkened from the shower and now dripping onto her shoulders. She wrapped herself in an apricot-coloured bath sheet and stood for a minute with her eyes closed, inhaling the warm, fragrant vapour. Then giving herself a mental shake, she towelled herself dry, turned the shower back on, cleaned the walls and tray, and walked naked into her bedroom.

She carefully turned back the duvet to air the bed and set about her routine moisturisation of her lightly tanned body. As she slowly massaged her warm, smooth skin, she listened to the bird song outside, which never failed to give her pleasure. She selected clean underwear from her dressing table drawers: nothing flashy – just ordinary daywear: cream with an understated floral motif of the same shade.

She turned to the wardrobe, indecisive as her eyes skimmed the contents. Not trousers – no, not a skirt and blouse either… she pulled out two cotton summer dresses and held them side by side, her head cocked like a curious robin. Considering… It had to be one or the other. She put back the slightly shorter one, which had an eye-catching geometric design. The chosen garment was more subtle and subdued: blue with a small white floral pattern, loose fitting and sleeveless. She stepped into it, zipped up and looked at the effect in the mirror. It fell just below the knee: fresh but demure. Just right! She stepped back out of the dress, laid it on the bed and set about drying her hair.

Twenty minutes later, her dry hair restored to its glossy, honey blonde colour, Christine re-clothed and swished open the bedroom curtains to let in the light of a brilliantly sunny morning. Beautiful! The birds were still singing away and not a cloud in the sky.

In the kitchen she switched on the kettle and busied herself making her usual breakfast: fresh grapefruit, two slices of brown toast and instant coffee. She enjoyed a leisurely meal, then washed up, leaving the kitchen as immaculate as usual; not so much as a knife out of place – one of the benefits of living alone, she thought.

Christine wandered aimlessly from room to room adjusting a curtain here and a picture there, ensuring that everything was in its proper place. Her clothes from yesterday evening were already washed and now in the tumble dryer. She would run an iron over them as soon as the cycle finished and put them straight into the relevant drawers and wardrobe.

She'd made a great effort *not* to think, but to give her full attention to those commonplace, routine jobs she had carried out. Yet, as she sat with her second coffee of the morning, she felt her resolve slipping away and she could not help herself. Barry! It always came back to Barry. Her life had not been the same since that first encounter… and he was responsible for the situation in which she now found herself.

He had certainly been a charmer: slim, tanned and well muscled, not quite six feet, which made her five feet two seem diminutive, dark hair and eyes and a mischievous grin. God's gift to women! She had certainly been swept off her feet. How amazed she had been that he had chosen her when he could have had his pick of so many more glamorous women. They'd had some good times in those early days. He'd taken her for some lovely meals, to the theatre a couple of times and for peaceful romantic walks on the beach and by the river. He'd always been a bit too hands-on for her liking but nothing could have prepared her for the first time she went to his house and what was to follow. He'd said that he wanted to cook her a special meal and he had!

They'd had a lovely bottle of Chenin Blanc with their Dover sole and things were comfortable and relaxed between them, until it became evident that Barry was looking for something more than the usual kisses and caresses. When he made the move – she just froze! "Er no! I'm not ready for this yet Barry," she'd explained. "We've only just known each other for a few weeks."

"You'll be fine – just relax," he'd replied without stopping, his hands sliding beneath her clothing and feeling their way over her now taut body.

Christine, whilst she lacked experience in the love-making department, had still known that this was not what she wanted and was now feeling tense and anxious. "No," she'd repeated, "please stop. Please Barry!"

In response Barry had pushed her back on the sofa and rolled heavily on top of her, pushing his erection against her, while his mouth worked its way over her neck and breasts. She'd tried to push him away but he pinned her down roughly and pulled at the neckline of her dress, and her bra, exposing one of her breasts.

"You do want it," he said harshly. He unzipped his trousers and pulled out his penis, reaching for the hem of her dress.

"Please stop," she implored again, "I am not ready for this, Barry. Please let me sit up. We'll talk."

He had simply clamped his mouth firmly over hers so that she couldn't speak, one arm across her neck restraining both shoulders while the other hand tore at her clothing. She had heard and felt her dress tear and seconds later her bra was unfastened and wrenched from her body. When she had tried to struggle, Barry had just become rougher, gripping her, vice-like and punching her into submission. When he forced himself inside her the pain was unbearable, coursing through her whole body and ending in a silent, suffocated scream.

She'd bled profusely! Well, he'd taken her virginity in the most violent way so it was no wonder! Maybe you always bled the first time anyway... she didn't know...

Christine hadn't gone straight to the police, a delay she'd lived to regret. She'd walked, or rather staggered, home with no underwear on and only her torn dress and a thin jacket covering her. Barry had quite literally thrown her out, calling her a slut and a cock-tease. For the latter he'd told her, she'd "got what she deserved".

She was thankful that it was dark, as with blood trickling down her legs and tears down her face, she stumbled forward, each step causing a burning pain deep inside her. It had been a relief to reach her apartment safely: to close and lock the door behind her. She'd stood for some minutes with her back against the front door, crying hysterically, shaking uncontrollably.

Eventually she'd gone to the bathroom and stripped off the few clothes she had on, dropping her tattered dress straight into the bathroom waste bin. She had turned on the shower and stepped in, allowing the warm water to course over her body. Not hot enough to wash the events of the evening away! She remembered turning the temperature up, watching the diluted blood pooling around her feet before being washed down the drain forever. Later she'd regretted that too, but at the time she could only think of scrubbing every bit of Barry from her body and her life. Then, eventually scourged to her satisfaction and wrapped in her dressing gown, she had phoned Charlotte.

Charlotte had listened to Christine's tale of woe, interrupting the sobbing with increasing outbursts of expletives and angered comments. "I'm coming straight up to see you," she'd said. "And him!" she'd added darkly. "I'll be there in about..." a pause while she consulted her watch... "four hours. Try to get some rest in the meantime Chrissy. I know you won't sleep."

As good as her word, Charlotte had arrived at a quarter to six that morning. They'd hugged long but silently at the door and then Charlotte had led Christine, tearful again, to the sofa, made her comfortable under a travel rug, and gone into the kitchen to make coffee.

"Tell me it all again!" she had commanded once they were settled together on the sofa, and Christine had. Shaking as she poured out the sordid events of the previous evening, interspersed with her own bouts of tears, and the occasional question from Charlotte, she told all.

When Christine had run out of words and tears, Charlotte had said gently, "You should have gone straight to the police, you know Chrissy – while there was still 'evidence' on you."

"I couldn't!" Christine started sobbing again, her breathing becoming erratic and her chest heaving. "I had to get home – to feel safe. I had to get rid of everything to do with him!" She shuddered, running her hands feverishly over her arms and legs.

"But you've washed away valuable evidence, Chrissy."

"I've still got the marks though. Look!" Christine had shown Charlotte the ugly bruising on her neck, upper arms and breasts. "There are others!" she added ominously.

Charlotte grimaced, and sat deep in thought for a while, occasionally nodding as if to affirm something to herself. Christine sat in vacant silence, trying hard not to think. At last Charlotte said, "OK – I think this is what we should do..."

Christine had gone to the Police Station later that morning, alone, and with her torn and stained dress exactly as Charlotte had instructed her. She'd undergone some dreadful questioning at the station in a tiny, shabby-looking room, which made her feel as if she was a criminal. Later she'd seen a female "Liaison Officer" who was kinder, but she'd still had to submit to the ordeal of an examination and photographs. She'd felt "soiled" all over again, and that had just been the start of the trauma. As soon as she'd returned home – back in the shower again. Would she ever be able to stop trying to wash it all away? One thing was certain she'd never be able to wash the memory away! She wondered if she would feel any better when Barry was behind bars.

In due course forensic evidence had revealed traces of semen on Christine's dress, which was subsequently identified as Barry's, but while he admitted sex, he denied charges of rape, insisting that the act was consensual.

Christine's mind jumped to the trial and she could visualise it in detail as if it was yesterday:

Barry sitting there on the other side of the court: smart, sombre suit, tie and hair immaculate, talking in a relaxed and easy manner with his solicitor. He turned and fixed her with a stare charged with challenge. Christine lowered her eyes. Her own solicitor, Lauren Kendall, touched her gently on the arm, "Don't worry Chrissy, we'll get him sent down for what he has done. Just try to relax and remember your answers to my questions. It doesn't matter if you get upset – that is only natural under the circumstances. Just don't let Harker confuse or intimidate you – he'll try. That's his job!"

Christine nodded. Lauren had instructed her to dress smartly but simply. "Nothing the least bit provocative or sexy," she'd told her.

"I don't own anything provocative or sexy!" Christine had replied.

So she'd worn a high-necked, soft grey/green dress, with a matching short sleeved jacket over it; not new, an outfit she wore regularly for work and felt comfortable in. Polished black shoes, wristwatch and a simple gold bangle completed her outfit. Her nails were short, unvarnished and immaculate.

And the dreadful debacle had begun...

Barry's solicitor had been awful. Between he and Barry they'd made her seem like a tart and a pervert, who liked rough, kinky sex. Harker was both sarcastic and aggressive. He had asked her the most intimate questions and then twisted and turned her answers inside out. He made it seem as if Barry was the victim: an honest, hardworking soul who had been misled into raunchy sex by a manipulative, demanding, depraved woman, who had then turned the tables on him.

He'd also made a big issue about her not going straight to the police station that night. Her vital mistake, just as Charlotte had predicted, and her biggest regret! She just hadn't been thinking properly. How could she? She'd been so hurt and traumatised, and she'd just had to get home – to safety – get those soiled remnants of clothing off and wash him completely away. Luckily, and only thanks to Charlotte she had salvaged her dress and taken it to the police station with her. They had, eventually, been able to confirm the "presence" of Barry on the dress, but even so Harker had still managed to twist the facts there in Barry's favour.

Then after making mincemeat of her, Harker had led Barry gently through the cursed evening, where the "accused" was able to relate how he had prepared a lovely meal, in what he had hoped was a romantic setting. No they hadn't been drunk. No they hadn't on any previous occasion had sex together. They'd been building up their relationship gradually: walks, cinema, theatre, quiet drinks... and yes, he'd hoped that the evening would have culminated in Christine spending the night with him. He thought that he loved her and that she might be "the one". He was in fact full of hope about a future together.

He'd gone on to tell the court that he'd been surprised when she had made the first move towards intimacy, and having done so, began to urge him on to be rougher and rougher with her. He'd wanted to please her so had complied as best he could with her requests, nay demands.

When Barry had been asked by Harker whether Christine had also been rough with him – "Oh yes!" he'd replied evenly, and gone on to describe: 'Claw marks down his back and chest' – bites in some 'fairly intimate places.'

Lies! All lies!

When cross-examined by Lauren Kendall as to whether he was able to produce any evidence of this Barry scoffed derisively, "Of course not! I didn't exactly think I'd need any. Or do you think that I might have photographed things at the time? I'm not the pervert here!"

As he'd walked to resume his seat by Harker, Barry and the solicitor exchanged satisfied looks, Barry also managing to throw a brief triumphant glance in Christine's direction. She'd scowled back.

In addition Barry's friends and colleagues had one and all given character references as to his being "a great guy", "honest, hard-working, responsible", "a bit of a one for the ladies but harmless" and "a good sense of humour".

And Barry had got off! Walked away amidst his friends and Harker, a wide grin of triumph on his face. She'd stood with Lauren watching them heading for the local watering hole, "The Honest Lawyer" – what a joke! An oxymoron if ever there was!

Gina and Melanie, two friends who had attended the court to support Christine had wanted to take her to lunch, but she had declined. She had just wanted to get home and be alone for a while. She was stunned: incredulous at the verdict, and she needed time to come to terms with the fact that Barry had apparently walked away unscathed, character seemingly intact.

Later she'd phoned Charlotte…

Now, two years on "insufficient evidence", "of good character" and "no previous history" still bounced around in Christine's head. For the same two years she had suffered snide comments casting aspersions on her honesty, integrity and morals, and cruel jokes at her expense. She regularly endured the boringly repetitive "Hey Chris, fancy a bit of rough tonight?" or "I'd ask you for a blow-job but you might bite my tackle off".

She hadn't had a boyfriend since Barry – didn't want one – didn't know if she ever would. Or whether she would ever be able to forget that fateful night and get on with her life.

Then, just recently she'd seen him. He looked just the same: the last two years certainly hadn't aged him! She, Gina and Melanie had been finishing their meal in The Black Swan when he'd walked in. He was alone and made for the bar. Christine had immediately shrunk back in her seat in the booth that the three of them occupied, and nudged Melanie, who'd nodded. She'd seen him too.

"Let's go," Christine had said.

"No Chrissy, you can't spend your life running away. He can't see you back there, and we'll keep our eye on him."

Barry was eying up a group of girls at a table in the far corner who were obviously on some kind of celebration. At last he made eye contact with one of them and smiled. The girl might have been eighteen years old, medium height, slim, with huge blue eyes and long blonde hair. She returned the smile, then looked away. Barry continued to stare, now more specifically at the blonde girl.

Christine's immediate thought was "Hunter finds prey! Singles out the most vulnerable!"

Further smiles were exchanged, until the whole group were casting furtive looks over to the bar. Barry's first move had been successful. He spoke to the barman and nodded his head towards the party. Money changed hands, and a few minutes later a bottle of champagne in an ice bucket and a tray with six glasses on it were delivered to the girls' table, the barman saying something conspiratorially and gesticulating towards the bar. Blondie looked over and gave him a radiant smile, which he returned, waving his hand in a deprecating manner. Further discussion at the table!

Blondie stood up and approached the bar: a few words, smiles, giggles, and then she returned to her friends with Barry in tow.

"Mission accomplished!" thought Christine. She started to worry. How many? What if this girl was his next victim? She looked so young – even younger than she herself had been when she had met Barry. Could she do something to stop the train of events? And what could she do?

She caught Gina and Melanie gazing at her anxiously and realised that she'd retreated into her own world. Had one of them asked her a question, she wondered?

"Just worrying about that girl," she said by way of explanation.

"Well don't," cautioned Gina, "there's nothing you can do that won't have repercussions of one sort or another."

"Maybe there is," said Melanie getting to her feet. Blondie had just picked up her shoulder bag and stood up. "Go outside both of you. Start walking down Cartmel Street to the taxi rank. I'll catch you up. Go! Quickly!"

Melanie grabbed her own bag and headed for the ladies cloakroom where Blondie had just disappeared through the door.

Gina hustled Christine out of the pub and around the corner, Barry now too engrossed in his present company to notice either of them. They walked briskly in the direction of the taxi rank and were nearly there when Melanie came flying along behind them.

"Sorted!" she exclaimed. "At least I hope so."

"How come?" asked Gina.

Melanie chuckled. "Just gave Blondie a friendly word – told her that Barry was married, and that of course, he would deny it. I told her best give him the brush off without him knowing why – cause less trouble that way. She thanked me."

The three of them laughed as they boarded the taxi.

Later that night though Christine wasn't laughing. She realised that without Melanie's intervention, that young girl could have ended up in the same situation as herself two years ago. Someone still could! He'd got away with it once…

On impulse she rang Charlotte. "It's time to act!"

Christine rang around the regular group: Moira, Cathy Louise, Gina and Melanie suggesting a girls' night out.

"No special occasion," she'd said. "Just ages since all six of us could make it."

They'd settled on the following Tuesday as convenient for everyone, though they'd agreed that it would not be a late night as most of them had work the next morning. Cathy had said that she would book a table for 7.30 at The Red Balloon, one of their favourite haunts and one where they were well known. As far as Christine knew Barry played squash on Tuesday evenings after work, so there wasn't much chance of seeing him at The Red Balloon, which in any case was on the opposite side of town to him.

Later she rang Charlotte and told her of the arrangements.

Wednesday Afternoon

Christine had ironed and put away her clean clothes. She had made herself a salad sandwich for lunch and was sitting enjoying her after lunch coffee when the doorbell sounded.

She opened the door to behold a tall, fair-haired man, about forty, she guessed, and a younger woman, maybe late twenties with short dark hair. Both were smartly dressed and as the man addressed her, both held out warrant cards. Police officers. DI Paul Scott and DS Susan Ferguson. Christine looked perplexed when they asked if they could have a few words, but gestured them into the living room and turned off her CD player.

"Can you confirm that you are Christine Finlay, please?"

"I am. Is something wrong?" Christine looked from one face to the other for clues. The detectives introduced themselves even though Christine had already read the names on their warrant cards.

"Shall we sit?" asked Susan Ferguson, "We just have a few routine questions that we'd like to ask you."

Once they were all settled, and the two police officers had declined the offer of coffee, Paul Scott began. "Christine, can you tell us where you were yesterday evening? Say from about 6pm."

Christine was taken aback. "Why? Has there been an incident or something around here?" she asked tentatively.

"No not around here exactly," continued Scott. "Can you please just tell me where you were between the hours of 6pm and midnight?"

"Well, for most of that time I was out with friends. We were at The Red Balloon having a meal."

"Can you give us some times?" asked Susan taking out a notebook and pen.

"I was here at six o'clock and I left at about ten minutes to seven to walk to the pub. We were booked for 7.30." Christine paused. "What is this all about?" she asked, a little irritation showing in her voice. "Has something happened? Just tell me!"

"Let's just get some basic information down please and then we'll give you some details." Scott replied easily. Susan sat, pen poised over her notebook. "What time did you arrive at the pub, Christine, and who were you meeting there?"

"It must have been around 7.25, I think and three of my friends were already there."

"Names please," prompted Susan.

"Moira Philpotts, Louise Taylor and Melanie Hart. Oh God, has something happened to one of them?" shrieked Christine.

"No, no nothing like that. You said three of your friends – were there others?" asked Scott.

"Yes, there were six of us altogether. Gina and Cathy arrived together just after me. Gina Davison and Cathy Marsh," she added.

"We'll need addresses and contact numbers for each of them," said Scott. "Can you provide that information?"

Christine nodded, still looking anxiously from one detective to the other. "Will you please tell me why you want this information? What has happened?"

Susan Ferguson looked across at her senior officer, who cleared his throat, then began: "All in good time, let's just get all of the details of your movements last night, shall we? Now, between 6 and 6.50 where were you?"

"Here, getting ready to go out."

"Alone?"

"Yes."

"And between 6.50 and 7.25 you were walking from here to The Red Balloon?"

"Yes."

"Will you please describe the route you took Miss Finlay?"

Christine sighed then taking a deep breath. "Along Cedar Road to the junction where it meets Beech Avenue. I turned right just past The Copper Beech pub, then went all the way along the West Road to the end to The Red Balloon. OK?"

"Did you see anyone on this route?"

"Well, yes several people, I suppose."

"Anyone you knew?" interjected Susan.

"Not really," Christine thought hard. "A couple of people I said hello to in passing…" She hesitated. "A man walking a golden retriever, who I've seen before – he might remember me, and the newsagent along the West Road who was locking up his shop. I sometimes get a newspaper there so he probably knows me by sight. Other than that, just strangers…

"There were quite a few people around the Copper Beech area and a few kids running the streets but no one I could describe." Exasperation. "Why would I take any notice?"

"It's OK," said Scott. "Let's move on to your time in The Red Balloon. You were there from 7.25 until…?"

"11.15," said Christine immediately. "Most of the girls had work this morning so we couldn't be too late."

"During that time did you leave the pub at all?"

"No."

"Did any of your friends leave the pub at any time before 11.15?"

"Er yes, Louise and Moira left at eleven o'clock because that's when their taxi arrived." Christine watched as Susan Ferguson checked back through her notes.

"What about the rest of you? How did you get home?" asked Scott.

"Well, none of us live that far away so we walked. We all set off together, then part of the way down the West Road, Gina and Melanie went off towards the Grange Estate. Gina lives at Cotters Green and Melanie lives in Dickens Wynd. Cathy and I walked together past The Copper Beech and down Beech Avenue, then I turned off and came along Cedar Road. Less than five minutes by myself. When I got home Mr Sykes downstairs was sitting at the window. He's about eighty and he doesn't sleep very well. I waved to him. Now what is this all about?" finished Christine crossly.

"One more detail Christine and then I will explain to you why we have had to ask these questions," said Scott grimacing.

Christine nodded sulkily.

"Can you describe what you were wearing yesterday evening?"

"A red dress, black sandals – I had a grey jacket with me but I didn't wear it. It was a lovely evening. Oh, I put it on to walk home as it had got a bit chilly. Small black handbag – shall I show you?" She jumped up and after a minute reappeared with a red dress on a hanger, black strappy sandals dangling from one finger and a tiny black evening bag under her arm.

"Nice!" said Susan, smiling.

Christine laid the outfit over the empty armchair and sat down again. She looked at Paul Scott expectantly.

"Barry Robson was found dead in his home this morning," Scott announced.

Christine sat motionless, staring at the detective, a multitude of mixed emotions clambering over each other in her head. "Well," she finally said, "I'm taken aback by the news but I can't feel sorry, not after what he did to me…" her voice trailed off. "Was it a heart attack or something? An accident? Suicide?" she asked tentatively.

"We are treating his death as suspicious," said Scott gravely.

"Oh my God! You mean a murder – and you think I might have done it?"

"At this stage, Miss Finlay," formal again, "we are simply gathering information about any person who we feel may have had a motive, in the hope that we can eliminate non-relevant information from our enquiry."

"So you're saying that I'm a murder suspect?" Christine retorted angrily.

"In these early days of an enquiry we cannot afford to rule anyone out – everyone is a suspect if you like – but what we will do now that we have this information from you, is confirm with your friends your whereabouts yesterday evening and hopefully eliminate you from our enquiry. By the way," he added, "do any of the bar staff at The Red Balloon know you?"

"Yes," confirmed Christine. "Jimmy Black was behind the bar all night. The waitress who brought our food was new since we were last at the pub, but I imagine she would probably remember our group."

Susan Ferguson, who was still scribbling furiously, looked up briefly and asked, "Would you get me the addresses of your friends who were with you last evening please?" She looked questioningly at Scott, "and then we'll take our leave?"

In another ten minutes the two detectives were satisfied that they had enough information to progress their enquiry and left the flat.

Christine remained where she was for some minutes, mulling over the last hour. The rape had never been mentioned, but she was absolutely certain that the police officers had already familiarised themselves with all of the sordid details – and yes, she did have a pretty good motive for wanting Barry dead. Maybe a few other women did too for all she knew. Well, it would appear that Barry had been killed yesterday evening – so they would discover that she was nowhere near the crime scene for the whole of that time. No opportunity!

She realised that she had not asked how Barry had met his death, and they hadn't offered that information. Well, she couldn't feel sorry. How many women, and girls (yes girls – she thought about that girl he had tried to pick up in the Black Swan), had he given similar treatment to? Maybe he'd "got what he deserved" the bastard!

After a while Christine roused herself, got up and put her dress, bag and sandals away, then got her jacket, shoulder bag and a small hessian shopping bag and went out. She walked in the opposite direction from her route last night. First she called at the post office, bought stamps and made a quick call from their payphone, then went next door where she picked up milk, a pre-

prepared salad and a fresh brown loaf. That would do her for now, she was back at work tomorrow and she would call at M&S on her way home.

Paul Scott and Susan Ferguson had spent two days interviewing Christine Finlay's friends, the staff at The Red Balloon and Mr Sykes, who told the detectives over and over what a lovely girl Chrissy was. They had also found the man with the golden retriever, thanks to Mr Patel the newsagent, who knew him as a regular customer: Neil Harris and Barney came in every day for a newspaper and a freebie gravy bone!

Now they were awaiting the pathologist's report, but in any event it seemed that they could rule out Christine Finlay from their enquiry. Her every move on Tuesday evening was accounted for by several people. She hadn't even gone to the ladies toilet in the pub alone: on one occasion she had been accompanied by Gina Davison and the other by Cathy Marsh. One and all, the girls had agreed that Christine only left the lounge twice and each occasion had been for no longer than five minutes.

A pretty watertight alibi if ever there was one. They had accumulated ten statements including the barman and waitress at The Red Balloon, all confirming Christine's presence during the period when they believed Barry Robson was killed. Now they just needed confirmation of the time of death, but the doctor had already given them parameters for that. It looked as if Miss Finlay was out of the picture and they'd have to start looking elsewhere.

Robson's neighbours had already been interviewed but would now need re-visiting. Information about the deceased's friends and work colleagues would have to be obtained. Back to the drawing board!

"Let's check current and ex-girlfriends out," suggested Susan. "It sounds like he had plenty from what his neighbours said, and given that he was once accused of rape…"

"Good idea," agreed Paul, "and we should know more about the murder weapon soon. Unfortunately it seems as if it might be an ordinary kitchen knife from what Doc said – nothing out of the ordinary."

Charlotte had been searching for a cheap holiday for a few days now and eventually found what she was looking for: a fortnight in Malta. Funny – she'd never heard of anyone in recent times going there. Quite popular when Mam and Dad were young! They'd been a few times. Well, she would go and see what it was like.

She'd had her hair cut short two days ago – first time ever! And she'd had some low-lights put in. Different!

She couldn't ring Chrissy, of course, and she hadn't even seen her the last time she was up North. She couldn't very well do that could she? Chrissy would be all right now though. The last time they had spoken – only briefly – she could hear the relief in her voice. Christine had always been the quiet, vulnerable one and Charlotte the more independent, bossy one! How could two identical twins (and they really were identical) have such different temperaments? They'd even had the same tastes in clothes though, and both looked well in a little red number!

She had always looked after Chrissy, and she always would. A last glance around the flat and Charlotte shouldered her rucksack and headed out.

One Week Later

Charlotte sent Christine a postcard from Malta.

> "Having a good time.
> Hotel ok, sea and scenery wonderful.
> I really liked your friends –
> a good loyal crowd. Love C."

Christine read it, shredded it and dropped it into a litter bin in town.

Epilogue

Paul Scott and Susan Ferguson had turned over every possible lead. Other ex-girlfriends of Barry Robson had been traced and questioned. A couple of them admitted that their relationship with him had become rough and violent, although none had come forward and reported rape. They had simply ditched him as soon as possible. Slight motive perhaps but nothing conclusive and both detectives' gut feeling in each case had been one of insufficient motive and no supporting evidence.

Barry's friends and colleagues had grieved the loss of "a friendly, popular guy" who would be "a great loss to us all".

Without a doubt Christine Finlay fitted the frame with regard to motive, but her alibi for the entire timeframe had been gone over with a fine toothcomb and proved to be completely solid and unbreakable.

The case remained unsolved but not closed and eventually was filed away as a cold case.

Amber Alert

Amber stood at the side of the bypass watching with impatience the never-ending stream of cars, interspersed with a variety of laden heavy goods vehicles. A gang of motorcycles in various vivid colours streaked past, overtaking the four wheelers and ten wheelers alike, and weaving in and out of the lanes. No wonder everyone called this The Mad Mile!

She was late already and she just couldn't catch a break. She knew that she shouldn't have spent so long with the ponies, but they looked forward to her going to see them with their little weekly treats, and she looked forward to seeing them even more. Today she had taken them two carrots and an apple each, then fed them with handfuls of lush grass picked from the verdant hedgerow on the opposite side of the bridle path. They had already eaten their way through most of their field and so were always grateful for the longer, sweeter grass that they could not reach.

Amber wished they were her ponies, but she didn't even know to whom they belonged. To her knowledge no one ever came to see them, so she'd given them names of her own and now when she called them they came thundering across the field to see her. She'd called the two mares Ginny and Tammy, and the small grey gelding, she'd named Rory.

Frustrated, Amber glanced at her watch. She was definitely going to be in trouble now. Her anxious eyes darted from side to side, weighing up the speed of the traffic each way, one foot hovering at the kerb edge ready for even the slightest opportunity to cross. "After the red fiesta…" she told herself. The gap in the eastbound lane wouldn't provide much of a window of opportunity but she thought she could do it. Frustration turned to hope, then just as she was on her starting blocks, she saw "the man". He was on the opposite side of the bypass and he appeared to be staring straight at her.

She hesitated, just long enough for her to lose the chance to cross. Amber looked him in the eye and he looked straight back at her. She frowned. She was sure she had seen him last Saturday afternoon when she was returning from the pony field. She recognised his outdoor clothing: walking boots, a pair of light-coloured cargo pants and a dark green waterproof jacket. Come to think of it, she thought she'd seen him before that: same place, same clothing, same intense look. She felt a surge of panic. Was this more than a coincidence? He was still watching her. She noticed something dangling from one hand; it looked like a piece of rope… The traffic was still streaming past, which offered no one the opportunity to cross. The girl made up her mind in an instant, and turned away to the right, heading towards the underpass, some three hundred metres away. When she looked back, the man was gone!

Amber started to panic again. Was he also heading for the underpass from the opposite side? Would they meet in the dimly lit passage under the road? Stranger danger! She had to get through the tunnel before he got there. Another glance… she saw no one. Amber started to run.

As she got near to the gaping mouth of the tunnel she slowed and looked furtively around her. No sign of anyone! Still anxious, her heart pounding, she cautiously approached the sombre entrance – no one. With relief she sprinted through to the other side, acutely aware of the traffic noise above drowning out any other sound. She almost collided with a lad on a bicycle just turning into the underpass from the town side and she let out an involuntary scream. The boy swerved, shouting an apology before he disappeared through and out the other side. Seeing no one else in the vicinity Amber slowed a little and jogged the rest of the way home.

By the next Saturday, the effects of her previous week's shock had worn off, and Amber set out after lunch with a carrier bag laden with carrots, apples from the tree in the garden and some left over bread for the ponies.

It was a sunny autumn afternoon and she stayed a long time after all the food was gone, sitting on the fence and idly petting first one pony then another. This was idyllic. Quite suddenly Amber became aware that the light seemed to be going fast and she jumped down, gave Ginny, Tammy and Rory each a last handful of grass and a pat, then set off across the fields that took her back to the main road. As she approached her usual crossing place, the road was predictably busy and most of the vehicles already had their lights on although it wasn't yet quite dark. Amber saw the man immediately, standing at the opposite kerb side, watching her approach. Instinctively she altered her course to the diagonal, making for the subway again. Out of her peripheral vision she caught sight of another movement and let out an involuntary cry. Then she realised it was just a small, greyish dog passing by. Stand down! No threat! Her mind was still racing though, and her heart hammering, as she walked at an increasingly brisk pace. He must be waiting for her. Why?

Amber thought about the rope dangling menacingly from his hand and shuddered. She broke into a run, terrifying herself with thoughts of what his intentions might be, and what she could do if the man was waiting for her in the tunnel, where the noise of traffic above would drown out any commotion from within.

As she got close to the dingy subway entrance, she slowed down and crept surreptitiously forward, feeling the blood pounding in her head as she did so. She cautiously ventured a look and was relieved to find the tunnel empty. Taking a deep breath, Amber sprinted as fast as she could through the underpass, keeping herself in the centre of the path all the way through, and maintaining her pace for more than a hundred metres beyond the other side of the road. Gradually she allowed herself to slow a little and take a good look around. No one! Definitely no sign of "the man".

Although gasping and shaking, Amber allowed herself a little smile as she thought of her PE teacher, Miss Walker, and how pleased she would be with her recent 200 metre sprint. She was sure that she had just achieved a personal best.

Despite her concerns and fears, Amber could not stop seeing the ponies. She had formed quite a bond with them, and the highlight of her week was the afternoon she spent in their company. After feeding them today she had spent most of her time trying to untangle Ginny's mane, which was full of knots and assorted vegetation. She was, however, careful to take her leave at an earlier time, as the afternoon darkened on the approach of the equinox. As she made her way home now at 4.30 it was almost dusk, the light fading and the traffic every bit as bad as usual. Even at a distance from the main road, she could see the constant stream of headlights rushing past, equally bad in both directions. The Mad Mile!

Amber had more or less resigned herself to the extra 300 metre walk to the underpass and back almost the same distance on the other side to reach the estate on which she lived. However, in spite of her latent fear, she could not stop herself venturing so far along her normal route towards the bypass, peering into the distance for any sign of a figure on the opposite side of the road. "The man" was nowhere in sight. It was too early!

With sudden determination and change of plan, Amber made straight for the road, confident that she could be across and home before he appeared. As she arrived at the kerb side, darting looks all around her, there was no one to be seen. The passing drivers, intent on the road seemed not to notice her as she hovered on the brink of indecision as to when to cross. A couple of times there had been a brief gap in the westbound traffic, but none at a similar interval in the opposing lane. Amber was becoming increasingly impatient. She could have been almost at the subway by now.

Suddenly there was an opportunity! Cars were approaching in both directions, but she was confident that the gap would be sufficient to allow her to cross. She stepped out. Panic! Headlights! Full beam! A car bearing down the centre of the road, overtaking the row of westbound vehicles… and in the midst of it all, the briefest glimpse of "the man" standing across the road.

A heavy thud and a scream almost simultaneously, and then strange noises in her ears as everything turned distant and hazy… Then black!

Amber awoke in a strange bed. She gazed at the unfamiliar high ceiling, then cast her eyes left to behold the anxious faces of her parents, both of whom were sitting at her bedside, their hands tightly entwined and watching her intently.

"She's awake!"

"Nurse, nurse!" her mother stood and leaned towards Amber's face. "Can you hear me, love? It's Mum." Amber's eyes flickered and she nodded her head slightly.

"Thank God," said her father, burying his face in his hands.

A nurse arrived at the other side of the bed, calm and smiling. "Amber, you're back with us. Great! Don't move too much, just lie still for a few minutes until the doctor gets here." As she was speaking she checked the monitor readings and the cannula in Amber's hand, nodding and scribbling simultaneously.

"The man saved me… I thought he wanted to kill me, and he *saved* me," Amber whispered faintly.

The nurse looked at Mr and Mrs Cartwright and murmured soothingly, "She may be confused for a while, so don't worry. It's fairly normal after a trauma."

The doctor arrived and the Cartwrights were ushered away from Amber's bedside and into a family waiting area, where an auxiliary nurse made them coffee.

"What man?" asked Pam Cartwright as soon as they were alone.

"I don't know," answered her husband. "There was no one else at the scene according to the police and ambulance crew. Maybe it's part of the confusion. A hallucination brought on by shock?"

"But do you think that there might have been someone there, and maybe they ran off? Amber said the man saved her."

"She also said she thought he wanted to kill her, I don't know what that was all about."

"We'll have to wait until she is a bit better before we can ask her about it," conceded his wife.

"Maybe she won't want to talk about it, or maybe her brain will block the trauma out and she won't even remember what happened." Chris paused. "You know, I've been wondering – given all the reports on the accident, she seems to have come out of it comparatively well."

"Comparatively well?" shrieked Pam. "You must be joking!"

"Pam," interrupted Chris. "She is alive! She could have been killed! She could have had multiple fractures – brain damage – be still in a coma! Need I go on?"

Amber was home a few days later, having undergone extensive physical examination and daily tests of her vision, hearing and motor skills. She had been quiet and pensive, and was still suffering from her grazes and bruising, but knew that she had been lucky that her injuries were so few. She was experiencing periodic flashbacks to the scene that Saturday afternoon: the car headlights, the man she had grown to fear standing on the other side of the road. Then, the suddenness of the impact – not with a car as she had expected in those split seconds, but with the man himself, hurling himself into the path of the oncoming traffic and, seemingly half shoving and half lifting her through the air towards the kerb she had just left. Brakes screeching! Doors slamming! Her ears pounding and then everything seeming far away, muffled and dreamlike – then nothing!

Try as she might, Amber could not remember the aftermath of the accident. In the turmoil of her head, the man seemed to be gone from the scene. Was he hurt because he had tried to save her? Had he been in hospital at the same time as she had, without her even knowing? It occurred to her that she should have found that information out and thanked him. Another scenario suddenly played through her mind: what if he had been killed trying to save her? The more she thought about the scene and subsequent accident that afternoon the more she became convinced that this must be the case. Every time she had mentioned the man saving her, her parents had been dismissive, immediately drawing her away from the subject. On one occasion her father had told her that there was no other person or pedestrian involved in the accident, and no witnesses other than the three motorists who had stopped at the scene, one of whom had called the emergency services.

"You were very confused when you initially came round in hospital," he said by way of explanation. After that all discussion was discouraged.

It was two weeks since that fateful afternoon, and Amber had become more and more convinced that the man, whose name she still did not know, had in fact, lost his life in saving hers. Her parents were trying to hide the facts from her and she thought she knew why: guilt! She was responsible for the man's death. Well she did feel guilty! She felt guilty that she had harboured bad thoughts about him, convinced that he meant her harm. Another facet crossed her mind. What if he had a family? If he had died, what must they be going through? It was all her fault. That's why her mum and dad evaded all her questions – they were trying to protect her from guilt and shame. Instead of killing her, she had killed *him*!

It occurred to Amber the next day that there were no newspapers lying about the house. That was unusual. She decided that her parents were definitely keeping something from her. While her father was at work and her mother out shopping, Amber went to the recycle bin and took out the discarded newspapers, sorting them into date order. There were only nine papers: the bin contents must have been collected last week when she was still in hospital. Nevertheless Amber checked through each issue, but found nothing about her accident, apart from a reader's letter urging traffic calming measures to be taken on that stretch of road and pointing out that this had been a subject of contention for some years now. She guessed that she was old news by now, replaced with newer and more earth shattering stories.

Another idea occurred to Amber. She went to her computer and powered up. The Northern Echo website was familiar to her, as she had used it to help her with a school project a few months before. She typed in the 24th September, the Monday following her accident. Bingo! She was on the front page! At least the car wreck was on the front page, and her name, age and details of her injuries given. The next two days provided progress reports, but made no mention of any casualty other than herself. The final sentence in one report caught her attention. Another person had previously been killed on the same stretch of road. It was an Alan Watson, a man of 51 years. There were no further details apart from the date: August 2002.

Having plenty of leisure time on her hands Amber searched the Northern Echo online archives for information regarding the accident involving Alan Watson. It was fairly easy. It had made the headlines on 28th August 2002:

TRAGEDY! HIT AND RUN DRIVER KILLS LOCAL MAN

A nineteen-year-old female driver hit a pedestrian on the Springfield bypass road at six o'clock yesterday evening. 51 year old Alan Watson of Chapel Walk, Springfield Estate was killed outright by the silver VW Golf, travelling at "well over the speed limit": the testimony of four separate witnesses to the accident. Tracey Kindle, the driver, drove on, leaving a scene of devastation and trauma behind her.

Mr Watson had been walking his dog, Tilly, a Bedlington terrier, when she was spooked by a loud bang and slipped her lead. She ran terrified, but Alan had managed to find her on the other side of the bypass. She was so frightened that he picked her up and was carrying her instead of putting her lead on. Both he and Tilly were killed.

Miss Kindle was later apprehended by the police, at her home in Rosemarket Place, where she lives with her parents. Breathalyser and subsequent blood tests revealed that her alcohol intoxication was over three times the legal limit and the police estimated her speed as approximately 75 mph. Miss Kindle is currently remanded in custody for DUI and failing to stop at the scene of an accident. It is surmised that she will be charged with manslaughter as a minimum. Miss Kindle and her parents were not available for comment.

Further story on Page 4

There was a photograph of the scene on the front page showing a crumpled body on the road and a dog lying only feet away.

When Amber scrolled to the appropriate page, she gasped in shock. There was a picture of Alan Watson, in the prime of his life. He was sitting with his dog on a park bench, which bore a brass plate. She read the caption, which revealed that the photograph had been taken the year before, when Alan had dedicated this bench to his wife who had recently died of cancer. The inscription read:

In loving memory of Alice Watson
This park gave her the greatest pleasure
18th July 1952 – 10th April 2001

It was him! Amber stared at the picture, taking in the details of his build, his hair, the slope of his shoulders. There was no doubt in her mind. But he was dead! He'd been dead for nine years now. She scrolled back to the front page of the newspaper and looked at the picture of the body lying in the road. How could she be doing this?

She zoomed in until she could see the man's clothing – and although the photograph was black and white, she was certain that the jacket and trousers looked the same: dark jacket and light pants! Definitely! Clutched in the man's hand was a piece of rope. Amber looked closely. It was a dog lead!

Amber shivered: she felt as if she had seen a ghost. She had seen a ghost! She was sure of it.

That evening Amber recounted her story to her parents, and whilst they were attentive and concerned, she could tell that they didn't really attach much credence to her tale. Even when she showed them the Northern Echo extracts from 2001 and 2002 they simply exchanged glances with each other and shook their heads.

"You're still in shock," said her father. "Don't worry about it, love, you'll soon be able to put it behind you. Try not to think about it – just be glad you are alive."

Later Amber, still frustrated, pondered on her experience. The man she saw was real, she was absolutely sure of it. The figure had physically pushed her away from the speeding car. A solid impacting with another solid! There was nothing the least bit ethereal about him. She had seen him and felt him, and yet the picture in the 2002 newspaper of Alan Watson definitely was him. He was dead!

And that was the start of it! Amber discovered that she could see people that others could not! She was out shopping with her mother when an elderly lady crossed the High Street in front of a bus. Amber shouted in panic as the bus started to pull away from the bus stop. Everyone turned and looked at her quizzically, including her mother, who asked, "What was all that about?"

"I thought that lady was going to get knocked down," gasped Amber.

"What lady?" asked Pam, "There was no one there."

"I saw her, she walked right in front of the bus as it was pulling away," Amber exclaimed. "How did you not see her?"

"Because she wasn't there, Amber."

Everyone seemed to put it down to the trauma of the accident. Amber's parents took her to see first their GP then to another partner in the practice. From there she was referred to a mental health specialist: a psychiatrist, who after several months of therapy and counselling arrived at the same conclusion as everyone else. They all said "trauma", but she interpreted that as: they thought she was crazy, mental and hallucinatory.

Eventually Amber simply pretended that it had all just disappeared and the she was "fine now". She had started visiting the ponies again, but under strict instructions, always used the subway. She had not seen Alan Watson again, but she had no idea whether or not that was significant. She speculated that he might have been able to foresee her accident, and because of his own fate had come from the "spirit world" to intervene on her behalf. Was that mental? What if, what had happened to her: the accident, the affirmation in her own mind that she had seen and indeed been rescued, by a ghost, had opened some kind of ethereal door, so that she could see the spirits of the Departed? That sounded crazy even to her!

Amber couldn't equate terms such as "phantom", "spectre" or "ghost" to her experiences. She had seen *people*! They seemed real! They seemed alive! But other people didn't see them.

One afternoon Amber was walking along the riverside path with her friend Emma, when she encountered a small boy with clothes and hair soaking wet. The day was dry and sunny and she assumed that he had just perhaps fallen in the river. She asked him if he was all right.

"Who are you talking to?" asked Emma, as the child walked right past them.

"Did you not see that little boy?" returned Amber incredulously.

Emma returned her own incredulous look. Then both girls turned, but neither of them saw anyone on the path behind them. The girls stared at each other, neither wanting to be the first to speak.

"Come!" said Emma tugging Amber by the arm. She dragged her towards a wooden bench and they sat. She gave Amber a look of bewilderment then said tentatively, "Amber, I think that you can see ghosts! The hairs on my neck are standing up at the very thought but this is not the first time I've thought you were talking to yourself. You can see figures that other people can't. You saw a boy just there, but I couldn't see him. Why?"

"I don't know," admitted Amber thoughtfully. "What I see are real people, or they are to me. They don't look as I'd imagined ghosts would look. They're not shadowy, or wispy, or translucent... or scary. In fact they seem to me as real as anyone else. Solid! And I can't tell the difference, Emma, and *that's* what scares me. I mean, why me?" She paused. "I feel as if I am going mad, and other people already think I'm crazy!"

"Perhaps it's to do with your brush with death?" suggested Emma. "Maybe because you came close to the 'other side' those on the 'other side' feel they have a link with you."

Amber considered this. "But what can I do? How do I tell if other people are real or not? And how can I stop it happening?"

Emma mulled over the problem for a few minutes. "Well, if I am with you, I can tell you whether a person is real or not. We could have a sort of code… I know! Any time you're not sure if a person is real, just say 'Amber Alert' to me and I'll say 'yes' if I can see the person and 'no' if I can't."

Amber thought about this. "That could work, I suppose, but it doesn't solve the problem at times when you're not with me."

"Well you could do the same with your mum. I mean she already knows that you see things – people, I mean," added Emma hastily. "It could save her from being embarrassed by you talking to invisible beings when there are other people around. In fact all your friends and family could help you. Same code: 'Amber Alert!'"

"Sounds feasible," agreed Amber. "But do you think I'm going to spend the rest of my life like this? Not being able to tell the difference between reality and 'phantomsy'?"

Emma exploded into laughter, then quickly became serious again, "I honestly don't know, Amber. Maybe with more experience you will be able to tell the difference, or perhaps at some stage they will all just go away. It could be that you are just vulnerable at the moment."

Amber was nineteen and the last six years of her life had been a nightmare. Not that she bumped into ghosts on a daily basis, but she was on tenterhooks or Amber Alert all the time. Just in case! Strangely her days were more disturbed than her nights. What a fallacy that spirits were night-walkers! Utter rubbish! She'd met them hurrying along busy, bustling streets at rush hour, crossing the road, in the local park, once on a mid-morning train and once at a local youth club.

When she was fifteen she'd stayed in a hotel in Tothill Street, SW London, with her parents, and while there had an encounter with a girl about her own age, in the hotel itself. Amber was alone, walking along the long second floor corridor on her way down to the hotel restaurant, when a teenage girl emerged from room 203. So suddenly and silently did she appear that Amber startled like a filly. As the two girls passed one another Amber smiled and said "Hello" softly. The girl returned the greeting in a similar fashion without turning her head or altering her step. Amber turned and looked behind but the girl was gone, the long corridor behind her empty. "How could she have covered the distance so quickly?" mused Amber. As she reached the door to room 203 within only a few strides, Amber realised that she hadn't heard any sound of the door being opened or closed. Yet the automatic locking system of the hotel doors was a very audible series of clunks and clicks! She wondered…

Downstairs the next day Amber chatted casually to the young receptionist on duty, asking about the other teenager staying in the hotel. She hoped to meet her and perhaps pal up during their stay… was she staying in room 203? The girl paled, and tight-lipped, told Amber that room 203 was currently vacant and that no other teenager was at present staying at the hotel.

Amber had been at university for almost a year now and that had posed more problems than enough. The college building was over 300 years old: very beautiful architecturally, ecclesiastical in appearance and with plenty of history within its solid grey walls. The gardens were extensive and varied, colourful throughout the year and very well kept. Although very interested in the history and foundation of the ladies' Church of England college, and the plethora of renowned previous students, lecturers and Principals, Amber was particularly concerned with certain "legend and folklore". The college had three ghosts!

The "Grey Lady" resided in the West Bailey wing of the building, and was generally sighted early morning in the vicinity of one of the bathrooms. Apparently a maid from the nineteenth century had hanged herself there and it was surmised that she and "The Grey Lady" were one.

The East Bailey and Chantry contained narrow, low corridors and quaint, but poky, rooms with low ceilings, long since turned over to student accommodation. The heavily leaded windows were tiny, and the rooms and corridors alike, gloomy even in the height of summer. Very atmospheric! How could a ghost *not* live there?

There were in fact two phantoms putting in regular appearances: The "White Lady" and "Not the White Lady". It was hard to say which of these spectres provoked the most terror and hysteria among students. The "White Lady" walked the dim East Bailey corridor at night and was a constant source of upset and fear among those residents returning to their rooms after evenings out or making night-time bathroom excursions. The narrow passage way was closed off at each end by a half glass, half wood sliding door, so students generally felt trapped inside with the ghost.

The corridor had been exorcised and blessed by the Reverend College Chaplain and the Reverend Religious Knowledge Lecturer together, after one occasion of mass hysterics at 2am, which found all the occupants of the East Bailey in the reception area in a varied array of night attire, and passing round a bottle of cognac to countermand the shock.

"Not the White Lady" resided in The Chantry, an equally spooky gallery of student rooms. She (or he?) was not sighted as often, which was possibly the reason for the "ghost with no name", identifiable only by the fact that she/he was definitely "Not the White Lady". Encounters in The Chantry therefore were far more dramatic and terrifying because of their infrequency, and descriptions of the spectre varied wildly.

Amber was heartily sick of the three ghosts! Not that any of them had made themselves known to her. She hadn't seen any of them. However, troubled, or sometimes excited students, now repeatedly came to her with their histrionic tales of sightings. It began when her friend, Tina, whom she had met during her first week at Uni, (and whom she had subsequently confided in, asking her to be her new "Amber Alert") had one day brought a petrified fellow student to her, asking if Amber could help her.

So Amber had tried to explain to the traumatised Becky, her own experiences, beginning with her accident and the fortuitous intervention of Alan Watson. She emphasised that in all her subsequent personal encounters with the spirit world, none were harmful, and indeed most were just non-events – people going about their own business as any passer-by might.

After the Becky counselling session, word spread like wildfire among those first-year students living in the hall of residence, and Amber found herself subjected to an increasing amount of interrogation and general interruption to her study time. Before long third-year students were also knocking at her door, and on one occasion Miss Milner, the residential House Mistress, who was also the Senior Geography Lecturer, asked for an appointment to discuss her own experiences of the "Not the White Lady" ghost.

Reluctantly, Amber had also taken part in a number of "ghost watch" sessions in all three of the "haunted" areas of the college. She had encountered nothing, and her colleagues had expressed disappointment in her abilities.

"Listen!" said Amber crossly one afternoon to a gathering of students who were scathing and discontented with their lack of ghostly result from the previous night, "I didn't ask for any of this! Not from you and not from the Dead. I don't know why I have this connection, but I'd rather not have it. It makes my life miserable, and sometimes I feel as if I don't know who is real and who is not."

"So you're saying that your ghosts just look like normal people? Not ethereal?"

"Not dressed in clothes from, say, a hundred years ago, or a Cavalier or something?"

"Not materialising through walls before your eyes?"

Incredulous questions came thick and fast. Amber raised a defensive hand. "Let's move to the ground floor Common Room where we can be comfortable, and I will tell you everything I know – which isn't much," she added.

She began by describing her initial sightings of Alan Watson, and her fears of his intentions, leading up to her accident and the discovery beyond. Her audience were now completely captive, one girl hanging on every word and scribbling furiously. Amber pointed out that she had never seen Alan Watson again. The frenzied writer looked up and interjected, "Perhaps in saving you, it saved him also and allowed his spirit to rest properly? Maybe he had no reason to appear again."

Another voice broke in, "Or does he only appear when needed? Has he averted other accidents in the same place?"

A cacophony of discussion ensued. When a lull finally settled over the group, Amber continued. She described the woman who had stepped in front of the bus, the child, dripping wet on the riverside path and the teenage girl in the London hotel, as examples. There had been numerous others, of course, but she didn't have a couple of weeks to spare.

"What I want to tell you is that all of these 'beings' for want of a better word, looked to me like tangible, real people. There was never an occasion when I thought 'this is a ghost!' At the time, I could not distinguish them from anyone else around me. Often I would have other people with me who didn't see the figure. Back home I had a school friend who would try to keep me right and save me from embarrassment and now I have Tina doing the same. If I say 'Amber Alert' it means I can see someone who I suspect might not actually be alive and I'm waiting for confirmation or otherwise from whomever I'm with. My life has not been easy, I can tell you."

"But you are so matter of fact about it," piped up a girl on Amber's left, "you don't seem scared."

"I'm not," admitted Amber. "There are times when it can be a bloody nuisance, and sometimes embarrassing if I speak to someone I think is alive and visible to others, and it turns out they're not! Another thing…" she added, "the majority of my experiences have been in broad daylight, some in busy places where there are other people about. It's not spooky and it's not scary! It's just weird. Also, I've never come to any harm from any of the contacts."

The girl at the back of the room, who had been continually scribbling away, looked up. "Have you ever tried to call a spirit to you, Amber?" she now asked.

"No. I haven't," replied Amber. "Well only once at the request of another person." She added, "I think I have more than enough contact with them as it is."

"Wouldn't it be better though if you had more control over the 'apparitions'?" questioned the scribe. Various group members nodded agreement.

"You could help others more, that way," volunteered a girl named Kath, "you know, bereaved people and such."

Amber hesitated, looking around the whole gathering, then decided to speak frankly. "I once went to see a medium," she confessed, "about two years ago now. I was in the Sixth Form and I was so fed up with seeing people I didn't want to see, and not knowing if people were real or not, alive or dead, that Emma, my school friend and I made an appointment to meet with a medium to see if she could help me." She paused.

"What happened?" urged Kath, "Did you connect with her in some way?"

"Well, the woman, Lavinia, was older than me, about thirty, I guess, and the meeting was in the dining room of her home. I just wanted to talk to her really, about my experiences, and find out why they were happening to *me* and whether I could do anything to stop them. I wanted to ask her how she dealt with people from the 'other side'." Amber made speech marks with her fingers.

A silence had fallen on the room and the entire group stared at Amber expectantly, hanging on her every word. "Lavinia assumed that I wanted a 'sitting' to hear a message from someone departed from my life. The room was dimmed and three scented candles were burning on the table. We sat: Lavinia had a number of stones and crystals before her and asked Emma and I each to choose one and hold it in our hands… so we just went along with it. We didn't want to offend."

"What happened?" breathed Kath's friend Sophie.

"Not much," said Amber wryly. "I felt that the room was all about trappings and creating an atmosphere. Eventually Lavinia told me that there was an elderly man in the room asking for me by name. She asked if it could be my grandfather. I told her that my grandparents were all still alive and so she thought it may be a great-grandparent."

"Did you see anything?"

"No."

"Did you feel a presence?"

"No."

"Do you think that there was anyone there?"

The questions came thick and fast.

"What I think," said Amber slowly, "is that, given my life for the last six years, if my great-grandfather had anything to say to me, he would have chosen a direct route. He would have shown himself to me, and would not have chosen to go via a third party."

"What happened next? Tell us the rest of your story," the Writer looked up from her notepad, pen poised at the ready.

Amber looked at her curiously. "Well, Lavinia said that the spirit was moving away and that she had lost contact. At the end of the 'séance' if that's what it was, she was quite normal and apologised for the brevity of the meeting. She said that spirits could be quite temperamental. Then I told her that the reason I had made the appointment was really so that I could share my experiences with someone who had similar ones and perhaps get some advice on how to deal with it in everyday life."

"Go on!" urged voices, as Amber paused for breath.

"Was she any help?" a voice from the corner asked.

"Not really," continued Amber. "After a pretty lengthy discussion I got the impression that she wasn't very happy with me, or rather at the way I'd arranged the meeting. Then, just as we were leaving, a small girl, maybe about three or four years old, came into the hallway, I assumed from the kitchen maybe. I said hello to her, but she just stood looking up at Lavinia. I asked Lavinia if it was her daughter and she stared at me really strangely, and then looked all around her. Next thing, Emma gave me a huge dig in the ribs, and suddenly I knew that only I could see the child."

A heavy silence hung over the room. Amber looked around at the wide eyes and gaping mouths and continued her tale.

"'*What can you see?*' Lavinia asked me almost aggressively: I described the child to her: a little girl about three or four, with dark curls and brown mischievous eyes. She was wearing a green dress and had a green ribbon in her hair, black shiny shoes and white socks.

"Without a word Lavinia went upstairs and returned carrying a picture in a frame. She showed me the photograph it bore: the same little girl, perhaps slightly younger, wearing a red dress and clutching a brown and cream coloured fluffy dog. *'My daughter Jennifer: the last photo I have of her before she died'.* Her eyes filled with tears. *'She was wearing a green dress and hair ribbon the day she died'.*

"Oh God, I'm so sorry! I said to her. She went on to tell me that Jennifer had been going to a friend's birthday party. In her excitement to get there, she had jumped out of the car before Lavinia could stop her and started to cross the road. She had run straight into the path of a white van and had been killed instantly.

"I remember Lavinia saying to me *'Why would she appear to you and not me?'* and I didn't have an answer for her."

"Perhaps it was because of your own accident," speculated the Scribe, looking up from her notepad.

"Yes," agreed Tina. "Your brush with death has possibly made you more receptive to the spirit world. Do you think that all of the people you have seen have been victims of some kind of accident or violent death?"

"I'm not sure about that," said Amber, "some, yes! But with others, I haven't really been in a position to judge. I've quite literally seen them in passing."

"What about Lavinia?" asked another voice. "What happened to her? Did she ever see her daughter?"

"No, not that I know of," admitted Amber sadly, "she kept asking me to try and summon her, and I did try, but I couldn't. She was very determined, always wanting to meet me, and turning up at different places I went, to the point where I felt as if I was being stalked. She even confessed to me that she had never seen a ghost in her whole life: that her 'enterprise' as a medium was just that: a moneymaking business.

"Her life had fallen apart after Jennifer's death. She and her husband had split up, and she had no job and little money.

Establishing herself as a medium put her in touch with other bereaved people, and in 'helping them' as she put it, she made them feel better and earned herself some money. And she just might by some miracle connect with her daughter.

"Basically she was a fraud, and she wanted me to go into partnership with her, because I could see things and people that she couldn't. That's one reason I am here: at the opposite end of the country to my family!" finished Amber darkly.

"I can't help but feel sorry for Lavinia though," said Kath, "just imagine wanting so desperately to see your child again. It must be hell!"

"But where would it stop?" questioned Becky. "Would she just keep wanting to see Jennifer again and again? Would the child's spirit never be able to rest?"

Everyone stared at Amber expectantly. "I don't have any answers for you. I've told you everything I know, and I don't have any control over these happenings. I don't want them to happen, and I certainly don't want to try and make them happen to order. I haven't got a gift: I've got a curse!

"I don't know why I haven't come across our College Ghosts any more than you do. If they don't want me to see them, then I'm glad about that. Maybe it means that the 'curse' is lifting. If not then my story has no end…I'll be constantly on Amber Alert!"

Amber shrugged, and stood, effectively terminating all discussion.

The Scribe closed her notepad.

Two weeks later the end of term College Magazine published their winning story entitled: Amber Alert – A story with no end.

By Elaine Thew

Epipheny and Atonement

Hal was in Boxonia. He was planning and co-ordinating a military campaign against the rebels in the surrounding Paleno hills. He was arguing with himself: maybe it was taking a sledgehammer to crack a nut, but those undisciplined, thieving vagabonds needed teaching a sharp lesson and he was going to make sure they got their come-uppance! Sure there were some tough individuals up there, but the real men of steel were only a handful. The majority were a bunch of weak hangers-on, carried along in the wake of a few no-good, rabble-rousing, shit-stirring bullies. Take out the top men: that was the way to do it! Go in hard and fast. Make an example of the leaders in front of their men. The rest would soon disperse or surrender.

He surveyed his troops. They were good and they knew it! Hal knew he could count on his Generals to carry out his plan of attack, and they in turn had absolute confidence in the unquestioning obedience of their men. He estimated that they had an advantage of number some ten- or twelvefold. They could not do anything but succeed!

Hal was in Bochsanarch. He was briefing his men for a raid on the valley of Boxonia. The Boxonian force outnumbered his small band of vigilantes by at least ten to one. Poor odds for an ill-equipped band of "soldiers" for want of a better word, against a well-drilled, experienced army, trained for fighting with top-notch weaponry, "And", he thought, "a damned good Leader!"

His own men had simple weapons, some old issue rifles, a few handguns, a variety of knives. But they had something else to be reckoned with: pure recklessness. These were men with nothing to lose: they'd already lost everything and lived for revenge! He had complete trust in their loyalty and their capacity to kill. Every one of them would take their commands from him. And they would take no prisoners!

"Hal your tea's ready," called his mother.

"It would be!" muttered Hal under his breath and then "Coming Winnie!" in a louder voice. He took a last look at the formation of his troops and then hurried downstairs taking the stairs two at a time and jumping the last four.

His mother looked up at the familiar thud. "Less of the Winnie! It's Mam to you!"

"Okay Winnie," grinned the lad, sliding into his place at the table.

"Have you fed the rabbit?"

"Yes, and it's Boxer to you, Winnie!"

"You're a cheeky young devil!" but she smiled indulgently. "Right – it's homework straight after tea, then. *Before you go out!*" She finished with emphasis.

"Oh fuck off!" Hal muttered in a low voice, followed by an audible "Yeah, Yeah!"

"And you can cut out that language, lad. I'll 'fuck you' if you're not careful!" She brandished the bread knife.

Hal smirked. "I don't think so, Winnie! What do you think Dad?" as his father sat down opposite him.

"I think you are an insolent, disrespectful, little sod!" but he was laughing.

"There's Dancing Boy at the gate," said his father, just as Hal was swallowing the last mouthful of his pudding. Hal looked out of the kitchen window and waved to Nick, who was hopping and pacing about impatiently, waiting for him to appear.

"I think that lad's got worms or something. He can't keep still for more than ten seconds," said Mrs B absently, as she was pouring three cups of tea. Hal carefully slid out of his chair while his mother's back was turned, and sped out of the door and down the garden path.

"Quick!" he hissed, grabbing his friend's sweatshirt as he passed him at a sprint and dragging him along. The two of them raced down the street, turned the first available corner, and took cover in an overgrown wilderness of a garden, lying on their stomachs under a thick leafy shrub and laughing hysterically.

"God, you were like a rat up a drainpipe!" gurgled Nick helplessly.

"I have to be to get past Winnie. I can't always out-smart her, but I can out-run her." Hal took a few deep breaths. "Okay, let's get moving – the light is just about right."

Both boys shuffled out into the open and peered cautiously about. "No Winnie!" said Nick, and they headed swiftly for the other end of the street.

Another ten minutes saw them at the foot of the pit heap. The locals still called it that, even though it had for some years been a huge grassy hill and was now clad in hawthorn, blackthorn and elderberry. The bushes were wild and unpruned. The paths few and little trodden.

It was dusk and in the dim light, rabbits were feeding everywhere, unconcerned by the presence of the two lads. Hal scrambled under a particularly dense and prickly hawthorn, cursing as he wriggled further towards its centre and felt its thorns tearing at his clothes and bare arms. "Here!" He pushed the gun out towards Nick, and scrabbled his way back out. The rabbits were still feeding.

"You said I could have first go, didn't you? Remember?" said Nick, anxiously.

"Yeah – course I do!" nodded Hal.

Hal always felt sorry for Nick. He never seemed to be able to get anything. He never had any money. He came from a big family, whose father was constantly out of work due to ill health and they never had a bean. On the other hand, no one ever seemed to be bothered about what Nick was up to. He was lucky in that respect: no Winnie to contend with! He could stay out till whatever time he liked. His parents never bothered much when people complained about him. He hadn't even got into trouble when he had set the house on fire with a lighted firework through his family's own letterbox!

There was no way that Nick could have ever got hold of an air rifle though, he would never have had a tenner to give Jim Watson. Hal always had plenty of money: some of it legitimate pocket money, some – well – small amounts that Winnie would never miss. He hadn't dared take the gun home though. His mother would have had a blue fit. So would his dad for that matter. Still, it was safe enough here: no one ever came this far out except Nick and himself. No one would ever find his gun. He knew loads of hiding places! He could even hide it from Nick if he wanted to.

"Go on then. Make it a good'un! If you miss you'll have scared the arses off all those rabbits and you'll not get a second chance for ages." Hal was itching to handle the air rifle again. It was a BSA Airsporter .22, under lever, tap loader. A dream come true! He'd practised holding it, loading, aiming, and shooting at bottles, cans, and home made targets. Just about anything really! He was a good shot! He knew he could pot a rabbit or a bird but he'd promised not to shoot anything live until Nick was there. Both of the boys were gun mad, and crazy to kill something. He'd promised Nick first shot at a live target, to make up for the fact that Nick would never have a gun of his own.

Carefully Nick positioned the rifle, using the hooded foresight as Hal had shown him. He took aim at one of the bigger rabbits some twenty yards away. He was trembling with concentration and excitement. "Come on, mate," said Hal in a low voice. "Pull yourself together, you're shaking like a second hand Cortina! Aim at the head not the body – you want it dead not running around screaming!"

Nick gripped harder and slowly pulled the trigger. His body recoiled as the gun discharged and jerked upwards. Rabbits ran in all directions and vanished into the hillside in seconds.

"Shit!" muttered Hal, and then, "Sorry, mate! You couldn't help it!"

Nick handed the Airsporter sheepishly to Hal. "Thanks pal, sorry I fucked up! Your turn – that is, if we get another chance."

"Here – have a fag, whilst we're waiting," said Hal, rummaging in his pockets and producing a bent cigarette. Nick scoured his own pockets and having eventually found a match, struck it on a stone and lit up. Hal never ever smoked, but he managed to keep his friends supplied with cigarettes from the corner shop where his mother worked.

The air was still as Nick smoked and Hal practised taking aim at stones. All was quiet except for a medley of blackbirds and chaffinches making a last foray before dark, and at last the rabbits wandered in dribs and drabs into the open. It was almost dark and Hal was on his mettle, immediately positioning the gun and taking aim at one little creature after another. Finally he selected his victim, a large rabbit about forty yards away, and gave a slight nod to Nick to indicate his intention. No trembling here! He actions were purposeful and controlled. His hands were steady as he lined up the target with his sights and squeezed the trigger. His body jerked only a little as the noise shattered the tranquillity of the hillside. Rabbits fled in all directions.

"You missed!" said Nick in incredulity.

"Yeah!"

It was dark when Hal let himself quietly in the back gate. He moved stealthily to Boxer's hutch and opened first the padlock and then the door. The warmth and sweet smell of the straw drifted out as Hal reached inside, feeling for the soft furry body within. Gently he lifted the animal to his chest and caressed him tenderly. The rabbit was relaxed: unafraid. Hal murmured soothing noises as he carried the rabbit into the house with him. He closed the door as quietly as he could and began to tiptoe upstairs. The living room door opened suddenly: the light from the room falling directly on to the staircase and the boy.

"Where the hell have you been? I've been worried sick about you."

"We've just been playing around the pit heap. Anyway it's only 9 o'clock," said Hal with his most penitent smile.

"It's pitch dark," retorted his mother, "and you've still got homework to do."

"Sorry Winnie – I'll do it now."

Hal continued upstairs and into his bedroom, placing Boxer on the floor once he had closed the door. "Choose your side and go and inspect your troops, my man, whilst I scribble some words about the Hundred Years War to pacify Fred Wharton tomorrow." The rabbit hopped into the middle of the Bochsanarchists and nibbled at the imitation grass on the Paleno Hills.

"So you're with the anarchists today, are you? Then the die is cast, and the Boxer Rebellion will be successful!"

The rabbit wandered down to Boxonia leaving a trail of droppings behind him and felling half a dozen soldiers with a powerful kick from his hind legs.

─◦─

It was Sunday afternoon, with an autumnal nip in the air, and Hal and Nick were sitting huddled close to their campfire discussing tactics. They'd spent every evening last week practising with the Airsporter. On stationary objects they were becoming competent but the real bugbear was their lack of success with moving targets. Hal had even bunked off school a couple of days without Nick knowing, and spent all of his time on the pit heaps, caressing and handling his gun, taking aim at absolutely anything that moved – not firing too often because he needed to conserve his ammunition. He'd sat silent and motionless for hours: watching, studying, concentrating! He'd crawled through the long meadow grass: peering at the feeding rabbits and testing how close to them he could get before they gave alarm and scuttled away bobtails flying for cover. He'd shot a rat at fairly close range and watched it writhe for a full minute before a final shudder left it limp and lifeless. He'd thrown it into the pit pond to find out whether it would float or sink... All the time he was learning as much about the gun as he could – its capabilities and its limitations – his own limitations, and all the time his technique and accuracy improved. He was good!

Hal had been instructing an attentive Nick for most of the day. They'd shot at bottles and cans, targets they'd pinned on young trees, taking the gun in turns with a great sense of fairness. Then Nick had shot a rabbit, not dead! Hal had grabbed the gun from him and put a second shot into it quickly and finished it off. Late in the afternoon they'd collected kindling and built themselves a fire. Next to shooting, starting fires was Hal's greatest enthusiasm. He was particular, bordering on fussiness about its construction, and wouldn't allow it to be lit unless plenty of dry wood and the like had been assembled in advance, ready to feed the flames. They'd thrown the rabbit onto the fire and watched it burn with ghoulish fascination. Hal had a long stick, which he used as a poker, and kept under a hedgerow close to the rifle's hiding place. Only Hal could poke the fire!

Nick, in awe of Hal's knowledge and his capacity for producing lighter fuel, paraffin, aerosol sprays, and even petrol, was happy to be commanded in their use, and soaked up the instruction like a sponge. He sat now, contentedly smoking one of the cigarettes Hal had presented him with earlier, listening to his friend ruminating on the difficulties of getting enough practice in with live targets.

"You've wasted loads of pellets on sparrows. They're too small at this stage, we need practice on creatures with a decent body mass. Give us more of a chance: enough time to aim properly! Rats and rabbits are okay – but you only get one shot at it and they all scatter. You could wait an hour to get a shot at another one! No we need some slower rabbits 'til we get really good! Or deaf ones!" He laughed.

"We've got two rabbits out our back," volunteered Nick suddenly. "They'll be useless at running, 'cause they've never been out of their hutch for years. We could use them. For practice, you know."

"What shoot your pet rabbits?" exclaimed Hal frowning.

"Well, they're not really pets! Nobody bothers with them now. They're just a bloody nuisance. Probably no one will even know they're gone for ages."

"You sure you don't want 'em?" asked Hal.

"Sure." Nick was getting excited. It would be great to contribute something towards their operation instead of always being the "poor relation" and relying on Hal for everything. "Let's do it!"

"When?"

"Tomorrow night after tea?"

"No, not enough time or light. We need to plan it carefully. Got to do things properly." Clearly Hal's mind was now racing way ahead of Nick. "Next Saturday, two o'clock! That'll give us a bit more practice and time to get everything we need. We'll have a fire afterwards!"

They broke camp soon afterwards, Hal carefully stamping out the fire which had burnt low to a few smouldering ashes while they had been talking. He replaced the rifle in its hiding place, and having kicked a few twigs and leaves over it, the two lads set off down the hill and back to the village.

Saturday morning seemed interminable to Nick! All week there had been secret shooting practices, and each evening Hal had brought some item or other with him to stash "on site": matches, carefully wrapped up in polythene, a small container with some liquid in it – inflammable, Nick guessed, a knife, two bottles of Double Maxim! Purloined from the shop where Winnie worked, Hal explained.

"To celebrate!" he'd said.

Now Nick was holding a cardboard box containing the two ex-pet Dutch rabbits. Hal leapt over the gate and joined him and together they headed for the pit heaps.

"I've had an idea!" announced Nick. "It's about the rabbits."

"Go on," said Hal with interest.

"It's a survival experience, you know – pretend we have to survive in the wild: kill our own dinner and all that. Cook them on the fire and eat them – just like you'd have to do if you were marooned on a desert island or something." He looked anxiously at Hal for signs of approval.

Hal pulled a face. "OK then, I've never had rabbit before, have you?"

"Yes," said Nick. "Now and again we have a rabbit pie at home. They're pretty good! Kevin's dad shoots them sometimes and my mam gets them for next to nowt from him."

They arrived at their usual spot and Hal retrieved his gun and all his stashed rations, while Nick collected kindling for the makings of a fire.

"OK," said Hal. "It's your idea so what are we going to do?"

"Well, we shouldn't use the gun," explained Nick, "'Cos in the wild we might not have one. We'll have to rely on our wits, our hands and our knives. I've brought mine." He slipped a flick-knife out of his jacket pocket and displayed it."

Hal put his hand around the knife in the bottom of his pocket, but left it there. "Explain more," he said.

"Well, we let one rabbit go and one of us has to catch it and kill it. Then the other one gets the second rabbit, to do the same. You can catch it and kill it how you want, then we get a fire going."

"We'll have to do it as a survival game then," said Hal, "I can't just stand here and do that! You know, in cold blood? I'd have to feel desperate."

"Righto, we're on a desert island, that's the sea!" Nick pointed to the pond. "We've been shipwrecked and we're starving, 'cos all the rations have been lost, so we'll have to see what food the island can provide."

"Let's try it then," agreed Hal.

They stripped down to their T-shirts and underpants, and plodged into the pond until they were thigh deep. They turned, as one, and looked at the "shore", role playing their struggle from the ocean with groans, curses and staggers. Dripping wet they climbed onto the "island", looking furtively about in every direction. Plenty of grass and trees, no houses or settlements, or indeed any kind of habitation! Just as they'd suspected!

"We can make a shelter there," said Hal pointing to the pile of kindling already collected. He picked up his jeans from the ground and felt in the pocket. "Luckily I've got some matches and they are still dry. Good job I wrapped them in polythene before we jumped ship," he crowed.

"But what the fuck are we going to eat? I'm bloody famished!" yelled Nick excitedly as he pointed at the cardboard box containing the two rabbits.

Hal opened the top of the box and lifted one rabbit out, then closed the lid again. "Oh look! There's a rabbit. With a bit of luck there'll be plenty more," he shouted as he placed the little creature on a patch of grass, twenty feet away from where Nick stood. He stepped back and nodded to his mate. Nick flicked open his knife and began to move stealthily forward. The rabbit nibbled grass unperturbed, making a couple of small hops as it did so.

Suddenly Nick pounced, throwing himself on the rabbit and pinning it down. It screamed in fright, and, in panic and frenzied role play, Nick stabbed wildly at the struggling form. The rabbit shrieked longer and louder, trying to free itself by kicking out with its hind legs. Again and again Nick stabbed the terrified animal, arterial blood gushing over his hands and arms, until it stilled in his grasp. It lay motionless, looking tiny and pathetic. Nick was breathing hard, his eyes wild, his face spattered with blood and his arms dripping red.

Hal looked on in silent horror. After a few moments Nick stood up and picking up the fresh corpse, hung it over a tree branch. "Before rigor sets in," he explained. Then, breathing deeply he bent to the box with the remaining rabbit and lifted it out. "Your turn!" His expression conveyed a challenge.

He placed the rabbit in a patch of clover, but unlike its unsuspecting mate, its eyes and ears were alert with awareness of danger and fear, and it thumped at the ground. "It's gonna run! You'd better be quick," hissed Nick. Still Hal stood motionless. Nick ran and scooped the creature up, then deposited it in Hal's hands. "Right, I've caught it, now you kill it!" he urged.

Hal looked about him uneasily, then quickly, making up his mind, he hurried to a large boulder, grabbed the hind legs of the animal, and with as much force as he could muster, swung towards the stone, smashing the head and breaking the neck. One haunting scream and it was over. At least it was quick! He dropped the rabbit and turned away. Nick scooped it up and hung it beside its mate, then washed his bloodied hands and arms in the pit pond.

The lads stared at each other for a long minute, then Nick clapped Hal's shoulder and said, "Good one, mate, now let's get the fire going. Don't forget we're starving! We have to survive."

Silently they got to work, heads down, studiously ignoring each other, and soon had the usual good blaze going. While they waited for the embers to gain heat, Nick retrieved the rabbits. "We'll have to skin them," he muttered.

Together they clumsily hacked at the bodies, removing heads and feet and fur in a deluge of gore. Both had paled at the experience, holding back retches, neither wanting to admit his revulsion to the other. At last the job was completed in a fashion, which at best emphasised their lack of ability and experience. Blood and innards were strewn around in disproportionate quantity to what remained of the two sad little bodies.

Somehow the leadership had changed this afternoon, and Nick took charge of the situation, sharpening two sticks on which to cook the "meat" as it had now become, over the fire. He arranged them carefully and with all the solicitousness of a master chef, while Hal busied himself with raking the piles of gory body parts, giblets and stained, bedraggled fur further away from them with a tree branch. Nick had searched among the bloodied mess earlier and picked out two rabbit feet, still fresh from the kill. He dipped them in the pond, washing off the excess blood, and placed them on a stone to dry. "We keep one each," he announced. "Trophies!"

They sat by the fire with their Double Maxim, and a brooding silence hanging over them, as Nick turned the roasting meat this way and that. Suddenly Hal noticed two rats tucking into the rabbit entrails with gusto, and his hand reached automatically for the rifle beside him. He slid two pellets into the gun and locked it. Slowly and carefully he took aim, then squeezed… One rat keeled over: a head shot, whilst the other scarpered out of sight. The rat's legs continued to move so Hal put a second shot into the chest. Dead! Definitely!

"Wow, that was brilliant!" congratulated Nick.

Hal walked over to make sure the rat was definitely a goner and to check out his points of entry, then strolled back to the fire, some of his lost composure regained.

"The other rat's back out," whispered Nick excitedly. "Can I have a crack at it?"

Hal handed over the Airsporter and the tin of pellets. "Take your time," he cautioned.

Nick loaded, then aimed carefully, and holding his breath, squeezed the trigger. A small "phut" and the rat was writhing about on the ground. "Take the second shot," ordered Hal, and at the second "phut" the rat stilled.

Nick jumped up to check it out, delighted with his success. "And now to celebrate!" he said, lifting the cooked rabbit from the heat. He handed Hal one stick, waving the other about to cool it. Now that the moment had arrived both boys looked subdued and apprehensive, turning the charred corpses in their hands. "Together!" said Nick, and each watching the other they raised the meat to their mouths. Each took an uncharacteristically small bite, chewing slowly and with expressions of distaste. Nick swallowed! Hal spat!

"Urgh…"

"That's shit!"

Hal let his carcass fall to the ground.

Nick threw his into the fire, retching as he did so, to rid himself of the piece he had swallowed.

"My God, what have we done?"

"What a waste! All that for nothing."

They looked about them at the dying fire, the mess of entrails and miscellaneous body parts, and at a crow now pecking at a rabbit's head. Neither even had the stomach to take a pot shot at the corvid. "Let's go," said Hal suddenly. "Now."

Nick kicked and stamped at the fire while Hal stashed the gun again, then they set off homewards without another word.

Hal felt sick! He picked Boxer out of his run as he crossed the yard, cradling the rabbit in his arms tenderly. He could hear the television blaring and he crept upstairs silently without disturbing Winnie. Once in his room with the door shut, he sat on the bed, still nursing the warm little bundle of fur. He trembled and sobbed, trying to draw what comfort he could from the rabbit who had been part of his life for so long: his best friend through the dark evenings of winter. With him through all his past Boxonia adventures! His mascot!

Stroking Boxer, and fondling his long, silky ears calmed Hal a little and he gazed with love into the dark trusting eyes. He would never, ever hurt Boxer. Suddenly he felt his gorge rising, and first placing Boxer carefully on the floor, he then darted downstairs, out of the back door and across the yard to the toilet, where he threw up repeatedly until nothing remained but streaming eyes and strings of sour saliva hanging from his lips.

He kneeled on the cold floor for several long minutes, then having cleaned his face and struggled to his feet, he made his way back indoors. Winnie caught him as he crossed the kitchen. "What time do you call this? Your tea has been stone cold these last two hours."

"Don't want any," mumbled Hal. "I've been sick and I'm going to bed. I've been back ages," he added. "I went straight upstairs. Boxer's up there now."

"What's up?" asked his mother. "Do you think it's something you've eaten?" She sniffed the air as he passed her, "You've been drinking, you little bugger!" she said accusingly.

"I have Winnie – a bottle of beer that's all. And I feel crap, OK? Don't worry, I won't do it again!" He made his way upstairs and flopped onto his bed. Boxer was settled contentedly on the corner of the rug, so he left him there.

Hal didn't sleep. He was too tormented with thoughts of what he had done, and every time he looked at Boxer he began to cry again. The couple of times he began to nod with sheer exhaustion, his mind filled with piercing screams and warm arterial blood, and he jerked back to consciousness with an involuntary scream of his own. He wept and shook in turns. He felt nauseous but had nothing left in his stomach, and he lay wondering whether Nick was feeling the same as he did.

At first light Hal picked up Boxer and crept stealthily downstairs. He put the rabbit back in his run, gave him a carrot and a bowl of pellets, then let himself quietly out of the gate. When he got to Nick's house there was no sign of life, so lifting the clothes prop out of the corner of the yard, he used it to tap on Nick's bedroom window. The curtains parted a fraction and a hand acknowledged his presence. A minute later Nick came out of the back door, pulling his shirt on as he did so. Hal put his finger to his lips and nodded towards the back street. Only once they were clear of the houses and on route back to the pit heaps did they stop and look at each other: a look of mutual understanding coupled with self-loathing. No word passed between them, but Nick grasped Hal's arm, and Hal squeezed Nick's shoulder in return. They walked on in silence, neither of them wanting to be the first to speak of yesterday.

They arrived by mutual, unspoken consent back at the crime scene and regarded the charcoal remains of the fire. The two rabbit feet they had saved as trophies were still where they'd left them to dry, and they looked at them now with shame and disgust.

"Let's bury them," said Hal "For the rabbits."

"Yeah," agreed Nick. "It's the least we can do."

"We must have been mental!"

"They didn't deserve what we did to them, did they?"

"No, poor little buggers."

Between them they dug a hole, using stones and hands, tears falling freely as they did so, then carefully, almost reverently they carried a rabbit foot each and placed them side by side in the grave.

"We should say something," said Hal.

"Sorry!" said Nick looking down at the hole.

"Sorry!" echoed Hal tearfully.

Together they filled in the grave and then gathered a handful of dog daisies each, the most prolific flower on the heaps. They laid them over the tiny grave, then stood subdued in a minute's silence. As they turned away Hal muttered, "We can't ever tell anyone about this. It must be a sworn secret between us. Do you agree?"

Nick nodded, his eyes still downcast.

"We must do something symbolic," continued Hal, "something that will stay with us all our lives and bind us together forever in our secret, and make us better people."

"Like Blood Brothers!" ventured Nick. "A spilling of our own blood and a mingling of it with each other's."

Hal produced his knife and they solemnly conducted their ritual, cutting themselves, touching palms, and letting the blood drip over the rabbits' grave, making a silent promise to each other and to all creatures.

The next day Hal bunked off school. He went out at his usual time for the school bus, haversack over his shoulder, weighed down with a couple of school books, his swimming kit, his father's heaviest hammer and the short handled axe used for chopping sticks for the fire. From a distance he watched the bus leave, then turned away towards the pit heaps again. Once there, he retrieved his gun from its usual hiding place, and took it with him towards the pit pond. There he sat for a while, the Airsporter across his knees still in its case, watching the still, clear water and pondering on his next course of action. He'd first thought about selling the air rifle. He knew he could probably get more than he had paid for it, and was certain that either Kevin or John would be keen to get their hands on it. However... people get guns to kill things! He'd thought about chucking it into the pond, but it could easily be seen by any kid going for a skinny dip. No, he'd decided that the rifle had to be part of a sacrifice. An atonement!

Slowly he opened his haversack and withdrew the axe and the hammer. He hefted each one in turn, then settled on the weight advantage of the hammer. Hal took the Airsporter out of its case and balanced it at an angle against a large rock. He stood back and looked at it one last time, remembering how excited and proud he had been when it became his. Then he remembered all the rabbits and birds he had shot with it, and it now filled him with horror and disgust. He grasped the hammer firmly and rained frenzied blows down upon the barrel until it eventually warped and bent. Then he swapped the hammer for the axe and set to work on the stock and every bit of the mechanism he could damage. At last he was satisfied that it was beyond repair and could never again be fired upon any animal, then he threw it into the deepest part of the pond. Even if retrieved it would be no use to anyone.

He sat for the longest time, staring at nothing and trying also to think of nothing, but all the while he was reliving the previous two days, and waves of nausea and guilt swept over him. He wept as he had never before wept! He thought of every creature he had killed, and those through inexperience that he hadn't. He thought of the pet rabbits and he thought of Boxer. He found himself imagining what he would do to anyone who hurt Boxer... and he loathed himself more...

Gemma stood outside the door. She had been crying and her face was tear-stained, but she was hopeful that Mr Bridges, the Bird Man, would know what to do. Everyone went to Mr Bridges if an animal or bird got hurt. People said he was the kindest of men and would always help a creature in need. "Mr Bridges," she called, and then more loudly and urgently, "Mr Bridges!"

Harry looked out of the living room window, then hurried to the door. He opened it quickly and looked down at the anxious face of the little girl, who was cradling a blackbird in both hands.

"I couldn't knock at the door," she explained. "I was scared I'd drop him, or he'd get away. My mum said you'd know what to do."

Harry carefully took the blackbird from her. "Come in and close the door behind you," he said, turning and taking the bird through the house to his small kitchen. He sat down with the male blackbird resting in his lap, feeling its tiny heart pulsing in fear as he gently explored its neck and wings for injuries.

"What happened?" he asked.

"I was going over the bridge and a car came through the village. The blackbird tried to fly across the road and got hit. It was lying in the road, but it was still moving so I ran and got him when the car had gone."

"You are a kind and brave girl, but you could have got yourself run over as well." All the while Harry was checking the blackbird out, extending his wings and legs one at a time and watching reactions. "I think he might be lucky: no breaks as far as I can tell, so he's probably just in shock."

"What can we do?" asked the child. "Will you be able to save him?"

"Well, I hope so," replied Harry. "Let's just sit quietly with him for a while to give him a chance to recover. You hold him for a minute until I get something that might help him." He placed the bird in the girl's lap and showed her where to put her hands. "We don't want him trying to fly just yet, or he may hurt himself more by trying to get out of the house."

Harry went to a kitchen cupboard and withdrew a tin, which he opened to reveal a selection of first aid materials. He lifted out a small bottle and opened it. The lid held a dropper, which Harry squeezed, allowing a small amount of liquid to be sucked into the fine glass tube.

"Keep very still," he told Gemma. "Just hold him firmly, but don't squeeze too tightly." She nodded. He opened the delicate yellow beak slightly with a pair of fine tweezers and allowed one drop of the solution to dribble inside.

"It's called Rescue Remedy," he explained. "And it helps creatures to recover from shock – people too!" he added. "Useful stuff!" He re-capped the bottle and placed it on the table. "Now we just wait. You sit with him like that, so that we are not passing him back and forth and upsetting him. Let's just sit quietly for a few minutes and see if it helps him."

Several minutes elapsed and Gemma felt the bird trying to move beneath her fingers. "I think he's getting better," she whispered excitedly.

"Good! Don't leave go of him. I'll take him from you," said Harry, every bit as elated as the child. Between them they transferred the bird to Harry's more experienced hands. "Now, let's go into the garden." He nodded towards the back door, which Gemma opened.

Man and girl stood side by side at the top edge of the lawn, the blackbird now becoming restless and attempting to move his wings and make a bid for freedom.

"I think we can let him go now. He's ready," said Harry, and holding his hands aloft released the blackbird. He soared confidently upwards and over the garden fence, and they both watched him across the field until he disappeared.

When Harry looked down there were tears in Gemma's eyes. He took her hand, "Well done Gemma, you saved that little creature's life."

⁕

Later, when the little girl had gone home, delighted with the small bird book that Harry had given her, Harry had a few tears of his own. Thank God there were still some parents who taught their children to care about wildlife. He mused for a long time about the past and his own misspent youth: his epiphany and his penance…

Over the last forty years he had tried to do his bit for the local wildlife. He'd rescued more hedgehogs than he cared to remember, especially in the late autumn, when there were juveniles about who would not make their body weight in time for hibernation. Every year his garage became the home to three or four hogs over the winter: each one given a name, and marked so that their progress could be monitored after their release the following year.

There were always birds too: RTAs, those who had flown into windows, or any injured birds he had come across during his walks. They all came home with him and he did the best he could for each and every one. All casualties seemed to end up at his door, either via neighbours, local children, and sometimes not so local children. Word seemed to get around that he would do his best to help and would take any unfortunate creature in. Luckily for him he had a vet who would help him and treat all wildlife free of charge. Andrew was a godsend and he'd taught Harry so much over the years, that many treatments he could now undertake at home.

Harry smiled to himself as he thought of "Walter", a feral pigeon he had picked up tottering about in the town centre. Thanks to Andrew's prompt, and as always, free help he had nursed the injured bird back to health. It had been touch and go in the early days and he'd had Walter for several weeks. A friend had loaned him a small dog cage and Walter had, for that period, completely taken over his life. He remembered it as if it was yesterday, that feeling of exhilaration as he released his feathered friend from the top of the multi-storey car park, returning him to his own environment. He had flown down onto the roof below and Harry had been on tenterhooks watching him, then, seeing a flock of feral pigeons circling, Walter had lofted and joined them. What a moment! Harry had been good for nothing, tears coursing down his face, as Walter became just another dot in the distance. The measure of success!

Of course not all the stories had such happy endings, and Harry sat re-living some of those. A few years ago he found on his travels, and brought home a female blackbird who'd had an injured wing. He'd had taken care of her for ten days, in which time she had *progressed to flying in the house and coming to him for food. Although she was quite tame, Harry knew that he had to release her back into her natural environment before she became too reliant upon him. He'd resolved, with a certain amount of reluctance, to set her free the next morning. He was sure she was ready, and got up at an early hour, when there would be other blackbirds in the garden. When he'd come downstairs, however, he found her to his dismay lying dead in the cage he'd always put her in at night. He was broken hearted.*

He blamed himself for keeping her too long. He'd just wanted to be sure she was strong enough. He'd beaten himself up with "what ifs". What if he'd let her go the previous day when she'd seemed so healthy? What if it hadn't been raining that day: a contributory factor to keeping her another day? Would he have let her go? Could he have let her go? What if he had let her go and she had died? He wouldn't have known – would that make it any better?

He needed to torture himself – it was part of the penance!

The rabbits were the worst. When myxomatosis hit the area, he would regularly find sick rabbits on his walk, just sitting, in the final stages of the disease, blind and unable to move and dying a slow, horrific death. He couldn't leave them like that. There was only one thing to do: make the end quick. He shuddered as he remembered the first time. He'd looked around but there was nothing he could use but his own hands, and he still had graphic memories of his every move, from scooping up the tiny trembling form and caressing its soft fur, to sitting on a tree stump and holding it in his arms long after the deed was done, and finally laying it to rest in the long grass of the hedgerow. He'd taken to carrying a walking stick during the myxomatosis period to assist in the final act, instead of using his hands, and he still wept after each one, apologising to the creature over and over.

Harry struggled to his feet and went to his study, where he kept a diary of sorts. He sat at his desk and wrote an entry for today in longhand, describing the visit from Gemma, and the successful rescue of the blackbird. One more for the list! He wasn't a typical diary keeper but he maintained a record of all the birds and animals he had tried to help over the years, carrying his totals forward to each new diary. He recorded both successes and failures, and although he was elated by every creature he managed to save, he needed to acknowledge to himself that he had tried his best for each and every one that came his way. Win or lose it was the taking part that mattered. Gemma was the heroine today but at least he'd helped.

Harry looked back over the entries so far for this year. In the spring he had picked up a young fox that had been bumped by a car. Its leg was torn, but he'd taken it straight to Andrew who had mended it and in due course sent the fox to a rehabilitation centre for wild animals. It was now returned to the wild. He'd also been able to release three hedgehogs that he'd cared for over the winter, and he'd found a baby moorhen struggling through the long grass more than a hundred yards away from the river. Not a parent in sight! He'd really taken a chance with that one when he'd taken it back to the riverbank. He was sure that left to its own devices it would never have successfully made the journey, and as the area was popular with dog walkers he worried that a dog would catch it. As it turned out he was able to find a distraught parent bird, calling and calling, and with the help of his lawn rake, he was able to lower the chick to the reeds. As soon as he retreated the parent came to reclaim her baby. What a moment that was!

Harry turned to his summation and altered the total to include the blackbird. There was no pride in his action. It was a simple reckoning, and he knew that for him it would never be enough…

Twenty Tiny Tales

Rabbits 34	Hedgehogs 27	Moorhen 1
Foxes 5	Woodpigeons 3	Kingfisher 1
Squirrel 1	Kestrel (female) 1	Common gull 1
Blackbirds 789	Feral pigeons 2	Herring gull 1
Starlings 9	Blue tit 1	Frogs 4
Song thrush 1	Crow 1	Lambs (main road) 2
Robin 1	Goldfinch 1	Calf (river) 1
Pheasants 2	Sparrows 4	Pony (escaped on road) 1
Horse/foal (giving birth)	Ferrets 2	

One Week Left

I sat absolutely stunned! Even though it wasn't exactly a surprise, when the doctor actually put it into words, it brought the stark reality of the situation home. I had realised the inevitable some weeks before – I'm not totally stupid! Over the last few weeks everyone around me had been careful to appear bright, cheery and positive, in their blue and white starched uniforms, discussing the next phase of the "treatment" with me, and only voicing the truth in their hushed voices when they thought that I was asleep. In short the matter was that I felt that I probably had only as little as one week left. The doctor had of course been suitably tactful and erred on the side of optimism. I sat reflecting: perhaps in a way it's better to be told you've got one week to live than six months.

I wanted to be discharged. After all it's *my* time and it's pretty precious to me right now. After a rigmarole which involved seeing all kinds of medical and counselling staff, and signing forms (as if it mattered!) I finally got my own way. I was going home: there were things I wanted to do! I'm sure that at some time everyone has debated in their heads what they would do if they only had a limited time left to live. It's the same sort of thing as fantasising about what you would do if you won a million! Let me tell you here and now, it isn't real! You wouldn't do any of those things!

So here I was at home. I wasn't incapable, but I'd had to agree to a daily visit from a nurse. They'd wanted one to stay with me full-time but I wasn't having any of that! My God – they'd be forever washing me and making me a "nice cup of tea". I had better things to do with a week than that!

At first I was filled with all sorts of noble thoughts and ideas about what I would do! Then reality kicked in again. This is *my* week, no one else's! I'd already made my will, so that's okay, and who cares anyway? (After all I'll be gone.) I'd no near relatives left and the few remnants of family I did have, were scattered about the globe. They probably wouldn't even come back to fight about their share of the money let alone for the funeral! I couldn't say I'd blame them either; I don't suppose I'd go shooting off to Australia or even Italy if one of them were to pop their clogs. What are solicitors for anyway?

I'd wasted half of the first day of the rest of my life already just trying to get out of hospital. So now what? I made a cup of coffee and sat with it, thinking about how to put the remaining six to better use. Maybe I'd like to go to a few places – old haunts! There was only one individual I wanted to visit – one thing I really wanted to do. Well, I'd do that tomorrow to make sure that I had the strength to do the one thing that was important to me and then I would spend the rest of the week travelling as far as I was able. A few trips down memory lane are called for. Money was, of course, no object now! For the first time in my life the cliché "you can't take it with you!" meant something real! I'd get a taxi, or several taxis for that matter! In fact I'd get one now and go to the bank – I'd better pay my way with "readies" this week – so much easier under the circumstances.

I rang for a cab straight away and ten minutes later was on my way into town. I stood in a queue at the bank impatiently…

seven minutes before my turn came! I suppose half of these people had nothing better to do: chatting about the weather, having futile conversations on their mobile phones just as they are about to be served: "Yes, darling I'm at the bank now. I'll bring some milk in with me, blah blah, etc!". Did these people not realise that they were wasting their lives on trivia?

I took out a pretty large sum, really, considering it only had to do six days – but – suppose I managed to squeeze an extra couple out of Fate? I wasn't going to have anyone saying I hadn't paid my way right up to the end! How embarrassing it would be not to have enough to pay your taxi driver. I'm not having anyone saying things like that about me when I'm gone!

I got back into the taxi noticing as I did so that the meter had clocked up a considerable amount more during the waiting period. Funny how the habits of a lifetime still come back – so what, if it had cost nearly five pounds just to keep him waiting at the bank? My ten minutes were more precious than his if he did but know it! "Where to now, mate?" he asked.

I gave the matter some consideration. I'd originally decided to start on my plan of action tomorrow… isn't that just like we human beings? Tomorrow is always good enough! Suddenly the proverb "the way to Hell is paved with good intentions" jumped into the forefront of my mind with a clarity that was frightening. Well, I didn't feel completely at Death's Door today as I'd predicted I might, so I made a snap decision. "Drive me on to the coast road and head up the Northumberland coastline, I'll give you more specific directions when we get somewhere near where I want to be."

"It'll take me best part of an hour to get there – you won't have much of the day left," replied the taxi driver.

"That's okay. It will be long enough, and I don't mind travelling back in the dark if you've the time before the end of your shift."

"Anything you say, mate. You know what they say – he who pays the piper, etc."

We were travelling north within a few minutes. It's funny how you suddenly become very conscious of the time everything takes. It took eight whole minutes to get to the outskirts of the town and away from seething masses of people all rushing to shop in their lunch break, or maybe hurrying home at the end of their shift. There seemed to be a major urgency about it all and I wanted to shout and tell them to slow down and to enjoy what they had while they still had it! The only person who needed to be in a hurry was *me*. At least, I wasn't really in a hurry – there were very few things I really wanted to do, but I was going to make sure I did the things or *thing* that mattered the most!

On the journey, George, the taxi driver, and I got on first name terms. I asked him about his hours of work and explained that I would like to engage him for a few days, on a full-time basis, to act as my chauffeur. I'd pay him in cash at the end of each day.

"Fine by me," he said. He explained that he did a "school run" each day but that from 9.15 onwards his time was mine as long as I was paying. He seemed delighted at the guaranteed work. I said that it would just be for a few days, but didn't elaborate.

Once we were on the more rural roads I tried to take in as much scenery as I could, looking out of each window in turn, my head turning back and forth like an umpire at a tennis match despite the acute pain. I didn't want to miss anything. I'd always loved this part of the country, but I now felt acutely how much I'd taken it for granted. Yes, I'd appreciated it in a general awareness sort of way: the green patchwork effect of the fields in summer and the gold and red of the trees in autumn… I remembered the first signs of blossom on those same trees of the many, many Springs I'd travelled this road, and the sight of the snow-covered boughs in winter. I had the big picture all right, but now I was conscious of noticing so many other little things that maybe I'd overlooked before: a tiny wren flitting rapidly through the hedgerow like lightning, a small patch of early celandine at the side of the road, tiny buds of hawthorn just starting to show – mere fragments of green peeping through the dark wood!

I had travelled these roads so many times as a matter of course – all in a day's work, so to speak!

Even on those few very special journeys on this road – journeys which weren't work related, journeys with Donna sitting beside me, together we'd enjoyed identifying the very varied bird life, and seeing rabbits feeding at the side of the road in the knowledge that they were safe because of the lack of traffic – and lambs! Fields and fields of new born lambs! Donna had loved to see them gambolling about – it never failed to excite her! Then as we got nearer and nearer to the sea and could smell it on the air, Donna would get so excited and I loved to see her face, positively glowing as we drew nearer and nearer to our very own secret place.

Oh how I wished the clock could be turned back, not because I would want do anything differently, not where Donna was concerned, at least! We had loved each other, right up to the end. All I wanted was to be able to re-live some of those times again and cherish each one. They were still vivid enough in my mind and I was doing the next best thing. I could almost feel her sitting beside me... and soon enough I would be with her. I could not deny that I had been very lonely since she'd gone.

At my first glimpse of the sea my heart leapt. Maybe not the last glimpse of the sea I'd ever have, but most certainly the last from here and in this way. I asked George to pull over for a few minutes and just sat quietly looking all around me, taking it all in, and remembering... I wound the window down and breathed in the sea air. It was mild for the time of the year and I reflected that this had always been our favourite time to come up here. So few people about and no noise except the sea's own haunting noises in the distance and the call of the gulls as we got nearer to the coast.

I wound the window back up and directed George to the tiny single-track road I wanted him to take. Once we were on that road everything came flooding back. That last journey up here with Donna! Saying Goodbye! I knew each bend in that road. It had been a solitary journey back. I doubted whether even the return journey today would be as lonely. In a way I felt I was closer to her now than I was then.

I asked George to follow a sandy track on the left, which led to the middle of the dunes and when we got to our destination, a tiny flat spot only big enough to take one car, he turned with a puzzled look as he brought the cab to a halt. "Is this it, mate?" he enquired, obviously thinking that I was off my head.

"Yes, this is it George," I said, "and you may take an hour off now, for which I shall pay you of course!"

"There's not exactly a lot to do around these parts," he grinned. I must admit I couldn't exactly see him going for a long walk. He must have weighed at least twenty stone.

"Oh you don't have to stay here, you can go back to that last village. It's about two miles away, and they boast a pub and a coffee shop. Just come back for me here at about five o'clock"

I watched George pull away, then I turned towards the sea. I knew that I wouldn't be able to walk far, but I needed to make my way through the dunes by our favourite route until I could see the water's edge. After that it would just depend on how much strength I had left how far I could go. It was pretty tough going on the soft dry sand, and even the slightest undulation of the ground was hard work for me in my present condition, but I soon forgot all that when I was finally stood on that last dune, with a clear view down to the sea and along a stretch of three miles or so of clean silvery sand with not a soul in sight. Here

Donna would run down to the sea whether the tide was in or out, and splash about in the waves until I caught up with her at the water's edge.

I'd never been back here since that last time with Donna. It had all been too painful to remember. Yet somehow now despite my very real pain, I felt inside a pleasure and a tranquillity in coming here. It was like coming home! We'd walked the full length of the beach for the last time, and then I'd returned – alone!

I stood now, staring at the waves breaking on the sea and thinking of that last walk along its edge. I'd talked quietly to her all of the time telling her why I was doing it this way, and I knew that she understood. We talked the same language, Donna and I, and dreamed the same dreams! I'd told her that nothing could really separate us, however many miles were put between us. After I'd scattered her ashes the length of the beach and watched the tide coming in and washing over the still damp sand, I buried the little bio-degradable box that had held them, knowing that it too would return to the sea in due course. I remembered how empty yet peaceful I'd felt.

I knew that I could not manage to walk the length of the beach today, but I was determined to at least get to the water's edge for a last time. Luckily the tide was not too far out. I made my way slowly down "our" sand dune and across the expanse of dry sand. Once I reached the line of pebbles and then the damp compressed sand the going was easier – I could almost see Donna dancing in the breaking waves, her hair blown on the breeze and her legs all wet. I stood there: the water lapping around my feet and thought of her and talked to her.

She was here! She always would be! Life had not been the same without her, and from the moment she was gone I had wanted to be with her…

I was still there in the same spot, when I heard George calling to me, asking if I was all right. I hadn't heard the car return. He started to walk down the beach towards me and I waved him back to the car. I couldn't have anyone else intrude upon these last few minutes. I stood for a few more moments and then struggled slowly up the beach. When I came to the climb up the dunes, I thought it would take me forever. I wasn't sure if I could make it... not that that mattered to me now! I got to the top, almost wishing that I hadn't. I could see George sitting in the car. I turned and looked for what I knew was a last time at the sand and the sea, both stretching for miles.

Suddenly I saw Donna! She was waiting for me, dancing in the sea the same as usual... I knew what I had to do... I turned back to the car and threw my wallet as hard as I could towards it... all debts paid, George!

Summoning all of my strength I "ran" or at least staggered back down the beach, never taking my eyes off Donna...still she waited, as I knew she always had. I splashed through the waves and beyond. We belonged together, Donna and I – a man and his dog!

The Luck of the Devil

He'd always been a fit bloke. He walked and ran, played squash, trained with weights three times a week and generally looked in good shape. He'd weighed in at 210 pounds before the accident.

He looked at himself now in the mirror: a shadow of his former self: a wraith at 174 pounds! His face was ashen – his eyes were sunk deep in their sockets, his colour all gone after weeks and weeks indoors in hospital. They'd tried to put him back together, and many would think they had succeeded. His upper body was as good as new – at least it would be once he'd got back to the dumbbells. He could do that both sitting down and lying down. No permanent damage they'd said… a broken shoulder, a few broken ribs, a punctured lung… All now on the mend.

Then the doctor had given him the not so good news! His legs had been too badly crushed. He would eventually, they hoped, be able to walk again, with sticks, etc. He would be given a wheelchair for the next few months, and physiotherapy. As he sat, staring at a reflection, which he hardly recognised as his own, snatches of the conversation came back to him.

He knew that the hospital staff had done as good a job as humanly possible. The surgeon had been nothing short of amazing and all the nursing staff zealous over his post-operative care. There had been no negligence there! But you had to have something to work from. How could you repair damage caused by twenty minutes under the weight of a combine harvester?

The day of the accident was still vivid and lurid in his mind. He'd been on the Fireblade, taking one of his short cuts along the back roads to Ellie's to avoid the busy Saturday traffic on the A167. He knew every contour and gradient in the road and got a real adrenalin buzz from leaning into some of the most acute bends at an awesome speed. He'd always tried to beat his personal best, and had got his time down to just under nine minutes door to door.

That particular Saturday they'd had a row on the telephone earlier in the day. He was expected for lunch, and had almost decided that he wasn't going to turn up, and then had relented at the last minute. He didn't even know why. Theirs was a complex situation, both having been in previous relationships, but despite all of the difficulties, he knew that their lives were now somehow inextricably linked. He knew that Ellie felt the same about it. They'd come too far: overcome too many misunderstandings, weathered too many storms, gossip and rumours to throw it all away. So that was why he was tearing along the country road on that particular Saturday, throwing the bike this way and that into and out of the many bends, not however, with the usual exhilaration that he felt. His mind was only partly concentrating on the ride: the rest of it was going over the hasty words spoken on the phone on both sides.

Suddenly as he rounded a wide, sweeping, right-hand bend, the road partially obscured by trees and an overgrown hedgerow on the inside of the curve, he was confronted by a wall of green: a colossal and slow-moving combine harvester was immediately in his path. The breadth of the vehicle took well more than half the road width, leaving him nowhere to go. He was upon it in an instant. He braked as hard as he dared and felt his rear wheel slide from under him. He tried to throw himself and his bike clear of the giant machine, and almost, but not quite, made it. Before he knew it, he and the combine had made contact! The machine came to rest upon one of his legs. The other leg was trapped under the Fireblade, which in turn was pinned in place by the leg that was under the combine harvester.

The next half hour or so was a blank in his memory, but he remembered the paramedics allowing him to phone Ellie whilst he was lying in the ambulance. He couldn't bear to think of her sitting alone, waiting for him to arrive for lunch, and perhaps believing that he'd decided not to bother because of their previous argument. They'd spoken few words during that call and both were in shock! She'd simply ascertained which of the two local hospitals they were taking him to and rushed straight there in her van, arriving there as quickly as the ambulance, and meeting him at the rear doors as the two paramedics lifted him out.

All that was weeks ago and here he was, about to be discharged. Eventually! He was going to Ellie's so that she could care for him during his convalescence. She'd visited him every day for as long as the hospital would allow and had already had to tell him that his precious Fireblade had been written off by the insurance company. He'd asked about it as soon as he'd seen her the day after the accident and by her description of its condition, the subsequent news was not unexpected. The whole thing had been a long, traumatic haul, which had taken its toll on both of them, but at least they were going to see it through together. She'd taken it badly when he'd first told her of the permanent damage to his legs. She knew how much his fitness and his motorcycling meant to him. They'd spent the last few days putting a brave face on for each other, but each knew that the other was undeceived.

Ellie drove him home, his new collapsible wheelchair in the back of her van. Both of them were making small talk until they were in the privacy of the house. Only then did they allow some of their emotions to flow freely.

Over the next few weeks Les attended the hospital regularly for physiotherapy. Ellie always went with him, encouraging him every step of the way. But after the sessions, once home, they were both despondent and often tearful. Each tried to be optimistic and encouraging to the other, but they both knew the truth of the matter: that although he might eventually be able to walk, albeit with sticks, he would never be able to return to the same active lifestyle he'd always had. He'd never be able to ride a motorcycle again.

Again and again Ellie would watch him trying to walk unaided in the house, his face set with a mixture of grim determination and severe pain. She would be there when he flung himself down on the floor banging it with his fists in sheer frustration at his own weakness and inability. Les knew that she lay in bed each night with silent, hot tears trickling down her face as she hurt inside for him, unable to help him. He hurt inside for both her and himself. What kind of life together could they now have?

He'd tried to talk to her about it, to explain how he felt. He'd urged her to leave him and try to find someone else: a whole man, not an invalid. He'd tried to explain that he couldn't possibly marry her now – it wouldn't be fair! And he'd carefully broached the subject of how worthless he felt his own life now was, and how he couldn't live for years and years like this: a cripple. He'd tried to put it to her in an oblique fashion, but she'd seen exactly what he was driving at. She would! They'd always had a certain telepathy right from the early days of their relationship, and sometimes he felt she could see right inside his head. She was shocked, of course, and yet not really surprised at his thoughts, and she'd told him that she didn't want a life of which he was not a part. She couldn't live without him, and he knew himself that this was true. They had become so essential to each other, their lives so inextricably linked. He could remember her exact words: "We belong with each other, right to the very end".

It hadn't taken him long to formulate his plan. He'd persevered with the exercises and after two months of physiotherapy three times a week, had been discharged. No further sessions. He knew then that this was as good as it was going to get. The hospital staff wished him a cheery farewell and lots of luck: only the three-monthly check-ups now! He smiled wryly as he left on his sticks, Ellie at his side as usual.

Once in the car, on impulse he said, "Take me to Tillsons on the way home, if you don't mind." Tillsons was the motorcycle shop from which he'd bought the Fireblade.

"Do you think that's wise?" Ellie asked. "You know what it will do to you, seeing all those bikes."

"I'll be fine, I promise! All I can do now is look. Don't deprive me of that."

So they'd gone to Tillsons. They'd been greeted by the staff there, all of whom knew Les well. "What on earth have you been up to?" the Manager had said upon seeing him on his sticks. Les duly told them all about the accident and they'd joked with him and asked him how many lives he had left now. He'd laughed and joked back, and then he and Ellie had wandered around the shop together. Only she knew of the lump in his throat and saw the tears well up in his eyes as he looked the sports bikes over, and she knew that he was recognising and trying to accept the fact that he would never ride one again. He pointed to a scooter; a little 125 model and said, "What about that next time then?"

"No good," she said. "No room for me!"

After only about twenty minutes, a very short time for them to be in any bike shop, he'd said, "Well we'd best be off then." He stopped to purchase a *Motor Cycle Magazine* on the way out, telling Gary, the assistant, that he was going to look for a "new" bike, when he got home.

Once in the car and on their way, he felt Ellie glance sideways at him, care and concern on her face. He continued looking straight ahead, not daring to make eye contact. They arrived home (for Ellie's home had become his home, he was so helpless himself now) in silence. As she went to put the kettle on, he lowered himself into a chair and opened his magazine. When she came in with two cups of coffee, he had found the motorcycle "for sale" section and was browsing it intently.

"Don't you think you are being rather cruel to yourself?" she ventured.

"Let me be the judge of that," he'd replied curtly and she'd said nothing else, but she hurt inwardly for him and wished he didn't have to bear it alone.

"Sorry, I know I'm a miserable bastard. I can't help it," he'd apologised. "I just want to look, you know. I might see an old bike for a few hundred that I can just tinker on with. I can sit down to do that," he added, "I do appreciate how much you have done for me. I just need to cope with this in my own way."

Later that afternoon she heard him telephoning and enquiring about a motorcycle: a Suzuki Bandit 600, a few years old but at seemingly a surprisingly low price. He asked her to take him to inspect it. The bike had had a bit of a nudge and the tank was slightly dented, an indicator light was broken and the paintwork was scuffed. The owner, a twenty-two-year-old lad, had come off it and it had unnerved him. He wanted a quick sale.

With a bit of negotiation Les got the Bandit for £700. "It will do me fine for what I want," he'd said. They arranged to collect it two days later with help from Les's friend Andy, who rode it to Ellie's after she'd dropped him off. Les seemed very pleased with his new acquisition and Ellie began to think that maybe it was a decision for the best, even if Les couldn't ride it, messing about with it would at least keep him involved with motorbikes.

Once he was taking it apart and putting it back together he seemed much happier than he'd been for the last few weeks, and the two of them began to settle into a new, if rather tamer lifestyle. Les seemed engrossed in his task. He replaced the indicator light and checked the machine over mechanically, tuning it here and there, and waxed the chain. He had told Ellie that he wasn't bothered about the paintwork and she was quite surprised. She couldn't help wondering what was going to happen when he'd made the bike roadworthy again. Would the fact that he couldn't ride it cause him even more anguish? Would he simply sell it and buy another one to do up? She was worried!

Les was using his weights regularly again, and his upper body was beginning to return to something like it used to be. He exercised his legs, working almost feverishly, concentrating particularly on his ankles, which had taken the weight of the combine harvester. He had some flexibility back but not sufficient strength in them to bear his own weight unaided. Still he persevered...

His moods fluctuated dramatically: some days he was very depressed and others he seemed almost exhilarated, bordering occasionally on hysteria. More than once he'd told Ellie that he couldn't go on living this sort of life for the rest of his days. At other times he spoke almost in a joking way about an early death and said that it would be far the best way out for him. He would upset Ellie when he spoke like this and she would tell him how much she loved him and that she couldn't bear the thought of life without him. Then he would hold her to him and tell her not to worry: it wouldn't come to that.

One Sunday morning soon after the bike had been declared sound, Ellie walked into the hall to find Les coming downstairs in his usual way now, on his behind, dressed in his leather bike jacket and a pair of old jeans. He'd thrown his boots downstairs before him and was retrieving them to put on. "What do you think you are up to?" she asked.

"I'm just going to see if I can give the Bandit a short spin to test it," he'd said.

"I don't think so!" She'd expected this day for some time now and was ready for it. She knew that Les would want to get back on two wheels, especially if they were sat there in the garage doing nothing other than being ready for use and willing him to climb on. "You can't, love – I know that it's hard for you to bear, but you're not up to it. You could kill yourself, or someone else for that matter."

"I won't kill any one else, I promise you," he'd said emphatically, a strange look on his face. He pulled her to him and kissed her, almost savagely at first and then gently as he said, "I've got to do this, I think you know that." He added, "I love you and I know you love me. If you do, you'll let me do this one thing."

The girl looked at him and knew the truth. She knew now, what he'd known all along, and what he'd been planning for so many weeks. Les couldn't live this strange new life of helplessness and dependence on other people. He'd always been a free spirit. That's what she herself had admired in him. A life of imprisonment, for that's what it amounted to for him, could never be. She understood! She turned and went out of the room. When she came back she was carrying two crash helmets. She handed him his and began to put hers on.

"No!" he shouted. "You've still got a life, Ellie. I'm the one who hasn't! I want you to have a happy life, unfettered by a crippled husband!"

"Without you I haven't got a life, Les. We do everything together, don't we? How can I let you do this alone? You don't think I want to face life without you, do you?"

They'd argued and then clung to each other, each stating their own case to the other one. Eventually Les had said, "I can't do this to you. You won't be able to stop me from going out on the bike tomorrow or the next day – I'll just have to choose my time more carefully, that's all!"

She'd pleaded with him – not to prevent him from taking his own life, but for not giving her the right to also choose for herself. Eventually, broken by her tears, he'd agreed. "We won't need those," he'd said, pointing to the crash helmets on the floor. Together they got out the Bandit and put it on its prop stand on the drive…

They held each other closely for a minute before mounting. They wanted the same thing: freedom together. Once on the pillion seat, Ellie put her arms around his middle and hugged him close. Les knew that he wouldn't be able to ride far, but he'd already chosen the exact place of the "accident" – a bridge over the same country road where he'd had his previous crash. It had huge concrete pillars on either side. Perfect for what he had in mind! He didn't discuss the details with Ellie, the less she knew the easier it would be for her. He only hoped he had the bottle!

He rode carefully the hundred or so metres along the main road, praying that he wouldn't get pulled up by the police for not wearing a helmet at this stage. A left turn then took him onto the B road he needed and relative safety. Safety? He had some difficulty managing the manoeuvres with his feet but he knew that in any case the pain was not going to last for long. He could feel the tension in Ellie's body as it pressed against him: usually she was so relaxed on the bike! He pulled into the side of the road and turned around. "Are you sure you want to go through with this?" he asked. She nodded. He kissed her lightly on the lips and said, "I always knew you had guts, kid. I just always thought you had more brains!"

She squeezed his hand in reply and forced a smile. "I love you, so take me with you wherever you are going."

Les nodded, turned and gripped the throttle with his right hand. He revved up and let in the clutch… He felt Ellie's head on his left shoulder as the bridge came in sight: he glanced at the speedometer – 90mph and accelerating…

⁓

Some 35 minutes later, when the paramedics, summoned by a local farmer who had come upon the scene of the accident in his tractor, had made their assessment of the casualties, they called the hospital to give advance warning: "One casualty to bring in. A motorcyclist: male about 40-45, with severe head injuries, multiple fractures of arms and one leg, concussed and unconscious. The woman pillion didn't make it: dead on arrival at the scene of the accident. Neither of them wearing crash helmets!"

He looked down at Les as he switched his radio off. "You've been bloody lucky mate!" He shook his head.

That's What Friends Are For

They'd just extended their holiday by another week. The weather had been glorious for the last three weeks and it looked as if it would continue... in any case what had they to rush home for? Newly retired! New motorhome! Idyllic setting...

Lynn sat with her glass of orange juice watching the birds and rabbits feeding harmoniously upon the banquet of assorted seeds, nuts, fatballs and mealworms she had just arranged for them. Her book was in her lap, but she couldn't concentrate on it: the activity outside her window and the amazing, ever-changing sunrise had between them captured her whole attention. The sea, only sixty yards away, was calm and only gently rippled, a diaphanous surface with a streak of sunlight across the middle: it was as golden as the sky. Was this retirement? How much better could it get?

They'd been here before and Ardgowan Bay had become their favourite place to be, but in the past their stay had been time-bonded. Now, they had nothing to rush home for. Lynn stared out at the sea and sky: the tiny beach was deserted save for the gulls and oyster catchers busily picking their way along the shoreline. It wasn't unusual to see the head of a grey seal bobbing in the water beside the passing cormorants.

After a while she heard Chris stirring and looked towards the double bed in the rear of the van. Breakfast time…

It was 9.30, they'd breakfasted, showered, tidied the van and were sitting outside in shorts and vests, facing into the morning sun and occasionally glancing sideways at each other, with huge grins cracking their faces. This was the life! Lynn looked at her husband expectantly; his eyes twinkled as he said, "Another day in Paradise!" – his usual morning quote. She had to agree though.

They had just finished their coffee when Lynn's mobile phone rang. She picked it up and saw that the caller was Jane, her friend who looked after their house in their absence. Jane lived ten minutes away, but walked her dog Barney every morning on the riverbank near where they lived. She called at their house on route, checked the house, adjusted the blinds and filled the birdfeeders in the back garden.

"Hello Jane," said Lynn quizzically into the phone.

"Lynn! I am at your house now and someone has been in," came the panicked voice of Jane. "I'm in the porch, with the hall door open, and I can see that the kitchen window has been forced."

Lynn looked aghast. "Oh noooo," she moaned, then more urgently said, "Call the police, Jane. Don't go in by yourself, you don't know what you might find. There might still be someone in the house. Don't put yourself at risk."

"Okay," whispered Jane cautiously.

"Just get on to them immediately. I'll give you a few minutes to get hold of them and I'll ring you. Meanwhile we will get packed up as soon as possible at this end, and obviously we'll come straight home."

"Right," said Jane. She sounded stunned as she rang off.

"We've been burgled!" Lynn quickly recounted the conversation to Chris with eyes full of alarm.

"Oh My God! Poor Jane. Fancy walking in to something like that! Is she all right?" he asked, paling visibly.

"She's getting on to the police now," Lynn replied. "We need to pack up and get on our way home as soon as possible. We can't let Jane deal with all of this. I've told her not to go any further into the house until the police get there… for her own safety," she added.

"Good thinking," agreed Chris. "The place could have been trashed, or she might unwittingly disturb something important to the police investigation. And we can't let her endanger herself if anyone is still lurking about. The bastards!" he couldn't help himself. Shock was quickly being replaced by anger.

They worked feverishly, moving everything from the worktops into cupboards and locking the doors, ensuring nothing could fall when they were on the move. Chris went outside to load the chairs and water containers into lockers. He dismantled the birdfeeders, emptying the contents onto the grass to keep the wildlife going for a while.

Meanwhile Lynn went to inform the wardens of their sudden, enforced change of plan, apologising for cancelling the week they had only just booked. Once sorted, she rang Jane, who informed her that the police would be out as soon as possible, but that it could be an hour.

"I'm so, so sorry that you are having to deal with this, Jane. We are ready to set off now, but it's going to take us four to five hours to get home from here. Is there any chance you could wait until the police arrive? Maybe they can make the house secure until we get home. That way you won't have to wait for us to arrive. I'm just so sorry that you've walked in to something like this."

"I'm all right," responded Jane, "I've rung Andy to come and collect Barney for me. You know what Mr B's like, and he *will* bark at the policemen."

Chris climbed into the driving seat, fastened his seatbelt and started the engine. Lynn continued, "Jane, we're on the move now. I will keep phoning you with a progress report of our whereabouts, and if the police need to talk to me, tell them they can do as I'm in the passenger seat. Make yourself a coffee."

"I'd better not," replied her friend, "I'm not touching anything until the police are here. Talk to you soon, and please drive safely. I will stay here as long as I am needed and I will not leave the house vulnerable, so don't worry."

Lynn and Chris travelled the first ten miles in complete silence, both too shocked to broach the subject first. Eventually Chris spoke. "I think you should prepare yourself for the worst, love, you know the sort of thing these oiks do, and I'm not just talking about theft."

Lynn shuddered. "I know, I've read about such things in newspapers, but don't you think that would help to catch whoever committed the crime? DNA and all that?"

"Apparently not, at least not in excrement, and they're probably clued up enough to know not to piss!" remarked Chris.

"What do you think they'll have taken?" asked his wife.

"Well, any cash that's lying about, for starters, but that won't be much, will it?"

"Actually I left £200 at home," she admitted. "The money Helen gives me monthly to keep for her. It's mounted up and I forgot to bank it before we came away. I always keep some by in case she needs it urgently." She paused. "It's well hidden though, in an old tin that used to have an arrangement of scented soaps in it. The tin is in the bottom of my wardrobe under pairs of shoes."

"Well don't build your hopes up! I wish you'd told me that you hadn't banked Helen's money. I would have brought it with us in a separate wallet or something. I bet they've taken my air rifle." He spoke the last words through gritted teeth.

"Probably," agreed Lynn. "What about the telly, and your laptop, and my jewellery? Actually you know, when you think about it we haven't got that much in terms of technology. No expensive equipment, and our TVs and the laptop are dated now. Our cameras are with us, so maybe we won't have much to interest them."

"I think they are more likely to trash the place if they haven't found anything they want," said Chris bitterly. "I rather hope they've found the £200 and pissed off."

Silence resumed.

They were between Castle Douglas and Dumfries when the phone rang. Lynn snatched it up. As expected it was Jane. "The police have been and gone. One of them is going to ring you with a crime number and to introduce himself to you, and I'm now waiting for a SOCO or a CSI, or whatever it is. They are going to test for fingerprints, etc and may have to take away anything they find with a print on it. I've been through the house with the police who've just left, and while the burglars have emptied drawers onto the floor and dragged the contents of cupboards out, there's no horrible stuff, if you know what I mean. A couple of things are broken, maybe been trampled on, but not much." She paused for breath. "Of course, I have no idea what they've taken, but the TVs are there. The living room looks fairly untouched apart from drawers and cupboard doors left open. The bulk of the mess is upstairs."

"What about my ornaments?" asked Lynn suddenly. "When Margie was burgled a few years ago they stole all her Lladro and her Swarovski crystal."

"Just a minute." Jane looked around her. "I can't see anything missing down here. All your china dogs are here, and the cupboard doors are open in the dresser so I can see your Wedgwood and Royal Doulton. Not sure about upstairs though."

The two women chatted for a few more minutes, each worrying about the other, then Jane said, "I'll have to go, more police are here. I'll ring you as soon as they have gone." The phone went dead.

Lynn spent the next few miles bringing Chris up to speed, then, they resumed speculation about possible loss and damage.

On the motorway, Lynn's phone rang again. It was the police. A voice at the other end introduced himself, stating his name and rank, and Lynn actually smiled into the phone. She grabbed her notepad and pen from the shelf in the dashboard and began scribbling: crime number, contact telephone number… "Can you just give me your name again?" she said. Chris heard a voice at the other end speak, though he couldn't make out the words.

A minute later Lynn lowered the phone to her lap. "Our police contact is called Glen Miller!" she announced. "I know, it actually made me smile, but it really is his name. If we let him know when we are home, someone will call to see us."

They'd been travelling for two and a half hours, and decided that they needed to stop for a quick break, regardless of the urgency to get home. Chris pulled into the caravan and motorhome area of the motorway services, and vacated the driving seat looking tense and distraught. He visited the bathroom at the rear of the van then sat in the lounge area with his head in his hands. Lynn also visited the toilet then opened the fridge and took out a bottle of water. She unscrewed the top and held the bottle out to Chris. "I'm assuming you won't want me to take up time putting the kettle on and making a brew, but you must have a few minutes rest, and a drink."

He nodded and took the offered water, drinking deeply. He passed the bottle back and Lynn also took a drink.

"Right, let's go!" said Chris standing up.

Back on the road, more speculation about the state of affairs at home.

During the second half of their journey, Jane had been back on the phone and informed Lynn that the CSI team had finished for the day and had secured the kitchen window before they left. She also told her that she would stay at their house until they arrived home. When Lynn protested, she overruled their concerns about her time and her lunch, confirming that her daughter, Dawn, had brought her a flask of coffee and a sandwich.

"I'm not having you walking in to face all this. I *will* be here for you," she finished.

They pulled onto the drive just before 3.30 and Jane was at the front door before they had even alighted. She pulled them both to her, hugging them and telling them how very sorry she was. Each of them was apologising to her simultaneously for the trouble it had caused her.

"Let me make us all a coffee," said Jane. "Have you by any chance got any fresh milk?"

"Yes," said Chris, and retrieved a carton from the motorhome fridge. While Jane made the coffee, he and Lynn wandered from room to room, not touching anything, but eyes roving everywhere, taking in those items still there and the general mess of upturned drawers and open cupboards with their contents pulled out.

"Where to start?" whispered Lynn anxiously, tears welling up in her eyes.

"By informing our insurance company," replied Chris vehemently. "Don't touch anything until we've spoken to them. They may want to send someone out."

"Coffee!" announced Jane appearing in the doorway with three steaming mugs on a tray. "Sit down and pull yourselves together a bit. I'll tell you everything I can about what has happened so far." She gave her friends a blow by blow account of the day, finishing with the fingerprint and footprint testing, and the CSI crew telling her that they had a fairly clear footprint of a Nike training shoe and some partial fingerprints on some small boxes that had contained jewellery items. The jewellery had been taken and the boxes discarded, so the team had bagged and removed them for testing.

"I've cleaned up the mess left after the fingerprinting powder as best I can," said Jane. "It was on the doors of the mahogany units, the door handles upstairs and on the kitchen table, windows, and windowsills. Oh and they spilled some on the living room carpet, but I've got most of it up. I told them the carpet was new! Anyway, I couldn't have you coming home to all that mess as well as a burglary."

Lynn got up, walked to where Jane was sitting and hugged her. "You are such a good friend, Jane. You've gone over and above the call of duty… and of friendship," she added. "Thank you so much. How can we ever repay you?" Her eyes filled with tears again.

Jane stood. "I'm going to go now and let you have some time to assess the situation, and find out exactly what has been taken. Call me any time you want to. I'll be thinking of you."

While Lynn went to the front door with Jane, Chris rang Glen Miller.

The police officer had finally left, and the insurance company had been contacted. Chris had informed them that he had a crime number, but could not at this stage give them details of what had been taken as they had been home only an hour and a half, most of it taken up with the police. The advisor, pleasant and suitably sympathetic, told him that the relevant claim forms would be posted out the next morning. He provided Chris with a company claim reference number and urged him to phone at any time if he required further assistance.

The shell-shocked couple agreed that they would tackle one room at a time, and began the task of sorting through their bedroom, methodically assessing contents of each drawer and cupboard, and compiling a preliminary list of missing items, as best they could. It was not easy and they began to wander from their agenda, checking other rooms for the things they were the most concerned about. Chris's rifle was there! His most valuable, single personal possession! His mother's jewellery box was also intact, at the back of one of his drawers. He breathed a great sigh of relief as his eyes wandered over the contents. She had only died a few months before, and he had selected all the important items he wanted to keep, before offering other pieces to family members and friends. The drawer had clearly been opened and rummaged through: a watch taken, thankfully not his best one, which he had with him on holiday, and was currently wearing.

It began a train of thought… Why would anyone leave the jewellery alone? Was it too ancient? Too difficult to fence? Too traceable? He began to sift methodically through each drawer and wardrobe. A new bottle of aftershave was missing, but everything else seemed undisturbed. Lynn was calling him from the small room she called her dressing room. He walked to the doorway.

"They've taken some jewellery, but not all, and my new training shoes, and Helen's £200 from the bottom of the wardrobe," she said holding out the empty tin.

"Just a minute," muttered Chris walking back to the bedroom. He returned in less than a minute holding an empty shoebox. "They've taken my new trainers too. I told you we should have taken them on holiday with us."

"We should," agreed Lynn, "better to have wrecked them on the stony beach than to have them nicked! She deliberated, "I wonder why they left the boxes? Especially if they were going to sell them on."

"Maybe they're just wearing them," remarked Chris bitterly.

Their eyes met, then Chris turned away and resumed his inventory of the bedroom contents. Lynn continued checking her jewellery.

Within a few minutes Chris was back at the dressing room door, full of disbelief and indignation. "You will never believe what they've taken!"

"What?" Lynn turned towards the doorway.

"Twelve dispensers of toothpaste, eight cans of antiperspirant, and seven bottles of the balm I use on my head." He paused. "But this is the weird bit: they've left me two of each! Oh, and I told you they'd taken my new aftershave, but they've left me the open bottle of Beckham that Eileen bought me. Is that thoughtful or what?"

Lynn grimaced. "Well so far on my list I have. the bracelet and eternity ring you bought me, the gold bangle my parents bought me when I graduated, the gold Accurist watch and five unopened bottles of perfume that I inherited from your mam; four J'Adore and one Chanel No.5, and my new trainers." She took a deep breath. "They haven't taken my Chanel No.19 or my new Hugo Boss 'Femme'. I had the two 'in use' bottles on holiday with me. Also they have left quite a bit of jewellery – only taken the expensive stuff. One watch out of three, and they obviously didn't want any of my more modern hand-crafted jewellery: just gold and diamonds!"

"More saleable and less traceable, I expect," mused her husband. "Finish this room as well as you can, and I'll complete the bedroom, then let's have a cuppa and a snack. I really can't face a cooked meal tonight."

An hour later, Chris and Lynn were sitting in one corner of a still messed up living room, a cheese and tomato sandwich each and a cup of tea and coffee respectively, both looking very deflated.

"I still can't believe this is happening," ventured Lynn. "I feel as if I'm in the middle of a crazy dream."

"Well I can assure you, it is no dream!" replied Chris, "but I do think we are both in shock. I'm starting to have some ideas though… are you?"

"I thought about the window cleaners!" Chris opened his mouth to speak, but Lynn gestured him to let her continue. "For a start they are new around here. Everyone in the village always used Jim. For years! Since he retired we all seem to have different window cleaners. Also…" she hurried on, "they had a different person with them just before we went away. When I paid Tony, he said that he had his uncle with him, helping out."

"Hmm," Chris pondered. "I'm not going to dismiss it out of hand, but I have been thinking that maybe one of the burglars was a woman."

"What makes you think that?" She looked at him curiously.

"The lack of mess, for one thing. A woman, whilst she might be a thief, would perhaps be a controlling force, knowing that trashing a home, and other dirty stuff, would have far more impact on the victims, especially a woman, than a few things being taken. And…" he added, "they've been selective. In the whole scheme of things, not a great lot has been taken."

"Well, I agree with that." Lynn nodded. "The TVs and your laptop and gun are still here. From what I can see…" she looked about her, "all my china, crystal, pictures, music centre and CD player seem to be here. I haven't looked closely at downstairs rooms yet though."

"How about we put another hour or so in and call it a night?" suggested Chris. "I'll make the bedroom shipshape and you sort the kitchen out ready for the morning."

"Okay, I think that I'll want to clean everything in the bathroom too. It doesn't look as if they've been in there, but you never know." She looked around the room. "You know, the worst thing is not what they've taken but the fact that they have been in every room! Rummaged through our most personal possessions! I feel violated!" She suddenly burst into tears. "None of this would have happened if we hadn't extended our holiday."

Lynn slept fitfully that night, waking continually from stressful dreams. Almost every time she woke, the place next to her was empty and Chris was prowling around the house. On the couple of occasions he was in bed, he was sat propped up by pillows, with a large hammer beside him.

When morning finally came, they agreed that they both looked dreadful. "Enough to scare any burglar off," Lynn smiled wryly.

The day was busy with further phone calls, visits from the police and one from a victim support officer. In between, the couple continued their inventory of missing items, also confirming those items they suspected would have been taken were still there, and speculating again on the nature of the break-in and theft.

Jane had called in from her dog walk to see how they were bearing up and to ask if there was anything she could do. Over a coffee, Lynn showed her the "missing" list so far.

"It's a bit weird but it could be a lot worse," said her friend. "It seems to me that these burglars must have been on foot, maybe with a car parked discreetly somewhere else. Let's face it, in this street there's a good chance someone would notice a strange vehicle parked on the front, and you've no vehicular access at the back: high fence, no gate and just a field. I'm not saying that they couldn't have got over the back fence, but they'd have to pass or throw everything over and the closest they could get a car or van would be a hundred yards away."

"Chris has more or less been along those lines," agreed Lynn. "He reckons, two people, one a woman, leaving by the side gate with hand luggage: two bags each."

"I'm looking at your list so far and I'm not sure that I would need four bags to carry it: a couple of sports bags, one each if there were two people, which wouldn't particularly draw attention to anyone. The gym's open until 11pm."

They discussed possible scenarios for a few more minutes, then Jane and Barney took their leave.

Gradually the house was beginning to look back to normal, the only significant damage being to the kitchen window, which would have to be replaced. The insurance company had supplied them with details of the double glazing firm they dealt with and an appointment had already been made. Chris was researching home security firms with a view to having a house alarm installed, and also, as a knee-jerk reaction they had been discussing moving house and selling the motorhome. Was this burglary going to ruin the rest of their lives? Could they allow it to?

Later that day Lynn, who had still been going through the contents of all drawers and cupboards, restoring everything to its rightful place, announced that her collection of 50ps had been stolen. She had collected special edition 50p coins for some years and had around eighty coins. She had some duplicates and also a few other collectable coins. They were all missing. As they weren't boxed sets or "first editions" she was fairly certain that the insurance company would only give her face value: little compensation in her opinion.

While cleaning the kitchen, she had also discovered a footprint on the wall below the windowsill, and directly in line with the broken window where entry had been made. The print was quite clear and looked to be a small shoe size, smaller than her own size five. Perhaps Chris was right about one burglar being a woman. Could it even be a child? Oliver Twist popped into her mind. She shook her head. No, more likely a woman: the most expensive items that had been taken were jewellery and perfume. Someone had been very selective. She phoned Glen Miller and told him of the shoe print, and he had promised that someone would be out that afternoon to inspect it.

Shortly afterwards Lynn suddenly had a terrible thought. Her mother's jewellery, which she had inherited! Far more beautiful and more expensive than her own, she kept it in a nondescript box in an upstairs cupboard, which housed old paperwork, Christmas decorations, rolls of wallpaper, etc. The jewellery was valuable but more than that, of great sentimental value. She raced upstairs, heaved the contents of the cupboard onto the floor and found the old tattered box at the back and still intact. She pulled it out, sat on the bed and opened it, gazing at the contents with relief. There weren't many pieces, but each one worth quite a lot and separately insured. They were all there and she gently caressed a few of them, thinking of her mum as she did so. She carefully replaced them in the box, put it at the back of the top shelf and filled the cupboard again, purposely making it look messy with numerous items of little consequence.

The next few days were hectic, with telephone calls, interviews with home security firms, police visits and a lengthy victim support meeting. Chris and Lynn were introduced to various types of technology and gadgets to make their home safer and less penetrable and they took advantage of all of them. They upgraded their external doors and locks at the same time as their kitchen windows were being replaced. An alarm was fitted, and Chris installed external security lights in a number of locations around the outside of the house and garden.

Gradually they had reached the conclusion that they could not allow their lives to be ruined by the burglary and that they must continue to enjoy their motorhome. Most of their friends had now been informed of their return home and the break-in and all had been very supportive, arriving with condolences, flowers and wine.

When their friend Helen arrived the following weekend, Lynn told her of the stolen £200 but confirmed that the insurance policy would cover it. "I would have replaced it anyway, you know that, but it's good news that it is covered." They went on to discuss the other items stolen, Helen showing total incredulity at the list. Chris, who had been talking to Glen Miller the day before, recounted that Glen had said the three most commonly stolen items were perfume, coffee and meat. All were able to be sold quickly in pubs.

"Well, at least your meat and coffee were all with you in the motorhome," chuckled Helen, "and they were considerate enough to leave you enough toothpaste and deodorant to be going on with."

"Let's talk about something else," said Lynn. "I feel as if all we've done since we got home is to tell the same story over and over. Change of subject! How is Dave and has he got any work yet?"

"A couple of days doing a guvvy job, but better than nothing. Cash in hand. He's got a few applications in and he's registered with an agency, but that's about it."

Helen's husband was frequently out of work, and Chris and Lynn knew that they often struggled to make ends meet. Luckily Helen's own job was stable, though she did have to work shifts.

They passed the rest of the evening talking about Helen's dogs, avoiding burglary related topics completely. As Helen was getting ready to depart she asked Lynn, "Are you going to start over collecting 50 pence pieces? If so I'll keep a look out for some."

"I'm not sure I'll bother again. It kind of knocks the interest out of you, something like this."

"Oh, I think you should try…"

When Helen arrived the next Saturday, her first move was to put three 50 pence pieces in Lynn's hand. "A start to your collection."

Lynn examined them. "Votes for women 1903 – a good one," she smiled, and looked at the others. "Battle of Britain 1940 and VC medals. Yes, I had all of these, but now…"

"Oh go on! Get collecting, and I'll keep a look out for different ones. That's what friends are for." She hesitated then asked, "Any progress with the investigation? Or with your insurance?"

"Not really. It's early days and these things seem to move very slowly. Chris hasn't got much confidence in the police I'm afraid." She glanced at her husband.

"No I haven't," he retorted. "These incidents need to be acted upon quickly. For a start, the perfume and toiletries were probably sold the same or the next night in the pubs. It's too late now and they're hardly traceable!

"And you know what? We told Glen Miller about the window cleaners, he went and had a word with them, and reported back to us that they weren't wearing Nike trainers. Well that's conclusive!" he finished sarcastically.

The evening passed slowly. Lynn and Chris hadn't any news to impart other than lack of progress with the investigation. Helen's husband was still unemployed, and Helen herself had been on nightshift and also worked some overtime. By 10 o'clock they had all run out of steam and Helen stood up to take her leave. She fished a £20 note out of her pocket and handed it to Lynn. "I'm still giving you money to save for me. I know you'll replace the other £200 for me."

"Of course I will," said Lynn. "It was my fault that it was in the house and not in the bank before we went away." They hugged each other and Helen went on her way.

―――

"Why does Helen still save money with you when Dave's not working? She never seems to need to draw any back out," asked Chris as they were getting ready for bed.

"I don't know – maybe she needs a safety net in case she gets made redundant, or maybe she doesn't trust him not to empty their bank account."

"Or maybe she's going to leave him?" offered Chris.

"I really don't think so. They do lead very different lives, but they just seem to rub along together. I've never really got along with Dave myself and I haven't seen him for years, but he always seems to be out of work. He's had loads of jobs, but never seems to be able to keep them. I've often wondered whether it's to do with his personality, which is strange to say the least, or whether maybe he just doesn't like work!" She shrugged.

~~~

The next three weeks were very busy, with new house alarm, kitchen windows and back door all being fitted. Jane popped in regularly to see how they both were, bringing them pieces of cake she had baked and little posies from her garden. She came for a lesson on how to work the alarm, and took a key for the new back door. "You *are* going to go away again," she said. "You can't let this stop you from having the lifestyle you've wanted for so long."

"But we feel awful about what you have had to deal with, Jane," said Chris, "and we definitely don't want you to be worried or uncomfortable about looking after the house."

"I'm fine with it. We're friends, and friends help each other. You take me to the vets with Barney when I need it. That's what friends are for!"

~~~

Helen continued her usual Saturday evening visits, and each week brought with her £20 and two or three 50 pence pieces. Lynn paid for her collectors items with ordinary 50ps or pound coins, and now she had acquired, via Helen, coins featuring The Commonwealth Games, Benjamin Britten, the Great Britain Olympic Swimming Team for 2016, The Centenary of the Girl Guides and the Isle of Man Christmas 2002. Well, she supposed, it was a start!

They still talked regularly about the burglary and also about the new security measures in place. Helen seemed anxious to know whether the police had made any progress with the investigation, so Chris assured her that whether the thieves were caught or not, the insurance company would still pay out the stolen £200, so she need not worry.

"No, I'm not worried about that," she replied, "I just wondered if they had anyone in the frame for the crime. Any clues for example?"

"Just the partial fingerprints and a training shoe print outside the kitchen window where they got in: a Nike size 8," volunteered Lynn, "and I also showed them another footprint on the inside wall under the window. They had missed that!" She continued, "It was a small print: I reckon either a 3 or 3 and a half. I had a size 5 sandal and I measured it against the print. The footprint was smaller, so I'm thinking that a small person got through the window first and put their foot against the wall to help them get down. Maybe the bigger person needed to give the smaller one a leg up, hence the size 8 prints immediately outside the kitchen window."

"Maybe it was a child," Helen remarked, "like Oliver, you know." She smiled.

"Already been on that," said Lynn.

"Well, whatever, I don't think the police are going to resolve this case," said Chris. "They had a suspect and they ruled him out because the training shoes he had on weren't Nikes. I ask you!"

"Was that the window cleaner you told me about?" asked Helen.

"Yes! Let's be honest it's the perfect job to get away with being nosey and sussing out people's houses," said Lynn tartly.

Chris interjected, "She's got me convinced, Helen. We specifically told them not to clean the windows while we were away, so that both side gates remained locked. It was a bit pointless not revealing our intended absence to them, because, let's be honest: if the motorhome is gone then so are we!

"Anyway the police talked to Tony and his 'uncle' and to our neighbours and it turns out that Tony was on holiday *apparently*. The uncle, however, did clean our windows, and because the gates to the back of the house were padlocked, he borrowed a garden chair from next door and climbed over to clean them. Well, why would a part-time window cleaner go to that trouble for an extra £5 – to be paid several weeks later, because whatever else, he knew we weren't at home." He paused, then added, "He could have even jemmied the window when he was 'cleaning' it. Then he returns that night, or another, we don't really know when – and lets himself and an accomplice in without any noise."

Helen nodded. "It sounds feasible, but it also seems as if they haven't got sufficient evidence to pin anything on him."

"The police are absolute rubbish," said Chris cynically, "this kid here has got more off than the lot of them." He gestured towards Lynn. "She even knows what time the burglars were here!" He looked expectantly at his wife.

"The lights were on timers: two downstairs and one in our bedroom. Most of the 'activity', we'll call it, took place upstairs. The bedroom light will have come on at a quarter past ten. I reckon they were in the bedroom at that time and the light will have momentarily alarmed them. Someone went straight over and switched it off at the wall. So two things… one the timer stops at the exact time that it was switched off, and two, the way the timer fits against the wall switch, you can barely get a finger into the space. My theory therefore: someone with a small hand, and I doubt whether even they could get a gloved finger into the space." Ergo a fingerprint! Were the police interested? No!"

Helen's eyes widened as she gaped at her friend. "Amazing! You should have been a detective Lynn. It doesn't sound as though they are going to get anybody for this does it?"

"They won't," sneered Chris, "and mark my words, I think they've stopped investigating already and moved on. A small burglary like this is of no importance to them. I'll tell you what, I wish I could get my hands on them. I'd give them the justice they deserve. They wouldn't be able to rob anyone else. In fact they wouldn't be able to feed themselves."

"Let's talk about something else," interjected Lynn. "We are worn out discussing it. She looked at Helen. "How are the dogs?"

Three days later Glen Miller phoned to inform them that he was closing the case.

Jane had persuaded her friends that they should go for another break in their motorhome. She had been very supportive throughout their trauma, and now that all the business was concluded and the house made as secure as was financially viable, she advised them to get away for a while to regain their confidence. Chris had latterly put even more security lights around the external walls, the latest ones flashing as soon as a person came within their range, and certain to draw attention to any would-be intruder. As well as the new door, windows and locks, the windows also now had a variety of individual alarms, and Lynn had "smart watered" all portable items of value. Additionally the whole neighbourhood was on red alert!

As usual Helen arrived on the Saturday evening before the start of their break, bringing with her a bottle of wine and three more 50 pence pieces. "I haven't brought my £20," she explained, "I didn't think you'd want to leave it in the house."

"I don't want to leave anything in the house," replied Lynn. "In fact I don't really want to leave the house! – but I know we've got to at some point."

"We can't let the bastards ruin our lives," Chris snarled. "I just wish I could get my hands on them. I'd certainly ruin their lives."

After they'd eaten, Chris elected to wash up, so as they were just past the solstice and the evenings were light, Lynn suggested to Helen that they take the dogs for a short stroll along the riverside. They walked in silence, watching the two collies chasing through the long grass. As the minutes passed, the lack of conversation was becoming increasingly uncomfortable until eventually Helen spoke. "Chris has taken the whole burglary thing very badly, even though very little of his was actually taken, hasn't he? I've never known him to be so aggressive. He seems hell-bent on revenge!"

"Well it's an awful thing, Helen, to have your home violated like this. Just the fact that someone has been through all your personal stuff! I'll admit that the actual value of what was taken wasn't immense but that's not the point. It's an infringement on your privacy – and there's still this weirdness about the things they took." She paused. "Chris's toothpaste! I ask you! He likes the dispensers rather than tubes. They're £3 in the supermarkets, but whenever they have them in the Pound Shop, he buys in bulk. So what are the thieves going to do? Sell them in a pub for 50p each? It's mental!"

Helen gave her a sidelong glance. "Maybe they just kept them to use themselves. It strikes me that the people who broke into your house were probably very badly off, to take such basic stuff. Also they obviously didn't want to make a mess or take anything that might be of sentimental value."

"How could they know what was and wasn't of sentimental value Helen? How can I ever replace the gold bangle my mam and dad bought me for my graduation? Another bangle won't do!"

"You never know, your bangle may still turn up…"

"I hardly think so! I've turned the house upside down. It has definitely been stolen."

"I was thinking of maybe at a jewellers – one who deals in second-hand gold and stuff."

Lynn stared at her derisively for a moment, then she said, "It strikes me that you're feeling almost sympathetic towards our burglars. Why?"

Helen's face flushed. "Well, I know what it's like to be broke. I'm not saying it's right, but I can understand people becoming desperate if they're unemployed and struggling to make ends meet."

They walked in silence again.

"I wish we'd just come home when we originally intended to," sighed Lynn, "and maybe none of this would have happened. We should never have extended the holiday."

"You can't say that..." replied Helen. "It could have happened on any of your holidays."

"It could," admitted Lynn, "but I can't help feeling that it was someone with personal knowledge of our whereabouts or intentions. For example the window cleaners knew how long we were going to be away, so surely they would have 'done the job' earlier in the holiday, instead of the night of the day we were expected home. They could have been caught in the act! So... I'm beginning to think *not the window cleaners*."

"So what do you think?" asked Helen cautiously.

"Someone who knew we had just extended our holiday," replied Lynn equally carefully, "someone who knew we wouldn't be back for a week. So that narrows down the field of suspects considerably."

"So who knew that you'd booked another week?" asked Helen.

"Jane and Andy, Alison and you! That's all!"

"But any one of us could have unwittingly mentioned it to someone else. You really can't think that any of your mates would do this to you."

Lynn studied Helen's face intently, then said slowly, "Let's just put some facts out there for consideration: Dave is unemployed, can't seem to hold a job down anywhere. We know he does 'guvvy' jobs. We know that when he was working, he'd 'acquire' materials from work: like the boiler! Let's just say that you probably told him we were staying away for another week: he would know if we'd told you, that it was true, and therefore safe. How am I doing so far?"

Helen's face and neck were now bright red, but she said nothing.

Lynn continued. "For all you plead poverty, you give me money every week to put in a savings account for you, and you've never needed to draw upon it even when Dave hasn't had work for months. I can only conclude that Dave contributes income from his extra-curricular activities. Come on Helen, we know that Dave is a wide boy, and we know he doesn't care for your friendship with Chris or me. The fact that your account now stands at over £2,000 – is this your way of money laundering? Because you do know that you may be every bit as implicated as he is."

"You haven't a shred of proof about any of this," shouted Helen, "and I could do you for slander!"

"Well you could try," said Lynn calmly, "but I would then have to prove that it wasn't slander but the truth. I wonder how you would feel about an investigation into your finances."

There was a pregnant pause and then Lynn continued. "Look Helen, we've been friends for a long time now and I don't want to think of you being implicated in your husband's wrongdoings, but I do want honesty from you. Does our friendship count for nothing?"

She took hold of Helen's shoulders. Staring into her eyes. "It was Dave, wasn't it?"

"Yes," murmured Helen sullenly.

"Did you know this before or after he broke in then?"

"Before! In fact if it wasn't for me, it might have been a lot worse."

Suddenly Lynn had an epiphany. "You came with him, didn't you? Size three and a half trainers – your trainers! How could you?"

"How could I not?" came the reply. "I made him be careful. I wouldn't let him trash the house, and I wouldn't let him take certain things. He only wanted things he could turn over quickly and I knew that the perfume was only recently acquired from Chris's mam's stuff. It was a sort of 'what you've never had you'll never miss' situation. The perfume was gone the same night, so were the trainers. Dave got the £200, so I took the 50ps so that I could give them back to you a bit at a time.

"I wouldn't let him touch Chris's mam's jewellery or anything that I thought was of sentimental value. He never even got near *your* mam's jewellery and stuff. I know where it is hidden, so as soon as he started to open that cupboard, I told him not to waste time on a cupboard that I knew was just full of old wallpaper, and Christmas paper and decorations."

She looked at Lynn plaintively. "I really did my best to control the situation. If I'd just butted out, he would have still done you over and I don't know what he might have taken, or done!"

"What about my jewellery?" asked Lynn, "It's not as if I had very much to start with."

"I just thought you'd be less bothered about that than your mam's stuff."

"Well, the bracelet and eternity ring were gifts from Chris and that's bad enough, but the gold bangle was from Mam and Dad when I got my degree. How can that be all right?"

Helen's face crumpled. "I'm really sorry Lynn. I can't get anything back, Dave's mate has already taken all the jewellery down to London, so it's probably gone for good."

"So why did he take all the toothpaste, deodorant and stuff? What profit could there possibly be in that?"

"I did it! Just to save having to buy it and I thought it was better to take things that were of little consequence to you, and could easily be replaced."

They'd almost completed their circular walk. Helen called the dogs and clicked on their leads. "I won't come in," she said, "and I'm really, really sorry about everything, but I did what I thought of as damage limitation. Whatever else, I couldn't have stopped Dave and I know how hard you've worked on the house. I also knew those things that meant the most to you. At least, I thought I did! So I did what I thought was right by you, and isn't that what friends are for?"

"Helen, you know that if you had needed money, I would have given it to you, plus you have £2,000 sitting in an account in your name."

"But Dave doesn't know anything about that. It's my escape route."

The two women looked at one another for a long time, hugged briefly, then Lynn turned away. "This is what's called a blind eye – acceptance of a situation you cannot do anything about. *That's* what friends are for!"

The Revenge of Benj

Benj, or Benjamin as he was originally christened, was ninety-eight now. He'd been considered good-looking and debonair once but time had taken its toll and his appearance now was unkempt to say the least. He hadn't much grey hair, only the bits that had been that silvery blue colour in his more youthful days. He hadn't had a haircut in a long while and he was a mass of matted curls, which hid both his eyes and ears. That didn't really matter too much to his failing, opaque and cataracted eyes and as he hadn't been able to hear anything for the last twenty-one years, he wasn't at all bothered by the quantities of hair that sprouted in and around his rather leathery ears. Thankfully and amazingly, he still had all his teeth though they were yellowed with age and in some places stained brown. His breath was putrid. Benj had always had a pretty volatile temper right from reaching adolescence, and even in his younger days when he'd embarked on one of his more determined expressions of wilfulness, the rest of the family knew better than to attempt to deter or hinder him. Benj was single-minded! He was The Boss!

He had lived for a great number of years, he couldn't remember exactly how many, with Lorna and Philip, Susan and Carole; the latter years with Lorna and Philip only, the girls having long since flown the nest. As part of this trio, Benj had finally settled into a life of routine and boredom. Not that he minded routine – his life was built around it. He liked to take his exercise at the same time every day. He liked his tea at 5pm on the dot and complained loudly and repeatedly if there was any delay. If he fancied an occasional break away from the monotony, he could usually introduce some new mischief of his own: some unexpected deviation from the well-ordered schedule of the daily family life. He could if he chose cause complete mayhem, and he seemed to rather enjoy this special power.

Lorna could usually be relied upon to rise to the challenge, pick up the Benj gauntlet and run with it. Sometimes, although she would never have admitted it, she actually enjoyed and covertly encouraged his little demonstrations of power and rebellion. She and Benj had long since arrived at a mutual respect and she would smile secretly to herself, and even take a certain pride in his natural arrogance, as he thrust his head forward and went full steam into some new exploit.

Philip was another matter. He liked and needed routine and order every bit as much as Benj. He was an accountant and a man of precise, almost military habit. He rose at 6.45 every morning, showered and dressed for work, went down to breakfast at 7.05, ate a bowl of porridge and one slice of toast with lemon marmalade, and drank two cups of tea. He set off for work at precisely 7.30, having exchanged the briefest of good mornings and farewells with both Lorna and Benj. Since the idiosyncrasies of Philip's working day at the office did not affect Benj one way or another, they are of no consequence and will not be described. However, he left the office at 5pm precisely and his average time of arrival at home was 5.27. It annoyed him that due to traffic variations he was unable to be more specific. Benj had already eaten his meal by this time, since he could not be prevailed upon to wait for Philip's unpredictable return. At

6.30 Benj took his evening stroll, after which as far as he was concerned, the day was over.

On Sundays only, Philip accompanied Benj on his morning jaunt. The route they took was "the Sunday riverside walk": different from the walks during the rest of the week but a repetitious weekly pilgrimage nonetheless. In latter months, however, they had often returned to the house on less than friendly terms, Philip moody and silent, Benj serenely smug, having thrown in a last minute variation on the route.

From Benj achieving his ninety-first year and Lorna her fifty-second, there dawned a realisation on that lady that life as she knew it had become almost as exciting as a stagnant pond. In short she wanted excitement! She began to rebel against the hitherto military approach of the family to each week, each day, each hour... Reluctant at first to take any initiative herself to change her lifestyle, she began to look forward to the surprise sallies that Benj inflicted upon them. She grasped each new opportunity he presented to her, with a spirit of adventure. Indeed the very unpredictability of Benj's nature meant that there could be a run of several days where the normal routine was strictly observed, but this could be followed by either a single day, or a series of days where any kind of normal timetable went straight out of the window. Walks were blatantly extended, new routes were daringly explored, and meals were served at ridiculous times!

Things reached a climax when one day Philip returned from work at the usual 5.27 to find the house and meal completely abandoned. The two truants returned at 5.50 to find Philip peeling potatoes in a great state of agitation. While Benj immediately collapsed in a heap in the lounge, Lorna guiltily took over the preparation of tea. The whole routine, however, was upset for the entire evening. The format of the conversation during tea was always strictly adhered to. First was a résumé of

Philip's day, including what he had eaten for lunch in the work's canteen. This was followed by Lorna's account of her day, which may have included details of her sojourn to the supermarket, library or bank, according to which day of the week it was. Benj's exploits and mood came last. By the time the family were having coffee, most of the affairs of a domestic nature had been covered and it was time to turn on the news and weather forecast.

Tonight, though dinner and small talk proceeded as usual (there had been enough deviation for one day!) the first 30 minutes of the news was over by the time Philip had turned on the television. He had to change channels for a later news slot to ensure that he caught the most important headline stories. He didn't recognise the newsreader, and the format of the programme was different. Everything conspired to annoy him. He sighed and tutted frequently, then switched off prematurely, muttering about being late for switching on his computer and doing his daily download. He gave Benj a disdainful look and went upstairs to the office.

This was only the first of many such occurrences. Lorna seemed different. She didn't seem to mind these alterations to their daily routine; in fact she seemed to be thriving on it! She began to introduce changes of her own. She served chicken chasseur on a Tuesday when Philip normally expected toad in the hole! She joined an art class, which commenced at 5pm on Wednesdays, thus affecting both Benj's and Philip's meals. She'd prepared everything in advance, of course, but it meant that Philip had to cook tea when he came home from work.

A few weeks after this, Lorna noticed an advertisement in a local charity shop for voluntary help. On impulse she went in and offered her services. That committed her to Monday afternoons and Saturday mornings. At home she told Philip that he would need to start the tea on Mondays and that she would take over when she came home. Although Philip did not "do" arguments (they were too time consuming), it would not be stretching a point to say that Lorna's peculiar behaviour went down like the proverbial pork pie at a Bar Mitzvah. He had said coldly that he would "give it a go". However, he hadn't bargained for Benj's lack of co-operation…

On the first Monday of Lorna's charity shop session, Philip arrived home punctually to find Benj pacing the floor like a caged tiger. His tea was half an hour late! It was nearly time for his evening stroll! Even if he had his tea now, it would hardly have time to settle before his exercise! Exercise on a full stomach was bad! Where was Lorna? In his agitation he accidentally urinated. Both he and Philip looked aghast for a second, then Benj hung his head ashamed and Philip looked embarrassed for him. Philip left the room without a word and returned with a bucket of hot water, disinfectant and a cloth. He soaked up the pool and disinfected the area. He was just rinsing the cloth and bucket when Lorna arrived home.

Excited and enthusiastic, she launched straight into an account of her afternoon at the shop, not taking in the domestic scene and the tense atmosphere at all. Curtly Philip said, "Could this wait until we have a meal on the table?"

"Yes, of course," agreed his wife. "Oh, you haven't even started anything yet!" as she glanced around the kitchen.

"Benj peed himself," said Philip in a low growl.

"Oh how embarrassing for him – poor old man. Is he okay? Tell you what, I'll make his tea quickly, and you put some rice on for us. I took two portions of chilli out of the freezer this morning and it's just to heat up."

They could hear Benj complaining again in the living room. "Come on Benj, I've got some roast chicken here for you. I know you can't eat chilli."

It was 6.25 before Lorna and Philip were sitting down to their evening meal. Lorna had opened a bottle of red wine. "To celebrate!" she said grinning.

"And what might we be celebrating?" asked Philip with an edge of sarcasm in his voice.

"My new job! It's brilliant!" as she launched into a detailed account of her afternoon.

"It's hardly a job though," said Philip when she eventually paused for breath. "It's not as if you're earning anything."

"Money! That's all you think about. Oh, it will be so worthwhile and rewarding!" exclaimed Lorna. "Now, tell me about your day."

It's far too late, and we've missed the news *again*," said Philip peevishly, "and I've got to do my download." He rose from the table.

"Well, Benj and I will go for our constitutional then," said Lorna, oblivious to her husband's mood.

As the weeks wore on the irritations in the Gurney household increased. For how much of it Benj was responsible, is uncertain, but an antagonism was building up between Lorna and Philip, like storm clouds gathering. There were arguments as never before; never directly about Benj, but he certainly featured in them with regularity. These confrontations were usually followed by long periods of silence, especially from Philip. Lorna's changed attitude to the family routine, which had stood the test of the last seven years, both confused and incensed Philip. His need for order, regularity and predictability in his life were vital to his well-being.

It sometimes seemed to him that both Lorna and Benj were ranged against him: each of them hell-bent on bringing chaos into almost every day. He tried resolutely to adhere to his usual daily timetable, only to be thwarted by an apparent lack of co-operation by either or both of them. Up to a point Philip was more inclined to excuse Benj his idiosyncrasies on the grounds of age and infirmity, although he did find some of his recently acquired habits intolerable.

A major source of annoyance was the newspaper. Philip had always laid claim to the daily newspaper before anyone else. It was his custom to glance at the headlines and finance pages over breakfast. He would then fold the paper very neatly and place it on the left arm of his armchair to peruse it more fully in the evening. Lorna rarely glanced at it during the day but if she did, she would ensure that it was folded the same way, and laid in precisely the same position. However, Benj had quite suddenly taken to picking up the paper from the doormat before Philip came downstairs, and having tired of it after a short while, would cast it aside and leave it in such a condition that Philip was outraged. After three consecutive mornings of this, he ranted at Lorna. "Look at the mess of this paper! Is there any need for it? Can't you do something about it?"

"For heavens sake Philip, you're completely overreacting. It's only a newspaper, and it's still all there."

"That's not the point! You know I like the pages to be neat and tidy! Even when the girls were at home no one ever touched the paper until I had read it. You'll have to sort it out with Benj. I don't know why he's suddenly started bothering with the newspaper at his age – he's never been interested in it before!"

He had gone to work that morning without even opening the paper, and fumed about it all day.

Far worse for Philip, though, was the sudden and inexplicable change in his wife, which he neither liked nor understood. These days she was rarely home when he returned from his day at the office. She made demands of him, which he felt quite unequal to. Her Saturday mornings in the charity shop meant that he was left alone with Benj and never did one Saturday pass without incident.

On Lorna's first Saturday in the shop, he found that he was expected to do some shopping for the weekend as Lorna had forgotten that she would be unable to do it. "You'll manage," she'd said, "I've written you a list. Oh, and I usually let Benj go with me for the ride."

By the time Lorna returned home mid-afternoon Philip was livid with rage, and Benj was nowhere to be seen. "Where's Benj?" she enquired.

"He's still in the car," spluttered Philip. "He's been in there since mid-morning. He absolutely refuses to get out – and he has totally embarrassed me in the ASDA car park this morning."

"Oh, what's he been up to now?" asked Lorna indulgently.

"Whilst I was loading the shopping into the car, he got out, and the next thing I knew, he'd got into someone else's car. What a job I had getting him out. Stubborn old bastard! There were children in the car, and they thought it was a huge joke." Philip paused for breath. "They had sweets and he was cadging them – he was positively disgusting! He had melted chocolate all over his face and the kids were giggling at him. I was *mortified*!"

"Poor Benj – he can't help being a bit absent-minded. At his age we just have to expect it."

"Poor Benj! What about poor Philip? *He* is becoming a damn nuisance! A bloody liability!"

"You'll be old yourself one day, and no doubt you'll expect a lot of tolerance then. Come to think of it, you do now."

"If I ever get like that I'll shoot myself," retorted Philip.

"I'll buy you the gun, dear. Do you think you can wait until next week?"

"You get him out of the car – or lock him in and throw the keys away," yelled Philip, and stamped out of the room.

Philip never took Benj shopping again. In fact he steadfastly refused to do any Saturday morning visits to the supermarket in case he saw anyone who had witnessed "*the incident*" as he darkly referred to it.

Relations between Philip and Benj were crumbling at a rate of knots, and relations between husband and wife were little better. Arguments had become a way of life. Lorna was rebellious, Philip inflexible! Lorna required new mental stimulation and was of a mind to go out and find it. Philip was staid and wanted the security of knowing every day would be the same as it had always been. Lorna was taking on new challenges: all of them increasing her independence and taking her to activities outside of the marital home. She was moving on; her life was changing, and Philip, unfortunately, was not. They were not so much drifting apart, as accelerating in totally opposite directions.

Whilst Benj was the subject of many of their arguments, he, himself seemed relatively unaffected by it. He continued to enjoy life at his own pace, oblivious to the disruption all around him. He was, however, beginning to realise that Lorna was spending less and less time with him. He was left alone while she went to classes and courses, and to her voluntary work. He didn't mind this too much – he often had a nap in the middle of the day, and if he wasn't dozing on the sofa, he would wander about the house, poking into all kinds of forbidden places. It was exciting! Confusing, but exciting!

What really bothered Benj most about the new regime was that his tea now appeared to be a moveable feast and likewise his evening walk. Lorna still accompanied him in the mornings, but in the evenings her timing was irregular and erratic. Sometimes they were late in their start times, he often felt unnecessarily hurried along and his old, feeble limbs were unable to cope. Once or twice he had fallen and had difficulty getting up again. When Lorna had tried to assist him, he had nearly taken her head off in anger. The worst thing of all, however, was the fact that Philip instead of Lorna occasionally accompanied him.

This was intolerable! Philip was less patient than Lorna. His pace was unsympathetic with a nonagenarian, and worst of all – he completed the route without uttering a single word. This was all Lorna's fault!

The walks were also a trial for Philip. He didn't quite have it in him to make Benj go out alone. The old codger might get lost or run over, or even forget where he lived, and ultimately that would result in more embarrassment for Philip, or even criticism for being irresponsible or uncaring. What was Lorna thinking of, upscuttling all of their lives like this. This was all her fault!

Lorna and Philip's eldest daughter, Susan, was married to a Spaniard and had lived in Spain for the last three years. The family, with the exception of Benj, was excitedly awaiting the birth of Susan's first child. (It didn't matter to Benj at all because he was unlikely to ever see the child.)

The child was born – a little girl, Lucia, and Lorna determined to go out to Spain for Susan coming out of hospital with the baby. There was no question of Philip accompanying her – he said that he could not spare the time from work, especially so close to the end of the financial year. Undeterred, Lorna booked her flight. Two days before she was due to depart, Benj became ill. He had a severe attack of gastritis: he'd had a bad dose of the runs, which had left his tummy still groggy and his legs very weak and unsteady. "You can't leave him when he's like this," Philip had said. "You'll have to cancel your flight."

"No way! It's not as if it's just a holiday. This is a *baby*. This is important."

"But I'll be out from half past seven in the morning until well after five – Benj can't be left all day when he's so ill and helpless. What if he takes a turn for the worse?"

"Jan across the road is going to look in on him at lunchtime each day and make sure he's got everything he needs, and if he does get any worse you'll have to take a day or two off work till I get back. Heaven knows I've done my fair share!"

"If it was that easy to take time off, I'd be coming to Spain with you to see my grandchild," retorted Philip, "and you know that I can't deal with anyone throwing up – I never could when the girls were small."

"No, that's the trouble, Philip, you don't do 'difficult' – you never have! Well, you'll have to learn if necessary. I'm going to Spain!"

And she had gone!

Benj hadn't taken a turn for the worse in Lorna's absence, but he had taken a few days to get over his "attack". As he regained his strength he became increasingly morose. Left to his own devices in the house, he wandered from room to room, feeling his way around the familiar furniture, his eyes only able to see dark shapes. Occasionally he misjudged distances and knocked something over, and he would grumble and growl as he tried to negotiate his way around it. He was unable to hear Jan letting herself in at lunchtime and was therefore usually taken unawares, jumping as she touched him to let him know she was there. She would make him a snack and check each room to ensure that any mishaps were discovered and obstacles removed. She usually left a note for Philip telling him of any difficulties Benj had experienced during the day.

Philip was having difficulties of his own. He had to get up thirty minutes earlier each morning to allow time to see to Benj and settle him with everything he might need before he left for the office. On his return Benj would invariably be complaining and requiring his tea immediately if not sooner. Then, Philip would have hardly finished his own tea when Benj wanted to go for his evening stroll. Philip accompanied him grudgingly, his own evening timetable completely abandoned. He hadn't always time to do his daily download, and on several evenings he simply flopped in front of the television. This seemingly innocent pastime, however, brought its own problems, and led to another "Benj incident".

After washing up one evening, Philip entered the living room, where he had left the TV on, to find Benj in possession of the remote control. Philip had gone to take it from him, and possession being nine tenths of the law, he was met by a stare of belligerence and malice. It was a "Don't you dare" stare. He withdrew his hand.

Philip sat down and stared at the screen, trying to identify the channel. Within five minutes, however, Benj clicked a button and changed the channel. He gazed vacantly at the TV for a couple of minutes and then wriggled uncomfortably and changed channels again. A jingle from a well-known advert was on. Philip would have sworn that Benj could neither see nor hear it, and yet he appeared to spring to life at it, apparently riveted to the screen.

Benj had never had a particularly long attention span, and now his concentration waned in the middle of the second advertisement. He fidgeted and changed channels again. Philip was practically apoplectic. Fearful of what he might do or say in rage, he leapt up from his armchair and bounded upstairs to the sanctuary of his computer room. He didn't venture downstairs again until Benj was sleeping soundly and the remote control had fallen to the floor. He clicked the television off and went to bed.

Philip couldn't wait for Lorna to come home. She had phoned only once, the day after her departure, just to say that she had arrived safely and that Lucia was beautiful. In spite of their strained relations, undeniably he missed her. His life was topsy-turvy, Benj was unbelievably demanding and Philip began to realise how much of the responsibility for Benj, Lorna took upon herself. Still, he told himself, it was her fault that Benj was with them at all. He hadn't wanted him to come to live with them in the first place! Well, another two days and she would be home, and he, Philip, would have some respite. Perhaps their lives could resume normality...

Over the two years following Lorna's redundancy, she had applied for numerous jobs without success. As time went on her enthusiasm for job hunting had waned and she had become more and more despondent about her career prospects. When she saw the advertisement for a local post in nursery education, she almost didn't bother to send for the details, even though it seemed to be exactly what she had been looking for a year ago. However, spurred on by her deteriorating marriage, and realising that the only way she could leave Philip was to be financially independent, she rallied, and before going to Spain, she sent off several job applications, including the nursery education one.

Lorna's break in Spain had given her some thinking time too. More and more she came to the realisation that the three-way relationship she was part of at home could only get worse. She and Philip had no marriage to speak of, and she simply could not live the rest of her life so miserable, disillusioned and poor. She'd tried to create a more fulfilling life for herself with her hobbies and voluntary work but she was still financially dependent on Philip. He in turn disapproved of everything she did that interrupted his own routine. He constantly poured cold water upon all her hopes and ideas, and berated her lack of earnings. In addition he and Benj were permanently at loggerheads, and she was endlessly pulled one way then another in an endeavour to keep the peace.

Obviously if she left home, Benj would come with her; he was her responsibility at the end of the day, but she had no idea how she would cope with him on her own, especially if she managed to find a job. It was unthinkable in her mind to put him in a home.

On Lorna's return from Spain, the family reunion was lukewarm, but a letter awaited her, inviting her to an interview the following week. She could hardly believe it – only her second interview in two years! She was simultaneously excited and terrified. Philip was dour and tight-lipped, and Benj was totally mystified and uncomprehending at what all the fuss was about.

It seemed like a miracle to Lorna when she was offered the nursery school job, and she accepted immediately with undisguised delight. When Philip came home that evening Lorna triumphantly presented him with her news and start date. His reaction was bathos at its best! "And what about *him*?" he said, staring pointedly at Benj, who was half-sat, half-laid on the sofa, staring unseeingly at the TV, and equally oblivious to the atmosphere.

"I'll sort something out. I thought you would at least have been pleased that I am going to be earning," retorted Lorna tartly. "Thanks for all your support!" she added sarcastically as she returned to the kitchen.

Lorna had slept in the spare bedroom since her return from Spain two weeks before. Even so she could still hear Philip's snoring from the main bedroom at the opposite side of the landing. Benj also regularly padded about in the night sleepless and confused, and she could hear him pattering on the tiled kitchen floor. On both counts Lorna slept fitfully, her ears attuned for the two sets of familiar noises. Several times a night she would wake and lie listening, for what seemed an eternity, frustrated at her waking, her mind unable to switch off from the latest "domestic".

She had woken at 2.15 to the usual background of noise. When she woke at four, her ears and brain were endeavouring to synchronise, when she jerked to a higher level of consciousness. Although Philip's voice was faint, there was no mistaking the urgency of his calls for help. Lorna stumbled from her bed and across the landing. Philip's body, only half covered by the duvet was contorted in pain and he was half groaning, half sobbing with pain and fear. Using all her powers of control to remain calm, Lorna asked him questions, trying to identify the location and nature of the pain.

"I think I need a doctor, or to go to the hospital," Philip's voice, stilted and barely audible, snapped Lorna into action. Uttering a few words of empathy and encouragement, she hastily grabbed the telephone and frantically dialled the emergency number. An ambulance was with them in less than ten minutes, and in a very few more minutes both were speeding to the local hospital, lights blazing and sirens wailing. Philip was stretchered and wearing an oxygen mask, while Lorna sat opposite him tense and watchful.

Even at 4.30am the A&E unit was busy, and it was some thirty minutes later when a duty doctor entered the sterile cubicle where Philip was laid, and carried out an examination of his chest and abdomen. The result was inconclusive, but his opinion was that the most sinister possibilities could be ruled out. "I don't think you've got anything more than a mild gastric disorder," he'd said, "I think you'll find that it settles down in 24 hours. You can use paracetomol for the pain. They shouldn't upset your stomach."

The doctor had confirmed that he was happy for Philip to be discharged, and soon they were heading homewards in a taxi.

There was tension between them, and Lorna watched Philip's face anxiously. His breathing still seemed laboured, and he continued to hold his middle, his face creased with pain. As Lorna helped her husband out of the taxi, she exclaimed in horror, "Oh, My God! Look at your face – it has the most awful rash!"

Back in the house Philip collapsed on the sofa. Benj was pacing about in agitation not knowing what was going on, or whether it was morning or not. Lorna opened the curtains and examined her husband's face in the natural morning light. The rash was across his forehead and consisted of blotches of an ugly purplish hue. She fetched a hand mirror so that Philip could see for himself. Perspiration was standing on his brow, making the inflamed patches glisten. He stared at his reflection, his eyes wide with panic. He knew that he was feeling worse every minute.

"Can you help me to get back to bed?" his voice was almost a whisper. One hand still clutching his abdomen, he rolled off the sofa, and crawled painfully to the foot of the stairs. Between them they managed somehow to get Philip back into bed, where he lay, curled up in a foetus position, silently shaking and weeping with relief and exhaustion. Reluctantly he took the two tablets offered by Lorna, and managed to swallow them with water. She covered him tenderly and sat beside him, resting her hand lightly on his shoulder. She was more shocked than she would have believed possible. She had convinced herself that her feelings of love and affection for this man had largely died, a process which had accelerated over the last few confrontational months. She couldn't have said now whether she felt love, or pity, or even just the empathy of one human being for another in the face of very real suffering… she just didn't know what she felt… probably fear most of all!

Lorna watched the minutes ticking slowly away on the alarm clock by the bed. She listened in anguish to Philip's smothered sobs and occasional faint moans as he was gripped by another stabbing pain. Now and again she heard Benj on his wanderings to and fro downstairs, knocking into furniture, clattering things to the floor. She knew that he was distressed, but he would just have to wait. Right now he was not her main priority.

Minute by minute Philip's rash was extending: first over his whole face, then down his neck and onto his chest. He seemed to be becoming delirious: talking nonsense and hallucinating. Lorna was frightened. At eight o'clock Philip's fever had not calmed, neither had he had any respite from his pain. With shaking hands Lorna dialled the emergency number again. She really felt that she was in danger of becoming hysterical, and tried desperately to keep calm, consciously concentrating on regulating her breathing. She asked for an ambulance to be sent ASAP, gave brief details and the address. She went back to the bedroom and sat beside her husband, taking one of his hands in her own. Hardly aware of her he drew away, clutching at his abdomen with both hands.

The seven minutes it took the ambulance to arrive seemed an eternity and Lorna repeatedly picked up her purse and keys to be ready for an immediate departure, only to put them down again to look out of the window. Minutes later as they sped for the second time towards the hospital, now with a different ambulance crew, Lorna endeavoured to explain the course of events since the early hours. These were relayed in turn to the hospital in preparation for their arrival. When the ambulance drew up at the A&E entrance, the paramedic team advised Lorna to go ahead to reception and confirm Philip's details, whilst they manoeuvred him from the vehicle onto a trolley and wheeled him inside.

This time Philip had the Senior Houseman's attention within five minutes, with two nurses also in attendance, carrying out various checks at the direction of the doctor. Lorna joined them in the cubicle to answer the various questions posed by Dr Pitchford, and was relieved to hear that it was his intention to admit Philip to an assessment ward for further tests and a fuller diagnosis. In too much of a stressed state to assimilate all of the information, Lorna locked onto the words "septicaemia". Suddenly a picture flashed through her brain of Sunday afternoon: Philip with an empty corned beef tin, about to put it in the pedal bin when Benj snatched it from him and Philip crying out in sudden pain. Blood on Philip's hand! She thought he'd made such a song and dance about it at the time. "Good heavens! It was an accident: he doesn't know what he's doing or why," she'd told him, and on further examination of Philip's hand, "only a slight break in the skin on the middle finger."

Lorna recounted these facts to Dr Pitchford. Could the septicaemia have been caused by that incident? The doctor was interested but non-committal. He noted it down on Philip's records, and enquired as he did so, whether Philip was covered or up to date with his anti-tetanus jabs. Lorna negated this and said he would probably need one.

The medical team was galvanised into action and soon had arranged for Philip's immediate transfer to a bed in a small, single room on the Assessment Ward. Once satisfied by this decision, Lorna waited until they were ready to despatch Philip, accompanied by a nurse, to the upper echelons of the hospital, and then reluctantly took her leave. She *must* go and attend to Benj's needs. Poor old sod would be wondering what on earth was going on. She assured Philip she would be back as soon as possible with the items he would need for a hospital stay.

She took a taxi home – more expense! Just when they could do without it! For the first time that morning she thought of work. She'd only been there for two days and now she was going to have to request some time off. What on earth would they think of her? And would they hold the job open for her?

She paid her taxi fare, watched the cab move off, and inserted her key in the door. As she walked through the hall and into the living room, she could hear Benj wandering about – he hadn't heard her and when she entered the kitchen it still took him a while to realise she was there. Poor Benj! He looked so old and frail and confused! How could he have changed so much and so quickly?

Suddenly the enormity of her problems and what the future might hold hit Lorna like a blow to her head. Dealing with the last few hours had drained her mentally and emotionally. She felt completely wrung out. She sat down, her face crumpled and tears rolled freely down her cheeks. After a few minutes she tried to pull herself together, aware that Benj had no idea what was happening, and was still going aimlessly between the downstairs rooms. She got up from her chair and began to prepare Benj's breakfast. Once he was busy eating, in an apparently unconcerned way, Lorna phoned Jan.

"Oh, Jan! Can you please come over? We've had an emergency through the night and Philip is in hospital." Her tears began again as she tried to explain.

"I'll be straight there. Don't say any more over the phone. Just go and open the door. I'm coming *now*."

Jan was as good as her word. By the time Lorna had stumbled her way to the door, Jan was already walking up the drive. She put her arms around Lorna and steered her back into the living room. "It's okay, love," she said gently. "What was it? Heart attack?"

"No – they think it's some kind of septicaemia. They've kept him in for tests. He has an awful rash – like an allergy. Oh, Jan, he's in *agony*."

"Right, now what do you want me to do? I can see to Benj – that's no problem. I know his routine now and I still have your spare key. Are you going straight back to the hospital?"

"Yes. I need to go back to Philip. Benj has had his breakfast. He'll probably grumble about upsetting his routine and won't understand why – but I can't help that right now. Do you think you could drive me to the hospital – I really don't want to do this alone."

"No problem! Let me just go back and check the house. You collect together the bits and pieces you need for Philip and I'll be back in five minutes with the car."

Within her promised five minutes Jan had drawn up at Lorna's drive in her Micra. On route to the hospital, Lorna recounted the events since early morning.

"Well he's in the best place now, Lorna. Leave it to the experts – they'll identify what it is. I expect they'll know in a couple of hours."

"It's just that he's in such pain, Jan. I can't bear to see him like that. The doctor in A&E thought it could be some form of septicaemia. I thought it might have been to do with the corned beef tin on Sunday." Lorna related the story.

Jan thought about this before replying. "If it's septicaemia or tetanus or something, it's more likely he did it gardening – maybe caught himself on a rusty nail. I wouldn't think that the tin would be rusty."

Jan parked the car and together the two women hurried through the now busy hospital corridors and up to ward 31. As they approached the small room, which Philip now occupied, they could see a number of medical staff ominously gathered around his bed. One of the nurses guided Lorna and Jan into an adjacent room and closed the door. "Hello Lorna, I'm Fiona and I'm going to be caring for Philip for now. I'd just like to explain what we are doing before you see him, then you'll understand what the various tubes and monitors are for. It's a bit of a shock for some people when they first come into a ward like this and they see so much equipment hitched up to their loved one." She went on to explain that so far they had put a couple of lines into Philip's arm to make it easier to take blood on a regular basis and to administer painkillers and other drugs as required. Several monitors showed the level of drugs, Philip's blood pressure and his heart rate. "I don't want to alarm you, Lorna, but early indications are that this is a form of meningitis."

Lorna stared blankly for a moment as the words sank in, and started to say, "But I thought the doctor said it was septicaemia…" She left the sentence unfinished, her voice trailing off to a mere whisper.

"Meningitis can be caused by septicaemia, Lorna," said Fiona. "We need to carry out some more tests before we can be sure, but we're trying to make Philip as comfortable as possible in the meantime. I need to alert you to this as you, yourself may be at risk if we confirm that it is meningitis that Philip has got."

"How much at risk?" asked Lorna fearfully. "I've been away in Spain for two weeks, where I've been near a new baby. I've been back home for two weeks now, but we haven't slept in the same room."

"You are at risk because you are living in the same house, Lorna. People who have had less contact with Philip, for example work colleagues, are not at high risk, but all the same you should let his employer know the score. Now, would you like to see Philip for a short while? We will be carrying out a significant amount of testing on him today and will have to keep asking you to leave the room, so you may want to go home and get some rest while you can. You can, of course, stay if you wish."

"Do you think he is in real danger then?" asked Lorna.

"Well there's no doubt about it, he is quite poorly, but we do not know at this stage whether it is meningitis. Early indications are that it is. If the tests confirm this, then certainly it is a life threatening condition."

"But in A&E this morning they just sent him home with paracetamol," said Lorna incredulously. "How could they not have identified it then?"

"We will have to investigate that through our own internal procedures, Lorna, but I cannot comment on it right now."

The next few days passed in a frantic whirl, which Lorna coped with in a dreamlike state…

Now as if things weren't bad enough, Lorna had been up all night with Benj. She had awoken to hear him pacing about downstairs, her bedside clock registering 1.45. As she lay a few moments, trying to get herself together, she tuned in to frenzied choking or retching noises, and shot out of bed, gathering up her dressing gown as she propelled herself downstairs. Sure enough Benj was throwing up. He had made it to the kitchen and the vinyl flooring was awash with a vile smelling, brown soup-like liquid. At least it wasn't all over the lounge carpet! He stood now, head down, looking thoroughly dejected.

Lorna gave a resigned sigh. "It's OK Benj, I know you couldn't help it."

His whole body was shivering, and Lorna felt so guilty about how much time he'd spent alone in the house recently. She found a blanket and settled Benj in his favourite armchair, swathing him in its folds. She set to cleaning the kitchen floor, whilst Benj, exhausted fell into an uneasy sleep. On finishing, Lorna felt drained herself, so fetching the duvet from her bed, lay beneath it on the sofa where she could be on hand if Benj needed her. The hours passed slowly, and at first light, Lorna pale and haggard, was up and about. A cup of tea helped, and she managed to get some boiled water into Benj. His breathing was laboured, his pupils dilated and he seemed very weak.

"Let's see if we can get you up – you're bound to need the toilet by now." She tried to get him to his feet but his legs gave way and panicking, she heaved him back into the armchair, where he slumped into a heap. Lorna made herself some porridge, then sat alternately clock watching and Benj watching. At nine o'clock she picked up the phone.

Her first call was to the hospital, to check on Philip. The answering nurse confirmed that he had passed a "reasonable night", but was unable to provide any other information until after the doctor's rounds, which commenced at ten. No change there then!

Having ended the call, Lorna sat for a few minutes musing, then decisively punched in a second number. The phone was answered immediately and Lorna described to the receptionist Benj's symptoms. "He's very old and there has been a lot of deterioration recently. I'd like someone to come out as soon as possible," she finished.

"It will be about 11.30 to twelve o'clock, after morning surgery," confirmed the voice, before the line went dead.

Lorna sat, phone in hand, watching Benj. He hadn't moved. He looked so small and frail, and quite unlike the feisty, robust character he used to be. Tears rolled down Lorna's cheeks as she remembered what fun they'd had over the years. How sad that it had come to this. The worst thing of all was the loss of dignity.

As the morning dragged on Lorna became more agitated and distraught. She really couldn't cope with much more! She thought about her new job, and how much she had looked forward to a new start: financial independence and maybe a whole new life. "In your dreams!" she told herself. How could she deal with a full-time job now? She sat and wrote a letter of apology and resignation, propping the sealed envelope on the shelf by the front door ready to post. In a strange way she felt relieved. One less thing to worry about!

The doorbell rang at 11.50 and even though she'd been on tenterhooks expecting it, Lorna visibly jumped. Benj was oblivious: he hadn't heard the doorbell for the last couple of years – at least. Lorna opened the door and stood aside to let Angela Hill and an accompanying nurse, whose name she did not know, pass. Few words were exchanged. Angela took out her stethoscope and knelt in front of Benj, who only then became aware of her. As she sounded his heart he gave a low grumble and began to struggle in an attempt to get away from her. She rose and stepped back to give Benj some personal space, simultaneously nodding at the nurse, who handed her a pair of surgical scissors from the bag. As she bent again, she took hold of Benj's leg and began to trim the hair. He went ballistic! There really was fight in the old dog yet!

The vet had jumped back from the bared teeth, and now filled a syringe with sedative, which she quickly jabbed into Benj's hindquarters, trickling the liquid in. The drug quietened him within a minute and Angela resumed her work on his front leg, finding a vein and applying the requested euthanasia. Benj stilled and Lorna wailed, throwing herself on Benj's small lifeless body. Vet and nurse stood in the background for a few minutes, allowing Lorna her last goodbye, then having made all necessary arrangements, took their leave with Benj on a small stretcher and covered with a blanket.

Lorna sat and wept. How much worse could life get?

When she visited Philip that afternoon, she recounted to him the events of the night and morning, while he sat stony-faced.

When she had finished her tale of woe, she looked at him tearfully, but with expectation of some sympathy.

"They said I might lose one of my feet!" was all he said.

Lorna stared at him in disbelief, not quite knowing where to put this piece of information in the whole scheme of things. "How come?" she eventually responded, feeling totally inadequate.

"Apparently not unusual in these cases, if in fact it is meningitis. They can't seem to make their minds up." Philip muttered bitterly. "I may not be able to drive again – or work for that matter. The end of my career, I think!" His body slumped and his face contorted. "I suppose it's a good thing you've got a proper job now," he finished.

Lorna didn't dare volunteer any information about the letter of resignation she had just posted, and an uncomfortable silence prevailed.

Three days later Philip's left foot was amputated! When Lorna visited the following day she found him full of hell. "I've been thinking about that bloody dog," he shouted as she walked into his room. "He's caused all of this."

"How can that be?" asked Lorna tentatively.

"He bit me, didn't he?" I told you at the time he had, but no, you insisted it was a cut from the corned beef tin, which by the way, wouldn't have happened if *he* hadn't tried to snatch it away from me. Whichever way you look at it, it was *his* fault. But he *did* bite me. I know it!... and think about the condition of his teeth: green and disgusting, and probably teeming with bacteria!" Philip flung himself back against his pillows, tears in his eyes. "Meningitis! Amputated foot! All because of a dog bite. What a stupid, cantankerous old git he was: I'm glad he's gone."

Lorna tried to choke back her own tears, but finally, a huge sob escaped. "None of it was Benj's fault. He couldn't help being old. His eyes and ears were failing and we didn't give him the attention he deserved. We're all going to get old, aren't we, and hope that when the time comes someone will care about us?" She looked questioningly at Philip.

"Well I can't see me getting to a ripe old age now, can you? And I'll tell you something, if I wasn't always kind to Benj, he's certainly had his revenge! Anyway, I kept you and the girls for years, and I've kept you and financed your stupid ideas these last two years, so now it's your turn to be the breadwinner." He glared at his wife.

Later that evening, as Lorna was sat at home, alone, she pondered on how it had ended with Benj. Her decision had been impulsive, and her reasons the wrong ones. She hadn't been fair with Benj: she'd put herself first and now she felt riddled with guilt. Maybe it had been "near his time" but she couldn't cope with the demands made of her: her new job, Philip in hospital, and herself rushing back and forth between the two dependants. It wasn't Benj's fault.

She sat thinking of the future. No job! No dog!… and she couldn't leave Philip now could she? However much she wanted to… Her chances of independence and a new life had gone. She turned to the Situations Vacant in the evening newspaper… Yes, Benj certainly had his revenge on both of them.

The Power of Pain

My left shoulder had become increasingly painful over a period of weeks now. Having a history of neck problems and also a previously frozen right shoulder, I was fairly certain that I had a trapped nerve, and had gleaned from earlier courses of physiotherapy how to identify the exact location of the problem. One very helpful and effective physiotherapist from the past had shown me how to free the nerve in my neck and part way down my shoulder blade. This had proven to be extremely useful on those occasions on which I had unthinkingly turned my head quickly, twisted my neck, and experienced a sharp, acute pain at a very specific point.

Twice previously in my life I had been given a surgical collar by the hospital, to wear on each occasion for several weeks. The first time was a result of whiplash following a car accident, and a couple of years later following an incident with one of my dogs, when we had been running together and he crashed into the back of my knees, causing my legs to leave the ground and the back of my head to be the first point of contact with the said ground. The collars afforded me some relief during the weeks, and on one occasion, months that I had worn them, but in fact did nothing to resolve the problem. In each case I still needed physiotherapy.

In later years when I had an injury, which resulted in a frozen shoulder, it took several weeks of physiotherapy followed by a cortisone injection and then a little more physiotherapy to regain normal mobility.

Now I found myself with neck and shoulder problems again. This time it was my left shoulder giving me trouble, and the nature of the pain led me to believe that I had a trapped nerve: one I couldn't reach to eliminate the pain. I tried all my usual exercises to no avail, and the pain, which had gone on for weeks was wearing me down. Our GP surgery had recently advertised that it had brought in a system of self-referral to a physiotherapist who was seconded to their practice from the local hospital. Presumably this was to cut out the "middle man", in this case the doctor, for cases where patients had recurring problems and knew that another session of physio would resolve or alleviate the pain. I decided to give this a try, confident that I had identified my problem and could locate the area of pain accurately. I duly made an appointment with "Rachael".

My husband accompanied me because I am partially deaf and sometimes need another pair of ears, and also on the basis that he might be able to learn exactly where the nerve trapping was occurring and observe how to release it (as I had so often done myself when the nerve was at an accessible place in my neck). We believed that this was a way of economising our use of the NHS: "for the greater good", you might say.

Rachael didn't seem particularly pleased to see us, staring hard at Rob as he followed me into the treatment room. Her first remark, before I could introduce my husband and inform of his reason for being there, was "Have you just walked in off the street?".

We were both taken aback, and as the patient, I explained why Rob was there. For some reason Rachael still did not seem pleased. She turned to her computer and began typing. After a minute or two, she half turned towards me and began asking the usual information questions. This took twelve minutes.

Rachael then stood and asked me to stand facing her and perform some basic arm and shoulder movements. As I carried out these tasks, I informed her of the exact point of extension where my pain kicked in and also where it became unbearable. She then asked me to lie on my back on the treatment bed and used both palms to press my left shoulder, shaking her head and commenting that she didn't know why my shoulder should be so stiff. And that was it! She informed me that my twenty-minute consultation was up, handed me two forms; one a feedback questionnaire for the session I'd just had and the other a referral form to send to the hospital if I wanted to self-refer there. Apparently self-referral for physio at the surgery itself was a "one-off". She virtually chased us out of the door!

A further week passed while I deliberated on what to do. My pain levels were probably no worse but certainly no better after my three to four minutes of "treatment". My arm and shoulder mobility was, however, becoming more restricted and I felt that my lifestyle was becoming inhibited: using the vacuum cleaner caused a great deal of discomfort and cleaning windows was equally difficult. Worst of all though were the simple but personal tasks of dressing and undressing, washing and drying my hair, and washing my back in the shower. I did not want to become dependent on, or a burden to, anyone.

During this time two of my friends had told me of a private physiotherapy practice in a neighbouring village. One friend had used the practice personally for a back problem and another had a relative who had had treatment from the same person. Both came with glowing reports. I decided to give them a ring.

I secured an appointment for three days later, with their apologies that I could not be fitted in any sooner. Having now spent months in pain "three days' time" was great news to me.

Monday 4pm came around and Rob drove me to the practice in the next village: a converted cottage, which housed two physiotherapists and one masseuse. We sat for a few minutes in a quaint little waiting room with half a dozen assorted chairs, an ancient log burner and equally ancient fire irons, and walls covered in strange modern art: vivid colours with a cycling theme.

I was duly called into the treatment room by a physiotherapist called Terry. First name terms immediately! Rob came with me as he had done at the surgery, in case I required assistance with hearing. No problem!

I talked with Terry, showing him where my pain was worst, and how far I could extend my arm in various directions before the pain in my shoulder and/or neck became intolerable. Within a very few minutes he had identified my condition as bursitis. I had never heard the term before. He went on to explain the existence of sacs filled with a lubricating fluid between tissues such as bone, muscle, tendons and skin, their purpose being to reduce rubbing, friction and therefore irritation, and bursitis being the inflammation of such a sac. Bursitis could affect the shoulder, elbow, hip, knee or Achilles tendon.

He then asked me to lie on the treatment bed and he proceeded with a very "hands-on" approach, which involved both pressure on my left shoulder and various movements of my left arm and both shoulder and elbow joint. At times it was excruciating to say the least but I was determined that if this was the way to cure the problem, I could live with it. On several occasions it caused me to gasp, or hold my breath to stop me from crying out.

During this, Terry continued to ask questions, regarding previous problems and treatment, exercises, anti-inflammatory medication, etc. I recounted everything I could remember of my neck problems and frozen shoulder, including the cortisone injection and physio, which had put the latter right. Finally I arrived at Rachael. I told him of my experience although I did not reveal any names, but Terry pressed further when I said that the therapist was seconded from the hospital to the surgery.

"I used to work there," he explained. "How old was she and was she blonde?" I told him that she was dark-haired and called Rachael. "Oh, I know Rachael," he said, "and I know that she is very 'hands-off'." He went on to say, "When I was doing my Master's degree she was actually one of my tutors, and she used to ask *me* how to perform some of the various techniques."

"Well she obviously hasn't got her head around them! She really was useless," I countered.

The session was painful, but I certainly felt as if I had had physio. Terry gave me three exercises to perform through the next week, with strict instructions on frequency and number of reps, warning me not to overdo it and only to push to the point of pain. Next session, same time next week!

I carried out my exercises religiously, three times a day, with four reps of each per session: first standing straight with my arms by my sides and moving my shoulders to try and bring my shoulder blades together. That was okay. The second exercise involved taking my left hand with my right hand in front of me at waist height, arms straight, then raising both arms up as far as I was able, just pushing the pain barrier a little. I pushed! It hurt!

The third exercise initially caused me a great deal of pain: left arm out to the side at shoulder level, with elbow in a right angle, and palm of hand facing forward. Holding the right-angled position, I had to try to move the whole arm back using the shoulder joint. On the second, third and fourth reps, I had to raise the elbow and upper arm a few inches and then repeat the backward movement. Excruciating, but I forced myself to go through with it.

I couldn't believe how much it took out of me, but I persevered, shoulder and elbow painful for a long while after each session, and residual throbbing right through my arm.

―⁂―

I'd had six sessions with Terry. Same time each week. I also had to continue my exercise regime at home, increasing the reps to five and adding another exercise to my routine. The new exercise involved reaching behind my back with my right hand, grasping my left hand and gently pulling it across my lower back, as usual, until I hit the pain barrier. This was the worst!

Terry was encouraging, every week telling me that he could feel a difference and that I was making progress. At every session he would pull my left arm a little harder, as if he was trying to disconnect it from my shoulder, and then, holding my upper arm firmly, and my elbow in the 90 degree position, he would pivot the elbow first one way then the other. I'd always believed that I had quite a high pain threshold, but I really began to feel that this was like a form of medieval torture. The sudden gripe hit the shoulder and the elbow simultaneously, and pain coursed down my arm to my wrist. At the end of the session I felt wrung out and my upper arm ached perpetually all week, feeling as if a heavy weight was permanently upon it.

I was still determined to continue my own physio at home, however gruelling it was becoming. Terry knew best and he'd told me that it was the road to improvement. I longed to be able to do normal things again, like fasten my bra at the back instead of the front, and wash my hair properly. So I knuckled down and got on with it.

Eventually in the seventh week, when the agony in my shoulder had never let up between physio appointments, and I was experiencing either throbbing or sometimes numbness in my upper arm and at times acute pain down my arm and in my wrist, I was persuaded by husband and friends collectively that I should also see a doctor. One and all they thought that I should have seen some improvement and experienced some relief from pain. As it was now wearing me down considerably, I conceded. The doctor immediately gave me some stronger anti-inflammatory tablets and referred me for an X-ray. Meanwhile I continued my physiotherapy sessions with Terry but they were still extremely harrowing.

The results of my X-ray came back with the word "unknown" on it. I was referred for another, and also for an MRI scan. I began to think that I had a trapped nerve in my scapula area. The second radiograph showed a "subluxation", which was a partial anterior dislocation of the shoulder. This surprised me as my shoulder was not noticeably displaced, but I was assured that these things could go unnoticed. I studied my frame in the mirror, comparing shoulders but could see no difference. I wondered though... surely an experienced physiotherapist would be able to detect such a thing? Apparently a displaced bone or joint can put stress upon the bursa thus causing bursitis, but if this was the cause of my problem Terry had not explained it. And surely he would have done something to rectify the dislocation first!

Maybe I didn't know enough. I tried to find out more on the internet: not something with which I had great familiarity. Firstly I googled "bursitis", and the description sounded about right. I could only assume that in my case, the damage had occurred through repetitive strain or minor impact: maybe then, from dog training over the years, as I used to take in problem dogs, the most common problem being pulling on the lead. They were frequently strong, adolescent dogs, which had simply never been lead-trained by their owners when they were young. I certainly wasn't aware of any sudden or serious injury, but of course I was getting older and probably tendons, etc were less likely to cope with the stress. I noticed in my research though, that the main cure recommended for bursitis was rest, and anti-inflammatory medication. Was this "hands-on" painful physiotherapy not the answer? Certainly I seemed to be getting worse with my physio sessions.

I then attended an MRI scan to identify any soft tissue damage. It revealed that I did have ligament damage: a high rate of lesions to the gleno-humeral ligament. There was also evidence of injury to the axillary nerve. My GP subsequently told me that I may wish to consider Arthroscopic surgery but that the success rate on such an operation was poor. I needed time to think about that!

When I got home, I again tried to glean further information online, and I discovered that the manipulation and the manual traction techniques used by Terry, in particular the "adduction of arm" which involved an external rotation of the forearm whilst holding the elbow at 90 degrees could actually cause neuro-vascular complications. Was this what I had?

I read on and found that another of the techniques that Terry had used was called the Milch operation. It was described as an extension of the external rotation system, involving the arm being pulled into an overhead position and gentle rotation applied.

It was anything but gentle!

So was Terry inept? Was he a qualified physiotherapist? I began to wonder… maybe I could check out his qualifications online. I was becoming a little more able to use the internet.

I realised that I didn't know Terry's surname. All I originally had was a telephone number from my friend. I put in the name of the practice and hoped for the best. It came up with the names of the three partners: Neil Kimber, Alice Wetherall and Terry Everett. Each had letters after their names and further research confirmed that they were genuine certifications. I felt quite proud of myself.

Terry had a BSc in physiotherapy, was a member of the Chartered Society of Physiotherapists (CSP) and was registered with the Health and Care Professionals Council (HCPC). So, Terry was not a fraud! His qualifications were genuine. He must know what he was doing, and he must be aware of the risks involved, none of which were explained to me. Now what? Where did that leave me?

After brooding for nearly a week on what I could do, I decided to see my GP again and ask him what I could do, if anything, about Terry. Was he responsible for giving me more problems than I had when I first consulted him. I also needed to find out more about the surgery to rectify the damage caused.

As I sat in the waiting room, I noticed Rachael appear from one of the corridors and head for the room marked "Visiting Practitioners". As she closed the door behind her, I read her name in the slot on the door: Mrs R Everett.

Suddenly everything became clear.

Charity Begins At Home

Jessie was a slightly built, elderly but sprightly woman, a mere four feet eleven inches, and for an eighty-two-year-old, as bright as a button and as fit as a lop. Her silver hair, rather too long for her age, was generally tied back in a loose ponytail, or occasionally when she was going into town, was fastened in a neat bun at the nape of her neck. For her town expeditions she always dressed in the same grey wool, three-quarter length coat: her only "proper coat", and which despite the three-quarter length, still dwarfed her. Additionally she always carried the same large, black handbag: a patchwork affair of soft leather pieces, and she pulled behind her an old tartan, two-wheeled shopping trolley, which invariably contained a thick plastic bag of birdseed to feed to the town centre's feral pigeons.

Jessie's shopping excursions were fairly predictable. She visited both of the "Pound" shops and all of the charity shops, of which there were many, sometimes buying old rugs or blankets for the dog, and an occasional cardigan or book for herself. She'd had a bus pass for as long as she could remember, so her ventures down town cost her very little. She'd also found a small, basic, but clean, café in a side street, where a cup of good strong tea cost her only one pound, and because she was a regular, Ron, the elderly gentleman behind the counter, often placed a custard cream or a gingersnap on her saucer 'free gratis'. Being a woman with a great sense of fairness, she had on occasion brought him a particularly nice pullover she'd found in one of her much-visited charity shops. Hence they'd become good mates!

This morning, after her browsing, where she had spotted a "must-have" Gucci handbag in the Mind shop, and had her usual tea break in Ron's Café, Jessie sat on a bench in the small park area in the middle of the High Street. She carefully rearranged her shopping trolley contents, placing the Gucci bag in the bottom and placing the birdseed on top of it. She distributed handfuls of seed around where she sat and in less than half a minute, she was surrounded by pigeons of all colours and markings. Some even came to feed from her hand, which delighted her. Noticing the activity, a few starlings and house sparrows joined the feeding frenzy.

Occasionally during these visits, a passer-by would make a scathing comment about "encouraging vermin" and Jessie would immediately defend her actions and her feathered friends as "all God's creatures" and "they're not doing you any harm". Today, however, the park was empty and peaceful, so she sat serenely for about twenty minutes. Once she had generously distributed the whole kilo of seed, Jessie took her bag and shopping trolley and wandered to the bus stop for her bus home.

Once home, Jessie was enthusiastically welcomed by Prada, her small, black and tan dog, a crossbreed obtained from the local dog rescue centre three years ago. Together they shared a toasted teacake (sometimes it was a couple of crumpets or a cheese sandwich), after which they made for the riverbank for their usual afternoon stroll. Practically every new person that Jessie met asked her dog's name, and smiled or laughed when she told them. She would then explain that the Dogs' Trust had named three abandoned puppies, and that at that particular time they had been using the letter P. Prada's siblings were Pernod and Perry.

Jessie had now changed from her "town clothes" into an old black, quilted nylon jacket, a pair of black stretchy trousers and a pair of well-worn, "sensible" black shoes. She still carried a handbag: a different one from her town bag, but just as large, and distinctly the worse for wear. It was crammed to the top with doggy treats and biscuits of every imaginable kind, the front pocket holding a quire of doggy pick-up bags.

Both Jessie and Prada were familiar and much-loved characters on the local riverside walk, well known to both dogs and owners. Canines "in the know" would spot Jessie from several hundred yards away, and speed off to her with a total disregard for their owners' commands or pleas. The handbag was the focal point, and Jessie never disappointed! Even the more elderly canines with failing eyesight, could detect their favourite person's scent, and tottered towards her, noses twitching.

The sleeves on Jessie's jacket were often stained with mud or saliva from overzealous friends, but she didn't mind. Her popularity pleased her, and in any case her jacket went into the wash every Saturday after her second walk, emerging spotless in time for her Sunday morning expedition (usually the busiest walk of the week, with regard to her canine fan club).

Today was Thursday so her coat was looking a bit the worse for wear but Jessie didn't care. First on her walk she met Charlie, a black cocker spaniel, who bounded over to her enthusiastically, plonking his rear abruptly on the ground in front of her and staring pointedly at the famous handbag, his head slightly cocked to one side and his ears forward. When he saw the first biscuit appear, he immediately offered Jessie his right paw. She smiled, politely took it, and rewarded him with a gravy bone. She took out another biscuit, shook the offered left paw, and gave him that too.

Next she was spotted by a pair of boxers, who were known locally and affectionately as "The Kray Twins". Not quite so well mannered as Charlie, they shoved him aside and proceeded to cavort in front of Jessie, pushing at her arm and her bag with their loose slavering jowls, their behinds wiggling back and forth, and knocking into each other. "Sit Boys!" said Jessie firmly, and their bums hit the ground immediately and simultaneously, whilst eager faces stared at their benefactor with expectation. Jessie held out a biscuit in each hand to The Krays, then threw another one to Charlie who was hovering behind them. He caught it deftly, then quite satisfied, all three dogs careered off together joyously.

Meanwhile Prada had been quietly examining molehills, knowing full well that she need not get into competition for any treats. Her home was full of them! Together she and Jessie proceeded as far as the footbridge over the river, where they turned and followed the same route back, Prada ritually playing with her ball on the return journey. They were almost back to the point where Prada had her lead put on to walk through the streets home, when suddenly, and seemingly from nowhere, came Jazz the Weimaraner, as mad as ever despite her three score years and ten. She almost knocked Jessie over in her enthusiasm and delight at seeing her Best Friend, and began barking manically because Jessie did not have a biscuit ready. "Quiet!" Jessie turned her back on the dog until she located a chew stick in her bag, Jazz whizzing around the hundred and eighty degrees until she faced both Jessie and the chew stick, her motion causing strings of drool to fly through the air. "Jazz sit!" commanded the sliver of a woman, and Jazz promptly obeyed, her eyes like gimlets staring at the treat in Jessie's hand. Jessie might be her best friend, but food was her Master! Jessie only exposed the very end of the treat, making Jazz ease it gently from her closed fist. A practised manoeuvre for a snatchy dog!

Jazz's owner had by this time joined Jessie, smiling indulgently at the tableau. "She's more obedient and gentle for you than she is for me," he remarked and Jessie smiled knowingly. They chatted for a few minutes about the weather and complete dog food, then parted company.

Once they were home Jessie changed the water in Prada's bowl and made herself her afternoon latte, which she carried through to the living room, together with two biscuits, one for herself and one for Prada. After they had partaken of their coffee break, Prada delightedly finishing the last of Jessie's coffee, Jessie retrieved the Gucci handbag from her shopping trolley in the hall. Having inspected the outside thoroughly and revelling in the excellent condition of it, she took a deep breath and opened it. The inside had a wonderful satin lining, which was immaculate. Seated at the bottom of the main compartment were a brown leather purse, a hairbrush and comb, a small case containing a manicure kit and a wad of tissues. Wide-eyed, Jessie carefully lifted out each item, examining them and placing them one by one on the arm of her chair. In a zipped compartment in one side of the interior, she found a bunch of keys, with one hundred pounds in twenty pound notes folded discreetly beneath them. She gasped in amazement! Another pocket revealed a small case holding a mirror and a handbag-sized bottle of Dior perfume. Jessie unscrewed the top and sniffed at the intoxicating scent. Next, slotted into a pen-holding loop was a slimline, silver Parker pen. Her eyes lit up: Jessie loved a good pen and she slid it through her fingers gently, into a writing position and tried it on the edge of her newspaper. It contained a fine point, black refill: "beautiful!"

After a few moments of gazing wondrously at the bag and its contents, Jessie took up the purse and opened it. She tipped the coins onto the floor in front of her, and then eased out the notes. The total came to £113.76 – not bad! Plus there was the £100 "emergency money". She transferred the purse contents to her own purse and put the £100 into the drawer of her welsh dresser.

She then removed all of the cards from the slots in the now empty purse: a visa credit card and a Barclays Bank debit card, each bearing the name L. V. Burton and a Debenham's card with Mrs L. V. Burton. There was also a Marks and Spencer Sparks card with no name on it, but a signature on the back. Jessie got to her feet again, retrieved a pair of scissors from the kitchen, stood over the rubbish bin and cut all of the cards into tiny pieces. She did have some scruples and would not have wanted the cards to fall into the wrong hands. By tonight there would be vegetable peelings and other waste on top of the pieces, so that would be fine. All in all a pretty good day!

On Monday the following week Jessie set off for town in her usual attire. In her trolley she had a carrier bag full of items she intended to take to the Age UK shop: a couple of skirts, a pair of shoes she had bought in the market then found they were too uncomfortable, two paperback books and a Gucci bag. That weekend, at the local supermarket, she had spent £10 on a variety of biscuits and treats for her riverside friends, and a further £20 on tins of dog food and boxes of Gravy Bones, Markies and Shapes, and put them in the collection box for the local dogs' home. Whilst she was unloading them from her trolley, a couple of people who were chatting nearby commented on her kindness and generosity. She had smiled and said, "We all have to try and do our bit."

Once she had alighted from the bus, Jessie went straight to the Age UK shop, where she handed over her bag of donated items to a grateful volunteer assistant, who took them straight through to the back room. Jessie headed off to Poundland for some toothpaste and antiperspirant, then went for a wander around the Blue Cross and Marie Curie charity shops. She didn't see anything to attract her there, so she put three pound coins in each of their donation boxes, which received smiles and thanks from the personnel on each counter.

Off to Ron's for a cup of tea next! As soon as the old gentleman saw her come through the door, he called a cheery greeting and turned towards the tea urn. Once Jessie was settled at her usual table, Ron hobbled over with her cup of tea and a Tunnocks caramel wafer. "A special treat today!" he announced, "a thank you for those lovely warm gloves you found for me last week."

Business was slack so Ron joined Jessie at the table for a few minutes chat. Then, tea and biscuit consumed, Jessie handed Ron a pound coin (an understanding between them that he must take it), thanked him, then grasping her handbag and trolley made her way to the door.

"See you on market day?" called Ron after her.

"Definitely!" replied Jessie with a smile and a wave.

She checked her watch and decided that she had time for two more charity shops. "Not Mind," she said to herself. "Not this week anyway!" She crossed the road and headed for Barnardo's: a lovely shop, with a few but not too many people browsing inside. Jessie wandered slowly around, stopping to examine a few items of clothing here and there. Suddenly she caught sight of a small, china, two-cup teapot, which she instantly recognised as Wedgwood "April Flowers". Making a beeline for it she squeezed past a couple of women holding dresses up against themselves, and looking about for the full length mirror. Jessie pointed them towards the back of the shop beside the counter, then turned her attention to the teapot, cradling it in her tiny hands. Yes, she would have it! It was so pretty and delicate. She picked up the tan Marks and Spencer shoulder bag from the floor, popped it under her arm and headed for the counter herself.

The two ladies with the dresses had retreated behind a curtained area to try on their coveted items, so Jessie placed the teapot on the counter, while she scrabbled in her bag for £3.50. As the assistant busied herself packaging the teapot in bubble wrap and sorting out 50p change for Jessie, the latter lifted out her birdseed, discreetly placed the Marks and Spencer handbag at the bottom of her shopping trolley, replaced the birdseed on top of it and then balanced her teapot, along with her previous purchases of toothpaste and antiperspirant on top of the seed. Taking her change with thanks, Jessie manoeuvred her shopping trolley into one of the aisles and left the shop as three more women descended upon it.

With no time for another charity shop now, Jessie headed to the park to feed the birds. Within a few minutes, she was surrounded by her beloved pigeons, more arriving all the time. They strutted and pecked at her offerings whilst she looked on with affection. She sat serenely, watching them and thinking about St Francis, her favourite saint. Nothing gave her greater pleasure than knowing that she could help them and other wildlife for whom mere survival could be so difficult. When her kilo of seed had all gone, Jessie stood, collected her belongings, and made for the bus stop. On her way she stopped to buy a Big Issue and to put £2 into the upturned cap of an elderly chap sitting huddled on the ground in the subway.

That afternoon, Jessie and Prada had met no less than six members of their riverside fan club, Prada patiently waiting while Jessie doled out canine treats of every description, catering from Yorkshire Terrier to English Pointer in size requirements. Once home, they shared a latte as usual, then Jessie went to retrieve her latest acquisition. The bag was a tan leather shoulder bag, exactly the same as Jessie had seen in M&S during the winter months, worth about £50, she thought. It had pockets all over it, so Jessie decided to begin with the two on the front of the bag before opening the main compartment. She found a lip salve, lip gloss, a nail file, an emery board and a blister pack of paracetamol. She turned her attention to the rear pocket, which, it turned out, was brimming with receipts from all kinds of stores: supermarkets, clothes and shoe shops, a local department store and Boots the Chemist. Jessie binned the lot, then proceeded to the main compartment of the bag, where she found a purse, a separate Next cardholder, two combs, two pens with logos of charity shops: one Blue Cross and one Macmillan, and a pocket diary. Jessie opened the purse to find £65 in notes and £4.73 in coins. Not bad – better than nothing! She transferred the money to her own purse, then examined the cards in the leather holder: two bank cards, a Morrison's More card, a Debenham's card (with an expired date on it) an RAC card and a library card. Following her code of ethics Jessie cut each card several times and placed them in the kitchen bin, along with the diary, and combs. The pens went into her "everyday" pen drawer.

A last small zip pocket in the interior of the bag revealed a driving licence, the photograph showing a good likeness to one of the women trying on dresses in Barnardo's, her name Mrs Sandra Jenkins, the same as the bank cards. The licence card also of course included the address of the holder, and Jessie contemplated returning it anonymously to the owner in the post. After deliberating on the possible risks, however, she decided against it and placed the card in an envelope which she had simply addressed DVLA SWANSEA. Either it would get there, or it wouldn't.

She now had two purses and a handbag to donate to the charity shops in town next week.

Jessie's son, Stephen, always came for his tea on Wednesdays, so she'd had a busy afternoon after her walk with Prada, making pastry for a steak pie and peeling vegetables to accompany it. The pie was now in the oven and the table already set. She placed the vegetables in the steamer over the already boiling water as soon as Stephen walked through the back door, carrying a bunch of alstromeria.

"There you go Mam: prezzie!" He handed her the flowers and bent to pat Prada, who was capering around him with the teddy bear that Jessie had bought her in the PDSA shop a couple of weeks ago. "Something smells pretty good."

Jessie found a vase and quickly arranged the flowers, then hugged her son. "Thanks, Son, they are lovely."

They chatted over dinner about Steve's job in car sales, and his wife Susan's shift work as a staff nurse. "She'll probably get here next week with a bit of luck," he concluded. When Jessie got up to make the coffee for them, Stephen moved to an armchair.

"Now let's have a look at your bank statement, Mam, and make sure you're still afloat," he said as he settled himself and took out his glasses. His mother brought in the two mugs, then went to the dresser and withdrew an envelope, which she meekly handed to him.

"How are Alice and Thomas?" Jessie asked. She rarely saw her grandchildren these days. Adults themselves now, they both had families of their own and neither of them lived very close, their jobs having taken them away from the North East of England some years ago.

"Oh they're both okay. Susan spoke to Alice at the weekend and they've just booked a holiday in France. Thomas has applied for another job: a promotion in the same department, so we'll just have to wait and see."

He began to study Jessie's finances. "Looks like you're doing all right now, Mam," he looked up at her and smiled. "I guess you've learned your lesson: that you just can't keep giving all your money away to charities. All those begging letters! Sometimes as many as three a week – they had you insane, and nearly bankrupt."

His mother looked wistfully at him. "I know you are right Steve, but I was getting lots of mail about cruelty to animals which upsets me greatly. Some of the photographs they sent were dreadful. They had me in tears, and having nightmares sometimes. Some of the horses and donkeys couldn't walk, they had been so neglected, and the dogs, especially those in other countries were skeletal, and even in this country, where we are supposed to be civilised, creatures that had been deliberately tortured." She started to cry at the memories.

"Mam," Steve got up to comfort her. "I understand, you know that, and it's why we agreed that you could have a monthly direct debit out of your account for two charities of your own choosing. Look!" he pointed to the bank statement. "I think £10 a month to each is very generous of you, and quite enough for someone whose only income is a state pension. Think of all the horses and donkeys, dogs and cats you are helping to save, and they are in this country, not hundreds of miles away. One person can only do so much."

Jessie nodded, still quite subdued. "Are you doing your bit, Stephen?"

"Yes, Mam, I'm doing Redwings Horse Sanctuary and The Salvation Army. I chose them because most of the money raised goes on the needy animals and people: 81% in the case of Redwings. Are you okay with that?"

"I am, son," she replied, "and thank you for taking some of the burden from me and helping out with some of the charities that mean the most to me. They need all the help they can get."

Stephen left an hour later, to make sure he was home for Susan finishing her shift. After his departure Jessie went through to her bedroom and rummaged through the contents of the lower drawer of her dressing table until she found the cheque book for her "other" account. The account that Stephen monitored was with Barclays, but she had opened herself another current account with Nat West, into which she could make cash deposits.

She took both the cheque book and paying in book for that account to the table, retrieved a pack of envelopes from the dresser drawer and began to work through a series of letters of appeal she had received requesting donations. She began with the Dogs' Trust because of them rescuing Prada and her siblings: a cheque for £20. Then came The Battersea Dogs' Home: well they did the same sort of thing – so another £20 cheque. Jessie counted the remaining letters; there were five, so £10 to each of them: the PDSA, the Mare and Foal Sanctuary, Hillside Animal Sanctuary, The Salvation Army and the town's local hospice. She felt that they were all very worthy causes and simply could not stop supporting them. These donations would take quite a slice out of the money in her "other" account but tomorrow she would take the £100 from the drawer of her dresser and pay it in. Sometimes she worried about what she was doing, but it was the only way she could continue to help those animals and people in need. In any case she would only target people who appeared to be wealthy enough.

She'd stopped telling Stephen about the letters she still received (about two every week), because she knew that he would go berserk. She had only involved him a few months ago, in desperation, because trying to help everyone was getting too much for her: she'd become overdrawn and very distressed about what to do. Now, having cancelled all her direct debits but two, and written to many of the charities to prevent them sending any further requests for money to her, Stephen monitored her monthly bank statements. He had told her that she should not now receive begging letters from huge international charities about crises overseas, nor should she receive anything to do with cruelty to animals. He had remonstrated with those organisations who had sent his elderly mother distressing photographs picturing emaciated and injured animals, which had upset her greatly, and which had caused her to empty her bank account.

Jessie completed her cheques and the relevant appeal forms, addressed the seven envelopes and put them in her town handbag ready to post the next morning. She also completed her paying in slip and slid the five £20 notes into the book beside it.

Thursday was market day. Jessie started at the bank, paying in the money to her earmarked account, and then she posted her letters. Charity obligations completed she meandered around the market stalls, stopping at the pet supplies stall to buy two kilo bags of pigeon corn, one bag for today and the second bag for Monday when she would be back in town. When the owner of the pet stall handed her the change from her purchase, she dropped it into the PDSA collection tin on his counter.

Jessie strolled along the street, handbag over her arm and pulling her shopping trolley behind her. She gazed into windows that she passed until she reached the RSPCA shop. During her browsing inside she found a book of British birds, which had excellent illustrations and was in impeccable condition. She knew that her great-grandson, Jamie, would love it. She tucked it under her arm and continued to scan the shelves, hoping to find something suitable for his sister, Amy, who was now three years old. She spotted a lovely butterfly mobile – just the thing! Each item was £1.50. Good, she liked to keep them both the same. She took them to the pay desk, paid over her £3 then popped another £2 into their donations box near the till.

Back out on the street, she pondered on which way to go. "Macmillan," she decided, as she hadn't been in their shop for a couple of weeks. They didn't take bric-a-brac or household items, but they did take clothes and fashion accessories, so that was all right.

As she entered the shop, she fumbled for the carrier bag in the bottom of her trolley. It contained, of course, the M&S handbag, the two purses and the Next cardholder. The young woman behind the counter, took the bag, had a brief look inside, and exclaimed, "That's wonderful, thank you so much." She handed Jessie a small lapel pin by way of showing her appreciation of the donation. Jessie pocketed it with a smile. She decided it was probably better not to browse in there today and headed off to Ron's for her cuppa.

As usual Ron was cheery, and delighted to see her, promptly delivering a cup of tea and two jaffa cakes to her table, and having a minute's chat before having to bustle back to the counter to serve other customers. Jessie sat quietly and planned her next two objectives: the Blue Cross and the Dogs' Trust, always favourites with her!

The Blue Cross shop was empty when she reached the door, so she decided to leave it until later, crossing the road and heading for the Dogs' Trust shop. There were a few customers there, so she casually took herself inside, scanning the shelves and clothes racks (and also the handbags!). No, nothing and no one suitable, she decided. The people there didn't look too well off themselves. She popped a small donation into their collecting box and left.

Back to the Blue Cross, which now had half a dozen people engrossed in the wares. Good! Jessie wandered towards a young blonde woman, maybe in her mid-twenties, her face heavily made up and her body suitably kitted out in "designer" clothes.

"Oh My God!" exclaimed the woman, dropping her multi-coloured bag to the floor, and pouncing on a teddy bear with clothes on. "It's a Steiff!"

She examined the bear closely. "Yes, it's the real thing! I'm having him!"

Jessie noticed the price label of £4 on one of the teddy's paws, and was dying to know how much the bear would be worth – it was obviously a collector's item. The girl grabbed up her bag, which bore the name Miu Miu, and went triumphantly to the counter, pulling out a five pound note as she walked. Jessie observed her from a distance. The cashier popped the bear into a bag and handed it over to the new owner along with £1 change, which the girl took without thanks and casually dropped it into her bag.

Jessie had cautiously looked at the bag but decided that although the name meant nothing to her, the design was much too noticeable for her purposes. She frowned as the woman sailed out of the shop, saying loudly to the world at large, "This is so going on eBay tonight!"

Well why couldn't she have at least given the Blue Cross the extra pound? Jessie put £5 in the Blue Cross tin, then hastened to the door. The woman was swinging down the street, a joyous bounce in her step. She turned into Costa, and Jessie impulsively followed her inside. At the counter the girl ordered a panini, a lemon muffin and a regular cappuccino, presumably her lunch break, and Jessie gasped at the cost, when she couldn't even give the Blue Cross her £1 change. And how much was she going to make selling that Steiff bear on eBay?

"Can I help you?" asked the lad behind the counter, looking at Jessie enquiringly, and poised ready with a cup and saucer in one hand.

"Er, no thank you," replied Jessie, "I can't afford a cup of coffee at that price, love. I don't quite know why I came in."

He peered over the counter at the old lady and said, "Here, my treat! Have one on the house. I'll bring it round for you."

Before she knew it she was at the table next to the girl with the Steiff bear, with a large coffee in front of her and a special Costa biscuit, all complimentary. "Thank you so much, son, you are very kind. I'll bet your mam is really proud of you." She smiled and he waved a deprecating hand as he retreated behind the counter.

"Enjoy!"

As she drank her coffee, which was really good, Jessie watched the girl to the left of her playing with her mobile phone as she ate her lunch. Then she rummaged in her Miu Miu bag, found a pen and notebook and began to scribble hurriedly in it. She glanced at her watch, exclaimed aloud and hurriedly swept phone, notebook and pen off the table and into her bag, immediately heading for the door.

Glancing across at the now empty table Jessie realised that the pen had actually missed the bag and gone onto the floor. She gathered her own belongings: handbag and shopping trolley, then bent down, retrieved the pen, and casually dropped it into her own handbag. She looked at her watch, saw that she was now running late and hurried off to feed her beloved pigeons.

After her visit to the park she still managed to catch her usual bus home and her afternoon was like any other: lunch and a walk with Prada, meeting some of their friends on the riverbank, and liberally handing out treats. Over coffee that afternoon, Jessie examined her purse contents. She'd spent £1 on her tea at Ron's and used £17 of her cash on seed and charity donations, but no spoils today to replace it! What a shame! She turned her attention to her newly acquired pen. She didn't know what make it was: not a Parker though. It was classy to look at: gold and platinum coloured and it was a beautiful writer – oh well, another one for her remarkable collection. She wondered whether the little Steiff bear was on eBay yet?

That evening the news showed an earthquake disaster in some small country that Jessie hadn't even heard of. The film footage was horrifying, showing children emaciated, injured, orphaned and homeless, which had Jessie in tears by the end of it. Later that evening an appeal was launched on TV requesting aid to the country, in particular to help the children. Jessie hurriedly wrote down the details: a telephone number by which you could make a donation with your bank card. No she couldn't do that! Then flashed on the screen an address to which cheques could be sent. Jessie managed to copy it down, then got up to check the balance in her "other" account: £205. Still as sharp as ever, she calculated her activity since the statement date. She'd written cheques totalling £90, and they were in the post now, but she'd deposited £100 cash just that morning – so £215 left. She opened her chequebook and with her newly acquired pen wrote a cheque for £50 to the relief fund, writing in her book the balance of £165.

The next morning Jessie took Prada via the postbox on their walk, posting the letter containing her donation. She'd have to raise more money, she told herself. There were so many people and animals in need. She still had a fair amount of cash in her purse from the previous week, so when she went to the supermarket she bought her own and Prada's food for the next few days, several additional boxes of biscuits for all their riverbank friends, and twenty four tins of Pedigree dogmeat and two 7kg sacks of complete food for the Dogs' Trust collection box in store. One of the shop assistants helped her to the charity box, placing the food inside for her.

"You really have got a heart of gold Mrs James," she said, "I'm sure you've earned your place in heaven!"

"Hey, I don't want to be doing that any time soon, I have so much more fundraising to do!" laughed Jessie.

The girl smiled. "See you next week then. Take care of yourself."

As she walked home Jessie considered the girl's words. Heaven? Hell? Who knew if the good deeds outweighed the bad, or vice versa?

It was Saturday lunchtime and Stephen had dropped in on his mother unexpectedly. It was his weekend off and Susan had already arranged to go shopping with one of her friends.

Both Jessie and Prada were delighted to see him, and his mother set about making a sandwich and a cuppa for them. Steve picked up the newspaper, flicked through it, then turned to the puzzle page. He glanced about him; there were always pens lying about somewhere in this house. Yes, there was one on the dining table. He rose and picked it up, returning to the armchair. A very nice pen! He examined it more closely then gave a startled gasp at the logo.

A minute later his mother came into the room carrying a tray with a plateful of ham, cheese and pickle sandwiches, and two cups of tea. Steve jumped up, took the tray from her and set it down carefully on the coffee table between them.

"Mam, this is a very expensive pen. Where did you get it?"

"I don't know, son, you know how many pens I have. I can't keep track of them all. Why are you asking?"

"Because it's a MontBlanc!" he exclaimed.

"That means absolutely nothing to me," his mother replied, averting her eyes. "It's a lovely writer. Is it more expensive than a Parker or a Papermate?"

"They're not even in the same league! I'll bet this pen cost at least a hundred pounds."

Jessie gasped. "What?"

"Come on Mam, think! Where did you get it?"

"Well actually, Steve, I just found it… when I was in town," she added.

"We need to take it to the police station then. I expect it's been reported missing: lost."

"Er… I've had it for ages though. Months. Maybe even a year or more," she stammered, "I can't see it ever being returned to anyone now, can you? Maybe it wasn't even reported to the police."

Stephen sat musing for a minute, then got out his mobile phone.

"You're not going to ring the police are you? I don't want the police to come here!" There was panic in his mother's voice.

"No, Mam, I'm just going to look on the Internet."

"Why? Do you think someone would have put an advert on the Internet? A 'lost' notice, I mean?"

Steve shook his head. "I'm just going to check out exactly what sort of pen it is, and how much it's worth. That could help me decide what to do about it."

He googled MontBlanc pens and scrolled through information about them. He picked up the pen, his eyes sliding from pen to screen and back. "I've found it!" then exclaimed, "Bloody hell! It's a MontBlanc Meisterstuck Rollerball: gold plated and costs £340."

Jessie's jaw dropped and she stared at her son, speechless.

He held up the pen in one hand and showed her the picture on his phone with the other.

"Please don't involve the police, Stephen, I really did just find it on the ground. I didn't steal it..." she cried.

"I'm not saying you did, Mam. I would never think anything like that of you. Maybe if you have had it for ages, there isn't any point in doing anything about it now." He sat silent for a minute, deep in thought.

Jessie's mind was now in overdrive: all that money for a pen! The girl! The Steiff bear! Suddenly she looked at her son, "Stephen, could you put the pen on eBay and sell it? It could mean a lot of money for a charity. Think of how many dogs it would feed, up at the home."

He stared at her for a while. "Mam you really are the kindest person I know. You only ever think about helping others, especially those in need, and especially the animals." He thought for a while.

"How about this? I will buy the pen from you. I would love a pen like this, but I could never justify spending over £300 on a pen when I have family commitments. Suppose I buy it for £150 and give you the cash to donate to whichever charities you want to?"

"Oh Yes! What a wonderful son you are to me." Jessie looked into his eyes and hugged him tightly.

"You made me what I am," he murmured as he took out his wallet and peeled off the appropriate notes. He handed them to his mother and she held out the pen. "Oh what the heck!" Steve reached into his pocket and withdrew his wallet again. He peeled off another £50, handed it to her, and then accepted the pen. "Doing my bit, just like you asked of me. I love you Mam."

"I love you too, Son."

After Stephen had departed, Jessie sat for a long while contemplating her actions over the last four months. In so many ways she wanted to confide in her son, but she did not want to offload the burden onto him. Also there were certain other things that she just could not tell him. He knew that she had suffered from acute pancreatitis and he had accompanied her on a couple of her hospital appointments. Together they'd found out that a high percentage of cases were brought about by excesses of alcohol, a fact that caused some humour at the time: Jessie telling the doctor that she only ever had an alcoholic drink at Christmas and maybe a couple of times during a year on special occasions, while Steve had asked her, "You're not a closet drinker, are you Mam?"

After a series of questions and discussion about her occupations, parents and diet, the doctor came to the conclusion that the most likely instigator of her condition was the many years she had worked for a shoe manufacturer, a small firm making a very special range of shoes. Jessie and another employee had spent their days using varnishes and other sprays in a very confined area: a small room dedicated to the finishing process. It was many years ago, before all the health and safety legislation had come to pass, and the risks were not known.

She'd now been diagnosed with pancreatic cancer, and had been told that it was inoperable, but that they could perhaps slow the progression of it down with chemotherapy and possibly some radiotherapy. She had refused both treatments. She'd suspected the outcome already and had deliberately attended this appointment alone, insisting that Steve didn't take any more time off work, so there was no argument about her decision.

"I think I've had quite enough exposure to chemicals in my life and I don't want any more." And that was four months ago, when she'd decided to increase her donations to deserving causes. After all she had a limited time to "make a difference" and as a result she'd become quite badly overdrawn.

Since then, of course, she'd put into operation her current plan for the "redistribution of wealth". She only ever took from people who looked, by their appearance and "accessories", as if they could afford it. And the charities got everything! Except the occasional pen, of course! Not one penny did she keep for herself: cash went into her "other" account and the only thing it was used for was to write cheques to causes who needed it. The money that went into her purse was spent on either birdseed or dog food, both for the needy, or distributed around the charity shops she visited and the homeless and down-at-heel people she saw about town. What else could she do? She no longer had savings, having already given away all of her money. Her house had been in Stephen's name for years now, which would simplify matters when she was gone. In fact he'd told her that her "estate" wouldn't even have to go through probate. Her main worry was Prada, but she knew that Stephen and Susan would take her. They both loved her, and she was only three years old – she would settle with them.

Jessie had sat for a long while, Prada's head on her knee, with those dark, liquid eyes fixed on Jessie's face in devotion, with just a touch of anxiety. She placed her hand gently on top of Prada's head and the grateful dog shuffled in a little closer, the tip of her tail twitching slightly. Finally Jessie said to her little companion, "Come on, lass, we'll go out. I ain't gonna change now. I can't." As Jessie stood, Prada bounded to the back door, wagging her tail and nuzzling her lead, which was hanging on the hook there. Jessie got out the biscuit tins, crammed her bag full of canine goodies, and shrugged into her mud and saliva covered coat. (It would go into the wash after her walk!) "Let's go!" she said, clipping on Prada's lead and opening the door.

First on the riverbank they met Charlie the "cocker" and Jazz the "weimy", their owners walking together. Both dogs charged over to Jessie, Jazz muscling in front of Charlie to be first in the sweetie queue. The latter simply sat off to one side of Jessie, looking up at her with patient expectation. She reached over Jazz, took Charlie's offered paw, and gave him his reward for good manners, then she proceeded to feed Jazz two chewy sticks, giving Charlie a couple more biscuits while the "mad weimy" was suitably engrossed.

Satisfied customers departed, Jessie and Prada walked on, meeting in succession Hamish the Westie, Jenna and Scarlett a pair of young Golden Retrievers, and Molly an elderly Irish Setter; all regulars! Each of them greeted Prada briefly with a quick wag of the tail, then Jessie with enthusiasm, delight and drools. All happily accepted treats, and when Jessie held up her empty hands in a "that's all" gesture, departed contentedly.

On their return journey Jessie and Prada met the Kray Twins, just after a gang of three border collies had departed from the sweetie shop. The boxers dashed up, skidding to a halt, with strings of saliva hanging from their jowls. As Lisa their owner approached, she beamed at Jessie and remarked, "All of the dogs love you Jessie. You are the most popular person on this riverbank."

"No I'm not," grinned Jessie. "This is!" She held up her tattered bag triumphantly, and all canine eyes were upon it.

"I still think that they love *you*," said Lisa. "Come on Lads!" she told the Krays, and satisfied with their treats, they galloped off together. Lisa followed them.

Jessie and Prada made their way home: coat in the washer, milk on for a latte, and an assortment of biscuits for both of them. "What a little gem you are," she told Prada, "you are so unselfish, even when other dogs are crowding round, devouring as much as they can. I hope we have a bit more time together."

She sat analysing her actions over the last few months, and trying to justify them in her own head. At last, she smiled at Prada and told her, "My name might be Jessie James but I like to think that I'm more of a latter-day Robin Hood – at least I hope so."

Epilogue

Jessie lived almost another year, continuing her "good work" almost right to the end. When she was eventually no longer able to go into town or to walk Prada, Stephen did her shopping and took over the dog walks. He wouldn't take Jessie's goodies bag out with him: absolutely not, but she did persuade him to take a pocket full of biscuits for her friends. Each time he came back, he sat and had a coffee with Jessie and recounted whom he had seen, and each time telling her, "I can't believe how popular you are, Mam! Well, actually I can!"

During her last weeks Jessie and Stephen had spent a great deal of time together and she had confessed all to him. He was shocked and appalled at the time, but the more he considered her motives, the more he came to terms with it. He couldn't do anything about it now, could he? He didn't want to see her spend her last days in prison, and even if that were not to happen, how could he let her leave the world with everyone talking about the bad things she had done rather than the good.

Let sleeping dogs lie.

Jessie had requested no flowers at her funeral, preferring all attendees to donate to charity. Stephen had promised to collect all donations and send them to her "regular" recipients. He couldn't bear for there to be no flowers at all though and after much discussion with Susan they decided to donate

£100 themselves and Susan crafted a wreath made from the honeysuckle in Jessie's own garden as Jessie had loved the scent of it, and she had once told Stephen that it was representative of "devotion".

On the day, the coffin looked particularly bare with only the honeysuckle wreath, and they wondered what people would think of them. Still, it was what Jessie wanted. Lots of her riverbank friends turned up: a dozen or more had their dogs with them and, obviously pre-planned, they formed a corridor on either side of the entrance to the crematorium. As the cortège passed, they each placed envelopes on the top of the coffin, their donations to animal charities selected by Jessie. Each envelope was accompanied by either a single flower: a rose or carnation, or a small unassuming posy: lily of the valley, forget-me-nots, and amusingly dogs roses and dog daisies, picked from the riverside. Jessie was now covered in flowers!

Representatives from various charities attended too, a large group of ladies and one elderly gentleman. They had obviously seen the obituary for Jessie in the newspaper and rallied to the occasion. Each lady was wearing a badge or an item of clothing showing the charity they represented, and one and all were wearing homemade armbands, which said "Thank You Jessie".

The man was dressed in a brightly coloured pullover and carrying a single red rose, which he placed gently upon Jessie once the pall-bearers had retreated, bowing before the coffin and then taking his seat. "Ron, of course!" thought Stephen.

The first piece of music was already by this time playing: "Everything is Beautiful". The service was short and simple, Stephen giving the eulogy himself in spite of the occasional stumbling over words, and at one point having to pause a while to get his emotions under control. He spoke of her impoverished childhood, her years of hard work at the small shoe factory, while bringing him up in a loving, caring way, and teaching him to love and care for animals and to help those people worse off than they were. He spoke of the years she had helped charities of all kinds and also confided what no one else up to this point knew: that she had given away all the money she had, and had bankrupted herself. He concluded by asking that they took a few minutes now to think of Jessie and what she meant to each of them, finishing with: "The next piece of music was going to be 'You'll Never Walk Alone' one of her favourites, but I decided that everyone would cry, especially me, so here is my choice, and I think it befits her!"

The music began: "If you want it, here it is, come and get it... you'd better hurry 'cause it's going fast..." Everyone laughed, then stood thinking of Jessie and her kindliness and beneficence, during the committal.

A few words of thanks were spoken in conclusion, and Jessie's final piece of music began: "Remember Me as a Sunny Day..."

And Two Bonus Tales

Scoop The Pool

It was the 134th year of the local agricultural show. The village that held it was very small: a population of just over five hundred, and it was still like stepping back into the early 1960s. That was what Irene and Hank loved about it and they spent a great deal of their time here, hoping to eventually buy a small property. Most of the houses were old terraces, many over two hundred years old and badly in need of update and repair. Those cottages situated alongside the river still had fixtures for flood barriers across their doors, and the barriers were put in place over the winter and also at other times of expected heavy rain.

Today, however, the sun was shining and the two huge fields used to host the show had tents, pens and rings erected, and were buzzing with excitement and activity. The day was to be filled with the judging of livestock classes, horse riding events, an Exemption Dog Show, Cumbrian wrestling, vintage cars and tractors, etc. all events taking place outside on the fields. The tents housed the entries for the industrial classes, which included home-grown vegetables and flowers, home baking of all kinds, jams and chutneys, art and crafts: one speciality being hand-crafted walking sticks and crooks, and a photographic section.

There were also a couple of stalls and roundabouts to satisfy the children, mobile kiosks selling food and drink, and of course, the ubiquitous beer tent.

Most of the locals made a great effort to enter some of the classes, and residents of other surrounding villages also took part, knowing that the folk of Liddleholm would in turn support their annual shows.

At mid-morning the day was warm and sunny, and the atmosphere expectant, friendly and welcoming. People were gathered around the various rings of their particular interest, conversing with both friends and strangers. The tents were closed to the public temporarily while the judging took place, then to be re-opened at 12.30pm to allow exhibitors to see how they had fared, and the general public to meander about making their own judgements on both the exhibits and the class results.

Groups of people were standing on the periphery of the dog ring, awaiting their classes and chatting to one another, whilst keeping one eye on the class being judged. Irene was waiting to compete with her friend's dog Pepper. Gill and Benny had a pet Border Terrier and had never entered a dog show of any sort, but Irene, who had always shown dogs in the past, volunteered to take Pepper in for a laugh, assuring them that she definitely stood a chance. She had already been awarded a third place and a fourth place in two of the terrier classes, and was awaiting her third class: Veteran.

Irene and Hank had both entered the photography section, between them trying to put entries into almost every category in support of the show. Irene was very pleased with most of her entries and had done fairly well in previous years. There were other very good local photographers too, and all were delighted if they won a first place in any class. Some gravitated towards black and white photographs, others to colourful skies, wildlife or portraits. Whilst slightly competitive, the general aura at the show was friendly, each admiring the others' entries.

While waiting with Hank and their friends Gill and Benny, Irene was chatting to a woman who was standing next to them outside the dog ring. She was wielding a large DSLR Nikon camera, taking the occasional picture of the dog exhibits, but waiting for the wrestling to begin in the adjacent ring. The lady, in her sixties, with long blonde, crimped hair was very friendly and garrulous, and kept making remarks about "what she could do" or "what she would like to do" with those muscular wrestlers as they limbered up before going into the ring. The conversation moved on to the Sixties: in particular pop music of the time, music festivals, especially Woodstock, and hippies! It turned out that Irene was only three years younger than Moira, as she'd introduced herself, and they'd liked many of the same things, especially the fashion of the time and their tastes in music.

Moira said that everyone in her "neck of the woods" regarded her as still a hippy. She and her partner had bought a huge piece of land, and farmed it, with all their animals being free range, and the couple were largely self-sufficient. They had also taken rescue animals in, which warmed Irene to her as she herself had taken in a number of rescue dogs over the years. Moira told her of a rescued horse she had taken on. He had been initially terrified of people and was still somewhat nervous of certain types, but she had won him over and now he was twenty-four years old. She explained to Irene where she lived and it seemed that her farm was in a fairly isolated area, with only a single track road to it and only one other farm adjoining her fields. It sounded idyllic, and was about 55 miles from Liddleholm.

Irene and her husband had an old camper van, and she asked Moira if she knew of anywhere they could stay around that area, as it sounded wonderfully tranquil. Moira immediately said that they could park up in one of her fields, and could be totally alone and undisturbed. There would be no electricity, but there was an external fresh water supply, and scenery to die for. As she was speaking, she rummaged in her bag, producing a pen, and asked Irene if she had anything to write on. Irene gave her the show schedule and Moira wrote down her address and telephone number, explaining to Irene the best route to take: over the fells, with single-track roads but absolutely stunning views.

"Just give me a ring if you decide to come." She added, "Your friends can come too if they like," nodding towards Gill and Benny.

Entrants for the Veteran class were then called for and Irene and Pepper entered the dog ring. By now Pepper had got used to being examined by the judge and she behaved impeccably. She won the class, and as well as a red rosette, she qualified for the Veteran Trophy, absolutely delighting Gill and Benny. She also had her photograph taken for the local newspaper.

Once the dog show was concluded Irene, Hank, Gill and Benny made their way to the tent housing the photographic section. The judging was completed and the tent was now open to the general public as well as the exhibitors. The four friends wandered around, looking at the photo exhibits and the prize cards attached to those which had received an award, each of them commenting upon whether they thought that the photograph was deserving or not. They were delighted to see that Hank had won the Novice class and also taken third place in the same class.

Irene had previously won the Novice class and was therefore competing with those at a higher level. She had been awarded second place in two of her classes and third place in another. She was, however, a little disappointed that the photograph in which she'd had the most confidence, had achieved nothing at all. "Ah well! C'est la vie!" These things were all very subjective. Her friends commiserated with her, but also congratulated her on her achievements in the other classes.

As Irene turned down one of the aisles to examine the results of some of the other classes, the committee member in charge of the photographic competition was handing out envelopes of prize money to those who had achieved first, second or third placings in their classes. He waved to Irene and handed her three envelopes: two containing £2 and one with £1. The woman behind Irene waiting to collect her prize money was Moira, the hippy lady she had chatted with at the dog ring, so Irene stood back and waited for her. As she turned towards Irene, Moira had a radiant grin on her face and she held up a thick wadge of small buff-coloured envelopes, about three inches deep.

"My goodness!" exclaimed Irene, "you have done well. What is your exhibitor number? I must go and look at your photographs."

By then Hank had also been awarded his prize money: £3 for first place and £1 for third. Together the couple meandered around examining those pictures attached with Moira's exhibitor's number 62. They found eight first place awards, five seconds and four thirds!

"Wow!" exclaimed Irene, "£38! She will have the most points in the show, and she has also been awarded the 'Best Photograph in Show'. That qualifies her for another £10 and two trophies."

"Some of her photographs are excellent," admitted Hank, "but some are a bit weird. Also they look as if they've had a lot of digital enhancement, which I would not have thought was acceptable in a competition such as this."

"Moira told me that this was the first time she had entered this show too, yet her photographs look extremely professional, don't you think?"

As the four friends were leaving the tent some time later, they ran into Moira again, coming from the presentation ring and holding the two trophies. As she approached them she raised both above her head, an exuberant look upon her face. They all congratulated her again.

"You've really scooped the pool!" said Hank.

Shortly after, they were allowed to collect their exhibits and leave the showground.

―――

There was much discussion as the four friends partook of their evening meal in Gill and Benny's camper van. Pepper's trophy and rosettes were on display in the front window, and Pepper herself was being continually patted, cuddled and asked, "Who is a clever girl?" She positively basked in the glory.

As they sat over coffee at the end of the meal, Irene picked up the show catalogue to examine the entry details. Moving methodically through the photographic section, she discovered that Moira Collins-Todd must have won almost every class she had entered and been placed second and third in the others. Weirdly though, the woman had entered the Novice class, which was for those competitors who had not won a prize before at the show. She was therefore eligible for the class, but had not even been placed.

Irene checked the address she had been given by Moira, against the catalogue details. Yes, it was the same. Moira must have really expected to do well, to travel nearly 60 miles to a little country show like this. She wondered idly if perhaps Moira was actually a professional photographer rather than a farmer, but she obviously lived on a farm, by her address.

After Irene had commented on her thoughts aloud, Benny volunteered the information that while she was in the ring with Pepper, he'd chatted with Moira and found that she had originally come from Gloucestershire, where she and her partner had a ten-acre piece of land, which they'd farmed in an amateur way for years, but had in recent years moved to Scotland, where they were able to afford a ninety-acre plot, and so turn 'full-time'. They had horses, sheep, pigs and five dogs and they grew most of their own food and fodder.

The four discussed the show results a while longer and then unanimously decided that it time to turn in.

The next morning, Irene was up and about early, as usual, and as she sat over first a glass of orange juice and then a coffee, she perused the show catalogue once again, coming across a list of judges in the front pages, complete with their addresses. The dog section judge had been a Mrs Crathorne, who had been a lovely lady, and very friendly with all her competitors, as well as patient and helpful to those who had never entered a show before.

The judge of the photographic section was Mrs Philippa Darrowby-Smith and her address was a farm near Galashiels, a good way from where they were at present. Irene sat frowning at the information for a while, the cogs turning, then she quietly got up and slid the road atlas out from the locker above her head. She turned to the page with a map showing north of where they were currently staying and found Galashiels almost at the top of the page. Amazingly the area in which the judge's farm was located was shown on the road map, not far from the town itself. Curiously Irene turned back to the show catalogue and found Moira's address. She placed its location on the atlas, a tiny place called Cloverfield, then double checked that of the judge, glancing also at the scale of the map.

Then she sat stunned!

She was turning over an unlikely chain of events in her mind. The two addresses were very close to one another. Both women were farmers. They probably knew each other. Surely they would attend the same market? They were obviously both photographers too. Moira definitely was, and Mrs Darrowby-Smith must be too, as she'd been asked to judge. Was it all a set-up? Surely not at such a small village show as this?

When Hank got up, he dressed and made off to the village shop to pick up a newspaper. Upon his return Irene had the breakfast ready, and once down to his last cup of tea, he opened the paper, knowing that there was some kind of disaster reported on the front page. He stared at the photograph, murmuring, "Bloody Hell!" then quickly read on. There had been a car accident as someone was returning home from yesterday's show. There had been two women in the car, one had been killed and the other had been taken to hospital with serious injuries. Both women had double-barrelled names, and were returning to Galashiels. No other vehicle was involved.

Hank stared at the photograph on the front page: a car upside down in what looked to be a deep pond situated close to the road. Another picture showed the fire brigade preparing to remove the vehicle from the pond, with an ambulance and a police car also standing by.

Hank read the brief description of the accident through twice, then passed the paper to Irene, pointing at the first paragraph on the front page. "Do you recognise those two names?" he indicated.

Irene took the paper, looking firstly at where her husband was pointing. "Yes," she said frowning. She then quickly scanned the two front page photographs. "Oh My God!" she gasped. "It's yesterday's judge and Moira." She paused as she took in the relevance of the situation. "They were travelling together!"

"Yes," agreed Hank, "and one of them is dead, the other one in hospital with serious injuries."

They stared at one another in silence for some time, the cogs turning in each of their heads. "It doesn't tell you much," remarked Irene, "but there will probably be more in tomorrow's paper. It says that it is Philippa Darrowby-Smith who is dead. She was the judge, and also the driver. Moira is alive, but who knows in what state?"

"Well," said Hank wryly, "I might have said yesterday that Moira 'scooped the pool', but it looks to me as if it was the fire brigade that did!"

The next morning's newspaper was obtained by Hank as soon as the shop was open. He hurried back with it and they sat together in the camper van poring over it. They discovered that Moira had been taken to Edinburgh Hospital as she had to have one arm amputated and also one side of her face and head had required sixty-two stitches.

Apparently both women were well over the limit alcohol-wise and an empty wine bottle and six empty lager cans had been retrieved from inside the car, along with a plentiful supply of marijuana.

The report gave the full names and addresses of both women, and also the fact that they were both farmers, their land next door to each other. Irene, of course, knew this but the journalist had obviously dug up further information: both women came originally from Gloucestershire and in their teens had attended the same public school.

Hank's concluding remark was that "for those two cheating ladies, that certainly was a Photo Finish!".

A Real Murder Mystery

2015

Jim was ninety-three years old and had been a widower for almost two years now. His wife had been eighty-six when he'd lost her to bone cancer which had latterly turned into leukaemia. Although he looked quite frail to those who didn't know him, underneath his dated clothing his frame was wiry, and he could walk for miles unaided by a walking stick or any other help. His grip and his handshake were still like a vice.

His son and daughter-in-law had always been regular visitors to Jim and Annie's small council bungalow. After his mother's demise, however, John and his wife began to go every day to make sure Jim was managing to look after himself. They had arrived one morning, shortly after Annie's death to find him very ill, weak, vomiting blood and unable to stand up. They had had to call an ambulance. As a result Jim ended up in hospital for three weeks during which time he suffered from delirium as well as malnutrition. However, that was behind him now and as well as John and Aileen, he now had a carer, Maureen, who went in twice a day to ensure that he had meals and medication at the appropriate times.

Although Jim had initially rebelled against having a carer, once he had got used to Maureen's presence, he looked forward to her visits and always had the kettle on for her arriving. He bought her a special coffee mug of her own for his house and plied her with cakes and biscuits, wanting her to sit and talk to him rather than doing any jobs for him. He had even told her that if he had been younger he would have liked to marry her, which had worried both Maureen and John.

Aileen fancied herself as a bit of a writer and used to like to talk to Jim about the past, taking notes as they spoke about his childhood years in the 1920s, moving house from the tiny pit cottage in the small mining community, his teenage years, his working down in the local pit and, of course, the war years. As well as being interested from a historical point of view, she wanted to write a short biography of Jim for her husband, who was very interested in finding more about his family history. The chat sessions that they had together revealed to John how little he actually knew about his mother and father.

Jim recounted a story of when he was nine years old and out in the fields at harvest time. As the crops were being cut, rabbits were running out of the harvested field looking for cover elsewhere and the men were shooting them. Jim, being a very resourceful child in an impecunious family, saw a large rabbit keel over and flop to the ground. He ran over and swiped the rabbit up, continuing to run as fast as he could to the gate of the field. Unfortunately five yards short of the gate the man who had shot the rabbit caught up with him and wordlessly took the rabbit, gave Jim a good swift kick up the backside, and walked away. All hopes of a rabbit pie for dinner were dashed.

Another tale, which Jim remembered, was the visit of a titled lady, not just to the village, but to his very house. Lady Nancy Astor was staying at "The Big House" in Croxdale, a nearby village. It was a Sunday afternoon and Lady Astor, another titled lady (Jim was unable to remember her name), and a young girl decided to take an afternoon stroll. Their wanderings led them to his village where they wished to see how the people there lived. They decided, rather high-handedly to "visit" one of the families and inspect the inside of a typical miner's cottage. Jim's parents' house was randomly chosen.

Jim's grandfather, Andrew (local pronunciation: Andra), had been into town to drink at the Red Lion, his usual Sunday lunchtime haunt. After the 3pm closing time he returned home to sleep off his drunkenness in the fireside chair, and was doing just that when the Lady Astor party entered his home. Apparently this lady was renowned for her condemnatory attitude towards people who imbibed, however, she was a self invited guest to the Ridley household, and Jim remembered her as gracious and friendly, chatting to Andrew while Jessie, his sister, took the young girl on a requested tour of the community and to the local brickworks. At the conclusion of the visit the family were thanked for their simple hospitality.

Because Jim was a redhead, the only member of his family with this colouring, one of the neighbours nicknamed him Rusty and the name stuck for the rest of his life, even within his own family. At eleven years old Jim left the village with his family and moved into a council house in an area of the town known locally as "Jerusalem", and at fourteen, left secondary school to work in the local pit. When war broke out he went to join up but was told that he would better serve his country by remaining in the mines.

He had countless stories about the war years, usually involving drinking in all the pubs in the town, getting totally inebriated and taking willing girls to the woods or down back alleys. (He even remembered their names.) During this time most of the young men were away fighting and the local young ladies had little choice of men. So Jim shone! He was an incorrigible philanderer. He recounted one story in particular (several times): a tale of the blackout period when he had undertaken some ARP responsibilities and had a small but powerful flashlight. He shone it on his friend who was "having it away" with one of the local girls in the narrow alley down the side of the pub in which they had been drinking. He had had a real good look and said that having identified her, he took her down the woods "for one" several times after that.

Also in those days Jim mainly rode a bicycle, although if he ever got the chance to drive any kind of vehicle he jumped at it. All these tales were fairly repetitive and Aileen kept prompting him to move on to other topics and later years.

Occasionally he would remember some incident from the early post-war years, usually to do with mining disasters, changing to working in a different pit, finding his favourite pub and "making it his own", and moving house again to a different street in the same town. For his age, his memory of detail was quite amazing.

One afternoon they had talked about these post-war years, Aileen scribbling away as Jim talked, and John interjecting with the odd question. They had reached about 1948 as far as they both could tell, and Aileen asked about his courtship with Annie, which had begun some time that year. Nothing! Perhaps in Jim's eyes, that wasn't appropriate, so instead she asked about their early married life from 1950. Suddenly Jim clammed up and just sat staring at the wall opposite: arms folded across his chest, his mouth pursed and his pale blue eyes torpid and expressionless, ignoring all prompts and questions.

John tried to remind his father of tales he had heard in the past about his mother going to the dances in their courtship days and Jim preferring to go to the pub until closing time then going down to the dance hall "The Rink" to pick Annie up and walk her home. "What a courtship!" finished John. Jim nodded, then resumed his "thousand yard stare" pose. Aileen looked at Jim's body language of withdrawal and signalled to John to leave it, and said, "You look tired, Jim. Let's leave it for today, shall we?" No reply! Shortly after they left for home.

Northern Echo Report: 26th October 1952

Teenage Girl Stabbed To Death

A sixteen year old girl, Mary Thompson, was found murdered in her home at 16 William Street, S--------- on the evening of 24th October. Her father Robert Arthur Thompson (known locally as Bob) on returning from an evening at the Red Lion on Station Road discovered her inert body. She was face down on the hearth rug and lying in a pool of blood. Her torso had multiple injuries believed to have been stab wounds.

In an interview with Bob Thompson, he reported that on discovery of the body, he had turned his daughter over on to her back in the hope that she may have still been alive. Then, ascertaining that she was dead, he rushed to the police station on foot as no one in that street had a telephone. He tearfully told us that his wife was away: staying at her mother's on Russell Street because the old lady was sick. He also confirmed that his elder daughter had recently married and no longer lived with them. He had left Mary in the house alone when he went off to the pub to play dominoes. It was his fault that it had happened! He was hysterical.

Bob Thompson was quite intoxicated when he entered the police station and at first the duty sergeant found it difficult to make sense of what the man was trying to tell him. He decided to retain him at the station and sent the local bobby PC Charlie Short out to the house to investigate.

It was revealed that Mary had been stabbed over forty times in her torso, the weapon penetrating several of her vital organs. Although the weapon has not yet been recovered, it is believed to be a knife with a blade five to six inches long; a smooth, double edged instrument.

Police are requesting that anyone who was in the "Jerusalem" area that evening, come forward if they saw anything out of the ordinary that they believed might be suspicious, or anyone who was a stranger to the area.

There was a photograph of the house below the report.

Northern Echo – Follow Up Report
28th October 1952

Have You Seen This Man?

The first part was a précis of the previous one, reminding readers of the basic murder details. Then...

Two neighbours have now come forward, separately, to report a bicycle leaning against the wall of the terraced house where Mary Thompson was murdered.

George Wilkinson of 14 William Street, next door to the Thompson family residence reported that as he setting off at 7.30pm to his local pub The Crown, he noticed a blue bicycle leaning against the wall between his own door and that of number 16. It had a cross bar so he suggested that it was a gent's bike.

Another neighbour, Margaret Carr who lives on the opposite side of the street to the victim's home, noticed the pushbike as she was leaving the house to go to the bingo, at about ten minutes to eight. She wasn't sure of the colour though, from that distance and in poor light.

The police have requested that anyone who noticed a cyclist in the William Street area between the hours of 6pm and 11pm on the evening of 24th October, come forward and ask to speak to Sergeant Alan Alderson. Any description of the cycle or cyclist would be helpful to their enquiries.

There was much talk all over town about the murder. Initially Bob Thompson, the girl's father was brought back into the station for questioning, as it was he who had "found" the body, and no one had seen Mary since around four o'clock on that fatal afternoon.

However, his whereabouts up until 5.30pm was vouched for by his employers at the Kenmir's furniture factory. Also, from 7.10pm until 11.00pm the regulars at the Red Lion verified his presence in the bar. That left only a small window of opportunity for the murder to have taken place. The time of death has already been calculated by the police doctor and coroner as occurring between 8 and 11pm on the night in question.

In addition, Bob Thompson was absolutely devastated: hysterical initially when reporting the murder to the duty sergeant, then so angry afterwards and hell-bent on seeking revenge.

The case was never resolved and was eventually closed.

2015

It was lunchtime and John and Aileen were meeting with Maureen in the local Starbucks. They had all been at Jim's bungalow that morning as a result of Maureen telephoning the couple and also her manager to explain that there was a problem with her client. She had subsequently stayed with Jim until the family arrived.

"The doctor has already been," Maureen had reported to them. "Jim's very confused this morning and it's most likely a water infection, so I've managed to get him to give me a sample. I'm going to drop it in at the surgery now and also get him a prescription for some antibiotics." She waved the prescription form in front of them.

It had all been a bit of a shock to John: seeing his father behaving so strangely and not even knowing who they were when they entered the house. Jim had walked away from the door muttering, "Not another effing doctor…"

John began to ask his dad questions in an effort to try and ascertain what the extent of the problem was.

"Dad, do you know who I am?"

"No!"

"I'm John, your son."

Vacant expression.

"Well, what's your name then?"

His father studied him carefully. "Jim. Rusty maybe?" he replied shrugging.

"Well done! What day is it?"

"Dunno! Christmas Day?"

"No Dad, it's Wednesday – just an ordinary day."

"Where's Annie?" asked Jim suddenly.

John looked dismayed. "She's passed away, Dad. She's been gone for two years now."

"Well she was sitting there just this morning," Jim replied belligerently as he pointed to the place on the sofa where his wife had always sat.

"No Dad, she can't have been. She's been gone a long while now."

"Well, she left me this, before she went out this morning," said his father crossly, picking up a boxed jigsaw puzzle and thrusting it aggressively at John.

"Er, right!" John took the jigsaw and looked anxiously across to where Maureen and Aileen were talking quietly in the entrance to the kitchen. Maureen came forward and smiled at Jim.

"I've got to go now Jim, but I'll be back again in a while. Aileen is going to put your meal into the microwave now. I'll see you soon." She nodded to John and whispered, "I've talked to Aileen, see you in Starbucks at one o'clock."

"Right, we'll be there."

Jim picked up a bag of sugar from where he had put it on the hearth and handed it to Maureen. "There you are lass, you'd better make it last a while. There's a shortage you know."

Maureen glanced at John, who was looking totally bewildered by now, and mouthed, "It's okay, I'll just humour him," and took the bag from Jim.

They were all in Starbucks now, swapping stories about Jim's behaviour that morning, and agreeing that he was very confused. Maureen was sure that it was the result of a water infection, but told them also that she believed that Jim was showing early signs of senile dementia. The three of them agreed that his memory of current and recent events was poor and that any arrangements made with him were often forgotten.

"Yet he can still tell me the same stories from the past over and over again, with great attention to detail," volunteered Aileen.

"That's pretty normal with dementia," confirmed Maureen. "Look: I've already got his prescription for the antibiotics so I'm going to go now and give him the first one. Would you like me to put in an extra visit for the next few days so that I can be sure he takes the tablets at the right times?"

"That would be great, if you don't mind," replied John gratefully. "We will go tomorrow and see how he is doing. Maybe you could do morning and early evening for the next few days and we can do lunchtimes?"

"Fine," agreed Maureen. "Encourage him to drink as much water as you can, while you are there. It will help his condition." The three of them talked for a few minutes more then Maureen took her leave.

A few days later the confusion in Jim's head had abated, although his memory was still poor.

The following weeks brought bouts of forgetfulness and also repeated water infections, which led to a more confused state of mind each time. It improved temporarily with the courses of antibiotics, however, underlying this, as Maureen had predicted, the dementia became more obvious. One minute Jim could be calm and cooperative, the next, when "accused" of forgetting something, acting irrationally or reproached for doing something that could be potentially injurious or dangerous, aggression would come to the fore, in the form of swearing, slamming doors and throwing things at people.

───※───

As John and Aileen were arriving at Jim's one afternoon, his carer Maureen had just left him and was halfway down the bank to her car. They stopped for a chat and an update.

"He seems quite agitated today," she said. "There were policemen in the street this morning. I'm not sure why, but maybe just delivering bad news to someone? I suppose it could have been a break-in, or a bit of vandalism? Anyway, they were over there," she pointed down the street to the left, and to the opposite side of the street from where Jim lived. "For some reason he seemed to think they were after him and he wouldn't let me in at first. The door was locked. He had his key in the door on the inside so I couldn't get in with the key from the safe." She paused.

"I knocked at the door, then on the window and eventually called through the letterbox, telling him it was me. Even so, he took quite a lot of persuading, and when he did finally open the door, he practically dragged me in and locked the door behind us. That was this morning and he was exactly the same just now on the lunchtime call. I have been there ages, and he's a bit calmer now, but he still thinks that the police are looking for him."

Both John and Aileen looked mystified. "I wonder if he will let us in," mused Aileen.

"I think I'd better go up there straight away and see what's got into him," replied John. They departed hurriedly, John telling Maureen that he would ring her later with an update.

The door was locked. John rang the bell, hammered on the door and shouted, "Dad it's us! Let us in." It took quite a bit of repetition before Jim finally came to the other side of the door. When he eventually opened it, he stood out of sight behind the door, then, once the pair were inside, hurriedly closed and locked it again.

Once in the living room John began to question his father about the events of the morning. Jim, however, was not forthcoming: sitting silently in his chair scowling, casting furtive glances at his son, then staring straight ahead at the blank wall for minutes at a time.

Aileen decided to go out of the room in case her presence was a problem. She announced that she would put the kettle on and make some tea. Once the two men were alone, John began to probe further.

"Why are you scared of the police, Dad?"

No reply.

"Maureen said that you thought they were after you. Why would you think that?"

Silence!

"Have you done something wrong when you went into town? Not paid for something perhaps? Maybe by mistake?"

"No!"

"Well they can't be after you if you've done nothing wrong, Dad. Anyway, they haven't come to your door have they? So they must have been to see someone else in the street."

They sat for a few minutes in silence again.

Aileen brought in the tea, and sensing the tension tried to change the subject to what Jim required in the way of shopping. She managed to obtain a few one word answers, though his mind was clearly elsewhere... bread... cheese... milk... ginger cake... a cherry pie. She made a list in her notebook, then, having finished their drinks, she cleared the cups away and went to collect Jim's washing to take home.

When John and Jim were alone again, and after another period of uncomfortable silence, Jim confided to his son, "I think it must be about that girl that I killed!"

John's jaw dropped. "What girl? Dad you haven't killed anyone. Don't be daft. There hasn't been anyone killed around here in recent times. It would have been on the news." He smiled at Jim. "And how could you be responsible? Good God you're ninety-three years old!"

Jim simply pursed his mouth and looked away.

Aileen came back into the room and placed a bag full of washing next to her coat and handbag. After a few more minutes of stilted, innocuous conversation, the couple took their leave. Usually Jim stood at the front door and watched them walk down the path to where the car was parked, waving until they turned the corner, but on this occasion, he shut the door immediately and they were still close enough to hear the key being turned in the lock.

The couple drove home in silence, John obviously preoccupied and brooding. When they got into the house, Aileen set the washing machine away with Jim's washing and made them each a latte. As they sat drinking their coffee, John told her what had transpired while she was out of the room. He looked really worried and his voice was shaky and unnatural.

After listening for a while, Aileen asked, "Are you concerned about your dad's dementia and that it is worsening, or do you really believe that he might have killed someone?"

"I honestly don't know!" He sat with his head in his hands. "Well think about what Maureen has told us about dementia. That people can remember things that happened years ago and it's the recent events that they can't bring to mind."

"Well just because your dad might be able to remember a local murder from the past doesn't mean he committed it."

"I know that, but there was a girl from around here murdered, a long time ago, before I was born. Everyone in this neighbourhood knew the family, and I don't think they ever caught the murderer. Also don't forget, my dad said 'the girl that I killed' – Dementia! Remembering things from the past accurately! What am I supposed to think?"

They talked for some while, Aileen trying hard to convince her husband that it was highly unlikely that his father was a murderer, and that the comment was all part of his dementia.

2000

In August 2000 flowers began to appear suddenly and with regularity on the grave of Mary Thompson in the York Hill Cemetery. No card or any sort of message was left with any of them and it led to speculation locally as to the donor. Mary's parents were both deceased and her elder sister and husband had emigrated from the UK to Australia in 1954, anxious to be away from the neighbourhood and the constant reminder of the family tragedy. There were no other relatives in the North East of England and no one owning up to being responsible for the tributes. It caused much gossip.

The Northern Echo picked up the baton and on 16th September 2000 printed an article on the 1952 murder case. They then appealed for the depositor of the flowers to come forward. No one did! The donor obviously wished to remain anonymous, which led to a certain amount of speculation as to whether it could be the murderer placing the bouquets, wreaths and posies out of guilt and remorse. The Echo continued to appeal for help in obtaining the identity of the placer of the flowers and people began to watch the cemetery in the hope of catching a glimpse or even a photograph of the said person. Someone also took photographs of the grave every time a new tribute was made, and sent them to the newspaper to print in the hope that a local florist might recognise their own work and be able to identify the purchaser.

Immediately after the newspaper appeal was into its third week and creating much attention, the flowers stopped.

John was at his parents' house one Sunday in September, and as they sat over a cup of tea, he casually glanced at the newspaper lying on the sofa next to him. It was dated the previous Thursday. As his father cleared away the teapot, cups, milk and sugar, John picked up the paper and scanned the main articles. His attention was drawn to the one reporting the flowers on a girl's grave, just up the road from where he used to live and quite close to where his parents' home now was. He studied it, frowning. His mother, as usual, just sat, vacantly staring at the wall opposite, and casually touching her hair to make sure all was in place.

John waited until his father came back into the living room, and questioned him about the article and the original incident of 1952. At first Jim seemed reluctant to engage in conversation, but as John asked various questions about the murder, which had taken place not far from where his parents had lived at that time, just before he was born, Jim eventually acknowledged that he remembered it, and that the girl had been stabbed to death in her own home, which was in the "Jerusalem" area.

John asked his father whether he knew exactly where the girl was buried. Jim replied that he knew it was in the York Hill cemetery but didn't know exactly where.

"So it seems like they never caught the murderer?"

"No, the father was pulled in for questioning, but they said he had... what's the word?"

"An alibi?" said John.

"Yes, that's it. His mates down the pub said he couldn't've done it."

"Did you know the family, then, Dad?"

"Well, I knew Bob, a bit, but we drank in different pubs. And I knew the lasses by sight."

"The youngest one was a lovely looking girl," interposed Annie, "never did much with her hair though," she said, glancing into one of the many mirrors and preening her own hair.

"So it's an unsolved crime!" mused John thoughtfully. "No wonder they're paying so much attention to the flowers on the grave."

"What! You think they might be able to catch the murderer after all this time?" asked Jim.

"Oh, yes. It's possible. The police always have records of what they call 'cold cases' in case the same thing starts up again. Also they have far more advanced technology these days. Forensics! Actually I wouldn't be surprised if they had already set up cameras trained on the grave in question." John glanced at his watch and stood up.

"I'd better make tracks now. I'll phone you through the week."

2015

John and Aileen were discussing for the umpteenth time Jim's dementia: Aileen trying hard to convince her husband that it highly unlikely that his father was a murderer, while John strove to remember the details of the reports in 2000 about the flowers on the girl's grave.

Eventually Aileen researched the Northern Echo website and managed to find the report that John had read at his father's house some fifteen years before, about flowers being placed anonymously on the grave of Mary Thompson. Once John had perused the article, he remembered having a discussion with his father about "cold cases", and Jim being amazed that they might still be able to identify the murderer so many years later due to more sophisticated methodology. He concluded by saying to Aileen, "I told him that they most probably had cameras set up in the cemetery, possibly focused on the girl's grave, to try and catch the person responsible for laying the flowers there. Interestingly the flowers stopped!"

"Maybe as a result of the Northern Echo report?" commented Aileen.

"Or maybe because of the conversation I had with my dad, when I read the article," replied John flatly.

The following afternoon saw the couple at the Crown Street Library in Darlington, not far from the Northern Echo offices. They researched the 1952 archived copies of the "Echo", which were still on microfiche. Without too much trouble they found a number of the original articles about the Mary Thompson murder. When John studied them he was shocked and appalled: "A man with gingery hair, on a blue bicycle!" he said in a low voice.

"You can't assume that it was your dad, John, just because of the ginger hair! And how would you know if he ever had a blue push bike, before you were born?"

"He did! He had it for years, right through my childhood years in fact, and it *was* blue."

"It's still not conclusive, though, John. No evidence then. Insufficient evidence now! Case dismissed!"

When they got home and were sitting over a cup of coffee, John began again: "You know, I've been thinking…"

"Oh, I know you have," interrupted his wife, "but the evidence is slim, in fact it's not really evidence is it? It's coincidence!"

"You know I don't believe in coincidence, so hear me out, please."

"Okay. Case for the Prosecution. Fire away."

"I've told you before that my parents did not have a happy marriage. Over the years my mother had several affairs and at one time in the sixties was going to leave my dad, taking me with her. It didn't happen though, and they'd been married for sixty-four years when she died, as you know. Even in her latter years, I've believed that she was "seeing" someone else, and as you also know, we found lots of "evidence" to that effect when we were clearing out her belongings after she'd gone. I think it's significant that Dad wanted rid of everything to do with her immediately after her death."

"Yes, I do know that, and I remember how upset you were on behalf of Jim, thinking that she had cheated on him all their married life. I also remember that she treated him like dirt, even in front of us, which was pretty embarrassing. He never retaliated though, and until recently, with the onset of his dementia and the subsequent aggression, I always thought of him as a mild mannered, courteous and chivalrous man: a gentleman!"

"So did I. I always felt sorry for him and wished that sometimes he would bite back. I even spoke to him about her once, several years ago now, but he just shrugged and said, 'It's just how she is: take no notice of her, I don't.' I didn't understand why they stayed together – but here goes..." John paused for breath then continued. "Let's go back to the war and post-war years. It sounds as if my dad had a bit of a reputation about town as a womaniser. He was quite keen to talk to you about his exploits, how he 'put it about', 'took girls down the woods', 'had his way with them' – yet get to the point where he met my mam and he wouldn't say anything about that: not about their courtship or their married years. It was almost as if his life ended then.

"Now my mam had a bit of a reputation of her own. You know how vain she was, and apparently the best looking woman in town in the forties and fifties – and maybe even later. Certainly all she could think about was her appearance, and going dancing. My dad only ever went to the pub, and so they led very separate lives."

Aileen nodded in agreement, thinking about those afternoons she'd spent trying to glean information from Jim about the forties and onward.

John continued, "My Aunty Evelyn has told us a few tales as you know: that my mother was, as she put it 'highly sexed', in other words, she put herself about. Evelyn also told me that Mam invariably spent all their money on clothes, so that sometimes they couldn't pay their bills and Dad had to borrow from his parents. She also said that in their early years of being married, Dad had been putting aside some money each week so that they could buy a television, then discovered that Mam had taken it and spent the lot on clothes and make up."

"Well you've never heard those sort of stories about her from Jim have you? It sounds to me as if they just accepted each other for what they were. Both seem to have had quite a reputation for needing sex, Jim taking it from anyone if the opportunity arose, and Annie giving it away freely to her many admirers."

"It's nauseating to think about your parents being like that," said John, "and my mother still seeing someone illicitly when she was in her seventies and eighties. Urgh!"

"And still thinking of herself as a glamour girl. Look how obsessed she was with her appearance, especially her bloody hair," exclaimed Aileen.

"Okay," said John. "Let's go back to 1952 when Mary Thompson was murdered. It was towards the end of October, almost exactly three months before I was born, so my mam was six months pregnant." He looked meaningfully at his wife. "So my dad wasn't getting any, was he?"

Aileen looked at him uncertainly. "So…?"

"Well Mary was supposedly a good-looking girl. Sixteen years old! Legal age! Maybe my dad tried it on with her."

"But there was no evidence of a sexual assault was there?"

"Not that I know of, but maybe things went so far and then she said 'No' and he just flew into a rage with her for leading him on."

"John, you have no evidence whatsoever to suggest that this was the case."

"Picture this: my dad was sexually deprived and frustrated. He's said that he knew the family 'a bit'. He knew where the Thompsons lived and where Bob Thompson used to drink every night. It would probably be common knowledge in such a small community as 'Jerusalem', so would the fact that the elder daughter had recently married and left home, and perhaps it would also be known that the girl's grandmother was failing and that Mary's mother would be with her and not at home. It was an old, stable community where everyone knew everyone else's business. Maybe he thought he was in with a chance of a leg-over because of the situation, and when it didn't come off, he flew into a frenzy! And don't forget; ginger hair, blue bike – pregnant wife!"

Aileen studied for a few minutes, going over the logic in her head. "I can see why you might have gone along these lines, but at the end of the day, it's all circumstantial, with a bit of imagination added, so I'm still going to say 'Case dismissed due to lack of evidence!'"

"Well, I'm going to put forward one more piece of information for you to consider, and you already know some of it. My mother was a thief! She got 'done' for shoplifting back in the sixties."

"I know, you told me that. Marks and Spencer – yes?"

"Yes! But what you don't know, and neither did I until I was talking to Aunty Evelyn recently – it wasn't a one-off! She had FORM."

Aileen's eyes widened and she stared silently at her husband. He continued, "I know, it was a shock to me too. Now remember clearing out my mam's room: all those clothes! Loads of jewellery, and bottle upon bottle of perfume, not cheap stuff either! Where did all that come from? They weren't very poor but they weren't exactly rich either. The goods were disproportionate to the income."

Aileen's mouth tightened as John looked intently at her, then she said meaningfully, "Well, they could have been *presents*."

He caught on immediately. "Yes, I've already been along that road, but she could also have been a kleptomaniac! Consider this: I don't think my parents loved each other, but maybe they knew too much about one another. If someone knows a very important and particularly distasteful secret about you, you aren't going to kick him or her into touch are you? You can't risk the vengeance of having your secret disclosed, can you?"

Aileen contemplated this for some while, hardly daring to offer up a response. Then she finally concluded: "The Jury's out on this one!"